AMERICAN HERO

Mack Bolan is a man committed to bloodshed and violence, yet he embodies the nobler reaches of human consciousness. He's the violent judgment in a violent universe, the tool of the balancing forces of nature, a cataclysmic answer to the cancer cells of man's destiny. He lives at the cutting edge of the human estate.

Bolan knows that he represents the sanctity of life and his enemies do not. Therefore, his task is clear.

"Mack Bolan stabs right through the heart of the frustration and hopelessness the average person feels about crime running rampant in the streets."
—*Dallas Times Herald*

DON PENDLETON's
MACK BOLAN.

BLOWOUT

A GOLD EAGLE BOOK FROM
WORLDWIDE.

TORONTO • NEW YORK • LONDON • PARIS
AMSTERDAM • STOCKHOLM • HAMBURG
ATHENS • MILAN • TOKYO • SYDNEY

First edition August 1989

ISBN 0-373-61416-0

Special thanks and acknowledgment to
Peter Leslie for his contribution to this work.

The cult of numbers is the supreme fallacy
of modern warfare.
—B. H. Liddell Hart, 1944

I am involved in an everlasting war, and I
believe that one man can make a difference.
—Mack Bolan

PROLOGUE

Mack Bolan stood looking down at the pool of congealing blood around his feet. Each time the neon arrow above the Black Tie nightclub entrance flashed, the dark pool of liquid leaking from beneath the body turned sickly green.

Even in midwinter, Hamburg, in northern Germany, was a city of green—green spires, shallow green roofs and evergreen trees pricking through the snow banked on either side of the lake that split the town from north to south. The doors of the white patrol car skating across the icy pavement toward the sidewalk were green and so, a darker shade, were the uniforms of the men piling out as soon as the car screeched to a halt.

There was a lot of blood: seven bullet holes in the victim's camel topcoat stared blackly up at the streetlight above the nightclub arrow. The blood itself turned black when the revolving amber light on the patrol car roof flashed out of sync with the arrow.

Twenty seconds ago that lifeless figure had been an indistinct shape hurrying past him toward the steps leading down to the nightclub entrance. A cab was still parked fifty yards away on the far side of the street with its engine idling. The exhaust roar of the killers' getaway car—a Golf GTi—still audible, dwindling away on the far side of the white roofs lining the maze of narrow streets that led to the docks.

Bolan shivered. Not at the impact of sudden death so close at hand—half a lifetime's fight against organized crime had inured him to that—but it was minus two Fahrenheit and the wind from the east was biting. The kapok-filled black parka he wore over his sweater and slacks could shield him from that frozen breath as long as he kept walking, but it was no proof against the numbing cold that rose from the ground the moment his limbs stopped moving.

Already a crowd was gathering at the scene of the shooting. The cabdriver came running, his feet sliding on the packed ice of the sidewalk; women in fur coats climbed the stone stairs from the nightclub; windows in the dark facades across the street blazed with light. There was a babble of voices.

"What happened?" someone asked in German.

"I heard the shots, I thought—"

"Three men in a Volkswagen."

"Only just paid me off after a trip from the Atlantic Hotel," the cabdriver announced to anyone who would listen.

"All right, all right," the cops called—there were four of them, their breath steaming in the arctic air. "Stand back there. Move along. Is there a doctor...?"

A thin elderly man in a snap-brim hat and a long black leather topcoat stepped forward and lowered himself on one knee beside the body. Two of the cops held back the curious onlookers, while a third walked over to retrieve a fur hat that had rolled away and come to rest against the frozen slush piled in the gutter. The sergeant in charge of the patrol helped the doctor turn over the slaughtered man.

Above the riddled camel coat Bolan saw short dark hair, cropped at the neck. Below the coat, checkered pants were tucked into brown leather boots with high heels. Leather gloves sheathed the hands that had clawed ineffectually at the sidewalk's frozen flagstones.

High-heeled boots?

Light fell on a livid face as the body was turned over. Staring eyes ringed with mascara, a gaping mouth outlined in scarlet, the camel coat falling open to reveal a heavy fisherman's-knit sweater contoured around two swelling curves, the lower part of the torso dark with blood.

The victim was a young woman of about thirty with the wide features and high cheekbones of a Slav.

CHAPTER ONE

The customized Cadillac was so long that the chauffeur had difficulty turning out of the lane that led from the red-light district onto the main drag.

A cast-iron post once used for hitching horses was at the corner of the alleyway, and to avoid scratching the ivory-white side panels, the driver was obliged to run his near-side front wheel up onto the opposite sidewalk. A slight thaw had come that afternoon, and puddles sat between the ramparts of slush. As the heavy, fat tire thumped back onto the pavement, muddy water splashed up and spotted the black nylons of a hooker patrolling in a fur jacket and tight leather skirt. The woman swung around, her painted face ready to scream abuse... and then, before the angry words could leave her mouth, she shrank back into a doorway, recognizing the car.

The tinted side windows were closed, but there was no mistaking the whitewall tires or the thin maroon trim circling the Caddy's waist. A monogrammed logo broke the trim in the center of each front door, and there were chromed fishtails below the vehicle's enormous trunk.

The wide main street was almost deserted. Soon it would be dark, and the winter sky was somber with the promise of more snow. The afternoon tourist trade was on the way back into the warmth, and the nighttime hard-liners were still stretching and yawning.

Reeperbahn—the "street of the ropemakers"—was notorious the world over, synonymous with sin and vice of every kind. It lay west of Hamburg's city center, an artery channeling traffic to the snob suburbs of Altona and Blankenese, leading the forty-ton, twelve- and fourteen-wheel semis away from the docks and the huge fish market.

It was an inoffensive-looking street, lined with trees, still showing the remnants of streetcar lines where the blacktop had worn thin. Certainly there were night-clubs, nudie shows, even an occasional sex bazaar strung out along its three-quarter-mile length between the botanical gardens and the Nobistor. But, as with the Boulevard de Clichy in Paris, it was in the warren of narrow, cobbled lanes on either side that the traffic in sex flowed fastest.

The district, known as St. Pauli, was described in the city's official tourist guides as "a quarter of relaxation and frivolities." It depended on how you relaxed and how frivolous you wanted to be.

In St. Pauli were the Grosse Freiheit, the Kleine Freiheit and the Herbertstrasse, discreetly shielded by hoardings forbidding admission to those under eighteen, where Hamburg's famous "shop window girls" could be ogled displaying themselves in anything from a flimsy nightgown to a black leather ensemble complete with boots, whip and spurs. Here were sex shops selling blue movies, hard-core porn and erotic toys. Here, too, could be found singles pickup bars, live sex on stage, gay Turkish baths and clip joints with telephones on each table where everything was promised and nothing given.

But none of these delights seemed to appeal to the occupants of the customized white Cadillac. The car glided past a twenty-four-hour bikers' clothing store, a gas station bright with neon, the Chinese Laundromat and a McDonald's steamy with the odor of frying onions. Then, turning left at the Hans-Albersplatz, it ran into a minor traffic jam.

Cars, delivery trucks and cabs were momentarily stalled as some stranger in town backed a beat-up Opel out from the fruit and vegetable stalls of an open-air market. There was a further halt while the flustered driver tried to nose his way into a one-way street against the traffic flow. The Cadillac's chauffeur permitted himself two short, impatient blasts on the twin-tone horn. Gradually the blocked vehicles dispersed and the big American machine hissed along the icy cobbles toward the river.

Two blocks inland from the fish market, the car stopped and the driver reached behind him to open the rear door. The man who got out was tall and solidly built, with a craggy face and a wrestler's shoulders. He wore pale brown boots lined with fleece and a houndstooth topcoat over his tweed suit. A Tyrolean hat with a bunch of feathers tucked into the band was pulled down over his low forehead.

He walked unhurriedly into a cul-de-sac, drawing on a pair of brown kid gloves. Despite the latent power in his big frame, despite the strength of his shoulders constantly shrugging within the topcoat, there was something strangely effeminate in his gait. The two ends of the unfastened topcoat belt flipped behind him this way and that as he walked. At the far end of the entry, four steps led between iron railings to a doorway in a peeling stucco facade. Above the doorway, white lettering on a frosted glass transom spelled out the words Club

Paradiso. The big guy climbed the steps and went inside.

In the street the Cadillac waited, its engine silently turning over. Blue smoke from the fishtails condensed behind it in the freezing air. The light thickened. Here and there along the darkening sidewalks, shop windows lit up. Behind them a ship's siren bleated mournfully on the river.

Fifteen minutes later the Caddy's passenger returned. He walked back to the car slowly, stripping off his gloves. When the chauffeur opened the rear door, he leaned down and handed a wad of hundred-mark bills into the interior.

"I steamed in and put the question real nice," he said hoarsely in German. "But the punk came at me with a shiv. Can you imagine? Ripped the sleeve of my coat and all." He held out his left arm, displaying a slit in the thick stuff reaching from the wrist almost to the elbow. "Course I had to teach him a lesson. Then the mother tells me there ain't but a C in the cash register. That earned him a kick. And even then I could only choke just under a couple of thou from the son of a bitch."

"Forget it, Hansie," a voice said from the back of the Cadillac. "We'll call by and pick up the rest at the end of the week. If he doesn't have it then, we'll send in the Team. Get back in the car now. There's work to do."

Hansie climbed in. The driver slammed the door, switched on his lights and pulled away from the curb.

Five blocks to the east, the customized car parked at the end of a cab stand near the St. Pauli-Landungsbrücken ferry terminal, and Hansie sauntered down a paved walkway between two tall redbrick buildings. Several of the houses fronting the passageway were shuttered and empty, but there was an ill-lit grocery store halfway along flanked by a secondhand clothes dealer and a cigar store whose grimy window displayed a selection of lurid pulp romances behind a wire grille. In the road at the far end of the passage, a young man was thumping one of the headlights on a stationary car with his fist. It was the same old Opel, a dark blue sedan, that had caused the Hans-Albersplatz tie-up. Now, it seemed, there was a bad connection in the electrical wiring.

Hansie turned into a doorway beside the cigar store. A girl in high-heeled shoes and a shiny black raincoat undulated out of the shadows. "Like to come home with me, darling?" she murmured. "Give you a good time."

He turned furiously toward her. "Do me a fucking favor!"

She stepped back as the light fell across his face. "Hansie! Christ, I didn't see you. I didn't know—"

"Who the hell do you think I am?" He slapped her hard across the face. "Take me for a mug again and you'll end up with a few scars. Now beat it, bitch. Take fucking ten. I got business in here."

"But, Hansie, this is my spot! Shit, the other girls—"

"Fuck the other girls. Now shove off before I really smack you."

She stepped past him into the alleyway and hurried off with her head lowered. In the light the brutish face was still scowling. "And tell your pimp to come across on time this week if he knows what's good for him," he shouted after her.

Hansie trod lightly down a wooden cellar stairway and shoved open a padded door covered in red felt. There was a worn patch above the handle where innumerable hands had rubbed the material through to the wood beneath. A stocky blue-chinned man with a bald head was polishing glasses behind a bar at the far end of the low-ceilinged room. Two dozen tables covered in red-checkered oilcloth stood around a tiny stage beneath a battery of photofloods.

"Hansie!" the bald-headed man exclaimed. "You're an hour early, my friend." He glanced toward the stage. "The three gays ain't due to start their act until seven. And the law's been leanin'—"

"Fuck your gays. As if they needed it," Hansie said conversationally. He walked across the room toward the bar, pulling on the brown leather gloves.

The bald-headed man licked his lips. "If you've come about the money. . ." he began nervously.

"You know damn well why I came, Rudi. Two grand, wasn't it? Well, the boss says you can add another century now, by way of interest."

"Hansie, I ain't got it. Honest to God, I swear it! You gotta give me time. For pity's sake—"

The big man looked around the room. He gestured at the tables beneath the pink-shaded wall lamps, the threadbare velour of two "discreet" booths behind the stage, the dials and knobs of a complex music center under the rows of bottles behind the bar. "You mean you got no clients? The girls don't pay up? The fags ain't coming across with their percentage? The mugs all took a vacation in East Berlin, maybe?"

Hansie smiled. Yellow horse teeth gleamed dully in the mirror behind the bar. "Come on, Rudi," he said. "Friends of mine been in this dump checking up this week. You had sixty-seven people in here last night and more than a hundred between midday and midnight on Sunday. Sprinzel's delivered you a case of Jack Daniel's and three of schnapps this morning, along with four dozen Canada Dry and a load of Cokes. And you're telling me business is bad?''

"I didn't say that. I...Ferdy Kraul's boys was in!'' the bartender burst out. "They smacked the wife around and threatened to break the place up. There was six or seven of them. They took all I had. I couldn't do anything else, Hansie. I couldn't.''

"There you are, you see,'' Hansie said softly. "That's what happens when you fall behind with the insurance payments. That's what you pay protection for—to help us stop loudmouth punks like that from turning a guy's place over. You better come up with the premium now in case it happens again.''

"Hansie, *I don't have it*. I told you. I need time. You gotta give me time.''

The big man leaned his hands on the bar and nodded genially. "That's a nice tape deck you got there,'' he said. "Let's have some music, huh?''

Rudi switched on the center and spun a knob beneath the illuminated dials. His fingers were trembling. At once the room was filled with the heavily accented beat of an accordion band playing a schmaltzy tango that must have dated from the 1930s.

"Louder,'' Hansie said. "I always like to hear a good tune.''

The volume of the music increased as the barman turned the knob again. "Hansie...'' he said.

The big man moved very quickly for a person his size. His two hands shot out to seize the lapels of the barman's jacket. Leaning back and flexing his arms, he dragged the guy facedown across the counter. And then, as Rudi cried out in fear and alarm, Hansie hauled him over and smashed his knee into the prostrate victim's face.

Rudi dropped to the floor, groaning. Hansie grabbed his collar and dragged him to his feet. The enforcer was as swift and as light on his toes as a boxer or a ballet dancer. One leather fist darted out and split the flesh over Rudi's cheekbone. A hook to the pit of the stomach doubled him over, and as soon as he straightened on rubber knees, a vicious kidney punch slammed into the small of his back. The edge of the enforcer's hand, hard as a plank, finally caught him across the throat.

The sounds of the struggle were drowned by the blare of accordions. Rudi's mouth opened and closed each time the blows thudded home, but the only voice audible was a nasal tenor issuing from the stereo speakers above the stage.

Hansie pirouetted around his victim as he began to fall, seizing him under one arm and behind the neck in a half nelson. Locked together, the semiconscious bartender and his attacker swayed between the tables in a grotesque parody of a ballet duet.

A knee suddenly struck the base of Rudi's spine, and the lower half of his body arched forward so that the corner of a table dug into his groin. As he was dragged back toward the bar, his legs jackknifed to ease the agony in his genitals. Hansie sped up the froglike convulsions with a well-placed kick to the ankle.

The song was lost in a shrill scream of terror that could be heard even over the amplified clamor of the accordions. Rudi was struggling desperately to free himself from the forearm that was now wedged rigidly under his jaw. Hansie had shifted his grip; the gloved fingers of his free hand held an open cutthroat razor in front of the barman's eyes.

Light flashed on the blade as he drew it slowly, almost caressingly, across Rudi's cheek. Instantly the thin trickle of blood from the split flesh over the bone was eclipsed by a curtain of scarlet masking the whole right-hand side of the wounded man's face. Hansie snatched his arm away before the red cascade splashed onto his sleeve, allowing Rudi to slump to the floor.

He catfooted around behind the bar, wiped the razor on a rag and stowed it in an inside pocket. He poured himself half a tumbler of straight bourbon and drank it slowly. Almost as an afterthought, he took the bottle by the neck and smashed it down on one of the glass shelves. The glass shattered, sending beer tankards and bottles crashing to the floor.

The song was finished. There was no more music, although the tape spools continued to turn silently. As Hansie walked to the door, the only sound apart from his footsteps was the hoarse sobbing of the man bleeding in front of the bar and the rhythmic gurgle of liquor splashing from one of the broken bottles. He paused at the foot of the stairs, holding the door open with the toe of one fleece-lined boot.

"Today's Tuesday, Rudi," he said quietly. "You got until midday Thursday. You won't forget this time, will you?"

It was dark outside. Snowflakes drifted through the pools of light cast by the streetlights. The Cadillac was waiting at one end of the alley. The ancient Opel was at the other, still stalled with one blank headlight. The young driver was in a glass phone booth nearby, stamping his feet to keep out the cold.

Soon afterward the young Opel driver pushed his way out and the door swung shut behind him. Turning up his collar against the falling snow, he bent over the front of the car. Whatever advice he had been given over the phone must have been good because the dead headlight flickered, then shone brightly almost at once. He slid behind the wheel and drove away.

His route led back across the canals that fed the waters of the Alster—the lake bisecting the city—into the Elbe River, past the baroque central tower of the city hall, into the aseptic geometry of the post-World War II commercial quarter east of the railroad station. He managed to keep the Opel's engine running as he waited to cross the stream of rush-hour traffic clogging the Glockengeisser Wall. But clearly it wasn't his day: by the time the old sedan had threaded its way through the four lines of honking cars, trucks, cabs and buses, the engine was spluttering. Two blocks beyond the station, in a small square off the Steindamm, it backfired twice and then died altogether.

The driver clambered out and levered up the hood to expose the carburetor and ignition leads. Snowflakes, falling faster now, hissed into oblivion on the hot exhaust manifold. He flashed a pocket flashlight among the wires and hoses behind the radiator. The little square was very quiet. Fresh snow, thickly carpeting the sidewalks, muted the sounds of traffic on the main streets.

On the opposite corner, the plate-glass front of a café-restaurant had recently been shattered, and jagged shards littered the trampled slush, glittering like diamonds in the lamplight. Through the gap, a desolation of smashed tableware and splintered wood was visible in the dim radiance of a single low-power bulb hanging from the ceiling. The place looked as thought a grenade had exploded in the entrance.

Feet crunched across the broken glass. A tall, muscular man wearing a brown houndstooth topcoat walked out of the ruined café and crossed the roadway to a convertible parked outside a church.

A customized Eldorado with whitewall tires.

The driver of the Opel straightened quickly and walked to a row of pay phones ranked against the wall of the church. The first stank of urine. In the second the instrument had been ripped from the wall and the handset broken. The third was usable, but the young man seemed to prefer the last, where one of the glass door panels was missing. Lifting the receiver, he dropped in coins and punched the buttons, but kept one finger pressed down on the cradle so that no dial tone sounded in his ear. Then, leaning his back against the door so that it swung slightly open, he listened.

The Cadillac was only a few yards away. He heard the click as a rear door opened. "What happened?" a voice asked from inside the car.

"Kraul again," the big man rasped. "Place has been gone over but good. Furniture wrecked, all the equipment fucked over. You never saw anything like that kitchen!"

"How long ago?"

"They split around seven. A whole team. We can't have missed them but by a few minutes."

"Yet there are no rubbernecks? No neighbors? No cops even?"

"Well, there wouldn't be, would there? They were warned off."

"What about Becker himself?"

A snort of laughter. "Not as lucky as Boris! Cashed in this time. Flat out on the deck behind the counter with his skull bashed in. I figure they came on too strong and croaked the bastard."

"Get in, Hansie," the voice ordered curtly. "Herr Kraul and his gorillas are going too far and I won't stand for it. What we need in this game is a little more planning and one hell of a lot more organization."

The door slammed, and the big Caddy hissed away along the icy asphalt.

The young man in the phone booth released his breath. He lifted his finger, punched out another number and spoke into the mouthpiece. "Kriminalkommissar Fischer. Wertheim speaking. Hello, chief? Yes, sir, I did. Subject under observation as instructed, but there's a jumbo-size wrench in the works. I'm speaking from the Becker Café now, and it seems Kraul beat them to it. I think you'd better send a squad car and an ambulance PDQ."

He listened for another thirty seconds, voiced a brief affirmative and replaced the receiver. The Opel started at the first twist of the key. He drove smoothly out of the square, the even pulse of the engine beating back from the snow-topped wall encircling the church.

In the far corner a tall man, as tall as Hansie but less fleshy, stood unseen in the shadow beneath a lime tree. Behind him a Honda 70 scooter leaned against a railing. As he wheeled the machine into the roadway, lamplight illuminated a determined chin and cold blue eyes beneath the hood of a black parka.

Mack Bolan had been an interested witness.

The Cadillac was running on Frankfurt license plates. Bolan had been tailing Arvell Asticot, the international drug baron, for days. Asticot was the reason the Executioner was in West Germany. And although the voice inside the Eldorado hadn't been Asticot's, the car was the same one that had collected the narcotics boss from his Frankfurt hotel and driven him north three days ago. The hunt was on.

CHAPTER TWO

The name of the young woman who had been shot outside the Black Tie was Edwina Mueller. She was a prominent women's lib activist and, at committee level, a leading member of the Hamburg Green Party—the ecologist political party that waged war on acid rain, automobile exhaust, factory pollution and the slaughter of animals for clothes and food. An increasingly powerful force in West Germany, the ecologists infuriated—and exerted growing pressure on—industrialists, farmers, shopkeepers and people in the hotel and restaurant business. They pulled a lot of votes. But a local party worker, Bolan figured, wasn't likely to be set up and then gunned down in the street for her views.

The police, according to the newspapers, had discovered nothing in her private life dramatic enough to provoke a murder attempt—especially a successful attempt by a professional hit team.

But Bolan couldn't help wondering if the bullets had been meant for him. If so, who had put out the contract? And how had they known he was in Hamburg? Or why?

Sure, there was a driver with Arvell Asticot's Cadillac when he followed it north from Frankfurt, but the drug lord didn't normally carry hired help of his own. Being strictly a one-man act was the main secret of Asticot's success: if nobody knew his secrets, nobody could squeal. And although the Executioner had made it to

Frankfurt in time to see him leave, at every other stop-over he had been one step behind, hitting town after the guy had split.

Negative, therefore, to the query: had he stumbled on the Executioner someplace along the line?

Okay, could it simply be that some Hamburg under-world boss had by chance recognized him, and without any specific intel on his motivation, determined to elim-inate him . . . just in case he *might* be onto a racket that was especially sensitive at the time?

It could. But Bolan figured it unlikely.

But if Asticot *had* somehow gotten wise to the fact that he was after him, it would be vital for the Executioner to take evasive action, particularly if the drug baron had drummed up local talent to protect him.

If that talent was acting on its own, if there was a general contract out for him, it was more vital still.

He decided he needed more information; he would head for the American consulate and set a few inquiries in motion.

Bolan was working one hundred percent unofficially; he would be disowned and left to the local police if he threatened to embarrass the U.S. government. But cer-tain facilities, equally unofficial, had been arranged by Hal Brognola. And there was a package to be collected that should have arrived at the Bonn embassy in the diplomatic bag, to be forwarded to Hamburg by air.

Bolan had checked into the Hotel Oper, a tall build-ing on the Drehbahn, not far from the southwestern corner of Lake Alster. For clients wishing to keep a low profile the place had advantages: it was, in fact, a multistory garage and parking lot with a lobby, wine bar and restaurant at street level, and a single penthouse floor of small, anonymous rooms below the roof. Once the chambermaids had fixed the rooms in midmorning, guests were on their own and could use the ramps that sloped between different parking levels to enter or leave the hotel without being observed, by car or on foot.

The U.S. consul general in Hamburg was comfortably installed on the Alsterufer, a wide roadway that skirted the western shore of the lake. Bolan had driven from Frankfurt in a rented BMW, which he had left on the lowest level of his hotel, ready for a quick getaway. But he decided to walk to the consulate.

It was no longer snowing, but frozen slush and packed ice, gray with mud, veneered street and sidewalk. The sky was a sulfurous yellow. Bolan passed the wedding-cake facade of the Four Seasons Hotel and strode toward the twin road and rail bridges spanning the lower part of the lake. The air that he breathed was so bitterly cold that it seared his nose and mouth. He wound a woolen muffler around the lower half of his face: as well as filtering out the worst of the cold, it helped make his muscular seventy-four-inch frame less identifiable among the hunched, wrapped-up pedestrians battling against the arctic wind.

Hurrying, he composed in his mind the open-coded message he would ask the consulate cipher clerk to transmit to CIA headquarters in Langley, Virginia. With the right access group and a for-your-eyes-only prefix, the message would be relayed straight to Brognola's office in Washington without being translated into intelligible words.

Bolan would ask for the most up-to-date intel on Asticot, with a printout from the Stony Man computer detailing the results of a trace designed to link him with the Hamburg underworld. He would also ask for a separate check on a woman named Edwina Mueller. And finally he would request Brognola to call him back at once by satellite.

Below the bridges, slabs of dun-colored ice knocked against tarpaulined skiffs moored for the winter by the boathouse cafés. But the narrow northern end of the lake, beyond the consulate, had frozen over completely, and there were children skating between the snow-covered gardens on either side of the ferry dock.

Bolan was directed to the consulate annex, one block farther north. The message was transmitted at once, but he was told there would be a delay before any reply could be expected. He picked up his package from the dispatch clerk and decided to take it back to his hotel.

Inside, he knew, would be a waterproof neoprene pouch containing skeleton keys, a glass cutter, a flat-bladed throwing knife in a leather ankle sheath, a wire garrote and—to avoid trouble at frontier or airline security checks—two Beretta 93-R autoloaders with quickdraw shoulder rigs. When he got to the hotel, he handed the package to the receptionist, asking for it to be stowed in the hotel safe. Then he returned to the consulate annex.

It was colder still when he emerged from the shelter of the modernistic skyscraper at the inner end of the Drehbahn. The wind had dried the top layer of snow into tiny particles that whirled like white sand along the swept flagstones, stinging his face when he came out from under the arches of the Colonnaden walkway. He zippered up his parka and strode toward the lake.

At the consulate annex he drew a near blank. The trace on Edwina Mueller was negative. Nothing known. Brognola had been called away to some unforeseen security crisis in Hawaii and wouldn't be back in his office for several days. And traffic on the satellite link was exceptionally heavy, the cipher clerk told him; he had no idea how long it might be before an answer to the remaining queries could be expected. There was, however, a sealed envelope that had arrived for Bolan by special messenger.

He broke the wax seals and slit the flap with his thumbnail. Inside there was an American passport, a press accreditation card issued and signed by the West German foreign ministry in Bonn and letters from the overseas editor of a photonews magazine in Chicago asking for follow-ups to current European political crises—in particular the opening round of East-West peace talks in Berlin. A strip of paper torn from a telex machine completed the package.

The message read: You might find these useful if you want to be in two places—or be two people—at the same time! Best—H.B.

The papers were in the name of Mike Belasko, a cover identity the Executioner had used before in places as far apart as Hong Kong and Northern Ireland. At the moment Bolan was using his Mike Blanski cover. It was sometimes wise to have a backup identity, though. You never knew what might happen.

Bolan figured it might flesh out his newsman cover if he did a half hour of sidewalk interviews, buttonholing fellow countrymen coming in and out of the consulate and asking them their views on the current round of East-West disarmament talks in Geneva and the possibility—for the umpteenth time—of the abolition of the Berlin Wall and the reunification of Germany.

He was questioning a group of consulate secretaries flouncing back from their sandwich lunches at the Alsterpavilion when he saw the guy: a tall, rangy character with a blue chin and flinty eyes in a face that looked as if frost had set in behind it.

Ferucco Lattuada.

Automatically the Executioner's mind started flipping over the sheets in his mental mug shot file.

A Syndicate man for starters. Son of Giordano Lattuada, a second-generation American born of naturalized parents who had emigrated during the great Sicilian exodus in the 1890s and settled in Chicago's Little Italy. Giordano had quit school when he was twelve, refused to work in the family pizza bar, led a local street gang and then became a legman for Samoots Amatuma when he was president of the Unione Siciliane in 1925. He was associated with Scalise, Anselmi and Frank "the Enforcer" Nitti in Capone's heyday and later worked as a hit man for Meyer Lansky in New York.

Ferucco, his son, was born sometime during World War II, which put him on the wrong side of forty. He had been recruited, Bolan recalled, by the Lucchese family soon after his old man vanished as the result of a quarrel with Teamster boss Jimmy Hoffa. Giordano's skeleton was probably still standing at attention forty feet below the surface of the East River with the legs ankle deep in a bowl of concrete.

Ferucco had succeeded his daddy as the family contract killer and was reputed to have chalked up a score totaling twenty-seven successful hits—about one a year since reaching voting age. He was supposed to have fled to Vegas when Lips Flanagan was run out of the numbers racket in Dallas. He'd been working for Flanagan at the time, and there were rumors that, on account of his Cosa Nostra connections, Ferucco had crossed him up at the instigation of the Syndicate men who'd taken over his pitch.

The last Bolan had heard, Ferucco Lattuada had rented a Beechcraft to fly him from Nevada to Mexico because he'd been tipped off that the IRS was after his balls on a tax evasion rap.

So what the hell was he doing in Hamburg?

Why would a well-heeled hood with connections be hoofing it past a frozen lake near the Baltic in a temperature of minus two Fahrenheit, when he could be lying on the beach at Acapulco with a rented blonde?

Bolan couldn't say exactly why, but he decided that question needed an answer. It could be that he himself needed to lay off the Asticot trail for a while, that he had to take a break from the boring legwork that had occupied his time for more than two weeks now. It was possible that he sensed a link between the mob-style shooting outside the Black Tie and the appearance in town of a notorious mafioso.

Whatever, he determined—since he happened by chance to have laid eyes on the mobster—to follow him for a couple of hours. The guy might of course be in Hamburg on some perfectly innocent business, buying Bundesbank Defense Bonds or visiting his Aunt Giovanna. On the other hand . . .

Bolan snapped shut his journalist's notebook, and hurried after Lattuada. The guy headed south, toward the city center. What had he been doing this far out along the lakeshore? He certainly hadn't been paying a courtesy call on the consul general, not with the IRS on his tail. There was a ritzy dining and dancing club, Die Insel, a little way beyond the consulate, but it didn't open its doors until evening. The rest of the property was residential. Bolan shook his head; maybe he would get a clue to where the mobster had been if he could find out where he was going.

His quarry was wearing a belted sheepskin jacket and a Russian-style fur hat with the flaps pulled down to cover his ears. For several hundred yards, where there were a few walkers negotiating the humped ice along the sidewalk, he was content to keep well behind. But as Lattuada approached the two bridges across the Alster, traffic—on the street as well as the sidewalks—grew more dense and the Executioner was obliged to close up. There were too many fur hats and sheepskin coats around to risk losing the guy down the steps of a subway entrance or crossing one of the bridges as the lights changed to release a flood of cars, trucks and buses.

There was a cab stand outside the entrance to the Four Seasons, and Lattuada shrugged off the doorman and jerked open the door of the first. Bolan was no more than a dozen yards behind. He shoved a couple of marks into the doorman's hand while the hood was climbing in, then signaled to the next in line.

"I know this sounds like a bad movie," he told the driver in English as he leaned in through the open window, "but I'd like you to follow that cab. No kidding."

The cabbie chuckled hoarsely behind the layers of woolen scarves muffling the lower half of his face and pulled the double-jointed bend of arm that his profession has developed to open a rear door. "*Jawohl*, Herr James Bond," he said. "Jump in and we shall see what can be done."

The doorman saluted and closed the door. The cab spun its rear wheels on the packed ice, pulling out into the traffic stream, and the driver took an encore on the arm-bend routine, sliding back the glass panel between him and the rear of the vehicle. He tilted his head backward. Bolan heard the gruff voice over the whine of gears and the diesel knock of the worn motor. "The man in front, does he know he's being tailed?"

"No way," Bolan said. He reckoned he could lay money on that.

"Would it tip him off if he saw you? Does he know your face?"

Bolan saw the point. He'd happened on a driver who used his head. Traffic was heavy, the surrounding streets were narrow, there were red lights. Keeping a screen of other vehicles between the two cabs might be a surefire way of losing Lattuada.

"He never laid eyes on me," the warrior said. "Wouldn't know me from the German chancellor if he did. You can close right up behind him and he won't suspect a thing, not even if you drop me off at the same street number."

The cabbie nodded and slid the panel shut. He strong-armed his way across the stream heading for the bridges, the Dammtor railroad station and the radio center, turned past the opera house and joined the slow-motion merry-go-round circling the Stephansplatz on the way to the wide parkway leading to St. Pauli.

At one point in the jam the two cabs were side by side, and Bolan stole a glance at the mobster. He wasn't sitting on the edge of the seat, or shouting at the cabbie or biting his nails. He was lounging against the seat with no expression on his blue-jowled face, taking an occasional peek at the gold Rolex on his wrist. He didn't look like a big-time hood planning a heist; he looked like a guy who was just beginning to become a little impatient because his cab was stalled in the Stephansplatz.

They made good time down the parkway and the Reeperbahn. And then, past the sidewalk whores wearing today's fashions and yesterday's faces, Lattuada's cab turned into a network of mean streets on the fringe of the fish market and put him down on a corner in sight of the river.

"Eleven marks fifty," Bolan's driver announced, switching off the meter.

He'd made a U-turn and deposited Bolan on the far side of the intersection. Smart guy. Bolan handed him fifteen marks. "Keep the change," he said. "Could be I'll need a reliable man sometime. Have you got a card?"

"My thanks. Yes, I do." The cabbie unlocked two layers of topcoat, thrust his hand inside a third and fished out a surprisingly crisp, clean pasteboard rectangle. "That's the number of the stand I work from," he said. "South side of the Atlantic Hotel. The other guys will take messages if I'm not there. The other number—the one written in ink—is where I live. But you'd have to make it early in the morning or after eight at night, unless you left word with the wife."

"Okay," Bolan said. "See you around maybe."

He tucked the card into his breast pocket and was hurrying after Lattuada, who had vanished up an alleyway, when the cabbie called after him, "One more thing, 007. Keep a fucking firm hand on your hip pocket while you're in this neighborhood!"

Bolan grinned and waved a hand as he turned into the alley. Lattuada led him out the far end, down a short street where dockside cranes showed above the rooftops and through an archway that led to a lane running parallel with the river. Then the mobster turned past a corner news agent and cigar store, and Bolan found himself in an area of the city that might well have been the backside of hell.

He'd been in a few crummy neighborhoods in his time, from Belfast's Sandy Row to the Amsterdam Oosterdok, from the shanty towns above Rio to Smoky Hollow and the Bowery. But for his money Andreas Bernersstrasse, in the St. Pauli district of Hamburg, had them all beat for sheer sleaziness. Halfway along there was a vacant lot, and the smokestack of a freighter was visible against the blank wall of a warehouse on the far side of the Elbe, but Bolan reckoned he'd never set foot in a place that radiated evil and the lowest depths of crime more directly than the 250-yard length of that German street.

There was no traffic. Most of the houses were shuttered, the paint on the woodwork cracked and peeling. The only store was a dirty bookshop with girlie magazines racked inside and the boss behind a one-way mirror. There weren't even any streetwalkers to be seen— just half a dozen guys propping up walls or slouched against rusted iron railings. Hell, the Executioner thought, ten paces away from Hamburg's answer to London's Soho, and here I am in the first reel of a Gothic horror movie!

He saw one mean-faced little runt in a cloth cap and a white muffler picking his teeth with a matchstick. Two more stared with blank eyes from a doorway at the end of a passage lined with stinking trash cans. The most sinister was perched on the curb like a vulture—a lean, stooped character with a hooked nose, a razor scar warping one side of his face and skin like used sandpaper.

None of them moved as Bolan rounded the corner. They didn't even turn their heads. But they were all watching him. For an instant he checked his step, wishing he hadn't stashed the gun in his hotel room.

Lattuada was striding into an entry fifty yards away. The icy wind hustled low clouds across the strip of sky between the rooftops and skittered torn strips of paper along the pavement. Nothing else stirred.

Then he thought: what the hell! This is Germany's second city, in daylight, in the middle of the afternoon; surely even down by the docks an inoffensive visitor can walk through St. Pauli without risking...what? A mugging? A knife between the ribs as the billfold is lifted? A beating because Lattuada had protection and nobody followed him?

Bolan shrugged. He figured he could take the whole damn streetful if he had a wall to back up against. He walked on toward the entry. He had seen some pretty low-down gorillas stateside during what he privately called the Mafia Wars, but even the meanest punks, even the most soulless killers had more human warmth in their faces than the human dregs he passed in Andreas Bernersstrasse that afternoon. The guy with the scarred face had the coldest stare he'd ever seen.

Bolan headed down a paved walk only five yards wide, lit by a single streetlight. Lattuada turned beneath an archway at the far end, just as the Executioner heard the sounds of a fight.

The squalid four-story row houses on either side of the alley were railed off from the pavement, with rusty gates opening on steps that led down to narrow, ill-smelling areas. In one of them was another of Hamburg's ubiquitous drinking clubs. An open doorway, garish with yellow paint, sported a sign decorated with palm trees and the words Coconut Grove. The noise came from someplace inside—the stamp of feet, voices shouting, the crash of furniture and breaking glass.

In that neighborhood Bolan would have normally quickened his step and closed in on Lattuada...if he hadn't heard the scream. It was a girl's voice, high-pitched and taut with terror. And if Andreas Bernersstrasse was a set from a Gothic movie, Bolan was now plunged into the world of comic strips, for the words he heard in German were as corny as speech balloons in a horror comic: "Help! Help! For the love of God, someone help me!"

The warrior hesitated. Lattuada was already out of sight; another few seconds and he would lose him. On the other hand, he didn't *know* that the mobster was in town to operate some criminal racket. Was it worth following up what was no more than a hunch when there was something wrong, really wrong, happening literally under his feet?

Before he'd made up his mind, the girl screamed again—and the scream was stifled halfway up the scale as though a hand had been clapped over her mouth.

That did it. The Executioner wheeled around, flung open the iron gate and charged down the steps.

CHAPTER THREE

It was the usual blueprint clip joint. After dark there would be a tout in a doorman's cap at the entrance to the alley, directing suckers to the yellow door with murmurs of, "Private club, *Meinherr*. Beautiful girls!" A showcase on the wall would display titty pix or girls with whips, none of whom would be performing—or would ever have performed—on the premises. Inside it would be the stock scene: canned music, dim lighting, a tired stripper who undressed four times each hour in four different "clubs" of the same type. There would be half a dozen overpainted and underclothed harpies at the bar, and a cocktail atmosphere combining one part cheap scent and one part wood alcohol with three parts stale perspiration.

Mack Bolan's introduction to the place was a little different. There were only four or five men in there, but it seemed to him like a company of U.S. Marines flushing hostile snipers out of a Vietnam foxhole. There was just one large room behind the yellow door, and the only light filtered through a broken shutter over the area window and down an inner stairway behind the bar. Dim figures heaved and threshed in the gloom. Bolan heard groans and grunts of pain and the thud of blows. As he burst through the door, he tripped over something soft and heavy and his feet crunched on broken glass.

The girl screamed again. She was struggling with a big man behind the bar, clawing at his face as he tried to lift her in a bear hug. "Shut that bitch's mouth, and get her out of here!" someone shouted in German.

The big guy shifted his grip and raised his fist. That was when the Executioner joined the fight.

The impetus of his entrance, plus the trip, carried him clear across the room between the antagonists. Stumbling over some piece of smashed furniture, he hurled himself toward the bar. The edge of the counter caught him across the hips, and he shot facedown across the polished wood as fast as a bank robbery getaway car. His head butted the girl's captor beneath the man's lifted arm—hard.

It wasn't enough to knock out the guy, but, coming unexpectedly out of the dark, the blow threw him off balance. He grunted, fell back a pace and loosened his grip on the woman.

By that time Bolan's hand had connected with an unbroken bottle lying on the bar. The big guy was now silhouetted against the light from the inner stairway. Bolan dived to the floor on the operating side of the bar, swung the bottle and connected with the base of the man's neck. He seized the girl's arm and dragged her away while her captor was staggering, then lashed out a second time. The bottle smashed on his thick skull, and he dropped in a Niagara of alcohol and shattered glass.

The battle was still raging all around. Bolan shoved his prize violently toward the stairs and yelled in his passable German, "Run! Get up there and keep going!"

Something slammed against his left shoulder, half paralyzing his arm. A blade sliced through his sleeve. Then he was climbing like a Fourth of July rocket and a voice below was screeching, "Don't let that cow get away!"

"Who the hell's that motherfucker?" someone else shouted.

"For Chrissake, what the...?"

"Kill the son of a bitch!"

"After them!"

And then the sudden pounding of feet.

Bolan was thankful there were no gunshots. He supposed both sides were scared of bringing down their own in any attempt to block a third party while the light was poor. He was faced at the top of the stairs with a short passage that led to the street-level front door—or a window that opened onto a refuse-strewn backyard.

Remembering the Andreas Bernersstrasse, he chose the window.

He held his two forearms up to protect his face and burst through the lower part in a running dive that carried him through and down to the yard in a shower of jagged glass fragments. Turning, he pulled the girl through the gap as the pursuit hit the top of the staircase.

Something whistled over their heads, shattering the upper half of the window on its way. Bolan staggered upright, clutching the girl's hand, and found his parka skewered to a packing case with a throwing knife. He jerked free and sprinted for an open gateway at the far end of the yard, dragging the girl after him.

This time two shots rang out, and he saw puffs of brick dust spurt from one of the gateposts just ahead of him.

"Don't shoot! We need the broad!" one of the pursuers yelled.

Bolan toppled over a stack of beer crates as he dashed past and then upended a trash can to roll behind him and block the hoods spilling through the broken window. He didn't look back; it would have wasted precious tenths of a second, and they hadn't seen his face yet. He was content to leave it that way.

Beyond the gateway a cobblestoned lane ran left and right. He grabbed the girl's elbow and turned right, because he saw that the lane ended there by the arch he'd seen Lattuada pass through. He reckoned they would be okay if they could just make it to a street with real people in it; the killers would hardly dare continue the assault and battery in broad daylight, with an audience.

Unless the audience came from the Andreas Bernersstrasse.

But there was still a way to go. The goons were no more than twenty yards behind. Gasping for breath, the fugitives ran between windowless brick walls, over stones greasy with nameless garbage, through an atmosphere sickly with the stench of rotting food.

In back someone slipped, cursed and fell. But the others were closing fast. Bolan imagined he could already feel hot, beery breath on his neck.

"Get the damn girl!" the same hoarse voice cried, farther back. "Smash that fucker's head in, but bring back the girl!"

A bottle shattered at the Executioner's feet. Something heavy hit him between the shoulders and dropped. Another knife hissed past his ear, struck sparks from the wall and fell to the ground. Then they were at the archway, turning into the blind end of a cul-de-sac at the far end of which he could see traffic, storefronts, men and women walking this way and that.

Even the blind alley was inhabited: the driver of a panel truck was delivering a rack of leather jackets to one of the buildings. Beyond it, a Cadillac convertible with tinted windows and whitewall tires waited with two wheels up on the sidewalk.

Bolan paid it no mind. Coincidence? He would worry about that later. "It's okay," he panted. "We made it, lady. You can relax now. We're safe."

It was true. Nobody had followed them through the archway. He slowed to a walk, realizing he was still clutching the girl's arm as fiercely as a drowning man, then released her. For the first time he had a chance to look at his prize.

She was a blonde with a pageboy hairstyle and a standout body. Right now a lot of her upholstery was showing because the green silk top she wore was ripped in several places and there was no bra beneath it. The bell of pale hair was mussed, there were runs in her nylons, and the black skirt was gray with dust all down one side. He couldn't see her face because she was shivering and her head was down.

He shrugged out of the parka and wrapped it around her shoulders. "Relax," he said again. "It's all over now."

She looked up then—Marilyn Monroe's younger sister before they told her about gin. But there was a graze on one cheek, her lip was split and pretty soon she would have a black eye. Somebody had been thumping this kid but good. "It's not over," she said tearfully in English. "It'll never be over."

"Ah, it may not be as bad as you think," Bolan soothed. They turned the corner, and he found they were only a couple of blocks from the street where the Black Tie was located. He took her elbow again and steered her toward a café. "C'mon. We'll wrap you around a nice hot cup of coffee with schnapps and you'll feel better. You had one hell of a shock and—"

"No!" she interrupted hysterically. "Not here. No- where around here."

"Okay, okay. No sweat." He raised an arm, and a taxi cruised into the curbside slush. "This lady's been in an accident," he said. "Take us to the nearest hospital as fast as you can." He opened the door and shoved her inside.

"I don't want to go to any hospital!" she cried as he sat beside her.

"Quiet," Bolan said in a low voice. "We're not going to any hospital. That's just a stall in case anyone's lis- tening. We'll get out wherever he takes us and find some quiet place nearby where we can talk."

The hospital was an ultramodern block behind a de- partment store across the road from the Altona subway station. There was a cafeteria on the second floor, and he piloted her to a table there, thankful to come in out of the freezing cold.

"I haven't thanked you," she said. "I don't know who you are or why you did it, but I have to thank you for getting me out of there. Why *did* you do it?"

"In my country we kind of feel a lady shouldn't be pushed around by a roomful of thugs," Bolan said lightly. "Who were they?"

"It was the Team," she muttered. Shivering again, she went on. "Charlie didn't have the money, and they said if he didn't come across by lunchtime today they'd...they'd break the place up and see that he never walked again."

"Charlie?"

"Charlie Farnsbarn. Oh, that's not his real name, of course, but that's what everyone calls him."

"What is his real name?"

"I don't know. Mackintosh? McKay? McEvoy? Something like that. Kind of a Scottish name, you know, although he comes from Trinidad."

"Trinidad? You mean he was—is, I hope—a black guy?"

She nodded. The tears were running down her cheeks. "Poor Charlie. I know the Coconut Grove was a clip joint, but he did run two other places, real classy clubs with a band and all. The Sugar Hill and Tondelayo's. And he's always been g-good to me." She was sobbing aloud now, her slender body shaking each time she caught her breath.

"What happened?" Bolan prompted gently.

"What happened? Well, they broke up the place, didn't they? They did what they said they would, the way they always do when the Yank is involved." The bell of blond hair tolled a silent knell. "I had a date with him at three-thirty. It was to audition for the floor show at Tondelayo's, but the fight had already started when I got there. Not the noisy part but the...I tried to run away but Hansie grabbed me. They wanted to take me with them. The Yank doesn't like witnesses, and they didn't know I was..."

She paused fractionally before she continued. Bolan was seething with questions, but it seemed best to let the vein run out. "They wrecked the place," she said, "and then they started on Charlie. Beat him up and then put the boot in when he was down. He managed to get hold of some wire on the floor and all the lights fused when he jerked it. Then he...he made a run for it, but they caught him." She bit down hard on her lower lip and her eyes closed for a moment. "They cut the tendons at the back of his knees with a razor," she said.

"That must have been Charlie I tripped over when I came through the door. If they hamstrung him, it's true—he'll never walk again," Bolan said.

"I told you. They do what they say. It always happens when—"

"Don't tell me," Bolan cut in. "When the Yank's involved. So who's the Yank?"

"Well, he took over when they began to ease out Kraul, didn't he?"

"You tell me. He's American? So what's his name? It wouldn't be...Lattuada, would it? And who the hell's Hansie?"

Suddenly she shook her head violently. "I don't want to talk about it," she cried. "Leave me alone. Why are you asking me all these questions? Who *are* you, anyway?"

"Let's just say an interested party," Bolan replied.

She was staring at him. "Oh!" she gasped. "You're hurt!"

He was, too. Technically. Although he hadn't noticed, blood had run down his left arm and congealed between the fingers of his hand. He remembered the knife or razor or whatever it was that had nicked his sleeve as he'd made his fleeting appearance on the stage of the Coconut Grove. Sure enough, the shirt was stuck to his skin just below the elbow and the muscle was stiff. He grinned. "It can't be serious," he said, "or I'd have fainted. Allow me to introduce myself. Mike Belasko of *World Review*."

For the first time the girl smiled. It looked good. "Dagmar Schroeder," she said.

"Nice to know you, Dagmar. You mentioned an audition...?"

"I'm a dancer."

"A stripper?"

She shook her head. "Specialty. I...don't wear too much to start with."

Bolan's lips twitched in a smile. A plump woman in a black dress and a starched white cap was standing by the table, notepad and pencil at the ready. "Two coffees, good and hot," he said, "and two schnapps."

"And a sandwich," Dagmar added. "Bratwurst on rye with butter."

"Make that two," Bolan told the woman. He'd had no lunch, either.

There was a column faced with mirrors beside the table, and the girl was staring at her reflection. "My God!" she exclaimed. "My *hair*! I must go fix it this minute." She stood up, clutching the edges of her torn silk top. "No wonder that waitress stared!"

"That goes for me, too. But we can't leave together. We'd lose the table. You go ahead, Dagmar. I'll stay and hold the fort."

He watched her walk away. In a far corner of the cafeteria a three-piece string orchestra sawed through *Tales from the Vienna Woods*. When Dagmar walked, her dancer's legs swung from the hip, but they were slightly bent at the knee. There was no corny swaying of her backside. This was a body, even after the humiliations of a donnybrook, that was aware of itself and what it could do, confident and almost arrogant in that knowledge.

The waitress had brought Bolan's order. Over the roar of the conversation and the clatter of crockery in the huge cafeteria, he was conscious of the fact that the three-piece had finished Strauss and was starting to dismantle Weber.

But music wasn't what was on his mind. What kind of conspiracy had he gotten himself mixed up in? Who were Hansie and the Yank and poor, loose-legged Charlie Farnsbarn? Was he right, thinking there could be a connection between Ferucco Lattuada and what sounded like some kind of German protection racket? Above all, if it was the menacingly named Team that had attacked Charlie, who were the guys fighting *them*? Friends of the hamstrung club owner? Men working for the mysterious Kraul? That was the next question he had to put to Dagmar.

Come to that, where *was* the girl? It seemed a long time since she'd left the table. Could she have passed out in the ladies' powder room? Abruptly Bolan got to his feet and made for the arch behind the cashier where the Damen and Herren signs hung.

There was a large woman in spectacles behind a table on the far side of the arch. She wore white coveralls and was reading an evening paper spread out on the table-top. "Not that way!" she protested in German. "You can't go in there! Yours is on the left. Can't you read?"

"A blonde," Bolan said, "about twenty-four. Medium height. She was wearing a black parka and something green underneath it that was torn. Her face was all bruised. Did you see her come in here ten, maybe twelve minutes ago?"

"Of course I did. I see everything. She was in a mess, poor young thing! I can't think—"

"Is she all right?"

"I guess so," the woman said, looking up over her spectacles. "She seemed fine. Gave me fifty pfennigs when she left."

"She *left*?" Bolan yelled. "Which way did she go?"

"You just missed her. She went down those stairs leading directly to the street half a minute ago."

He was already halfway down them himself. There was a line of cabs standing in the center of the roadway behind the entrance to the subway station. The cold struck him like a blow. Through snowflakes that were beginning to drift down again, he caught sight of a green sleeve as Dagmar Schroeder closed the door of the leading cab and it moved away.

"Taxi!" the Executioner shouted, stepping into the street, waving. "Taxi!"

A heavy hand fell on his arm. "A moment, *Mein-herr*, if you please," a voice said in English. "I am a house detective employed by the management and I have to inform you that I have observed you attempting to leave without paying for a meal that you ordered." The voice was somber. "I have to ask you to accompany me to the director's office...."

CHAPTER FOUR

It was crazy, Bolan fumed to himself. A goddamn house dick of all things! He tried to break free, but the grip on his arm tightened as the guy mouthed the formula required by the law. He was a big guy, too, as tall as the Executioner and three times heavier. Dagmar's cab was already halfway down the Königstrasse, and the lights had changed. An icy sidewalk was no place to try out techniques of unarmed combat. Besides, the guy was only doing his job. Bolan accompanied the man to the director's office.

The bill came to thirteen marks eighty. He rounded the sum out to fifteen marks, to placate the outraged waitress, and left. Back on the street, he went to the nearby department store and bought a new parka. It was snowing heavily now, and the traffic had begun to snarl up as the streetlights flickered on to shine through the whirling flakes. He took the subway back to his hotel, carried a fifth of Jack Daniel's up to his room and settled down in a comfortable chair so that the two of them could mull over the events of the past few hours.

First, though, he had to clean up. His shoulder was stiff and bruised where the blackjack had struck, but the skin wasn't broken. He was black-and-blue where whatever it was had thumped into his back during the chase down the alley. The wound on his arm was the worst, and that was three times nothing at all: a deep cut but clean, easily fixed by a shower, a dab of disinfectant and a strip of plaster. Once it was done, he poured himself half a tumbler of bourbon and put his feet up.

So, he thought, what had he gotten himself into? There seemed to be some kind of Mafia-style protection racket going on in St. Pauli, maybe in other Hamburg neighborhoods, too. That would have to be checked.

Lattuada was a Mafia hood who had certainly been involved in that racket—among others—back home. His presence could simply be a coincidence. Or something much more. Circumstantial support for the latter came from Dagmar Schroeder's mention of the Yank. But that, too, could be a coincidence. Since he happened to be tailing a fellow countryman when he met her, it was natural to make the connection, but he could be wrong: it could just as well be the nickname of some local punk.

Other questions looking for an answer: who or what exactly *was* the Team? Was the Yank their boss? Who was Hansie? Who was Kraul and how was he being "eased out"? What, if anything, had all this to do with Arvell Asticot?

Most important of all: why had the girl run out on him?

She was shit-scared. That was obvious. But there was something else, some undertone Bolan had sensed while she'd talked. What was that she'd said—and then hesitated? Yeah. *They wanted to take me with them. The Yank doesn't like witnesses, and they didn't know I was...* What? Somehow tied in with the guy?

Why had she clammed up just then? And on which side of the battle were "they"? The Team or the others? Whichever, why was it so vital to get the girl away? If it was just to silence a witness, they could have killed her before he had intervened.

One thing anyway was clear: whether or not Dagmar was allied to the Yank, whether or not the Yank was Lattuada, she was in there someplace with an angle; she was involved one way or another. More, Bolan thought, than just as an outsider who showed for an audition and found herself in the middle of a gang war.

Dagmar, in fact, was the one link between all the unanswered questions. He had to see her again and demand some answers. But how do you set about finding one young woman in a city of nearly two million people, if she wants to stay hidden? That was the toughest question of all.

The only lead he had was the name of the two other clubs she had mentioned, both of them belonging to the owner of the Coconut Grove. She wouldn't be at either of them tonight, that was for sure—not in the state she was in. But the management at one or the other might know her address.

Might. She knew the owner, but that didn't necessarily mean she was a regular at either. Or that they would release her address to a stranger if she was. She'd said they were both classy joints with house bands. It was on the cards that a dancer applying for a floor show audition would be strictly backdoor material anyway.

But leads were there to be followed. First Bolan checked the phone book. As he expected, her name wasn't in it. Before he went prospecting, however, he figured it would be smart to fill himself in on the local scene by using the one contact he had in Hamburg.

Freddie Leonhardt was the West German correspondent for *World Review*, the photonews weekly for which Mike Belasko was supposed to be a roving reporter. Michaelson, the magazine's foreign editor, was an ex-CIA field agent who played along with the deception because he was a golfing buddy of Hal Brognola's. From time to time high-powered diplomatic think pieces were published under the Belasko byline to keep the cover alive. And all *World Review* stringers were under a permanent obligation to offer every possible facility to Belasko any time he hit their territory.

In the case of the Hamburg man, there was a two-way interlock. Leonhardt's father had been a member of the Gehlen Organization—the Nazi intelligence service co-opted after World War II by the OSS and later the CIA for anti-Soviet work in the American zone, and especially West Berlin. Subsequently the son, too, was asked to pass occasional items of information on to Langley.

Bolan knew of Freddie Leonhardt's CIA connection, but the German was unaware of Belasko's real identity, and he had no idea that the life of the warrior with the cold blue eyes was dedicated to the eradication of crime and terrorism.

The only thing wrong with the setup from the Executioner's point of view was that he couldn't stand the guy at any price. Freddie had been to school in England, and then to Oxford, something he never let you forget. His English was fluent, all right, but it was so "British" that it would have made the queen of England reach for a blue pencil and rewrite his dialogue.

Freddie wore suede loafers and a yellow wool vest under his Prince of Wales checks. He kept his handmade cigarettes a hygienic distance from his face with the help of an ivory holder. A fob watch on a strap nestled in his breast pocket, there was a gold identity disk on his left wrist, and his graying hair curled just the right amount at the nape of his neck. It might have worked if he had been tall and willowy, but the image tarnished some when the cultured drawl on the telephone turned out to be no more than five feet four inches off the ground and inclining to plumpness.

Bolan thought him a dilettante, pretentious and unreliable. But he did know his stuff. He was a good journalist and he had an in. Bolan called him at his home, a nineteenth-century town house on the Isestrasse.

"But, my dear chap, anything at all," the unctuous voice intoned. "Didn't know you were in town, actually. Head office is getting bloody slack with the old service messages. But anything I can do to help, just say the word."

"There's a five-language brochure called the *Hamburger Vorschau* that I picked up at the hotel reception," Bolan said. "Tells you were to go, what to see, how to eat well and so on."

"Yes, old boy. They have them everywhere. Produced for the information office."

"Yeah," Bolan said. "The thing is, I want to check out two clubs, and they don't appear in the nightlife section. Or the phone book, for that matter."

"Well, you've come to the right door, squire," Leonhardt said. "On Hamburg nightlife yours truly is *the* jolly old expert. What are the names of these haunts of sin and the almighty dollar?"

"The Sugar Hill and Tondelayo's."

There was a slight pause before Leonhardt replied, "Are you sure you have the names right, old boy?"

"Pretty sure. Why?"

"Well..." The voice was guarded.

"Well what?"

"Well, I *know* them, of course. But I mean to say...my dear chap, you're not likely to find anything we can use for the rag *there*. They're run by blackies for a start."

"You mean they're specifically colored clubs?"

"Well, no, not exactly. Just the management and the band and some of the girls. But there's everything that goes with that. You know."

Bolan didn't know and said so.

"They're the kind of places that are *not quite*," Leonhardt explained. "I mean no one above the rank of assistant press attaché would dare go there. Drugged cigarettes under the counter in the men's room. Jewboys and their rag-trade birds who think they're cutting a hell of a dash. Daughters of the bloody Kraut aristocracy—what's left of it—on the prowl for spade dick. Middle-class radicals slumming in the cause of racial equality. Actually, some of the girls are practically tarts."

"You don't say!"

"Tondelayo's is smarter than the Sugar Hill, but they're both...well, not to put too fine a point on it, not much better than high-class whorehouses with music."

"I don't aim to put any kind of a point on it," Bolan said. "I just want the addresses."

"But the kind of people you want wouldn't be seen dead in either of them."

"What kind of people do I want?"

"Well..." Again the German sounded dubious. "Deputies, policymakers, johnnies in the diplomatic corps, the people you write about. If you ask me, you want something a little higher up the social scale. Try Die Insel, for example. All the top brass go there."

"Just give me the addresses," Bolan said.

Leonhardt sighed audibly. "The Sugar Hill's in a courtyard off the Albertplatz—that's a square behind the Hauptbahnhof, the main railroad station.

Tondelayo's is on this side of the Alster near the radio station.'' He spelled out the addresses.

"Fine," Bolan said. "Are they genuine clubs? I mean, do they check membership?"

"Actually they do. They ask to see your card and check it against a list at the door. Something to do with the drink laws and the fire regulations."

"I'm surprised you should know such a thing, a guy of your standing," Bolan said sourly. "Does a foreign press accreditation get you past the door at a private club?"

"No."

"Does a Hamburg press card?"

"Yes, as a matter of fact it does."

"Good. So grab yourself a cab, come on over and lend me yours."

"My dear fellow, I can't possibly do—"

"That's an order, Leonhardt," Bolan said curtly. He hung up.

THE ALBERTPLATZ WAS OFF the Steindamm, the tree-lined square where the Executioner had watched the man from the Cadillac report on the wreck of the Becker Café. And where he had first heard the name of Kraul mentioned. It was also the place where he had witnessed the young guy in the beat-up Opel so obviously, to a trained eye, keeping watch on the Cadillac, too.

He had seen neither the man nor the car since. Police shadow, private eye or lookout for Kraul, whoever he was, the tail remained just one more mystery in the web of intrigue surrounding the Executioner.

For his second visit to the square, Bolan again rented the Honda scooter. The snow was falling faster, and windshields were icing up. The streets risked becoming choked with stalled traffic, and the lightweight machine was easy to maneuver, to park and, if necessary, to wheel home if conditions became impossible.

The courtyard where the Sugar Hill was located was behind the church. It was a long, narrow slant of cobblestones fast whitening under the snowfall, where the double rank of parked cars surprised Bolan by its exotic flavor. He saw Ferraris, Stingrays, Jaguar coupes, an AC Cobra and a huge vintage Hispano-Suiza among the run-of-the-mill Fords, Volkswagens and Mercedes-Benzes blanketed by the whirling flakes.

There was a glass canopy over the club entrance, which was at street level, and there was a black guy with a Jamaican accent installed in the hallway behind an open membership register. Since there was no question of checking names against a list, Bolan was able to flash Leonhardt's press card and keep his thumb over most of the photo.

"Glad to have you with us, friend," the Jamaican said in English. "Always happy to see the gentlemen of the press. The bar's right on through." The bouncer standing behind him was black, too, but he didn't say anything.

"Is Dagmar Schroeder in tonight?" Bolan asked casually as he passed the desk.

The doorkeeper shrugged and shook his head. "Right on through, sir."

Bolan checked his coat and went through to the bar, a room at the far end of a long passageway with no doors. But the action was evidently in the basement below. From the top of the stairs Bolan could hear a small band that was really wailing, and crowd noises that meant the joint was jumping. A mulatto with frizzy, hennaed hair, a scanty sequined top and an impudent bottom was leaning against the bar.

"Hi, good-looking," she said lazily in English as he loped in. Bolan assumed Americans were regular patrons here. "You look like I could do with a drink," the mulatto slurred. "What you gonna buy me, man?"

"I always did go for the subtle approach," Bolan said. "Keep me in the dark a little longer and order for both of us. Beer for me."

Her name was Sally Ann, and she must have been all of nineteen years old. Downstairs she hooked her forearms over the Executioner's shoulders and draped four-fifths of her body, from the tips of the sequins to the tips of her silver sandals, against his husky frame. The top fifth leaned back with the head tilted and looked him in the eye. That was his guess: he couldn't actually see her doing it because there seemed to be eight hundred people jammed into a space the size of a Lincoln Continental, and the only light in the place came from a single lamp above the piano keyboard.

Dance was putting it politely. Couples stayed pressed together and shook while the four guys on the stage earned their money. The music was good, not so strident that it was almost impossible to talk.

"Isn't Dagmar in tonight?" Bolan had to press his lips against her ear to make himself heard.

"Dagmar?" The whites of her eyes gleamed up at him in the dusk.

"Dagmar Schroeder. The dancer."

"I never heard of her."

"I thought she was supposed to be part of the floor show. There is a floor show, isn't there?"

"If you can call it that. But it's only on Sundays here. Why mess with her when I'm here?"

"I have a message for her from her mother," Bolan said.

"I could add a PS that would help you forget that message."

"And just how would that read?"

Her fingers laced together behind his neck, but before she could reply there was a stamping of feet overhead and the guitar player stopped in midsolo. Immediately afterward Bolan heard a succession of sounds that were becoming disturbingly familiar: the noises of violent combat, breaking glass, splintering wood, shouts and curses. "Christ, it's not *another* police raid, is it?" someone near Bolan asked plaintively.

Knowing that the Sugar Hill belonged to Charlie, Bolan thought probably not.

Abruptly light flooded the room from wall brackets on three sides of the floor. He took a quick glance around. Being a private club, the place was exempt from fire regulations. Apart from a narrow doorway in back of the stage that led to a dressing room, the stairway was the only exit.

There was a lot of yelling upstairs in the bar now. Some of the men on the dance floor forced their way to the stairs. At least one was carrying a razor. A few women screamed. The band had already vanished, but there was a big guy standing on the edge of the stage telling everyone not to panic, that everything was all right. Bolan figured him for an optimist when all the lights went out, including the one over the piano.

In total darkness there was a moment's frozen pause in which the mayhem upstairs sounded unnaturally loud. Bolan unfastened his jacket and checked that the Beretta, which he had recovered from the hotel safe before he'd left, was sliding easily in its leather. Then, beneath an upsurge of voices suddenly exclaiming around him, he was aware of an undercurrent with a purpose, a whispering, a shuffling of feet. Somebody seized his arm and shoved him toward the stage. He tripped over the edge, cursing, and then Sally Ann's hand, which had stayed in his, jerked him impatiently forward.

It was one of the things he had noticed in dives all the way from Singapore to Cincinnati: the apparently effortless ability of jazz musicians to take an instant powder at the first hint of trouble. Including, no matter how cumbersome, their instruments. The Sugar Hill was no exception. Apart from the piano, the small stage was already clear. A cool breeze blew through the door behind it.

Quite a crowd of dancers was pushing its way through, but there was no jam-up—just an occasional staying hand and a few murmured warnings. The dressing room was pint-size. Beyond it, signaled by an odor of disinfectant, was a minuscule washroom... and yet this slow stream of customers seemed to be able to pile in there endlessly.

Bolan soon discovered why. There was a stepladder beneath an open trapdoor in the washroom ceiling...and those in the know, aided by club stewards, just climbed up and disappeared into the night. Clearly it was a tested escape route, established to help members avoid embarrassing encounters with the law. With that kind of organization, who needed fire regulations?

They surfaced in a narrow lane twisting back toward the Steindamm. The long passage that led to the bar must have penetrated another block, because the courtyard where Bolan's scooter and the exotic automobiles were parked was nowhere to be seen. Sheltering in a doorway while the outflow thinned a bit, Bolan turned to the girl. "Seems I owe you the other half of that drink we left back in there," he said. "Where do you want to go?"

Flakes of snow mantled the frizzy hair like the frosting on a Christmas tree. She took his arm. "We could try Tondelayo's," she said.

That was what he hoped she would say. In the circumstances it seemed a reasonable hunch. And if he was going to soft probe, asking questions, it would come easier if he was with a girl who was known at the club.

"Suits me," he said. "Is it far? We better grab a cab anyway. My parka's still down there—the second one I've lost today!—and you'll catch your death dressed like that."

"Not far," Sally Ann said. "Around the top end of the Alster, in the Harvesterhuder Weg."

As the taxi's radials bit through six inches of freshly fallen snow around the lakeside driveway, Bolan risked another question. "You figure it'll be okay at this place... Tondelayo's?" he asked. "I mean, the place belongs to Charlie and all that—they won't wreck it, too?"

"No, no," the girl said absently. She was staring at the blizzard lancing toward them through the tunnel of light carved by the taxi's headlights. "He's only part owner. Besides, there's a double payoff—city hall as well as the people who muscled in."

"You mean the...Team...chiseled him out of a piece of the action? And there's protection from the police, as well?"

Sally Ann let go of his arm. "I don't know what you're talking about."

"Ah, c'mon, don't give me that," Bolan needled. "What's the matter? You scared of the Yank or something?"

"Better to keep quiet about things like that." Suddenly the Danish accent was very strong. "You know something," the girl said, "we haven't had a snowfall this heavy since '84 when I was in school."

Tondelayo's was on the second floor of a narrow building that was a bakery at street level. "That's one up in favor of the management," Bolan said. "Basements are beginning to give me claustrophobia."

Freddie Leonhardt had been right. It was a ritzier joint than the Sugar Hill, but only just. The crowded bar was wider, garish tropical silhouettes decorated the walls, and there was waiter service at the tables around the dance floor. The six-piece band onstage boasted a drummer, too.

"You'll never guess why they opened over a bakery," Sally Ann said when Bolan had bribed their way to a table and ordered.

"No complaints about the noise, because bakers work nights anyway?" he offered.

"That, too. No, but the real reason is the smell. You can't tell grass from ordinary tobacco over the odor of baking bread. Not for sure. Did you know that?"

He shook his head. "I quit school young. So everybody lights up as soon as the ovens are fired?"

"Or before. Talking of which..." She shot him a sideways glance.

"Yeah?"

"I'm dying for a smoke right now."

Still playing dumb, Bolan raised a finger to signal a topless cigarette girl wearing fishnet tights.

Sally Ann's stare mixed scorn and disbelief in equal portions. "You have to be joking," she said. "Shit, I never figured you for a square." She shook her head. Then, compressing her lips, she left the table and flounced away to the ladies' room.

Two minutes later she was back, still frowning. "Not so cool," she said. "I shot a blank. So what's with you, Frank?"

"You get a lot of vintage Hollywood movies on TV here?" Bolan queried.

"I don't dig you. What's the pitch?"

He grinned. "Question of dialogue. But let it pass."

She was still angry. "All right," he said. "It just happens that I'm not in the habit of walking around with my pockets stuffed full of marijuana. Where I come from, it just happens to be illegal."

"Here, too, dummkopf. If you want to be stuffy about it, I mean. If you want to please the lady you're with, you go raise a couple of joints from Joe."

"I see," Bolan said. "Joe."

"The guy in the men's room," she said impatiently.

Bolan rose to his feet. He had no intention of buying drugs for anyone. He was in the business of eliminating the stuff from the planet, or at least making life hell for those who profited from the evil garbage. But "Joe" might give a lead or two about Dagmar. Penny-ante pushers got around and were easily bought. They made great snitches for cops. As for Sally Ann's request, he'd just tell her he couldn't find the pusher or that the guy was temporarily out of stock. Reluctantly he headed for the men's room.

There were a lot of people dancing now, but not so many that he couldn't identify the different categories of member itemized by Freddie Leonhardt. The only thing the Hamburg stringer had gotten wrong was the proportions: more than half the women were hookers with visiting firemen in tow. There were also a few kids who had apparently come to listen to the band.

On the far side of the floor Bolan buttonholed a waiter and ordered a second round. He figured another drink or two might make Sally Ann a little more talkative about matters concerning Dagmar and her associates.

"Right away, sir," the waiter said cheerfully. "Straight Jack Daniel's for two coming up. You'll find the men's room behind the office. Other side of the entrance."

"Thanks," Bolan said. He took a step, then turned back. "By the way, isn't Dagmar in tonight?"

The shutters came down over the dark face. "Dagmar?"

"Dagmar Schroeder. The dancer. I thought she was part of the floor show?"

"I don't know who you mean. We don't have a floor show. Now, if you'll excuse me, sir..."

The attendant in the men's room was a fat, bald Creole. By the time the Executioner had waited around for the place to empty, had hedged a little, slipped him ten marks and finally put the question, he had an eight-hundred-word Sunday magazine section piece on the guy's life story. Even then the Creole just shook his pale head. "I is des-o-lated, sir, but it can't be done."

"But I thought... One of the girls told me..."

"Sure, mister, sure. But I can't give you what I ain't got, can I? My supplier done let me down."

"That's too bad," Bolan said, not intending for a moment to buy any grass. He figured posing as a customer was the best way to get the guy's guard down.

"I know it, friend. You ain't the only one. But Dagmar didn't show tonight."

"*Dagmar!* Dagmar Schroeder? You don't mean Dagmar Schroeder the dancer?"

Down came another set of shutters. He pried them open a crack with another ten spot. "Tallish kid with blond hair. Pageboy cut. Pretty girl."

The fat shoulders shrugged. "Dunno. Just a chick who comes in and then goes out. Dagmar."

"You don't know her other name?"

"Mister, I don't even know if she *has* another name. I never heard nobody use one."

And that was as far as Joe would commit himself.

"You wouldn't know where I could contact her?" Bolan pursued. "Her address? Anyplace she hangs out? It's important. And it's worth another twenty."

Again the plump shoulders heaved. "Everything's important to someone, right?" The bills vanished. "You could try the Mandrake Root, Willi's Grotto, the Cellar, the Nussdorfer Weinstube. Some of 'em go there, daytimes. Sometimes."

Bolan didn't know if it was the right Dagmar, but he noted down the names. He'd paid for them, and it was the only lead he had.

Sally Ann sighed when he returned to the table with the bad news. "Guess we better go back to my place then, but all I have is a sack of low-grade hash from North Africa—none of that knockout Colombian shit that Joe peddles." On Joe's supplier, however, she couldn't—or wouldn't—add a word.

Bolan diverted his mind from Sally Ann's feminine charms. He had a list of addresses; he wasn't going to find out any more from Sally Ann, however appealing he found her kooky out-of-date image. And he certainly had no intention of passing the rest of the night fighting his way out of a hashish cloud. He asked the doorman to call a taxi.

It arrived almost at once, etching deep tire marks in the blinding white blanket of snow that filled the street from wall to wall.

The night was still blisteringly cold. "Keep that heater on full blast," Bolan told the cabbie. "Where am I going to drop you off?" he asked the girl.

"Drop me *off*?" She sounded scandalized. "Are you kidding?"

"Just tell the man the address."

She snapped out the name of a street on the far side of the botanic gardens and then turned on him furiously. "What kind of a heel are you?" she hissed. "All evening you let me think I scored, and then, when it comes to the crunch, here's Mr. Do-Right telling me good-night without even a kiss on the doorstep! What *is* this blow-hot-blow-cold routine, for Chrissakes?"

Bolan wadded a couple of hundred-mark bills and pressed them into her hand. "You'll have the rest of the night to think up an answer to those two questions," he said. "Okay, driver, the light's green."

The cab's diesel roared as the front wheels scythed through the soft snow carpet, then finally the tires gripped and they moved crabwise into the center of the roadway. "Thank Christ it's at least stopped falling," the cabbie growled, gingerly feathering the pedal.

They were still making less than fifteen miles per hour when they hit the intersection and the shooting started.

CHAPTER FIVE

The shots blazed out from two cars. One was at the head of a long line parked between the trees along the sidewalk; its roof, hood and windshield were so deeply covered that it was impossible to identify the make. At one side of the humped white shape a single shallow rectangle of black showed up where a window had been wound halfway down, and it was from the perforated muzzle of an SMG poking through this gap that the deathstream first belched.

The second car was a dark-colored Golf GTi. It was halted in the center of the cross street, the front and sides hatched open where snow had been clawed away to free glass and door handles.

Both windows on the passenger side were open, and gunfire flamed out from inside the sedan before the echoes of the SMG fusillade had been swallowed among the white-capped branches of the leafless trees. Two heavy-caliber automatics, Bolan thought, but he wouldn't have laid money on it because he had hit the cab door handle and dived into the roadway, pulling the girl with him, while the burst from the parked car was shattering the cab's windshield.

The fresh snow cushioned the impact, but the city blacktop was near enough to the surface to bruise knees, elbows, shoulders, and knock most of the breath from Bolan's body. He had bailed out on the side away from the killers beneath the trees because two autoloaders were less lethal than a single submachine gun—especially at a distance of more than twenty-five yards.

It was a good place for an ambush just the same. An overhead light slung on wires drenched the whole intersection in searing brilliance. The cab, lurching on for only a few yards after the initial volley, was stalled in the center of the wide space with the driver slumped over the wheel. The hail of lead that smashed through his chest had blasted open a door, and blood dripped darkly from the sill to stain the gray-white tire track below.

The Executioner and Sally Ann were isolated, half-buried in scuffed snow, fifteen feet behind the taxi. For the moment they were hidden from the marksman with the SMG, but they made perfect targets, black against the sparkling white, for the gunners in the Volkswagen.

The automatics fired again. Bullets gouged spurts of powdery snow from the unbroken carpet behind their heads. The killers didn't have the range quite right; they hadn't allowed for the "climb" of the heavy handguns, throwing the slugstream high.

Sally Ann had screamed as she was pulled from the cab. Now she hunched down, whimpering quietly in the shelter of Bolan's body. He lay on his back, the Beretta in his right hand, forefinger curled around the trigger. "Run like hell for the cab when I tell you, lie beneath it and *don't move*!" he rasped. Sighting coolly as the thugs in the VW tried for the third time, he raised his arms above his head and shot out the overhead light.

"Now!" he yelled at the girl.

She scrambled forward, scattering snow, sobbing for breath. A slug nicked Bolan's sleeve. Another took away the heel of his shoe, jarring his left leg. The overhead light faded to orange, turned red, died. Broken glass pattered down onto the cab.

Bolan was on his feet and running, plowing through the shin-high mantle of white in a desperate attempt to make the opposite sidewalk before the gunmen's eyes, temporarily blinded by the abrupt absence of brilliance, acclimatized to the ghostly half-light that would in very few seconds be reflected from the snow.

He tripped over the bank of frozen slush piled along the curb, stumbled and almost fell. Then he was vaulting an iron railing to drop down among the pale mounds of shrubbery in the front yard of a house on the corner of the intersection.

The snow had drifted here, and he got up on his haunches in its numbing embrace. Peering between icy branches, he could make out the dim bulk of the Golf and the cab marooned on a bone-white plain without depth or substance. The second car was no more than the termination of an irregular shape beneath bare trees silhouetted by light reflected from lights in adjacent streets. Above the Christmas-card rooftops a yellow glare from sodium lights in the city center showed up hurrying clouds.

Bolan had been quick, but not quick enough to escape detection. Livid flame stabbed the gloom surrounding the Golf, the crack of the shots curiously muffled by the snow. Bullets thwacked through the bushes on either side of Bolan, rattling the frozen leaves and tingling his cheeks with particles of frost. A ricochet whined off the iron railing.

He flicked the Beretta onto three-shot mode and fired two rapid bursts, aiming just above the flashes in the sedan's open windows. There was a loud cry. Bolan thought he heard a faint scrambling thump, as if one of the gunmen had been slammed back into the body of the car.

He was hidden from the SMG killer in the parked vehicle, and for the moment there was no more shooting. In the silence he was suddenly aware that the Volkswagen's engine had been quietly idling all this time.

Voices called out. A rapid exchange in German. The VW began to move. They were playing it the way the Executioner would have done himself if the positions had been reversed.

The sedan circled away slowly to the far side of the intersection, virtually out of the Beretta's effective range, turned beyond the taxi and began to approach the road that led back to Tondelayo's. At the same time a door slammed and there was a rustling of bushes beyond the railings by the parked car; the guy with the SMG, covered by his accomplices, was installing himself in the front yard across the road from Bolan. Once he was in place he could pin the warrior down while the VW moved in to finish him.

Bolan glanced swiftly around. Lights had come on in some of the houses bordering the intersection; in one or two windows figures were outlined peering down into the street. But the facade immediately behind him was dark. The window fronting the yard was shuttered and the entrance door was at the top of a flight of stairs—a position where he would provide a perfect target for the submachine gunner if he was to attempt a break-in to escape through the rear of the house.

From across the street, the SMG suddenly opened fire, shattering the calm with savage violence. The gunner hosed his deathstream right and left across the whole width of the yard, and Bolan only had time to fling himself facedown in the snow before the slugs streaked through the railings, splatted against the ironwork, and screeched off into the sky. Somewhere down the cross street an angry voice shouted from an upper story. The Golf accelerated and began to home in on Bolan's corner.

He bit his lip, going over the options. He quickly corrected that. There was no choice. He was cornered and the single chance he had was to tempt the opposition to empty their magazines and make a run for it while they reloaded.

Arguments against that were several: first, he didn't know the make of SMG and therefore the number of rounds in the magazine; second, ditto for the remaining handgun; and third, even if he did, it wouldn't be easy to make an accurate calculation of the number of rounds expended when the gun could have a firing rate of up to fifteen hundred or two thousand rounds per minute. In any case, he guessed the killers were professional enough to keep one gun operative while the other reloaded.

Bolan realized that this was one of the tightest corners he'd ever been in. Someone must want him out of the way very badly.

It followed therefore that his line of logic—even if he himself had no idea where it was leading—was taking him too close for comfort to...what? Who? Ferucco Lattuada? The protection racket linking the mafioso with club wrecking and the mysterious Yank?

Rule out any other answer. He would find out when he had fought his way out of the ambush...if he fought his way out of the ambush.

That was a big "if."

But negative thinking formed no part of Mack Bolan's intellectual armory. He would fight his way out. It was just a question of finding the right way to do it.

The answer was provided by a third party.

From different directions he heard over the rooftops the bray of two—no, three—approaching sirens. Someone in one of the nearby houses had called the cops.

There was a shout from the Volkswagen. A final volley from the submachine gun stirred the snow uncomfortably close to Bolan's face. The sedan slewed around in the center of the intersection, engine roaring, wheels scrabbling. A rear door opened and a dark shape tumbled out onto the roadway. The car braked by the railings across the street from Bolan's hideout, scattering snow. The man with the SMG leaped the railings and scrambled in the open door.

The Volkswagen accelerated away along the cross street, snaking crazily from side to side as the powdered front wheels fought for a grip on the icy surface.

Bolan had let loose a shot at the gunner as he dashed for the car, another at the Golf itself, careering away. He thought he might have winged the killer—had the guy stumbled slightly before he was dragged inside?—but he couldn't be sure he had scored. He was already out on the street himself and running.

He hoped to hell Sally Ann was okay underneath the stalled cab: he hadn't heard a sound from her since he'd killed the overhead light. "It's all right," he called. "On your feet and follow me. We've got to get out of here fast!"

There was no reply.

Bolan cursed. He couldn't believe she had been hit by a stray bullet: nobody had been firing in that direction. He sprinted past the body of the man thrown from the Volkswagen. Even in the poor light he could see the guy was dead; the lower half of his face had been pulverized by one of the Beretta's 9 mm bursts. "It's all over,

Sally!'' he yelled again. "Come out and start running!''

Once more there was no reaction.

The police sirens were much nearer now. One sounded no more than a couple of blocks away. Bolan skated to a halt in the cab's tire tracks. He dropped to one knee and peered beneath the trunk. Zero. No Sally Ann, alive or dead.

He ran to the front of the cab. The tracks in the snow told the story as clearly as a video. From the place where Bolan had pulled her out of the vehicle, the girl had crawled back beneath it, the way she had been told, dragged herself along and out between the front wheels, and then gotten to her feet and started running. The footmarks, widely spaced, led straight on from the cab and along the street the driver had been following.

And none of the killers had fired a single shot at her.

Bolan took in the rest of the scene with a swift glance. Even the dumbest cop could read what had happened at the intersection. An ambushed taxi, the driver killed, the passengers spilled into the snow. One passenger miraculously escaping, the other taking refuge behind the railings of a front yard. A gunman opposite, probably staked out in a parked car belonging to someone living in the block who was still unaware that it had been broken into. The getaway vehicle, spent shells buried in the snow, and a dead man lying at the crossroads.

Bolan shook his head. This was the second time he'd been left holding the bag at the scene of a murder. As far as the Executioner was concerned, he had two options: he could haul the murdered cabbie out of his seat and drive the taxi away, or he could run.

The cab would be quicker, but there were too many problems. Fingerprints on the controls as well as in back of the vehicle, the risk of witnesses, of the cab being identified too soon, the probability that he would be held responsible for the cabbie's death, too, at least until ballistics proved the man had been killed with a different gun. Bolan ran.

Planting his feet carefully in the wide tire tracks left by the skidding Volkswagen, he headed toward the next intersection, where late-night buses and homebound traffic had already flattened the snow enough to make pursuit of an individual trail impossible. Let the bloodhounds follow Sally Ann's tracks along the residential street if they wanted to play detective.

Running, as the nearest siren approached the ambush intersection behind him, Bolan wrestled with a single vital question. The ambush had been carefully set up; they'd been waiting for him. And they couldn't have had much time. They must have been tipped off the moment it was clear Bolan was about to leave Tondelayo's. Only two people could have done that accurately. Was it the doorman who called the cab, or was it Sally Ann herself?

CHAPTER SIX

The Mandrake Root was a cellar club beside the widest of the canals that connected the Alster with the Elbe. There was a simple bar and a couple of dozen tables with chairs. Most of the members at the tables—all of them men—were playing chess or backgammon. The only woman in the place looked like a retired schoolteacher. She was perched on a stool at one end of the bar, staring mournfully into a shot glass of schnapps.

The doorman was an expatriate Brit who had once been a street performer and then earned a meager living reciting Shakespeare to theater queues. Bolan learned that much just trying to get into the place.

When he got to the bar, he ordered a beer from a huge Russian with a tiny head and no neck. The chess players were engrossed in their games. The doorman, a short, shaggy man with a blotched red face, came and stood beside Bolan, then picked up a half-finished stein of dark ale.

Bolan laid a fifty-mark bill on the bar. "I have to contact a blonde, name of Dagmar Schroeder. A dancer. They tell me she comes in here sometimes."

"Aye," the doorman said. The bill disappeared. "But not in the mornings. You want to try the Nussdorfer Weinstube—or maybe the Kinderplatz, between city hall and the river."

Back in the open air it was several degrees warmer and the snowy sidewalks had already been trodden into muddy slush. He pondered the doorman's directions. Aside from the bribe, why was he so quick to volunteer information? Bolan knew that in places like these, sometimes no amount of money could pry information if they were ordered not to talk. How had he—or she—known Bolan would turn up at the Mandrake Root?

The question raised once more the other one that had been bugging him since the attack the night before. How had the killers known with such precision just when his cab was going to cross that intersection? The doorman or the girl?

If it *was* Sally Ann, that had to mean she was in with Lattuada, or whoever it was the Executioner was getting too close to, maybe that she had been staked out at the Sugar Hill as a deliberate decoy.

So how had they known he would *be* at the damn club? Indirectly through Dagmar? Because she had talked about her work as a dancer and they knew he wanted to locate her?

So why, in that case, the call for help? And, hell, what was this crap about an audition for a floor show when Tondelayo's didn't have a floor show?

Bolan sighed in exasperation. Two young women, two mysteries—and everything connecting them was contradictory! Turning up his collar against a cold wind blowing off the Alster, he hurried toward the Nussdorfer Weinstube.

It was a smoky, low-ceilinged basement near the radio station, crowded with wine-drinking liberals playing the bohemian game—guys with beards in clothes that didn't fit them, women with no foundation garments who looked as if they'd be happier sitting in dirndl skirts around a candle stuck in a Chianti bottle. Dagmar Schroeder, they told him, would be in Willi's Grotto.

She might have been. Bolan wouldn't know. Press card or no press card, they wouldn't allow him past the door because he wasn't a member. He trudged up the stairs, then asked the way to the Cellar.

There was no club. It was a cheap restaurant near the railroad station, sandwiched between a sexy lingerie boutique and a bicycle repair shop. The place smelled of french fries and garlic. Most of the tables were occupied by mechanics in blue coveralls from an auto tire shop across the street. Some of the hookers on the early shift were eating there, too, but none of them looked like Dagmar. The owner knew her just the same: she'd been there only yesterday for her morning coffee. He advised Bolan to try a café in Altona.

He discovered it was less than a block away from the café where the girl had run out on him. He also discovered that he now had a guide and mentor. The doorman from the Mandrake Root, surfacing for air, had homed in on a soft touch, seeing him pass again.

They went to an imitation drugstore near the Four Seasons, drank wine at the Alsterpavilion, switched to coffee at the Fischerhaus and escaped from the Kiss-Kiss Disco without swallowing anything at all. Waiters and barmen at all of them knew Dagmar. But, no, she hadn't been in today.

They ended up at a dockside saloon near the fish market.

Bolan was drawn to an argument at the other end of the bar. "Even if it does keep out the local trash," a beefy guy with a red face said angrily, "I don't see why the hell we should permit some goddamn American muscle into our German scene and organize a protection—"

"Helmut, you have to be realistic," a thin, dark man cut in.

"Realistic, hell. I'll allow that when you got a District, you got crime. You got the pimps and the pushers. You got the wholesalers. You got the cathouse madams and the villains who want to cut themselves a slice. So then you get the heavies, too. But I don't see—"

"You don't see from nothing. In a tough world and a tough trade you gotta put up with toughs. But can't you see it's better to have it *organized* so that, shit, you know where you're at—rather than being at the mercy of any two-bit punk old enough to carry a knife?"

"Right now I don't see too much evidence of organization."

"The chorus boys at the Opera tell me it's working out okay. They pay a regular subscription and their supplies always arrive on time. For Chrissakes, that's better than waiting around on street corners, isn't it?"

Bolan had heard enough. He asked a traffic cop the way to the Kinderplatz and found that it was a court-yard in back of a street market only two blocks away. On the way there he found that the temperature had dropped again. His feet crunched on ice and the freezing air was once more painful to breathe. He stopped off at a men's wear boutique and bought a wool scarf to wind around the lower half of his face.

At the market the roadway was jammed with house-wives searching for the best bargains among the barkers by their barrows of fish and meat and flowers. In be-tween fruit and vegetable stalls lining the sidewalk someone had stalled an ancient sedan. The driver was tinkering with the engine as Bolan pushed his way through the noisy crowd.

Through the arch that led to the courtyard, half a dozen doorways punctuated the forest of drainpipes climbing the sooty brick facades, and there was a delicatessen at one side of the entrance. He made the round of the doorways. Inside each there were plaques, hand-painted signs, business cards, sometimes even tarnished brass plates fixed to the walls. Bolan was familiar with the scene. On the upper floors there would be sweat-shops crammed with guest workers producing cheap garments for the rag trade, film processing laboratories, small-time attorneys' offices, hustling apartments—anything and anybody that went with low rent, one washroom per floor and the odor of bugs and dry rot.

He drew a blank until he made the fourth door. This one was closed and someone had slapped a coat of yellow paint over the flaking surface during the past few months. Five porcelain bell buttons were set into the brickwork beside the door, and there was a strip of card enclosed in a narrow metal frame under each. The building had clearly been turned into apartments fairly recently. The top card read: D. Schroeder—6th Floor.

He leaned on the bell. There was no reply from the interphone grille. He rang again, listening. Nothing. He knocked with his knuckles, as loud as he could. Nobody came. He stepped back a few paces and stared up at the top floor. Three windows under the eaves, all of them closed. He couldn't see anything beyond the glass, just the reflection of gray clouds hurrying across the sky.

The cold wind and the market noises were making his head ache. Apart from a sausage on a stick at the imitation drugstore he had eaten nothing since before his visit to the Sugar Hill the night before. He decided it was time to fix that. He went into the deli and ordered a coffee and a pastrami sandwich. Sipping and munching, he stared at the elongated reflections on the surface of a silver urn behind the bar.

Two attenuated market men slid around the curve of metal, flattened into grotesque dwarves as they passed behind him and sat down farther along the bar. The door opened again and a blonde, nine feet tall and thin as a pencil, appeared in the urn. Her deformed head raced across the surface as she leaned forward to speak to the guy behind the bar.

"Two on rye to take away, Fritz," she said hurriedly in German. "And a carton of hot coffee. Black."

Counterclockwise, Bolan spun slowly on his stool. "Yesterday, it was white," he said. "But then of course you didn't drink that, did you?"

Dagmar Schroeder stared at him with her mouth open. She had good teeth. "Oh, my God!" she said. But the recovery came quick. "I feel so bad. I don't know what to say to you, leaving you in the cafeteria like that."

Bolan nodded. "They missed you at Tondelayo's last night," he said.

"Tondelayo's?" If she was acting, she was doing it very well. The penciled brows knitted, the nose wrinkled, the blond hair swung as the head tilted to one side. "What do you mean? I wasn't expected there. I didn't do the audition. Charlie was in the hospital. You know that."

"They don't have a floor show, either. *You* know *that*."

The man behind the counter finished sharpening his knife and began carving the meat for her sandwiches. "What's this, they don't have a floor show?" Dagmar demanded angrily. "Why else would Charlie ask me to do an audition?"

"You tell me," Bolan said.

"Of *course* they have a floor show."

"Joe didn't think so. Nor did the waiter."

"Joe who? What are you talking about?"

"Joe said he missed your visit. The clients were disappointed."

She stared at him again. "What *are* you talking about?"

"Look," Bolan said. "This isn't getting us anyplace. I have to talk to you. Why don't we go take a drink in some nice quiet club, preferably at street level or even higher?"

"No!" Her voice was pitched so high that the market men looked up from their hot chocolates.

The counter clerk pushed a paper bag and a waxed carton toward her. "There you are, sweetie. Six marks seventy to you," he said in German.

"Take it out of this. Mine, too." The Executioner slid a ten spot across the polished wood, keeping his eyes fixed on the girl. She was wearing a tan raincoat, belted tightly at the waist, with the collar turned up. "You can help me," he said. "I have to talk to you. Please."

That one worked better. Muscles around the gray eyes relaxed. The flesh softened. Dagmar smiled. "Walk me back to my door?" she asked.

He swept his change off the bar and nodded. They left the deli and started to cross the courtyard. She took his arm. "I'm treating you very badly," she apologized. "After all, you did rescue me most gallantly from a really tough situation."

"So why won't you at least have a drink with me? Why did you run out on me? Why don't you give me honest answers to my—"

"Because I'm scared!" she interrupted fiercely. "That's why."

"So tell me about it. Maybe I can rescue you again."

She shook her head. They had arrived outside the yellow door. She turned to face him, still with one hand on his arm. "You don't understand," she said. "It's not safe for me to go anywhere. No place at all. I'm holed up in this grotty little apartment until the heat's off—if it ever is. I only come out to hurry over to Fritz's place for something to eat."

"Okay. So if you can't come out, let me come up to your place and talk." Bolan smiled. "Otherwise I'll just play watchdog, lie right here on your doormat and compromise you." He waved a hand around the yard. "Think what the neighbors would say."

The hand tightened on his arm. She smiled again. "That might be nice," she said. Bolan hoped the sigh she gave was one of relief.

He said, "Look, why don't I go over to the market, pick up some cold meat, maybe a little fruit, and drop by a wine store? Then I'll come right back . . . and invite you to have dinner at your own place."

"That would be great," Dagmar said. "But not to-night."

He frowned. "Why not? If you're hiding out . . ."

"There are things I have to do . . . phone calls to make . . . the place is in a mess. I don't know." Once more she sounded confused, a rabbit dashing frantically up and down the warren as a fox digs its way in.

"So I'll stick around for half an hour, give you time to straighten things out, come up later."

"No, no. You don't understand."

"There's plenty I don't understand," Bolan said. "Okay. But there's one thing I do know. You're in a hole, and I'm here to help if I can. I can see you're in big trouble. Some of it I've seen, some I found out, some I can guess. But just remember, any problem eases once it's shared."

"You're sweet," Dagmar said. She was standing very close to him.

"Sure I'm sweet. And I can be sweeter. But I can't help unless you level with me, and I guess there's nobody else standing in line right now, or he'd be here already and you wouldn't be in this mess. Believe me, I'm on your side... whatever it is."

"Of course I believe you. But—"

"So what's to stop us attending to the matter now, tonight?"

Once more the gold bell of hair shook from side to side, this time decisively. "There are things *I* have to find out, too. I can't explain, but I think I can sort out certain... problems... tonight. Come tomorrow night. Please. I'll tell you the whole story then. I promise."

"Well..." Bolan still wasn't very happy. "You promise?"

"All of it." She nodded. The gray eyes softened, glistened. "If we can find time. Among other things."

She put her arms around his neck and kissed him. "Nice Mr. Belasko," she said.

Bolan dragged his eyes away from the curve of raincoat above the tight belt and got out of there. He could still feel the trembling of her knees and the pressure of her breasts against his chest as he walked out the archway, stepped over half the engine from the old sedan, which the owner had laid out on the sidewalk, and zig-zagged away from the fruit and flowers.

It was only when he was back in his hotel that he re-called the car whose innards had been displayed on the sidewalk outside Dagmar's courtyard.

A blue, beat-up Opel sedan.

CHAPTER SEVEN

By dawn the next day the sky had cleared, but it was still bitterly cold. Bolan decided to treat the weather seriously. He bought a fleece-lined sheepskin car coat and a fur hat to supplement the woolen muffler he'd worn when he'd first hit town. Skintight calf-leather gloves protected his hands from the freezing air but left his fingers nimble enough to pluck the Beretta from its quickdraw rig and operate the autoloader's mechanism at normal speed.

He was aware now that thoughts of Dagmar threatened to occupy his mind for more time than the solution of the mystery surrounding her strictly demanded. And he had to remember the main reason for his presence in the city. He was amassing evidence—and hoped to collect a great deal more when he saw the girl—on the Lattuada deal, but he was no nearer Arvell Asticot than the day he'd arrived.

He figured he could maybe help along both cases by filling in the daylight hours before his date with some legwork. And for now that meant making a round of the bars and cafés in St. Pauli, keeping his ears open and trusting that his knowledge of German would hold him in good stead.

He spent most of the morning eavesdropping, but all he heard were complaints and common gossip. Finally he struck paydirt in two places.

"Regardless of what's said," the barman at the Zillertal confided to a busboy, "it does make life easier now that they're getting themselves organized, and that's a fact."

The busboy shuffled his feet on the tiled floor. "Bastards ought to be behind bars, the whole goddamn lot of 'em. Stuff the motherfuckers inside out, that's what I say."

"Well, don't say it too loud if you want to stay upright. No, but you have to admit, when Kraul and his lot were on the loose, and all of them other punks, you risked getting fucked over two, three times on the trot. Ask me, it's better this way. Once you come across, they let you get on with it."

Bolan had heard the same conversation before, almost in the same words. It crystallized his interpretation of the underground battle dividing the criminal quarters of the city.

In a bar near the Opera he heard two chorus boys in stage makeup complaining—this time about the dangers of life after dark.

"It's as much as one's life is worth," said the younger one, "trolling nights these days in that grisly Reeperbahn. You know what that bitch Rudi said—"

"I *know*, dear," the other interrupted. "But for once she was right, you know. One's behind has scarcely touched a seat these days before one is surrounded by Hansie and those big, rough men. It's too discouraging. Really it is."

Bolan whipped around from his position at the bar. The two dancers were just leaving. "Pardon me, uh, gentlemen," he said at the door in his passable German. "I happened to overhear you mention a personal friend of mine—Hansie...?"

"Hansie Schiller?" one of the chorus boys said.

"Right. I'm anxious to contact him, and I'm a stranger in town. I wonder if you could tell me where he lives, or at least some place he goes where I could get in touch?"

They looked at each other, penciled brows raised superciliously. "He doesn't exactly encourage house calls," the older one said.

"No, don't call him. He'll call you," his friend tittered. "If you *really* want to see him, you could try the Coliseum, of course."

"The Coliseum? Thanks." Having chanced his hand this far, Bolan decided to go the whole way. "Say, I don't suppose either of you guys know where I could fix myself up with a snort, do you? Or maybe just a little charge?"

They exchanged glances again. "You're a friend of Hansie's and you're asking *us*?" the younger one cried. "How droll can you be! Really!" he said to his friend as they flounced off toward the theater. "Some people!"

Apart from a couple of isolated references to the Yank, heard but unidentified in a bleak dockside tavern crowded with longshoremen, that was the sum total of Bolan's intel that day.

At seven o'clock he began his shopping. The Coliseum, wherever that was, could wait, as could Hansie Schiller and his connection with drugs, Lattuada, the Yank and their supposed relationship.

Bolan censored memories of loose, pointed breasts under a braless green top, a sexy, bent-knee walk, the promise in a certain kiss. He was seeing the girl because he needed information, right? He bought cold cuts, bread and two bottles of Alsatian wine. Then, he made his way to the Kinderplatz.

"I'll leave the yellow door open," she'd said, "but ring just the same, so I'll know it's you and I can open the one at the top. Three long and two short, followed by three short and two long. That's my private code. Special friends only!"

Bolan transferred the paper bag of cold cuts, and the bottles to one arm and thumbed the bell the way she'd said. Then, shouldering open the door, he lurched up the narrow stairway.

He couldn't find a switch for the lights as he cautiously made the fifth floor.

The hallway was completely dark. He'd heard no sounds from the other apartments as he climbed past: no voices, no radio, no street noises filtering through. All he could hear now was a dripping faucet and a creak someplace above as an old beam settled. There was a faint odor of fresh paint in the air. He sucked some in and started on the final flight of stairs.

As he turned on the landing he could see light around the edges of a door that had been left ajar at the top. Would she open it herself? Would she run forward and kiss him again, or would she wait for him to find her inside? The Executioner suddenly went cold. *If she was there at all . . .*

He had still heard no sound. She couldn't have run out on him again, could she? He shoved open the door and walked into the apartment.

She was there all right, and stark naked. The only thing on her was the knotted wool scarf with which she'd been strangled.

The body, still warm, lay on a divan, but he knew at once, before he saw the contorted, purple face, the staring eyes, the protruding tongue. There was something unmistakably final about the dead, that total lack of muscular control, the kinetic energy that knitted the frame together. The merely unconscious were never that way, even in deep coma. The unconscious sagged; the dead flopped.

The knot in the scarf was in back. The murderer must have been behind her. Someone she knew then? But why didn't she fight once she realized? Bruises on her wrists. Must have been two of them, one to hold her hands down, the other to...

That scarf?

His scarf!

Dagmar had been choked to death with the wool scarf he had bought two days before to keep the arctic air from searing his mouth and nose. As far as he knew, it was in the top left-hand drawer of the dresser in his hotel room, along with the Mike Belasko press card, a street map of Hamburg and a couple of spare batteries for his electric shaver.

What the hell was it doing here, sunk almost out of sight in the neck of a strangled dancer?

He wondered if he should call the cops. He hated just leaving her there. But did she have a phone? Involuntarily he half turned to look around the room—night table, closet, bookcase, a chair strewn with underclothes. The body slid off the edge of the divan and thumped onto the floor.

He turned back, but his left foot was imprisoned beneath the dead girl's hip. He stooped, some innate, inbred sense of decorum insisting he pick her up and place her back on the bed.

That's when the police burst in.

CHAPTER EIGHT

Bolan didn't catch on at once. Perhaps his mental reflexes had been momentarily numbed. And Fischer, the senior officer in charge of the squad, wasn't exactly an orator. He was solidly built, with a mustache, his voice was quiet, and he only used it for business purposes. His bleak face showed about as much expression as the Matterhorn.

Neither the young plainclothes sergeant nor the two uniformed cops with him had much to say to the Executioner, either. There were formalities to attend to, photographers and doctors and ambulance men to organize. It wasn't until the body had been removed and the four of them were left alone with the American that he became fully aware of the spot he was in.

"Why did you do it?" Fischer asked.

"Come again?" Bolan was sprawled on the settee in the living room. The two uniformed cops were blocking the entrance door. Fischer was pacing up and down, his sergeant squatting awkwardly on a pile of cushions with a notebook and pencil at the ready.

"Why did you kill her?"

Bolan sat up straight. "Me? You don't think...? But you can't be serious! I had a date with her. The door was open and I walked in and found her there. I was just going to call—"

"Don't waste my time, Belasko, if that's really your name. You expect me to believe an explanation like that when we actually caught you red-handed?"

Bolan opened his mouth to point out the craziness of the situation...and then saw it from their point of view. A dead woman, the body still warm. A foreigner standing over her with his hand on the scarf that had strangled her. They didn't know yet that the scarf was his, but it wouldn't take them long to find out. He was going to have to do some fast talking if he was to be back at his hotel by midnight.

"Look," he said reasonably, "why would I kill the kid? I don't even know her."

"You just said you had a date with her."

"Sure. I did. I wanted to know her. But she was scared. She—"

"Scared of what?"

"That's what I wanted to find out. She was mixed up in some kind of racket, kind of a local protection routine, I guess. Maybe with drug connections. I don't know. But I figured her for an innocent bystander and I was trying to help. That's why I came here. She was too frightened to meet me anyplace else."

"I suggest your reasons for coming here were quite different," Fischer said levelly. "However, motive becomes a moot point, a debate for judges and juries and lawyers, when the murderer is actually seen committing the crime."

"If your police doctor's half as smart as you are, the autopsy will show she was dead before I arrived."

"We don't know when you arrived," the sergeant said, writing in his book. "We have nobody's word for it but your own."

"Well, before *you* arrived then. What I mean is, it will show that I couldn't have been killing her when you came in. It'll show she died before that, and so much for your 'red-handed' accusation."

"Possibly. The body was warm. It's difficult for a postmortem to establish a precise time of death within the short period before it cools. In any case, if you weren't tightening the ligature when we saw you, you could have been in the act of removing it to destroy the evidence."

Yeah, Bolan thought, since it was mine, that would certainly figure.

"The important thing is that you were observed by four police witnesses at the scene of the crime—" Fischer favored him with a wintry smile "—in circumstances *suggesting* that you had just committed it. That's the mildest way it can be put."

"But why?" Bolan stood up abruptly, stooping to avoid the sloping ceiling. The two uniformed cops moved closer together in front of the door. "We were going to have dinner together. I'm asking you, does a guy planning to knock off a girl arrive loaded with groceries and bottles of wine? Does he?"

"He might—if he was planning to make the point you're making now. Or he might not have planned the murder at all. It might have been the result of a quarrel." He shot the Executioner one of the X-ray glances policemen use to signal a hit coming up. "If he was planning a seduction and she had other ideas, for example. I noticed there were bruises on her wrists."

Bolan was becoming impatient. "Just look at the stuff I humped up those damn stairs and—" He broke off in midsentence, staring at a table just inside the door—the table on which he had dumped the bottles, and paper bag when he'd come in. They weren't there anymore.

"Did any of your men move that stuff?" he demanded. But even as he asked he knew they hadn't. He had been in the room all the time. Even if he had temporarily forgotten about the provisions, he would have noticed if one of the cops had shifted them. Something else that had been worrying him surfaced. "Tell me," he asked, "how *did* you happen to show just when you did?"

Fischer shrugged. "Emergency call from the people in the apartment below. They heard a scream and the sounds of a struggle."

Suddenly, for the first time, Bolan had serious misgivings. He had obviously walked into some kind of setup. He recalled the loud creak he'd heard on his way upstairs. That had been no ancient beam settling. The killer or killers had been up there, someplace on that dark landing, waiting for him to walk into the trap before they left, taking his corroboratory evidence with them. They had already gotten into his hotel room and stolen the scarf, to tie him in with the murder. He wondered if they had actually made the emergency call from the silent apartment below Dagmar's, or whether he had been watched from outside and the call patched in someplace else.

How many other clues had they planted, pointing the Executioner's way? Then he had a chilling realization: they didn't have to. Not when he himself had spent the past two days leaving clues all over the city, asking for Dagmar Schroeder at every club, tavern and café. Probably, if they wanted the girl out of the way for some reason, it was those inquiries that decided them to pin the killing on him.

As for who "they" were, for once it didn't seem too difficult a question. Easier, certainly, than finding an answer to the mystery of the girl's own actions and reactions in the twenty-four hours before her death.

Both questions were soon—to quote the policeman himself—moot points. There were already guns in the hands of the uniformed cops at the door, but it wasn't until later, at the station house, that Bolan's misgivings were transformed into real alarm.

"You claim to be a special correspondent for this magazine in Chicago?" Fischer asked. He spoke like a man expecting lies.

"I *am* roving correspondent for *World Review* with special responsibility for foreign affairs," Bolan said.

"Yet you're carrying a German press card bearing another man's photograph and made out in a name not your own?"

Freddie Leonhardt's local pass, along with the Beretta in its shoulder rig, had been taken from Bolan when he was frisked.

"It's not my card," he said. "I borrowed it. The story sounds complicated, but I can explain exactly—"

"Where is your own card?" Fischer interrupted. "If you have one."

"In my hotel room."

"Apart from this, uh, borrowed card, do you have any means of identifying yourself? Can you substantiate your claim to be—?"

"Of course I do. Of course I can!" Bolan's voice was angry. "Telex messages and office memos addressed to me. Letters. Notes from my interviews. A driver's license. My passport." All these papers were part of the ID supplied to him by Hal Brognola via the diplomatic bag.

"Ah, yes," Fischer said. "A passport. And where would this valuable document be?"

Bolan sighed. "In my hotel room. Along with the press card, a checkbook and all the other stuff."

The policeman smoothed his mustache with a forefinger and nodded. "Just so. Odd, nevertheless, that a foreigner—and apparently an experienced journalist at that—should omit to retain such papers on his person while at the same time carrying a large-caliber automatic pistol in an extremely professional underarm holster."

"I wasn't expecting to face a police interrogation."

"Clearly. That's probably the truest thing you've said yet." Fischer paused for a moment, then said, "You have, of course, a Ministry of Interior permit to carry this weapon?"

Bolan was silent.

"Exactly. Well, Herr Belasko, you will, for the moment, remain here as our guest—" another cold smile "—while your claims are checked and further inquiries are made."

Bolan was locked in a cell. The further inquiries, he was to learn, were negative from his point of view. Neither the passport nor the press card was in his room. Nor could the law find any trace of a driver's license, a checkbook or a single scrap of paper relating him in any way to *World Review* or even bearing the Belasko name. The guy who'd stolen the scarf had been well briefed.

The frame was ingenious. Bolan wondered if he had been mistaken and Arvell Asticot, aware all the time that the Executioner was after him, was responsible.

That could wait. Just two things had priority now. To convince the police of his—or Mike Belasko's—identity, and to get out of there. Once they believed he really was a respectable American newspaperman, surely they would believe his story and he could go ahead with helping them find out what had actually happened at Dagmar's apartment, and why.

Bolan was determined to keep his real identity secret. He still had one trump card: the rented BMW that was parked on the lowest floor of the Hotel Oper garage. His Mike Blanski ID papers, along with a spare Beretta and the rest of the gear that had arrived in the diplomatic bag, were taped beneath the driver's seat.

Okay, so how to verify the Belasko identity?

There had been American Express checks in the pocket of his sheepskin coat, but Fischer said they could have been stolen. No supporting testimony. Cable Chicago? It was an explicit part of the deal with Michaelson that the *World Review* management would never be dragged into any trouble the Executioner had gotten himself into. The same applied to the consulate; Bolan knew he would be instantly disowned as an embarrassment in a situation of this kind. He hoped to hell there was no automatic feedback whereby the consul general was informed of the arrest of any American citizen.

The more he thought about it, the more he realized there was only one runner in the race—Freddie Leonhardt. He knew Belasko; he had met him. Technically speaking Leonhardt was working for him on a specific assignment. It seemed reasonable, then, to ask the law to rope him in, especially since he could explain the press card routine. He should also be able to verify Bolan's cover without involving Chicago.

But Fischer beat him to the punch. When Bolan was taken to the policeman's office the following morning, Leonhardt was already there, wearing a charcoal pinstripe suit, a paisley necktie and an embarrassed expression.

The office was in a steel-and-glass building loud with the clacking of typewriters. Fischer sat like a mustached Buddha behind his desk, with his assistant, the same young sergeant who had been with him the previous night, off to one side with the usual notebook. A uniformed cop, with the flap of his white holster unfastened at his belt, stood by the door.

"Perhaps we can wrap up this nonsense about who I am now," Bolan said. "Freddie, you can do that for me, can't you?"

For the first time he became aware that Leonhardt was avoiding eye contact. He was standing by a window, staring at gray stone and red brick. There had been a partial thaw during the night, and a thin sleet was washing blocks of snow down the shining slate roofs. The office was pretty gloomy, too, despite the ultramodern architecture—too many dossiers, too many scarred wood filing cabinets, not enough light. The walls were a bilious green up to waist height, a cold ivory above. "Do you know this man, Herr Leonhardt?" Fischer asked formally.

Freddie swung around. The sergeant's pencil poised over a blank page. "Yes, I know him. I've known him a few days."

"Can you identify him?"

"He represented himself to me as a journalist named Mike Belasko, who is employed by an American paper I work for sometimes."

"What the hell do you mean, 'represented himself'?" Bolan interrupted. "I *am* Mike Belasko and you damn well—"

"Silence!" Fischer snapped. "Please elaborate that statement, Herr Leonhardt." The sergeant's pencil was flying across the page.

"Well, I mean I was expecting Mike Belasko. The office had cabled me with instructions to help him all I could. And when this johnnie turned up, I naturally assumed..."

"Naturally you assumed this was the genuine article. Quite so. Are you saying now that subsequent events caused you to modify that view."

Leonhardt shifted his feet uncomfortably. "Not exactly. But..."

"Yes?"

"Well... he seemed to be going about his piece—an East-West situationer—you know, in, well, rather an odd way."

"Can you tell me in what way his behavior was odd?"

Leonhardt darted Bolan a glance out of the corner of his eye and then looked away. "Well, yes, I mean the story, that is to say the subject he was working on, had nothing to do with the places he went to. He kept asking me how to get to certain low-life haunts. St. Pauli and that kind of thing. And it...I wouldn't have thought that had any connection with the kind of articles he writes. That Belasko writes, that is."

"What the hell do you know about it, you snotty bastard?" Bolan rasped, half rising from his chair. "You don't know the first thing about the way an American paper works. You only have to look at the copy you turn in to see that. What do you know about interviewing the ordinary man in the street?"

The cop on the door pushed the Executioner down again. Fischer, who had listened impassively with his hands flat on the desk in front of him, now asked Leonhardt, "Was it to gain entry to these places that he took possession of your press card?"

Leonhardt nodded.

"And you gave it to him, despite the fact that the card explicitly states that it is nontransferable?"

The local news hawk flushed. "He was rather... persuasive."

"He talked you into giving him the card? He insisted?"

"I suppose so, yes."

"In view of this man's...unexpected actions since you first met him, have you now, on reflection, any reason to modify your original opinion that this is Belasko?"

"I, that is, I don't have any comment to make on that," Leonhardt said.

"Thank you, Herr Leonhardt. I don't think we need detain you any longer."

On his way out Freddie shot the Executioner a sheepish grin. "Sorry, old lad," he said awkwardly. "Got to own up in front of the jolly old beak, what!"

Bolan ignored him. "Okay," he said to Fischer. "Let's quit horsing around, shall we? This is a frame. Surely you can see that? Nobody in their right senses is going to leave themselves wide open like that—a foreigner without papers of *any* kind!—and then go around murdering dancers in St. Pauli. Come on now!"

"Murderers are rarely in their right senses," the policeman said equably. "Even if they were, the killing could be an impulsive act. The anonymity could be deliberate, a cloak for other illegal activities quite unconnected with it."

Fischer was a *Kriminalkommissar*, the equivalent of a homicide squad lieutenant or a British CID detective-inspector. He eyed Bolan coldly. "Whether or not you're an American reporter on an international assignment doesn't affect our evidence."

"What evidence?" Bolan demanded. "Apart from the fact that you found me in the apartment of a murdered girl—and the fact that someone has stolen my papers—there is no evidence. There can't be."

Fischer sighed. "Better tell him what we have, Wertheim." The sergeant flipped back forty pages of his notebook and cleared his throat. Fischer turned his back and stared out the window. "This is off the record," he told the sleet slanting down from the sky. "No notes are being taken. I should just like you to know the score. It may save time."

"Okay. Lay it on me," Bolan said.

"Observation kept over the past two months in the St. Pauli, Altona and Hammerbrook districts," Wertheim read aloud, "suggests that the following conclusions can be drawn. One, an organized system of extortion is in operation, mainly among the proprietors of drinking clubs, small restaurants, strip shows and quasi-legal gaming establishments.

"The system works like the so-called protection racket in the United States. That is, victims agree to pay the racketeers a certain percentage of their profits, or a fixed sum every week, in return for 'protection' against other, similar racketeers. In fact, the payments merely buy immunity from the attentions of those extorting the money. Failure to pay involves the wrecking of the establishment, sometimes with injury to the owner or members of his family. A second refusal results in more serious assaults, or in some cases even death."

Bolan was watching the man as he read. He was young, probably in his late twenties, with ginger hair, very pale eyes and a bristly mustache. He was wearing gray pants and a tweed sport jacket. Somehow his face looked familiar.

"Two," the young man continued, "although this crime technique has been practiced in Hamburg for some time, it has until recently been confined to isolated areas, with a number of small-time gangs each terrorizing comparatively few victims. Within the past two weeks the situation has altered. Today one highly organized group operates on a citywide basis. Other gangs have been eliminated or frightened off, and it is now thought that the newcomers also control gaming and prostitution and plan a greatly increased distribution of drugs."

Wertheim turned a page. His fingers were ingrained with dirt—or oil—and suddenly the Executioner remembered where he had seen him before. He was the driver of the beat-up Opel who had been tailing the customized Cadillac in the Albertplatz...and pretending he had a mechanical breakdown in the market outside the Schroeder apartment. Had he been keeping a special watch on the apartment? Or was he just briefed to watch St. Pauli as a whole? If so, Bolan wondered how many more of his own movements had been noted—and how incriminating they might seem, observed in the light of a murder investigation.

"Three," Wertheim said, "there was of course opposition to this crime cartel—principally from the St. Pauli gang led by Ferdinand Kraul. For a time the situation was fluid, with many establishments terrorized by both groups, but there appears to have been some kind of climax within the past few days and Kraul has not been seen since the sack of the Becker Café and the murder of its owner in the Albertplatz. Underworld rumors suppose that he was assassinated and his body dismembered and dropped into the ocean from an airplane,

but there is no confirmation of this. There is, nevertheless, virtually no obstacle now to the main protection
gang, known locally as the Team, ruling the whole of the
city's illegal population.

"Four, although it is well-known that the Team's
strong-arm enforcement squad is headed by Hansie
Schiller, their methods are so ruthless and so violent that
victims refuse to complain or prefer a charge for fear of
further reprisals. Schiller himself is a homosexual sad-
ist with convictions for robbery with violence, uttering
threats and GBH."

"What's GBH?" Bolan interrupted.

"In English, grievous bodily harm," Fischer said
without turning around.

"Five," the sergeant went on, "it is known that the
campaign resulting in the Team's success was masterminded by a member of the American Mafia, specially
hired to come to Europe and plan the operation. So far
this criminal's identity remains a mystery. He has only
been referred to by the nickname the Yank. He has,
however, been described as very tall, lean and dark, with
a Midwestern accent."

Tall, lean, dark, Bolan thought to himself. That has
to be Lattuada. It's just the kind of organization job he
could pull. At the same time he was forced to admit the
description applied equally well to him. Were they trying
to hang the whole Yank-in-Hamburg number on him?

They were.

The lieutenant swung back to face into the room.
"There is one more point." He looked expectantly at his
sidekick.

"Yes, sir. The leader of the Team is known to have
accompanied the enforcement thugs on a number of
bloody affrays in a white Cadillac automobile, registra-

tion number HH777-CDE. No description of this person is available, nor can a direct link with the American be proved. The Mafia man can, nevertheless, be shown to have had a liaison with a young woman having no criminal connections, but who is thought to have acted as a contact for him in certain activities concerned with narcotics." Wertheim closed the notebook with a snap. "The girl is…was originally a dancer. Name of Dagmar Schroeder."

Fischer picked up a sheet of paper from his desk and glanced at it. "You yourself," he said to Bolan, "were seen by the sergeant here to visit the Kinderplatz day before yesterday." He read from the paper. "'Subject rang the bell of the Schroeder apartment. When there was no reply, he went into the delicatessen known as Fritz's, where he was joined by Fräulein Schroeder. They emerged, apparently in the middle of a dispute, and returned to the apartment. Subject did not, however, go inside but left shortly afterward, having first kissed the young woman with an angry expression.'"

In the silence that followed those two revelations, Bolan heard the rumble of traffic, the greasy hiss of tires along a street veneered with melting snow, an occasional blast from a taxi horn. "I want a lawyer," he said.

"You'll have one," Fischer replied. He leaned forward, supporting his weight on arms lowered to the desk. "Look, Belasko, this isn't your turf. You may be a big noise in the Mob back home, but you don't know the form here. You just heard *some* of the stuff we've got against you."

"You've got zip against me," Bolan said. "You've got a load of facts concerning Hamburg crime. You've got gossip concerning *an* American. And you've got nothing substantial to connect me with either. You've got nothing to connect me with the Mafia. You can only connect me with Dagmar Schroeder because I was seen talking to her for five minutes outside her house...and, of course, through the murder frame. Any lawyer could blow your case wide open in ten minutes."

"Aha!" A hand came up and a finger wagged. "Maybe he could—if we were proceeding on a simple extortion charge. I'm not saying you would be wrong. But this is murder, and all that material is admissible because it tends to show character."

"You say this mafioso has been organizing your crime wave for a couple of months. I only hit town at the beginning of this week. The day before that I was in Frankfurt, and twenty-four hours earlier in Munich, with fifty witnesses who can testify to that."

"I don't doubt it," Fischer said. "It doesn't mean you couldn't have been here before, secretly, several times perhaps." He straightened and scratched the back of his thick neck. "Why not make it easier for yourself and come clean? There's no death penalty here. It would save a lot of time and trouble all around. I could block any extradition attempt in return, and you'd probably get away with ten years. We'd make it a *crime passionnel*. Otherwise..." He shook his head. "You may be able to frighten the petty crooks and the sex shop owners into silence when you're out on the loose. But once they know you're inside, the snitches will start coming out of the woodwork. Believe me."

Bolan didn't say anything. He just stared at Fischer.

The German cop sighed. "If that's the way you want it, we won't waste any more time. I'll make arrangements for a preliminary hearing. Wertheim, you better set up an ID parade."

SERGEANT WERTHEIM'S underlings had done their homework. There had been matchbooks from Tondelayo's and a couple of café bills in the warrior's pockets, and they had roped in the entire cast—the doorman from the Sugar Hill, the boss of the Cellar, the bartender at the Mandrake Root, the men's wear sales-clerk and the waiter and Joe from Tondelayo's. Even Sally Ann was there.

With one exception, all those folks could testify how eager he'd been to locate Dagmar Schroeder. And the exception would tell how he'd bought the wool scarf he was supposed to have strangled her with. If they suc-ceeded in picking him out of a lineup, of course.

They did. He was fingered by all the men except Joe, who swore he'd never seen any of the people in the lineup before—on principle, Bolan guessed. Sally Ann was the last to be shown into the room. Bolan was still wondering whose side she was on, and how much she had to do with his present predicament.

She walked up and down the line twice, shook her wild head and turned to Fischer, who was standing in back, smoking a short pipe with a large meerschaum bowl. "I never saw any of these gentlemen before," she said, "but I like the look of this one." She grabbed Bolan's arm. "I'll take him, thank you."

"This is no time for joking, Fräulein," Fischer said severely. "An identity parade is a serious matter. A crime may have been committed."

Sally Ann pouted. "If Comrade Gorbachev can frat-ernize with Americans," she said, "I don't see why I can't!"

She was at the door on her way out when Fischer said gently, "Since none of the men spoke, Fräulein, how did you know this one was American?"

CHAPTER NINE

A broad flight of steps in the center of a brick-and-sandstone facade led to the main entrance of the district courthouse. Inside there was a wide lobby with a marble floor. A staircase rose to the upper stories; the double doors to the courtroom were diagonally to the left.

The paneled, windowless room was surprisingly small. From his high rostrum the judge looked across his desk at a single polished bench running around the well of the court. Behind and slightly above were four rows of high-backed seats. The dock and the witness stand were level with the rostrum, one on each side. And apart from tables for the defense and prosecution, that was all: no juries were called at preliminary hearings.

It was ten-thirty on a damp morning, with the thaw well advanced and fog still veiling the trees around the Alster, when Mack Bolan was called to answer a charge of first-degree murder.

Police witnesses stood about on the black-and-white checkerboard floor in the lobby, waiting to be called. It was anticipated that the proceedings would take only a few minutes. After formal identification, the state would outline its case, produce witnesses and ask for a committal. The accused was expected to plead not guilty and reserve his defense, since there could be no question, on a murder charge, of bail being fixed.

In fact, the proceedings took even less time than predicted. The accused didn't plead at all. When he was

asked the customary question, he opened his mouth...
and was then seized by a paroxysm of coughing. He
spluttered an apology to the judge, said he was unused
to the northern climate and especially the fog, and then
doubled up with another fit.

During it, his right elbow jerked sharply backward,
catching one of the wardens with him in the pit of the
stomach. As the officer folded, Bolan lifted an uppercut from the floor to connect with the second warden's
jaw. The guy staggered back against the wall and began
to slide to the floor. But Bolan had already placed a hand
on the wooden rail surrounding the dock and vaulted
over it onto one of the lawyers' tables.

Papers, briefs, pens, document cases scattered as he
raced away and sprang to the floor in the tiny well of the
court. Two strides took him to the gate in the slatted rail
dividing the public benches from the officials, and then
he was only five feet from the doors.

The moment was well chosen. The court usher who
would normally have been standing in front of the
doors, barring the exit, had just opened one to call the
first witness in from the lobby when the Executioner
made his break. He was still off balance, half in and half
out of the court, when the accused man reached him.

Fischer was on his feet at the far side of the well,
shouting. The judge was banging his gavel. There was
confusion among the counsel and the newsmen in the
public seats, and three cops had started in pursuit from
the doorway leading to the cells.

Bolan shoved the usher violently out into the lobby,
skipped over him as he tripped and fell, and pulled the
door shut behind him. It only held up the pursuers for
an instant, but it gave the fugitive the time he needed.
Sergeant Wertheim, witnesses, one or two lawyers and

police on duty were standing on the black and white squares like pieces on a chessboard.

While the opposition milled around in the lobby below, Bolan took the shallow stone steps three at a time and raced for the second floor. He was past the mezzanine by the time Wertheim and his men made the bottom of the first flight, and his long legs increased the lead up the next and across the hallway above. The pursuit was further hampered by a spectator from the court who had run out into the lobby, then appeared to trip over the lowest stair in his excitement and fall in front of the uniformed cops. Shooting a rapid glance over the balustrade as he ran, Bolan recognized the guy—a longtime CIA sleeper, unknown to Freddie Leonhardt, posted to Hamburg under deep cover as an importer of mechanical toys from Berlin.

Had the boys from Langley been given covert orders to aid him if they could without blowing their own cover? Was the guy acting on his own initiative, one undercover man helping another, whatever their different objectives? Or was the stumble a coincidence?

No time to wrestle the question now. There was a cleaner from a commercial firm supplying towels to the offices on the third floor; she was leaning over the balustrade, peering down the stairwell to see what all the noise was about when Bolan appeared by the cart she had abandoned. He swung it violently around and sent it hurtling down the stone steps toward his pursuers, shedding towels, pails, brooms and bottles of cleaning fluid as it went. The woman screamed, but Bolan was already on the fourth landing by the time they disengaged themselves and made the floor below.

Panting, he glanced up the next flight of stairs and then along the corridors stretching left and right. Lower down, there had been people opening the doors of offices, curious to know what was going on; here, for the moment, the passageways were deserted. As feet clattered on the stairs, he came to a decision and ran swiftly to the corridor on his right. A few yards along, leading toward the rear of the building, there was another branching off to the left. At the far end of this was a door with a small notice announcing: WC—Privat. Bolan jerked the door open and slipped inside.

Gently he eased the door shut and shot the bolt. Gasping for breath now, he leaned his back against the panels and listened. The chase swept up to the fifth floor, hesitated, then split into separate sections. Footsteps receded, thumped overhead, stomped back down the stairs.

He heard Wertheim's voice: "Every door into every office, and the closets inside those offices!" Then Fischer, from farther away, shouted something unintelligible.

He looked around his refuge. Apart from the toilet and a sink with a cold-water faucet, the room was empty. Below and to one side of the toilet tank, which bore the name of a Ruhr ironworks in relief, was a small window. It was about eighteen inches square, just wide enough for a lean man to squeeze through.

Bolan peered through the grimy glass. The window looked out on an air shaft, fifty feet across and webbed with a complex of drainpipes emptying the guttering, sinks and bathrooms of the buildings surrounding it. He leaned his forehead against the glass, squinting sideways as he shielded the reflections with one hand. As he had hoped, a fat pipe ran down the wall close to the window, receiving the outflow from sink and toilet. It was only a few inches away. The odds were long, but it was the only possible escape and he had to take it.

There was just one thing wrong with the idea. The window wouldn't open. It was designed to open inward, but clearly nobody had used it in years, and the last time it was painted the cracks had filled and seized up solid.

Bolan heaved and tugged desperately at the small brass catch, cursing under his breath as the sweat ran down between his shoulder blades. Doors were opening and voices calling not far away. He couldn't even shift the lever operating the catch. Finally he snatched the hand towel from its bracket by the sink and smashed the glass with the wooden roller.

Outside the door someone shouted as the windowpane shattered. Bolan wrapped the towel around his hands and started to push out the fragments of broken glass still sticking to the frame.

Heavy footsteps pounded down the passageway. The handle of the door turned. The door rattled. Bolan stood on the toilet bowl, thrust one leg cautiously out through the window and sat astride the sill. Doubling up his body, he twisted the other foot out so that he was now draped over the sill with his head and shoulders inside and his legs outside.

The rest room door shook to a sudden impact. Bolan fed more of his body out over the sill, leaning his weight on his forearms and elbows. He stretched a leg sideways, feeling with his foot for the junction where the outflow from the sink ran into the drainpipe.

Wood splintered as somebody charged the door. Bolan found the junction with his toe, wedging the foot into the wide V and transferring some of his weight to it. Moving with care, he withdrew his head and shoulders from the window frame, feeling his jacket rip on fragments of glass still implanted in the wood.

The door shivered under another assault. Bolan was still grasping the windowsill with one hand, reaching now for a handhold with the other. His fingers touched the smooth, cold surface of the pipe and curved around it. He was spread-eagled on the face of the building with one leg dangling in space.

Inside, the bolt was split away from the jamb and the door burst open with a crash. The Executioner quickly transferred all his weight to the foot jammed between the two pipes, let go of the sill and clasped the drainpipe with both hands. He was hunched there when the beefy uniformed cop thrust his head, one arm and shoulder out the window. "You come back here!" the policeman ordered.

Bolan did not reply.

The cop compressed his lips. The situation was ridiculous.

He could just touch the escaped prisoner with his outstretched fingertips, but he couldn't grab him, much less support his weight with one hand if he did grab him. The most he could do would be to dislodge Bolan and send him hurtling to his death. He withdrew inside to ask for further instructions.

Bolan looked over his shoulder. That was a mistake. The air shaft, which was faced with glazed white tiles to reflect light into the lower windows, plummeted down sixty or seventy feet to an area at subbasement level. One careless move and he would end up with a broken back among the garbage cans.

Below the window through which he had escaped was another, and under that yet another. The floor plan of each story was identical, with the toilets one above the other to facilitate drainage. But even if he could slide down the pipe and make it into another rest room, the police would be there waiting for him long before he had made the difficult transfer to the sill and forced open the window. If, on the other hand, he could climb upward...

He tilted back his head and looked toward the room. There was one more washroom window and then, another eight or nine feet above, the guttering that ran around the shaft. The glazed tiles stopped at window height, leaving a wall of blackened brick.

And between the two was a stringcourse—a narrow, projecting ledge that ran along the face of the building. Bolan drew a deep breath. Mercifully there were ribbed rubber soles on his shoes.

Sergeant Wertheim's head and shoulders had replaced the cop's in the shattered window frame. "Don't be a fool," he called. "You'll kill yourself, man! Come on back in here and we'll give you a hand, but no smart tricks, eh?"

The Executioner still made no reply. He was levering himself up the drainpipe like a slow-motion frog. "We'll have a dozen men on the roof before you make the gutter," Wertheim shouted, "and you'll have run the risk for nothing!"

Bolan hardly heard him. He aimed to quit the pipe before he had gotten that far. If he could last that long. The air was moist, leaving a thin film of damp on the grimed surface of the pipe. Each time he tightened his grasp and dragged himself up a little higher, each time he gripped it with the soles of his shoes to maintain his position while he slid his hands farther up, the risk of slipping increased. The distance to the next junction in the pipe, below the fifth-floor window, wasn't much more than twice his own height—maybe a dozen separate maneuvers, flexing, stretching, gripping—but to the fugitive it seemed like a thousand feet.

For a moment he rested, watching his own breath condense on the shiny tiles. For the first time, exposed at that height, he realized how cold it was. To look down was impossible. If he looked, up, the gray clouds sailing over the roof gave him the illusion that the building was toppling toward him and made him giddy. The muscles in his wrists, calves and biceps were already clamoring for relief, and although the drainpipe was solidly cast and nine inches in diameter he had the recurring impression that it was about to pull away from the wall and crash to the ground with him still clinging to it.

Police now crowded the dormer windows above the guttering and crawled along the edge of the roof. Bolan gasped with relief as his fingers touched the pipe junction. Bathed in cold sweat, he pulled himself level with the window and rested for a moment with both feet in the V. There was a roaring in his ears: the voices shouting to him from above and below sounded immeasurably far away. Six more feet and his smarting eyes were staring at a row of bricks surmounting the tiles. Another agonizing sequence of pushes and pulls, then he was leaning against the pipe just below the gutter with one foot braced against the ledge.

The stone projection was three inches wide, the corner of the air shaft six feet away. Keeping one hand curled around the drainpipe, Bolan edged a foot out along the bricks. "For God's sake!" someone shouted. "Don't do it, man! Don't!"

Warily Bolan transferred his other foot to the ledge. He let go of the pipe and stood balanced on his toes, facing the wall with his arms spread. Gingerly, inch by inch, he moved away from the pipe.

Mack Bolan was only able to balance on the strip of stone because he was lean and muscular. With his arms flung wide and every available square inch of his body pressed to the damp brickwork, he advanced one foot a few inches, cautiously shifted his weight, brought up the other foot, moved the first again, thrusting desperately upward and inward with his calf muscles all the time.

His cheek lay against the wall and his eyes were fixed on the corner of the shaft. He knew that if he looked down he would fall, seeing the space that yawned between his heels. Even to turn his head and stare at the bricks would displace his weight enough to overbalance him. He felt as though the trembling of the blood in his veins was sufficient to shake him from his perch and hurl him into oblivion.

Sounds around him became exceptionally important, invested with terrible significance: the slither of his soles along the stone, the rasp of his jacket against brickwork, a scrape of boots above as some policeman followed his progress out of sight above the guttering, the hoarse, quick gasps of his breath. Loud enough to drown the world, these sounds became his lonely universe. Somewhere over the rooftops a clock chimed a quarter of an hour. Only fifteen minutes had passed since he had climbed the steps to the dock!

There was another drainpipe in the corner. Without it Bolan would have been lost. He clung to the smooth, cold, tubular casting for all he was worth.

The adjoining wall was part of a building two stories higher than the courthouse. Police following Bolan along the roof were therefore faced with a blank cliff of stonework; they would have to return to street level, run to the alley that led to the entrance of the next-door building and try to cut him off there, once they had checked exactly where he was aiming to get in.

It was the other building that had prompted him to make his near-suicidal trip. Plus the gamble that he could beat them to it. For the stringcourse continued around the corner, and above it on the next leg of his odyssey were windows. The nearest was less than three feet away.

Biting his lip, Bolan took a hand away from the drainpipe, and set out on the last few perilous feet, which somehow were the worst of all. Icy sweat ran into his eyes. A breeze sprang up from somewhere and plucked at his clothes. He was more than ever conscious of the chasm below him, of the hairline separating his life from his death. His calf and thigh muscles were on fire.

But at last the purgatorial journey was over. He stood in front of the window. It was open a crack at the bottom and there was nobody in the room beyond. Bolan thrust up the frame. As he lowered his outspread arms to grasp the sill, a fragment of the stone ledge crumbled under his weight and broke away.

Bolan fell.

His legs dropped into the void. His flailing arms struck the sill with an impact that ripped the remaining breath from his body, but miraculously one of his arms hooked over the sill and held.

For a dizzy moment he hung suspended over the air shaft with all his weight tearing at that arm. Then he managed to reach up with the other hand and find a purchase, lessening the strain.

Only on the fourth attempt was he able to will his muscles to haul him back up to a position where he could collapse over the sill and tumble into the room.

It was a small storeroom, not much larger than a broom closet, packed with cartons of cleaning materials and drums of detergent. Behind the door hung a dark blue lightweight raincoat—something a park keeper or a janitor might wear—together with a uniform cap with a shiny black peak.

Bolan put them on and opened the door. Shuddering slightly from the intolerable tension of those last few minutes of ferocious concentration, he was aware that he dare not let up for an instant; even from here he could make out the distant shouts of the pursuers, shouts that would grow louder with every second that passed.

The door opened onto a hallway. On the far side of the hallway were the doors of three elevators.

The whole operation was simple once it was under way. Bolan pressed the call buttons of all three cars. One arrived almost at once. The others whined upward from street level. Before they made half the distance he was riding down to the subbasement.

He heard the advance guard of the police squad clatter into the entrance and deploy up and down the stairs as he hurried out into the area at the bottom of the air shaft. Walking quickly to the building's fire exit, opposite the courthouse, he ran up the back stairs to the street. Five minutes later he was sitting on a bar stool in a tavern off the Alter Steinweg.

The place was empty. "Sir?" the bartender inquired. "What'll it be?"

"Beer," Bolan said hoarsely.

CHAPTER TEN

Bolan left the tavern and walked north, away from St. Pauli and the docks, away from the courthouse and city hall, but away also from the busy roads encircling the Alster. Mercifully, although his pockets had been emptied, there were a few bills sewn into the lining of his jacket that the friskers had missed. First priority for that cash had been the beer; the next was a change of clothing. After that it was a secret visit to the rented BMW, and back into the pursuit business with Ferucco Lattuada and Arvell Asticot at the top of the list. Add Hansie Schiller at number three.

Near the botanical gardens, Bolan found himself in the center of a crowd milling around half a dozen barrows loaded with fruit and flowers. Behind was a crowded parking lot surrounded on three sides by the tall, bleak facades of a hospital. He realized it must be the morning visiting hours.

At the end of the street sirens warbled. A green-and-white police car, and then another, roared down from the Reeperbahn direction and turned east. A third patrol advanced more slowly and stopped two hundred yards from the hospital. Three uniformed cops got out.

On an impulse, Bolan bought a bunch of dahlias and joined the line of men and women shuffling toward the hospital entrance. It was the best camouflage he could think of. In the wide, stone-flagged corridor leading to the stairs he stopped suddenly, hit by an idea. He could use the hospital not just as a temporary cover but as a positive step along the road he had to travel.

He turned around and went back to a glassed-in information desk by the doors. A middle-aged man in uniform sat over an admissions book behind the screen. Bolan waited while two women made inquiries about a relative with a broken leg. What *was* it that Dagmar had said? Or was it Sally Ann? He cast his mind back over the past few turbulent days.

That's not his real name, of course, but that's what everyone calls him....

Charlie, the hamstrung owner of the Coconut Grove.

Charlie what? Charlie Fairlawn? Charlie Fairbarn? Charlie *Farnsbarn*, that was it!

Bolan remembered that the guy, like the alto player at the Sugar Hill and the cloakroom attendant at Tondelayo's, was a West Indian. There were always Brits playing in the Hamburg clubs; the Beatles had made their name there. He guessed that Charlie Farnsbarn was some musicians' equivalent of John Doe or Jean Dupont or Billy Whatsit. But what was his real name? Had she ever said?

Kind of a Scottish name, you know, although he comes from Trinidad. Mackintosh? McKay? McEvoy?

"What can I do for you, friend?" The guy behind the desk was looking at Bolan's peaked cap. "Friend" was a concession, as one underling to another. He would help all he could, though the bourgeois would have to fill in the requisite forms.

"Kind of a problem," the Executioner said, doing his best, good though his German was, to de-Americanize his accent. "Would a guy who was injured, that's to say had an accident in St. Pauli, be brought here?"

The man pursed his lips. "Depends. What kind of injury? What part of St. Pauli? Which ambulance answered the emergency call? You don't know. Could just as easily be the Hanseatic General or Jerome Bonaparte in the Heidenkamps Weg. Not likely to be the Sisters of Mercy, though." He shook his head. "Too far east, see."

"Yeah. I get it. It *could* be here just the same? It was...a severe leg injury. Andreas Bernersstrasse."

The lips were still pursed. Breath whistled inward between them. The eyebrows rose. "It could be. Yes, from the Andreas Bernersstrasse. It could be. Date of admission?"

"The seventh. In the afternoon."

"Hmm. Mostly cracked bones that day after the big freeze. And auto accidents. They ought to sand the damn roads sooner." He turned the pages of the big book. "We'll give it a whirl, anyway. And the name?"

"That's the problem," Bolan said. "I'm not certain. I don't know the person very well. I just saw the... accident, and I wanted to know how the guy was getting on. He's a foreigner. Kind of a Scottish name. Mac-something, you know. The first name is Charles. Oh, and he's a black guy. From Trinidad."

"Foreign, eh?" The information clerk chuckled. "We don't log the color of their skins or where they come from. Not anymore." He was running a stubby forefinger down the column of hand-written entries. "Let's see...the seventh...Schwartz...Cameron, D. I.? No, that was the messenger from the British consulate with acute appendicitis. Mach, E.? Multiple internal injuries and a severed arm? Come to think of it, he was local. Truck driver had an argument with a shunting locomotive down at the docks. Anyway, you said legs, didn't you? Here! What about this one?'' The finger halted at the foot of a page. ''Macfarlane, C. J. F. Severe damage to outer hamstrings and adductor magnus.''

Bolan knew before the injuries were listed. Macfarlane was such an obvious candidate for distortion to Farnsbarn. ''That'll be it,'' he said. ''Is he still here?''

''Yup. Transferred from Emergency to General Surgical yesterday.'' The clerk wrote the name of the ward on a card and handed it through a pigeonhole in the glass. ''Second floor, turn left.''

''I'm obliged,'' Bolan said. ''Thanks a lot.''

''Any time,'' the clerk replied. ''I hope he appreciates the flowers.''

Bolan grinned and made for the stairs. Charlie Macfarlane was in a large general ward at the end of a long passageway smelling of chrysanthemums and rubber tubing with an aftertaste of ether. There were groups of relatives sitting or standing around the patients in their high, white-painted iron beds. Others stood uneasily in the corridor, waiting their turn. A woman cried softly behind screens masking one corner of the ward.

It wasn't necessary to ask a nurse where Macfarlane was. He was the only patient without a visitor and the only man who was black: a bulky Negro with iron-gray hair and thick lips that still bore the marks of a beating. He was leaning back against the pillows with his eyes closed when the Executioner sat down in a chair beside the bed. Behind Bolan, a stout woman was talking in whispers to an elderly man with one arm in a sling. Around the bed beyond Macfarlane several overdressed females fussed over a pale and sickly youth, arranging flowers in vases and fruit in bowls.

''Charlie?'' Bolan said quietly.

The black man opened his eyes. He dragged himself into a sitting position. "Who the hell are you? If it's the cops, I told you three times already I've nothing to—"

"Relax, Charlie," Bolan interrupted. "Take it easy. It's nothing to do with the law."

Macfarlane looked more frightened still. "An American! Shit, you're not—"

"No way." Bolan played his joker early in the game. "I haven't been sent by Lattuada, if that's what you mean. Him and me ain't exactly buddies."

The maneuver was successful; the gamble paid off. "Well, that makes you a buddy of mine for starters," the injured man said viciously. He gestured toward the foot of the bed, where a frame beneath the covers held sheets and blankets away from his legs. "They tell me I'll have to learn to walk again, with a steel fuckin' cage at first, and then leg irons for the rest of my life. I was an athlete, man."

"Okay, okay," Bolan soothed. "That makes two of us. Me, I'd—"

"What he do to you?"

"Only pin a murder rap on me, that's all. Nice guy."

"Hey!" Macfarlane reached for a crumpled newspaper lying between the bed and his night table. "It says here there's an American up before the judge this a.m. on a charge of—"

"He didn't wait to hear the result," Bolan said. "Charlie, I'm on the run. I don't have too much time. I'm trusting you because I have a hunch we're on the same side. And we both want to get Lattuada, right?"

"You can say that again."

"To put you in the picture, I got Dagmar away after they'd done the Coconut Grove, when you were already out."

"Jesus, I wondered what the hell... And then I saw that she had been—"

"Okay. Now listen, Charlie, I'll give it to you straight, the way it happened. After that I'd like you to answer one or two questions, if you would."

The man in the bed frowned. "Depends on the questions."

"Dagmar walked out on me a half hour after we left the Coconut Grove," Bolan said. "I spent the whole next day looking for her. I combed every dive in St. Pauli and Altona and some on the far side of the river. Finally I located her outside her own apartment and I made a date with her for the following night. For some reason she wouldn't see me that same night. We were going to talk about the Team and their racket. She was going to answer questions, too. But I never got to see her again. Alive, that is. When I showed for the date she was already dead, and every clue pointed my way, including some they'd stolen from my hotel room."

Charlie nodded. "That figures. It sounds like the way they work. Efficient."

"Efficient, as you say. Now I can understand why they'd want to pin the killing on me. I'm American, and Lattuada's description fits me. If I went on poking my nose, I could blow Lattuada and his connection with the racket. But why would they want to eliminate Dagmar in the first place, Charlie? Why?"

Macfarlane shrugged, then winced as the movement disturbed some dormant pain in his savaged body. "You tell me, man. They don't follow no rules."

"Okay. Let's take it from the top. Simple questions first. Lattuada and the Yank are one and the same, right?"

"Right."

"And he masterminded the campaign that put the Team at the top in the protection racket?"

Macfarlane nodded.

"The Team being led, so far as the strong-arm stuff goes, by this Hansie character?"

"Hansie Schiller, the iron fist in the fairy's glove, yeah."

"They were wrecking the Coconut Grove, and the Sugar Hill later, because you hadn't come across with the loot, right?"

The Trinidadian nodded again. "Bastards. As if they hadn't got enough, muscling in on Tondelayo's for a percentage. I said I'd see them in hell before—"

"Okay, Charlie," Bolan cut in. "So they took you up on it. They sent you to hell." He glanced at the injured man's feet. "But who were they still fighting after they'd put you out? Who were the other soldiers?"

"Friends of mine. Guys who have been strong-armed out of the same racket themselves. It was strictly a business operation, but they wanted to do it."

"Guys connected with Kraul?"

Charlie's eyes closed. "Who's Kraul?"

The Executioner let that one go with the tide. "All right. Now for the sixty-four-thousand-dollar question. Who *was* Dagmar? How did she fit in? What was her connection with the Team, and with you? She told me she'd come to see you about a spot in the floor show at Tondelayo's. The Sugar Hill, too. But there's no floor show at Tondelayo's, and only on Sundays at the other dump. How come, Charlie?"

A bespectacled nurse in a starched cap and apron wheeled a trolley loaded with enamel bowls and thermometers in glasses through the ward. She stopped by the bed beyond Macfarlane's. "Frau Meyer," she said severely, "I've told you before, only two visitors at a time! The others must wait outside and take their turn. It exhausts the patients."

"Dagmar was Lattuada's ex," Macfarlane said. "Nothing legal, but they were shacked up together awhile."

"And so?"

"Things were kind of tough after she walked out on him, and I helped her some. Found her the Kinderplatz apartment, fixed her up with a job, and like that."

"Were you laying her?"

"Not especially. I mean no more than anyone else."

"What was all this floor show routine?"

"That was just..." Charlie shrugged again, and winced. "It was like kind of a cover. Not that we needed one. But it gave her a reason to come and see me in case folks were nosy, see. She'd been a dancer once. Me, I was always saying I should start a floor show at Tondelayo's, expand the show at the Sugar Hill, like broaden out, okay? The story was that she'd come to discuss what kind of show it might be. You dig?"

Bolan nodded. "The guy in the men's room at Tondelayo's told me she was his connection for drugs. Or some girl called Dagmar was."

The West Indian lowered his eyelids and plucked at the sheet. "I wouldn't know anything about that."

"Look, Charlie," Bolan said urgently, "it can't hurt her now. I have to have the full story if I'm to nail Lattuada. It's tough enough as it is, being on the run. If I don't know the score, how can I help?"

"I guess you're right." Macfarlane sighed. The eyes closed altogether. "All right. Well, yes, to tell the truth we had a little business together. Being the boss, I couldn't afford to get caught with the stuff. Besides, I wasn't always there. Also the kid needed the money. You understand?"

"So you figured nobody would suspect a pretty blonde of being a pusher? And that was why you needed the floor show cover. Was this connection with or without the Team's knowledge?"

The man in the bed was silent for a moment. The pale boy in the next bed whined, "Please don't fuss, Mother. I've got plenty, really I have."

Macfarlane opened his eyes. The whites were the color of chicken fat. "That was the trouble," he told the warrior. "Dagmar's business with me was private. I reckoned those bastards were taking enough off me anyway."

"But they found out?"

"They found out. Lattuada was mad as hell because she wasn't using one of his wholesalers, and because we held out on him and he wasn't getting his cut. That was why they were told to take Dagmar with them when they'd fucked over the Coconut Grove, so they could choke the details of the operation out of her and louse it up."

"But they choked the life out of her instead, two days later. Why the hell should they have waited? Just to pin it on me? Why should they want to kill her anyway?"

"Don't ask me," Charlie said. "Maybe just because she knew too much. Maybe as a lesson to their own pushers. They play rough, those motherfuckers. Maybe because of something else, something we don't know about."

"Yeah," Bolan said slowly. "Maybe. She said she couldn't see me that night because she had to fix something, something she hoped she might be able to fix on the phone. *Was* there a phone in that apartment?"

Charlie shook his head.

"It doesn't make sense," the Executioner said. "It doesn't quite add up. Almost but not quite. From the little I saw of her, what you've told me figures, and yet there still seems to be something missing. If she was too scared to leave the apartment, and she had no phone, how could she hope to fix anything? And she *was* scared, too. That was genuine enough. Maybe there was nothing to fix. But in that case, why bother to tell me there was?"

"People aren't simple," Charlie said. "This was a complicated girl. She was a bit of a nympho, for starters. She couldn't say no. So she'd get herself in a mess and say the first thing that came into her head to get out of it. She'd tell you one thing in the morning, meaning every word of it, and then tell you something totally different that night, meaning that, too. Finally she'd get to believe her own lies, and lie again to explain that away." He compressed his bruised lips and shook his head once more. "That didn't stop her looking pretty, and it didn't stop fellows trying to make her."

"You're telling me all that crap about having something to fix could have been a stall? It was just that she already had a date lined up that night, but she wasn't prepared to admit it?"

"Maybe. Girls catch on pretty quick that there's a whole heap of men like to believe they're the only horse in the race. That doesn't stop the girls playing the field when they feel that way, but they have to hide it. And once you're on that kick, it becomes a habit, like anything else."

"Yeah," Bolan agreed. "A habit you can't kick." He shook his head. "You could be right at that, Charlie. It sounds too simple, but it does stack up with the details, as far as I know them."

"Let me bring you a nice piece of meat in a Pyrex dish," the woman at the next bed urged. "Boiled chicken they give him! And carrots any mensch she would have thrown them in the garbage can already!"

"What I can't understand," Bolan said, "is why they waited those two days. If it was so important to get the girl at your place, important enough to kill her, as it turned out, why didn't Lattuada go straight to her apartment that same night? They knew where it was, didn't they?"

"Sure. But maybe you're talking about two different things," Macfarlane said. "I mean, like the need to kill her may have come out of something that happened the night she wouldn't see you. Maybe it had nothing to do with what they wanted her for at the Coconut Grove. You never know."

The Executioner frowned. "It's possible. Only thing is, that would mean she was in some way, directly or indirectly, in contact with Lattuada or the Team on the night in question. From what you know of Dagmar, would you figure that was possible? Could she have been playing some kind of double game?"

"Dagmar never played any other kind. But the only person could answer that would be Lattuada's boss."

"Lattuada's *boss!* You mean . . . ? But who in hell is that?"

"You tell me!" Charlie Macfarlane said.

CHAPTER ELEVEN

On the following day, with the thaw continuing and sidewalks awash with gray slush, it started to rain before dawn and continued to rain all day. Mack Bolan awoke early in an atmosphere heavy with the odors of soot, diesel fuel and smoke from a coal stove that wouldn't draw properly. He had slept in a waiting room at the Hamburg train station among the handful of travelers condemned to catch the postal train to Lübeck and the Baltic coast and those who had arrived too late to make it home on the last buses or subway services the previous night.

Bolan himself had drawn a blank on his attempt to make the BMW in the hotel parking lot. Approaching the Drehbahn on a circuitous route when he left the hospital, he saw that police were stationed in pairs at both the hotel entrances and at the foot of the ramps leading up to and down from the garage floors. He guessed they would be covering the elevators inside, as well.

No dice, then, on his aim to locate Lattuada and the drug baron, especially since St. Pauli and other likely neighborhoods would be under intense surveillance from squads briefed to bring in the killer Belasko. He would have to lie very low until the heat was off.

It would even, he guessed, be unwise to check into some kind of lodging house in the suburbs. He wasn't too certain of German police procedure, and there was a chance that all registrations, as in France, were automatically checked out. A railroad terminal seemed as good a compromise as any. The cops would certainly be watching, but they would be at the barriers, casing the travelers leaving town and paying little attention to the floating population centered on the station itself. In any case it would be safer than roaming the streets on the day of his escape.

He passed the daylight hours in a movie theater, emerging to buy coffee and a bratwurst when rush-hour commuters flooded the station concourse. After that he returned to the theater until it closed at midnight.

Now, stiff from a few hours' sleep on a wooden bench, he limped downstairs to the washroom and splashed cold water on his face. Before he did anything else, he would have to buy a razor and a replacement for his ripped jacket. Buttoning his stolen raincoat against the downpour, he left the station with the city-bound office workers.

"Extra! Extra! Read all about it!" the newsboys cried into the rain at the head of the taxi queue on the approach ramp. "Wanted man in daring court escape! Read about his death-defying climb!" Bolan bought a copy and hurried to a cheap café on the far side of the street. Over coffee and a sandwich, he folded the paper to an inside page and read the lead story.

Skipping the sensationalistic introduction, which gave an accurate, if highly colored, account of his courtroom escape and the air shaft adventure that followed it, he translated from the German:

Kriminalkommissar Conrad Fischer, the detective who arrested Belasko, told our reporter, "He will not get far. All railroad stations, ports and airfields are being watched and we are already following a definite lead. I expect him to be back behind bars within forty-eight hours." The police description of the wanted murder suspect is: over six feet tall, of spare build, with blue eyes and dark hair. When last seen he was wearing a dark suit and was hatless, but it is thought that he may now be dressed in a dark blue raincoat and a peaked, military-style cap.

Turning to another page, Bolan casually removed the cap from his head and placed it on a shelf beneath the wall counter where he was sitting. There would be plenty of tall guys in blue raincoats on the streets today, many of them sparely built, and some of those lean men might wear military-style caps. But a combination of all three, together with an American accent, would be tempting fate. He had to get new clothes without delay, preferably garments that already had a used look.

The rain fell ceaselessly from a gray sky. The cold wind that drove the ragged clouds over the rooftops sent it gusting across the streets in squalls to splash calf-high from the streaming sidewalks. By the time Bolan located a used clothing store in a run-down neighborhood behind the station, his pants were sodden from the knee down and the raincoat was letting in water at the shoulder. It seemed a good enough reason to want a change of clothes.

"I just arrived from the north," he told the old man behind the counter. "The snow had changed to rain when I left, but not like this! I've got a lot of calls to make today. I guess I have to think of something a little more robust!"

Suits were impossible because of Bolan's height. Rather than draw attention to this, he went for separates: gray pants and a sport jacket in brown tweed. The pants were baggy around the hips and the jacket sleeves short, but he was able to choose them quickly enough not to draw attention to his difficulty with sizes. A tan trench coat soiled enough around the collar and sleeves to have been worn for more than one winter completed the outfit.

"Now what about these, sir?" the dealer asked, gesturing toward the pile of sodden garments at Bolan's feet. " I could give you a small discount if you'd care to—"

"No, no, the wife would kick up hell if I came home without these clothes. Thanks just the same." The warrior dared not admit his desire to rid himself of the telltale garments. As soon as he was gone, the dealer would see the rips in shoulder and lapels torn by the broken glass in the courthouse window. If he read the papers, or if the cops checked out secondhand dealers, he'd make the connection at once. And then the law would have an up-to-date description of what their quarry was wearing. Folding the jacket carefully, he wrapped it in the wet pants and raincoat and allowed the old man to package them in brown paper and string.

He walked out into the rain, bought a narrow-brim fedora at a department store and headed for St. Pauli. In a lane that twisted through a quarter of medieval houses near the river, he junked the package by a row of garbage cans stuffed with the fabric discards from a tailor's workshop.

St. Pauli was dangerous, sure, especially with the cops convinced that he was the mysterious Yank running the rackets there. But if he wanted to finger the murderers of Dagmar and wrap up the whole Mob scene, it was the only place to start. Maybe the law would even figure it was the last place a man on the run would go. It was a chance he had to take.

In a dockside saloon he sipped a beer and read the early editions of the evening papers. The accused foreigner in the St. Pauli Blonde case, he noted with satisfaction, had been sighted at the car ferry terminal linking northern Germany with Denmark at Grossenbrode. He had also been positively identified near the Kiel Canal, at Hannover airport and among the crowd in a Kassel beer garden. An early rearrest was expected.

It was difficult, just the same, for the Executioner to decide on a plan of action. The physical resemblance enabling Lattuada to frame Bolan would now work equally against the hood. Since the police description fitted him as well as the hunted man, he would probably lie low, for fear of getting hauled in himself, until the heat was off or Bolan was back behind bars. So how was a stranger in town to get next to him?

By hanging in there, hoping to pick up a lead, the way he had before Dagmar's death, and then following it up one hundred percent, Bolan thought. But first he had to find a base. He would search out a likely location, correction, the most *un*likely location possible, as soon as he dared recover the BMW from the hotel garage. Maybe a foreigner arriving in an expensive car at some country *Gasthaus* outside the city would get by. Meanwhile he would continue his round of the taverns in the red-light district, eavesdropping on the conversations around him, looking for a clue, a hint, a name quoted, that could put him on the right trail.

He was in a bar full of stevedores and off-duty hookers when a voice murmured in English just behind him, "Well, well. If it isn't my American friend."

Bolan swung around. It was Hugo, the doorman from the Mandrake Root. Bolan raised a finger to summon the bartender.

"If you'll take a person's advice, you'll leave this area pretty damn quick. The word's gone around and the Team's after your balls."

"What'll you have, Hugo?"

"Somethin' short, by the Lord's grace," the doorman replied. "For if we're not out of here in about two minnits, there'll be a hot time in the old town tonight, I'm tellin' you."

"A glass of Irish whiskey for the gentleman," Bolan told the barman. And then, "I sure appreciate the tip-off, Hugo. But what's going on? And why trouble yourself to warn me?"

"Brutal it is, my friend. I'll answer the second question first, though. It's just that you seem a right ould bugger, and maybe I've a soft spot for the underdog, too. The Irish in me, no doubt." He raised his glass and drank. "As for what's going on, why nothin' at all, nothin' at all. Everythin' has to be paid for. That's the way of it. And it seems you're havin' to pay for a certain, shall we say, curiosity and inquisitiveness that could inconvenience various parties who shall be nameless."

"And the price?"

"At bargain-basement rates, a beatin', a heavy one. In the higher price range, an unexpected encounter with the demon barber and his razor, or maybe even a headstone. Unless they just hand you back to the coppers."

"Would the nameless salesclerk answer to Hansie?"

"I wouldn't like to say," Hugo answered truthfully. "C'mon now, finish that drink and away to the toilets with you. I'll be joinin' you there in a minnit."

Bolan drained his glass and left the bar.

The window in the men's room looked out on a narrow passageway that ran down to the quayside. Bolan and Hugo dropped to the cobblestones and hurried through. It was almost dark, and a cold drizzle misted the pools of light thrown by the dockside lamps. Footfalls were deadened. Trucks moving away from a Greek freighter discharging a cargo of citrus fruit in cases appeared and disappeared in the murk as mysteriously as phantoms. Unless the east wind returned there could be fog again before morning.

"How the hell did they know I was in that particular joint?" Bolan asked. "I guess they did know, from what you say."

"Sure they knew. Did you ever hear tell of the Mafia, mister?"

Bolan nodded, grim knowledge written on his face.

"Well, that's what goes on here, in a manner of speakin'. I don't mean the protection lark. That happens all over, and not just with Sicilians. I mean like the old-time routine, the Black Hand and all that. There's an Italian colony here in St. Pauli. And Greeks and Turks and I don't know what-all. What the Yank does is put the Team onto them, mostly small shopkeepers, delicatessens, restaurants and that. He don't just put the bite on the clubs and the caffs. He's strong-armed all these foreigners into workin' as his legmen and lookouts, see. Once the word goes around in this part of town, every move you make goes straight back to His Eminence quick as a phone can be dialed. Likewise when a guy has to be collected for treatment, like with you this evenin'.''

"You heard they were coming to get me at that bar? That could be difficult, couldn't it? With all those people, and those girls? Or did you just hear the word, as you say, had gone out, and *you* happened to know where I was? You'd heard someone tell somebody, perhaps?''

"Sure, it don't pay to look closely at some things," Hugo said. "Isn't there a proverb or some such regarding the gift horse?''

Bolan shrugged and let it drop. It was enough, as the doorman had said, that he'd been spirited away unharmed. And, if nothing else, it proved the search, his search, was growing warm.

They crossed a busy street. The rain was definitely turning into a mist now. Cars swam past on the greasy pavement like fish in a bowl, their yellow eyes hooded. The few pedestrians they saw materialized and then vanished like wraiths. "I'm letting you lead the way. Where are we going?" Bolan asked.

"Somewhere a person can talk without bein' interrupted.''

On the far side of a narrow canal, soaring upward in the gloom, floodlights played on a single, spired Gothic tower surrounded by ruined walls. "Church of St. Nikolai," Hugo said. "Flattened by a bombing raid in World War II. Preserved as a monument."

Behind the church a narrow lane ran between two rows of old houses toward a small dock basin. Halfway along the lane a cul-de-sac led to the rear entrance of a warehouse fronting the wharf. As they passed the mouth of the entry, a huge American car, bleached white in the lamplight, turned into the lane and stopped. The rear door opened and two men got out.

Bolan recognized the car—the whitewall tires, the blinds masking the windows. He recognized one of the men. It was the vulturelike thug he had seen in the Andreas Bernersstrasse. The other was equally tall but more heavily built. He wore a brown houndstooth topcoat and a Tyrolean hat with feathers tucked into the band.

Too late, as they closed in on him, Bolan saw the cunning, and the simplicity, of the plan. Of course they couldn't snatch him in a crowded bar! Much better decoy him to a deserted alley through the use of someone he trusted. It was safer, too, than any attempt to follow him in the car and then hope to find an opportunity to shanghai him.

As the truth flashed through his mind, Bolan turned, but he was seized above the elbows in a viselike grip. The doorman's strength was astonishing. Before the Executioner could bring his unarmed combat expertise into play, the two hoods were beside him. The heavier one was buttoning a leather glove on his right hand.

Bolan struggled, but the vulture man flicked out an arm and hit him flat-handed across the throat. As the warrior gasped for air, the leather glove, balled now into a fist, pistoned once, twice, three times lazily, almost casually, into the pit of his stomach. The brute force of the blows momentarily paralyzed Bolan. He folded forward and dropped to his knees on the sidewalk.

The two men grabbed the Executioner under the arms and dragged him the few yards to the car. He turned his head as they bundled him into the rear. Hugo was staring at him, an unfathomable expression on his face.

Bolan winced, tried to say something, but could only croak unintelligibly. The rear door slammed, and the Cadillac accelerated silently away.

Slumped on the Caddy's rear seat with his arms crossed over his belly, Bolan tried to force air back into his lungs. Fingers twined in his hair, dragging back his head and jerking him upright. The gloved fist hit him again several times, always around the solar plexus or just above the groin. He tried to raise his arms to defend himself, but a hand slapped him repeatedly across the face, half blinding him.

The car stopped, started, slowed and stopped again. The window blinds hid everything but a blurred impression of lights passing, but the Executioner guessed from the total absence of echo that they were briefly out in the open, perhaps on one of the Alster bridges, heading east.

"Why...go on...slamming a guy...when you...already got...him?" he ground out between the blows.

"I like hitting people, dearie," the man wearing the glove said. His face was as bleak as an Easter Island statue, with granite chips for eyes. "Beside, we don't want no fuckin' cries for help while we're stalled in this goddamn traffic, do we?" He slammed another piledriver into Bolan's diaphragm.

"Right on," the vulture man said. "How about I tickle his eye with a shiv, Hansie?"

The gloved man shook his head. "Might as well enjoy myself and put him on the deck now. There ain't enough meat on this one to amuse me once we tear the clothes off him."

"You want the shiv?"

"Wise up, shithead. What d'ya think the boss'd say with blood all over the fuckin' seat?"

The car was rolling again. Bolan glanced around the interior. A glass screen separating the driver from the occupants in back was wound up and covered with blinds similar to those masking the windows. Although the body was customized, the layout of the car seemed to be standard.

The hoods had made two mistakes, perhaps overconfident because their quarry had been such an easy mark. Instead of neutralizing Bolan totally by sitting one on each side of him, they had crowded him into the far corner of the rear seat, leaving the Andreas Bernersstrasse thug on his right and the guy with the glove facing him on the tip-up occasional seat. Between the prisoner and the outside world, on one side, was only the door.

Bolan made his move. "I guess the fairy must be Hansie Schiller," he said to the vulture man. "I'm surprised to see a nice guy like you in such low company. You know, some of the shit that particular fruit grows in could rub off on you, and it sure as hell won't smell good."

The Executioner's head snapped back on his shoulders as the fist crashed against his jaw. "Sweetie, I don't like mouthy punks," Hansie said. He punched Bolan in the gut while the other torpedo held his arms. "Try this one on for size. It'll give you an idea of what's comin' if you don't shut up." The black glove slammed into the pit of the American's stomach again.

Bolan jackknifed forward until his chest was against his knees. He made gagging noises with his mouth. The hinges were at the leading edge of the door. The chromed handle beneath the armrest should open downward, he thought.

The Cadillac swung around a sharp left-hand curve and slowed. The two hoods swayed toward the center of the car, but Bolan had been waiting for just such a movement, and he leaned outward, against the thrust of centrifugal force. As if to steady himself, he shot his left hand out, hitting the handle and depressing it. The wide, heavy door suddenly swung open.

From his doubled-up position, Bolan somersaulted forward and pitched into the roadway. A confused impression of lights, wind, squealing brakes and the oily hiss of tires, and then he hit the wet pavement with his shoulder, rolling frantically toward the curb after the stunning impact, in case there was traffic following close behind.

Brakes screeched again. There was an angry honking of horns. Someone shouting something. Then he was on his feet, running for the sidewalk, dodging among the scatter of pedestrians in the misty lamplight. But the car made no attempt to stop. The door closed. The Caddy picked up speed and turned right at the next intersection. He had guessed right: they wouldn't try anything in front of witnesses.

He saw books in an illuminated shop window, a red sign spotlit above the doors of a tavern, another store displaying stationery and box files. He was in the Koppelstrasse, behind the Atlantic Hotel, less than a mile from his hotel on the other side of the Alster. It was completely dark now and the mist was thicker. He decided to walk there and try once more to gain access to his BMW.

When he got to the Hotel Oper, he saw two uniformed cops talking to the doorman and the hall porter beyond the glass doors. They were standing between the elevators and the reception desk. Each carried a Heckler & Koch machine pistol slung over his right shoulder with one hand resting on the breech. Bolan didn't want to try out his unarmed combat routines against a twin stream of 9 mm parabellum rounds pumped out at a rate of eight hundred per minute. He walked to the garage entrance.

The entrance and exit ramps were side by side. No police were visible. Bolan stole up to the ticket dispenser at the foot of the entrance ramp. He dodged past the striped barrier pole and advanced a few yards up the slope.

Above, on the first level, he heard a cough. Then a scrape of feet, a faint chink of metal as if, say, the buckle of a uniform belt had brushed against the steel casing of an autoloader magazine. He crept back down to the street.

No way.

In back of the hotel was an alley. On the opposite side of the narrow passage a fire escape zigzagged up the rear face of a modern apartment building. The block had a flat roof. Across from it he could see a parapet, the hotel's elevator housing bulked against the sky, a slope of shallow tiles. He moved to the fire escape and began to climb upward carefully.

More than half the windows passed by the iron stairway were lit, most of them with shutters closed or curtains drawn across to blank the interior. Inside one room with the draperies drawn back, a man and a girl were gesticulating, apparently in the middle of an argument; in another, a heavyset man sat at a table, staring morosely at a bottle and a tumbler half full of liquor. Bolan catfooted past like a shadow, his rubber-soled shoes making no sound on the metal grilles.

The fire escape didn't stop at the top floor but continued to roof level. Bolan stood on the railed platform and looked across the width of the alley at the hotel roof. The mist wrapped clammy hands around him, condensing on his eyebrows and the fur collar of his trench coat.

Beyond the parapet at the top of the hotel's rear facade, there was a flat area two or three yards across before the slant of wet tiles. He swung around. The roof of the apartment was flat all right, but the asphalt was dotted with obstructions—water tanks, ventilators, finned air-conditioning ducts, the housing that covered the exit from the emergency stairway.

The maximum straight-line run available to a man who wanted to launch himself across the gap between the two buildings was no more than six or seven yards. The gap was at least twelve feet across. With a greasy, soot-grimed wet surface to take off from and a parapet fencing in the landing space on the other side, it was obviously no go.

Bolan sighed and trod quietly back down the fire escape. As he emerged from the alley, a tan Mercedes limousine slid onto the Valentinskamp sidewalk and stopped beside him. A door opened, and he sensed a waft of heat seasoned with the odors of expensive leather seats and cigar smoke.

The man at the wheel was wearing leather, too, an expensively cut black suit with a white shirt and maroon necktie. He leaned across to the open door and said quietly, "Perhaps we could offer you a ride, Herr Belasko—up to the second floor of the Hotel Oper garage, for example?"

Halted in midstride, Bolan stared.

"We haven't officially met," the driver of the Mercedes said. "Let me introduce myself. The name is Kraul."

CHAPTER TWELVE

During an instant of hesitation, Mack Bolan saw that there were two stony-faced characters in the rear seat of the Mercedes, each grasping an automatic pistol fitted with a silencer. Both weapons were lined up on him. He got into the car and closed the door.

The Mercedes glided away from the curb. "All right," Bolan said, "I'll buy it. What's the pitch? What's this about a garage?"

"Oh, come, Herr Belasko," Kraul said, "let's not be foolish and pretend ignorance. You've spent a good half hour casing the hotel's entrances and exits in the hope of finding a way in past the police guards, so you can reclaim the BMW parked on the lowest level."

Bolan glanced at the man. Kraul's face was square-jawed, with deep lines etched between the nose and the corners of the mouth. His eyes, as far as the Executioner could see in the greenish light reflected from the instruments, were pale and slightly slitted. "If all that's true," Bolan asked, "why would you help me out?"

The German turned his head with a thin-lipped smile. "Let's just say it suits me to have you more mobile than you've been since you made your spectacular escape from the courthouse."

"And in return?"

"I ask nothing. Nothing, that is, that you wouldn't have been doing had you not been put out of the way on a trumped-up murder charge."

Bolan frowned. He didn't get it. "You've got a screwy sense of direction," he commented. "We were only a couple hundred yards from the hotel when you picked me up. We're a good mile away now, and heading north!" They had, in fact, just passed the arched bulk of the elevated Dammtor subway station, its huge windows gleaming dully through the mist.

"We can't just drive you straight in there," Kraul said irritably. "We have to go by my place first and make certain arrangements."

Bolan was silent. Maybe it wasn't a stall. After all, with two armed torpedoes in the back, the guy had no need to dream up the hotel parking scenario to persuade him to take a seat. The warrior decided to keep a low profile and play it by ear.

The Mercedes cut across to the lakeside drive, passed the neon lights of the Ferryhouse Restaurant and turned in between two gateposts topped by stone lions. The house at the end of the graveled approach was a three-story mansion with a pillared portico. A houseboy in a white jacket ran down the steps and opened Bolan's door as the car stopped.

The hoods with the silenced automatics were already out in the open, one on either side of the limo. "Perhaps you'd care to accompany our friends indoors while I put away the car," Kraul said. Bolan climbed the steps, crossed a marble hallway and preceded the two heavies into a room that looked like a library—two walls lined with books, white hide armchairs, a miniature billiard table, a log fire burning. The rock-faced hoods took up positions beside the double doors, their guns—.45-caliber Combat Masters, Bolan noticed—still in evidence. Soon afterward Kraul joined them.

In the brightly lit room, Bolan got a better picture of Kraul. He was lean, not very tall, with pale blond hair that arched above a lined forehead. About forty-five years old, the Executioner reckoned. "All right, I'm listening. Lay it on me."

"It's very simple," Kraul said. He fished a cigar from an inner pocket of his black leather jacket, unwrapped it and clipped the end with a gold cutter. "Georg, Nils, you can put the hardware away now."

The silenced guns disappeared, although the torpedoes remained on guard.

"The nucleus of the matter, Herr Belasko," Kraul resumed, "is this. Certain parties whose activities are, shall we say, inimical to my own methods of business are, it seems, on your own private hit list. Obviously, then, it is to my advantage to put you in a position where you can continue your own chase. Whether you like it or not, you'll be helping me."

"I get it," Bolan said. "Lattuada, Hansie and the Team have strong-armed you out of business. You figure if I'm free I can do your dirty work for you and leave you free to terrorize the District once more. Right?"

Kraul picked up a gold-plated cigarette lighter and lit his cigar. "Crudely put," he said, "but that, roughly speaking, is the position."

"You're in a crude business," Bolan said. "Don't think I rate you any higher than Lattuada. As far as I'm concerned, the whole damn lot of you, whether you smoke cigars or put the boot in for pleasure, should be six feet under."

The German smiled. He blew a plume of smoke toward the ceiling and subsided into one of the white hide chairs. "As long as I get what I want, you can think what you like."

"What makes you think I'll help you anyway, even if you do get me my car?"

"My dear fellow," Kraul protested, "use your head. You have no choice. You can't do anything else. To free yourself from the clutches of the law, you have to nail this American and prove he was responsible for the death of the young woman, the pusher who was once a dancer. And doing that, you *have* to be helping me."

Bolan's thoughts were racing. Unless he dropped the whole thing and got the hell out, the guy was right.

The Executioner never quit in the middle of a mission. Apart from nailing those who had framed him, he was determined to put an end to the evil activities of Lattuada and the scumbags working for him, not to mention the drug kingpin, Arvell Asticot. "What makes you think I wouldn't go after you just as hard once I'd made it?" he asked bleakly.

Kraul flicked a glance at Georg and Nils. "I'll take care of that when, and if, it arises," he said. "Just remember, we may temporarily be...inconvenienced, but I still have soldiers happy to do anything I say. Anything at all."

"All right," Bolan said, "so how do I get back to my car? And incidentally, how the hell do you know about it?"

"My influence isn't confined to Hamburg. You've been followed ever since you left Frankfurt. As you know, I've got a special interest in Lattuada and Schiller, as well as Arvell Asticot, so I keep an eye on their movements. I don't know exactly who you are, but I do know you're efficient, and for the moment that's enough for me. As for the car, the operation depends on the fact that, by chance, I have a BMW of the same model, in the same color, right here in my garage." The racketeer smiled thinly. "It may not have quite the arsenal concealed beneath the front seat, but with the help of a young friend of mine, I think it can prove useful." He raised his voice. "Very well, *Fräulein*, you may join us now."

An inner door opened. The girl who came into the room had dark skin, plum-colored lips and a wild hairstyle. She was dressed in jeans and a tight sweater that contoured her breasts. It was Sally Ann.

"Well," she said with her impudent smile, "look who's here—the reluctant lover himself...and a nonsmoker at that!"

He turned his back on her. "Perhaps you should know," he said to Kraul, "that Sally here can't be trusted. She's certainly well enough in with Lattuada and his thugs to walk unharmed out of an ambush, a crossroads attack involving an SMG and two automatics that murdered a cabdriver and could easily have finished me. I'm not even sure she wasn't the one who tipped them off I'd be there."

"Oh, you!" Sally Ann pouted. "You're still upright, aren't you?"

"Whatever," Bolan said, ignoring her, "she's playing a double game."

"I am well aware of it," Kraul said equably. "If we were in the espionage business, she'd be what you call a double agent. Herr Lattuada and his cronies use her to run occasional errands, to make the odd contact—"

"Such as setting up foreigners for a kill?"

"And in return, by permitting her to do this, I gain an eye and an ear, shall we say, in the enemy camp. So far, however, she's been unable to find an answer to the most important question."

"Which is?"

"Who hired that American mobster to come over here and disrupt what was a perfectly good business? Who, in a nutshell, is Lattuada's boss? It is hardly credible, I agree, but this is a complete mystery. Nobody knows!"

Bolan raised his eyebrows. This was the third time he'd heard the mystery man mentioned, once before by Charlie Macfarlane, once by the enforcer Hansie Schiller, whose fear of the boss's reaction had saved Bolan from being carved with a knife in the Cadillac. He said, "It wouldn't be Asticot, would it? He's certainly—" Bolan smiled slightly "—not unknown in the narcotics world."

Kraul shook his head. "Herr Asticot makes his money exploiting situations like the one we have in this city. One day he'll prove too clever and anger everybody at the same time, and that'll be the end of him. For the moment, however, he's kept his nose clean. But I can tell you definitely that he's not the brain behind Lattuada's schemes. There's too much risk of some of the dirt rubbing off on him."

The racketeer paused, tipping an inch and a half of cigar ash into an onyx ashtray. "I can tell you something else, since you're so anxious to locate Asticot...."

"What makes you think that?"

"Why else," Kraul said blandly, "would you have followed him from Munich to Frankfurt, and from Frankfurt here? I can tell you that at the moment he's in Lübeck, supervising the shipment of certain merchandise from a Greek freighter to a private individual. By chance, Lattuada is also in the same town today, but on quite a different mission."

"And you're hoping if I get my car back that I'll go after both of them?"

"I don't see what else you could do," Kraul said.

Bolan compressed his lips. It was clear that Sally Ann was a stalking-horse. And if he allowed himself to be dragged into the hunt, he suspected it wouldn't be long before he'd be the stalking-horse for both sides.

On the other hand, as the racketeer had pointed out, given the circumstances, what else could he do? "Suppose I go with this two-timing kid," he demanded. "What's to stop her turning me over to the other side, as one of her...errands?"

"The fact that I'd break her pretty neck if she did," Kraul replied. "And you'll have to take my word for that."

"Okay," Bolan sighed. "So what do we do?"

"It's quite simple. She drives my BMW into town. You'll be hidden in the trunk. She parks the car in the Hotel Oper garage, taking care to exchange a couple of words with the police on duty. They're not going to note the license number of a car going *in*—especially if it's driven by a sexy-looking woman."

Kraul's cigar was almost finished. He placed it in the ashtray. "Sally Ann kills an hour, maybe doing some late marketing. She returns to the garage and drives out. 'So long, boys,' she says. 'Try to keep warm, but don't do anything I wouldn't do!' She pays her ticket and leaves. You're still in the trunk. Only this time it's *your* BMW you're riding in. Later, some time tomorrow, I send someone in to collect my own car. He pretends that he lost the ticket and asks how much he owes, and so on. The car's clean, so no questions are asked. How does that sound, Herr Belasko?"

"Suits me," the Executioner said. "I can't find anything wrong with it. But let me make one thing clear. You can get back my car for me and the gear I need, but it doesn't buy you any immunity. I'm making no promises. I see no difference between you and Lattuada. If I succeed in putting him out of the way, it's in the cards that I might one day be chasing you just as hard. Is that clear?''

Kraul laughed aloud. He seemed genuinely amused. "Sally Ann," he said, "show our guest to the garage."

CHAPTER THIRTEEN

The keys of the rented BMW and the parking ticket were taped inside the sedan's rear bumper. Bolan was thankful he had taken this precaution: it meant the police had no idea he had transport, for there had been no evidence among the papers taken off him when he'd been arrested.

The only thing wrong with Kraul's escape plan was that the two cops on guard were still stationed at the top of the ramps leading to and from the lowest level, as they had been when the Executioner had first cased the place. And it was on that level that the BMW was parked.

There were no vacant slots nearby. No chance, then, for Sally Ann to drive out the "wrong" car without the cops noticing once she had done her shopping, especially since she had dutifully joked with the two guys on the way in.

She drove up to the fourth level and let Bolan out of the trunk.

"The important thing is to get the car out," he said when she had explained the problem. "That's the number one priority. I can make it with the stuff beneath the seat once we're away."

"Yes, but... I mean, like they have your description. And *I* can't very well go to that car when I get back, not when the guys have already seen me drive up to—"

"Okay, okay," he said soothingly. "No sweat. We'll take it for granted that neither of us dare go anywhere near that BMW while those guys are there."

"Then how the hell do we—"

"I said while they're there. What we do," Bolan said in a low voice, "is fix it so they're not there but someplace else. We decoy them away, long enough for you to make it to that first level, untape the key, start the car, pay your ticket and get out."

Sally Ann stared at him. "How?"

"We turn Kraul's plan upside down, or, to be precise, inside out. The plan had two aims: get me in here secretly, then take the car out openly. We'll reverse that. There are only two of us, and if one has to act as decoy, it has to be me...because you have to drive. So I'll show myself openly, lead them up to the top floor maybe, while you take a powder with the car. Okay?"

"You really figure you can hack it—" The girl stopped speaking as elevator doors clanged open. A young couple appeared at the far end of the level, started an Audi 80 and drove away down the ramp.

"Just leave it to me," Bolan said. "Have you got a watch on you? Right. Be back here at exactly nine-fifteen, at the foot of the ramp, ready to pay your ticket. You'll hear the noise when I make my play. As soon as you do, run up to the car. It's that simple."

She still looked dubious. "But that way your gun will still be in the car while I drive it—"

"I don't shoot cops," Bolan interrupted harshly. "We didn't all go to the same school as Herr Lattuada."

"Wouldn't it be easier if we *both* got into the car and crashed that little barrier pole at the foot of the exit ramp?"

"It might be if we had a bulldozer. The poles are steel. They're designed to stop folks crashing them. It's much simpler if you pay your mark, feed the release ticket into the machine so that the pole rises, and drive quietly out."

The hollow boom of an exhaust echoed up the ramp. An Opel Senator rose into view, turned onto the slope that led to higher levels with a screech of rubber and disappeared. Soon afterward they heard the slam of doors and the whine of an elevator.

"Just do as I said," Bolan said. "Wait for me at the end of the street when you're out, and I'll drive you back to Kraul's place before I head north."

When the girl had gone, he stole back down the ramps until he could peer around the corner and take in the lowest level. The two cops were sharing a cigarette at the top of the first slope. The BMW was parked halfway between Bolan's position and theirs. And, no, there was no way he could make the car without being seen. He went back up to the second highest floor.

At 9:12 he summoned the two elevators. One he sent up to the hotel on the penthouse floor. He wedged open the doors of the other with an empty two-liter oilcan he had found, immobilizing the cage at his level.

Two minutes later the unmistakable sounds of a struggle resounded throughout the garage. Bolan jumped on the hood of a sedan and thumped the roof. Back on the concrete floor, he uttered incoherent cries, battered the side of a panel truck that was parked opposite the downslope and hurled himself repeatedly against the body.

He smashed the truck window with his elbow and then, as the imploded fragments of glass were still clattering inside, he shouted clearly, "Help! I just saw him, the murderer! It's Belasko! The man who escaped from the courthouse! Help! He's trying to take my—"

From below he heard shouts and the stamp of feet. The elevator that was free went down toward the lower levels. Someone was running up the ramp. As Bolan had hoped, one of the cops was approaching on foot while the other took the elevator. He ran a little way down the slope so that he would be in view—enough to be identified—when the first man made it to the level below.

The cop appeared at the top of the access ramp, saw the Executioner there and yelled, "Stop, or I'll shoot!"

Bolan ran back to the upper floor. The earsplitting rasp of a machine pistol thundered among the parked vehicles; splinters from a concrete pillar hummed past his head.

He reached in through the broken window to release the truck hand brake, shoving the vehicle forward. The wheel was locked, but it ran down with increasing speed and crashed against the concrete barrier where the ramp curved, blocking the cop's pursuit. He jumped aside, cursing, and dropped to one knee, spraying a second burst up against the low roof of Bolan's level. But the deathstream missed the Executioner by several inches: he was already racing for the blocked escalator.

The second cage rose on the way to the top floor. As Bolan had guessed, the cops were trying a pincer movement, hoping to bracket him from above and below on whichever level he was. He kicked away the oilcan that was jamming the elevator doors, edged inside as they slid shut and pressed the Down button. A stream of slugs pierced the metal outer doors as the elevator car sank out of range.

One floor above the hotel entrance Bolan quit the elevator and ran down the ramp, past the barriers and out into the night. The BMW was waiting at the curbside fifty yards away. The passenger door was ajar and smoke curled up into the mist from the twin tailpipes.

Sally Ann was at the wheel. He leaped in and slammed the door. "All right," he panted, "we're on our way!"

The engine roared, and the heavy sedan laid rubber on the wet street and arrowed away toward the lake.

"Your friend Kraul," Bolan said as the BMW crossed the bridge at the northern tip of the Alster, "may have been forced out of the rackets in St. Pauli, but he sure knows how to take care of himself outside."

"Come again?"

"Take the situation as of now. Mercedes, BMW, something else in his garage under a tarp that could have been a Lamborghini or a Ferrari. A mansion complete with houseboy. Two bodyguards with silenced automatics. How does he get away with it?"

"Ferdy plays it real cool," Sally Ann said. "Personally speaking, he stays away from the action. You dig?"

"I'm talking about the law. If he bossed all the rackets before Lattuada horned in, how come he's not behind bars?"

"They could never pin anything on him. Like I say, he distanced himself. He knows every scam there is. Also, Ferdy pays his taxes."

"You mean he's in the clear with the local tax people?" Bolan was amused.

"Hell, no. He don't mess with that crap. He drops his bread at the right time, into the right pockets. Know what I mean?"

The Executioner sighed. "Yeah," he said, "I know exactly what you mean." Police headquarters, city hall, administrators in the state parliament, the routine was always the same, however many frontiers you crossed.

"In any case," Sally Ann said, "he never bossed *all* the rackets. He doesn't have Lattuada's organizing talent. There were always small-timers, punks, hoods from other cities, trying to muscle in. That was the price he paid for staying clear himself."

"He just sat in his beautiful house and let his gorillas kill on his behalf? Is that it?"

She shrugged. "If you want to put it that way."

"Can you think of any other way to put it?" Bolan said.

There was no reply. She turned off the brightly lit parkway into a wide residential street where the streetlights only swam at long intervals through the mist. "So Lattuada's got it all sewn up now, but Kraul aims to make a comeback?" Bolan asked.

"Of course."

"I did hear a rumor he'd been knocked off and his body dropped into the sea from an airplane."

"He started that himself," Sally Ann said. "There's a turnaround here. You wanna switch seats and collect the gear from under yours?"

"Okay," Bolan said. "This isn't the route we followed when we came into town, is it?"

She shook her head, braking the BMW to a standstill. "Out the front entrance, return the back way, approaching from a different direction. Routine."

From beneath the seat the warrior recovered his second Beretta, spare clips, a wire garrote, papers and the flat-bladed throwing knife he liked to keep strapped to his left ankle. He buckled on the autoloader's quick-draw leather and slid behind the wheel as the girl shifted to the other seat. "Wise me up on the lefts and rights," he told her.

The Kraul property was about four blocks away. Bolan saw the crimson reflections flicker on the underside of the low clouds when he was halfway there, but the mist, thicker still here on the northern side of the lake, muffled the sound of gunfire until he was within two hundred yards of the tall wooden gates that opened on a stableyard in back of the mansion.

He jammed on the brakes, cut the BMW's lights and engine and opened the door. "Stay here," he told the girl, "while I go see what's cooking. Don't move until I tell you, okay?"

Keeping close to the ten-foot-high wall surrounding the property, he ran to the open gates. Beyond them a big Ford had been run up onto the sidewalk, and behind that was the white Cadillac. There was a lamp on the far side of the street, and he could just make out the license number—HH777-CDE. It looked as if the Team was paying a call.

The shots were coming from the far side of the stable block. Above the roof he could see flames that must be spiraling up from a building somewhere in the grounds. Unsheathing the Beretta, he sidled into the yard.

Around one side of the block, a driveway curled through shrubbery toward the house. Some of the shooting seemed to be concentrated there. Bright flashes stabbed the dark and briefly illuminated patches of snow still lying beneath the bushes.

Bolan was ten yards inside the gates when he realized some of the shooters were firing at him. Brick dust from the wall stung his face as a near miss gouged the surface. Another slug struck sparks from the cobblestones by his feet, and a third smashed glass in a greenhouse behind him on the far side of the gates.

He flung himself to the ground at one side of a wooden bin full of coarse sand that was used to treat the yard when the ground was frozen. Half a dozen more bullets thudded into the box, and then there was a lull.

Were they stealing around the far side of the block to take him from behind? Advancing stealthily under cover of the bin? He didn't wait to find out. On elbows and knees, keeping the dark bulk of the bin between him and the shrubbery, he crawled back to the gates. Out on the sidewalk he rose to his feet and ran back to the BMW. The girl's face peered anxiously at him through the windshield. "Take it easy," he murmured. "The place is under attack, but you should be okay here. Wait while I check things out more."

He jumped lightly onto the sedan's hood and then the roof. The top of the wall was level with his eyeline, about five feet away. It was studded with shards of broken glass set in concrete. He stripped off his trench coat and flung it across the barrier, launching himself across the gap with an agile spring that landed him facedown across the wall. He heard the cloth rip, but none of the glass penetrated his clothes.

For two seconds Bolan rested there, the Beretta in his right hand, anticipating the sudden burst of fire from below, the numbing shock of a hit, a screaming ricochet. There was no sound, no movement. For the moment, at least, the gunmen seemed to have withdrawn.

Cautiously he rose half upright on the narrow strip of brickwork. There was enough light from the streetlight for him to see the reflected gleams where the glass was set. Still bent almost double, he made a crouching run for the shelter of a tall tree growing on the inner side of the wall, beyond the shrubbery. He dropped silently to the ground, picked his way carefully across a carpet of fallen leaves and skirted a patch of lawn that sloped down to the house.

From here, wide of the stables, he could see the fire— a pool house on the far side of an Olympic-size basin was burning furiously, with flames, sparks and black smoke roaring up into the sky. In the pulsating scarlet light he distinguished shadowy figures flitting toward the big house between clumps of vegetation.

The windows at the rear of the building were dark, but part of the driveway curving up to the portico in front was illuminated with light that streamed, Bolan imagined, from the long windows recessed behind the pillars. There was a burst of gunfire from somewhere inside the mansion: three short bursts from a submachine gun and a series of deeper, harsher shots from a heavy-caliber handgun.

On the far side of the driveway he heard a crashing of branches. Then someone screamed, followed by an answering volley from the dark. A bulky figure crossed the bars of light. Bolan thought he recognized the formidable shape of Hansie Schiller. The suspicion was confirmed a moment later when he heard the tough, yet slightly mincing voice bawl out, "Keep the fuckers pinned down until we blow it!"

There was more gunfire—twinkling points of flame, at least six if not more, from positions in a half circle around the front of the house. The SMG and the big handgun replied. It was quite possible that the goons who had accompanied Bolan into the house earlier were outposted someplace with their silenced automatics, waiting for a chance to make a kill without giving their own positions away.

Bolan moved into the darkest of the moving shadows cast by the burning pool house, traversing what he imagined to be a rose garden as thorns plucked at his pants and the tail of his jacket. He was approaching the corner of the building when an enormous weight smashed into his back and knocked him flat on his face. The impact jarred the breath from his lungs and sent the Beretta spinning out of his hand.

Pain flared through his kidneys, and he felt callused fingers scrabble for his throat as the man who had jumped him knelt on his back and groped for a stranglehold with both hands. The Executioner thrashed from side to side in an attempt to dislodge the guy, but the attacker was big, heavy and fast. The guy's knees clamped on either side of Bolan's waist, while his hands locked around the warrior's neck with the thumbs pressing remorselessly into the nape. He tore at the throttling grip, humping up his hips in an attempt to at least unbalance the man enough for him to get out from under. It was no more successful than the first try.

Bolan's senses swam. The crackle of flames and the concussion of firearms began to fade in his ears. The leaping orange light dimmed. Blood thumped in his temples as his lungs cried out for air.

One flailing arm swept across the flagstones paving the rose garden, and at the edge of a flower bed his fingers touched something cold, hard and sharp—a fragment of pavement split off by the frost. Grabbing it in his hand, he used all his remaining strength to arc his arm back and up toward the unseen face breathing beery fumes over his head.

The sharp edge of the stone homed in on flesh and bone. The attacker cursed, his hold slackened, and Bolan felt hot blood splash onto his cheek. The Executioner flung himself over on his back, gasping for air, and the hood was thrown among the rose bushes.

The guy yelled as the tough thorns tore at his face, hands and knees. Woody stems snapped. He struggled to his feet. At the same time Bolan leaped for the nebulous shape wriggling in the dark and struck out with his right hand held flat.

The hood took the karate blow on the forearm and launched a tremendous right that landed over the heart and sent the Executioner reeling. He followed through swiftly, bursting out of the rose bed to slam a one-two left and right punch to each side of Bolan's head.

Bolan staggered, crouching defensively as he sucked in air that seared his savaged throat. A sudden, brighter flare from the fire showed him the hood—a heavyweight with a jutting chin and glittering eyes—shaping up for a roundhouse blow that left the jaw, daubed with blood from a cut beneath one eye, wide open.

Bolan uncoiled like a steel spring, lifting an uppercut from hip level that connected like a battering ram and rocked the thug on his heels. It was then that the guy's right hand flew between the open edges of his lumber jacket.

Firelight gleamed redly on steel as the gun came out. The arm rose, pointing a metal finger. But Bolan had already ducked down to snare the throwing knife from its ankle sheath. He flicked the blade with deadly accuracy before the hood's finger tightened on the trigger.

The wide, flat, razor-sharp knife sank into the soft flesh beneath the guy's jaw. He tottered backward, arms flung wide, the trigger finger powering a shot that plowed uselessly into the earth. Then he slowly sank to his knees, twin streams of gore pumping out each side of the knife hilt, and keeled over onto his back.

Bolan stood over him. The man was gurgling blood, drowning in his own lifestream. The Executioner plucked out his knife, plunged it into the cold earth several times to cleanse the blade, resheathed it, then went in search of his Beretta.

The pool house fire was dying down, and he had to lie flat on the flagstones and squint along the surface of the lawn beyond before a glint of reflected light revealed the Beretta's location in the grass. He picked it up and hurried around to the rear of the house.

Until then Bolan had been of two minds. One band of evil men had been assaulting another, each of them bloodsuckers adhering to the innocent, terrorizing the inoffensive, reaping a black harvest from the fears of the weak. Normally in such a situation his inclination was to let them slog it out together...and the more dead left lying on the ground after the battle the better.

In this case, though, he was personally involved with both sides. The attackers had framed him for a murder, and now that he was at liberty, they were after, as the treacherous Hugo had said, his balls. They had already kidnapped and beaten him up once, and he had been lucky to escape. The defenders were every bit as bad. But Kraul had at least fixed it so that he'd gotten his car and gear back. The mobster had coerced Bolan into a line of action for selfish ends, but it was a line that happened to fit in with Bolan's own aims. That, however, didn't necessarily mean the Executioner was obliged to join battle on Kraul's side.

He had been content to stay on the sidelines until the lookout had jumped him. Now he was personally involved in this specific battle, too. Although he shrank from associating himself, even temporarily, with the ex-gang boss of St. Pauli, he would do what he could to bolster Kraul's defense.

He ran past a kitchen wing, in back of a conservatory and past the open carport to the far side of the house. There had been a lull in the shooting, but now, from behind a screen of bushes, he sensed activity all around the front facade. A match flared in the undergrowth, and then another. A larger flame sprang up. Hansie Schiller shouted something, and a voice answered from the far side of the front driveway near the gutted pool house.

There was a burst of covering fire from behind clumps of ornamental shrubs. And now several of the bigger flames wavered in the undergrowth. All the lights in the house went out. In the sudden darkness the flames rose into the air, moved faster toward the portico. One arched toward the facade, teased out of its own flight by the wind.

Bolan realized what it was an instant before it hit. The Team was attacking with Molotov cocktails. The first bottle smashed itself against a window, shattering the pane as the volatile gasoline spilled out and was ignited by the flaming paper. The second was hurled through the gap to explode in the room beyond. Immediately the room was an inferno. The curtains blazed. Upholstery and wall hangings burned. Flames streamed from the shattered window to blacken the facade.

A third bottle exploded at the top of the portico steps, setting fire to the doors. In the renewed outburst of shooting, a hood about to hurl the fourth was hit. The bottle dropped to the driveway at his feet and broke, transforming the man into a whirling column of flame that subsided, shrieking and thrashing, to the ground.

Over the sounds of battle Bolan now heard in the distance the urgent seesaw bray of fire department trucks and the warble of police sirens. Evidently Schiller heard them, too, for he was shouting again on the far side of the portico, urging some kind of action. A Molotov cocktail plunged through a second-floor window and erupted inside. Two grenades were flung through the glass of the entrance doors to explode with cracking detonations and billows of brown smoke in the hallway. Soon the entire front of the mansion would be a boiling holocaust of flame.

Coughing and choking, some with their clothes smoldering, men burst out of the house and engaged the attackers in hand-to-hand combat. Knives glinted in the light of the fire, clubs and blackjacks rose and fell, someone uttered a high-pitched, ululating scream. Sporadic shots still rang out, and there were motionless figures here and there on the ground, but it was difficult to distinguish friend from foe in the flickering red light.

Bolan saw two thugs drag the white-coated houseboy from the portico and set about him with knives. Folding down the Beretta's forward grip, the Executioner aimed carefully and blew one away with a single shot. Half a second later a three-shot burst sent the other stumbling off with a smashed shoulder. Hansie was flailing at a fallen man with an iron bar, but before the Executioner could line him up in his sights a knot of attackers carrying a struggling victim toward the flames came between them. It was then that he heard the shouts behind him.

He swung around and threw himself to the ground as muzzle-flashes split the dark fifty feet away. Slugs zipped through the leaves around him. He fired back, aiming for the spot where the two gunners had been, but they were already running toward the carport. There was a sudden exhaust roar, a shrill squeak of rubber and the high whine of gears as an automobile shot out of the port.

The big Mercedes that had originally picked Bolan up near his hotel rocketed onto the rear driveway, raced to the stableyard and turned into the roadway beyond. Bolan figured the boss was making his getaway. He hadn't seen Kraul during the combat, and it was predictable that the general would quit, leaving the soldiers to face the music.

For that matter, Bolan reckoned he should disengage. The sirens were very near now, approaching the front entrance. The two gunmen, having emptied their magazine without effect at the Mercedes, had disappeared. Schiller was calling the Team together.

Bolan ran noiselessly around the edge of the property until he reached the tree where he had jumped down from the wall. Dragging himself back up, he ran to where his trench coat still lay over the glass spikes. Schiller and his men were hotfooting it back past the pool toward the stables. Bolan could see pulsing blue light beyond the flames as the sirens died away. He jumped to the roof of the BMW and lowered himself to the ground.

The car was undamaged, but it was empty. Sally Ann had fled.

He shrugged. Had she taken off because she was scared? Had Kraul picked up his double agent on his way out of trouble?

It didn't matter. There were more interesting questions that required answers, he reflected as he started the engine and accelerated away before the goons reached their Cadillac and the accompanying Ford.

The first question concerned the lookout in the rose garden. He could easily have shot Bolan from behind before the warrior even knew he existed. But he had only produced the gun at the very last moment, preferring to rely on his physical prowess until he had lost hope. This implied, first, that the attackers had wanted Bolan alive; second, that they had known for one thing who he was and, for another, that he was going to be there.

The question led, paradoxically, to the mystery shots fired at him the moment he'd entered the stableyard. And fired only at him. Had those killers, too, been tipped off to lay an ambush? Bolan wondered just how much double-crossing Sally Ann was capable of.

CHAPTER FOURTEEN

Lübeck—thirty-nine miles northeast of Hamburg on the continuation of the high-speed E.45 freeway—was a port at the confluence of the Trave River and the huge Elbe Canal, nine miles inland from the open sea.

Why would a Greek freighter, presumably delivering a consignment of drugs to Lattuada or Asticot, choose to dock at such a remote and hard-to-reach berth? Why would a ship, which must have come through the Mediterranean and up the North Sea from the Middle East, or across the Atlantic from Central America, why would such a ship not stop off at Bremerhaven, Flensburg or even Hamburg itself? Why sail all the way around the Jutland Peninsula, through the Kattegat and the Skagerrak, past the southern boundary of Norway and Sweden and between the Danish islands, when four or five days could have been saved by calling at those other ports?

Could it be because Lübeck was at the head of an inlet forming the junction between the two Germanys? Because the far side of the narrow strip of water was East Germany? Because maybe the merchants of slow death were hoping to open up a new market?

Bolan would find out, if he could choke the truth out of the two underworld bosses before he blew them away. First, though, he had to locate the bosses themselves. And all he had to go on was Kraul's word that they were in town, that they weren't together and that although

Asticot was "supervising" a drug shipment from the freighter to a "private individual," the American was there on a different mission.

And that meant what? Hiring new muscle? Arranging an arms delivery? Searching out fresh talent for the whorehouses? Fixing some kind of smuggling deal? Exploring the East German connection?

Eighty percent negative on all questions. The first three could be done more easily, and with much better results, back in Hamburg. Any small port would do for the fourth, and there were plenty far more accessible on the North Sea coast. And if anyone was planning East German contacts, surely it would be Asticot, else why would his Greek freighter come all the way to Lübeck?

In any case, Asticot was the better lead: Bolan at least knew which part of town he was likely to be in. Lattuada was going to be more difficult. Lübeck was a city of a quarter of a million inhabitants, and although Bolan supposed there would be a red-light quarter near the docks, he had no way of knowing what other neighborhoods a displaced mafioso might favor.

He snatched a few hours' sleep in a highway rest area and drove through the outskirts at first light—a wasteland of roadside diners, gas stations, steelworks and steep-roofed housing developments. It was bitterly cold, the sky was covered in low cloud, and the vacant lots and mounds of rusting wreckage in automobile junkyards were still powdered with week-old snow.

Reading a newspaper as he sipped hot coffee at a hamburger stall outside a trailer camp, Bolan saw that more snow was forecast. Germany had beaten France two to one in the qualifying round of World Cup Soccer. A radical deputy had been killed by a car bomb outside his home in Turin; neofascist extremists were thought to be responsible. The Hamburg killer was now thought to have been involved in the deaths of a taxi driver and an unidentified vagrant at a city intersection forty-eight hours before the murder of the St. Pauli blonde.

Back in the BMW, Bolan drove past the fifteenth-century Holstentor Gate, around a city hall that was even older, between two churches with immensely high towers and on into the medieval quarter that clung to the waterfront. Here, among close-packed brick houses leaning together above the cobblestoned lanes, he checked into a small hotel, parked the car and walked toward the dock basins. The nighttime mist had vanished, but a thin, cold rain was falling.

The first part of his search was easy. He learned at the port office that there was only one Greek-registered ship alongside. It was called the *Aegean Queen*, and it was discharging a mixed cargo of citrus fruit, dried goat-skins and electrical components, that had been taken aboard at Le Havre, France.

Bolan located the freighter in a landscape of warehouses, mobile cranes and railroad tracks—a small, sleek, white-hulled craft that looked more like a rich man's pleasure boat than the battered and rusting tramp steamer he had expected. Part of the cargo had been discharged the previous day. Stevedores were loading wooden cases stacked on the quayside into a truck with the help of two forklifts. A seaman with a bullhorn was standing in the ship's bow, directing a crane driver who was lifting netted crates of fruit from the hold.

Between the *Aegean Queen* and a Finnish freighter unloading timber into a line of railroad flatcars, several groups of longshoremen stood smoking and talking, their cigarettes shielded from the rain in cupped hands. There was no sign of Arvell Asticot.

Bolan hadn't expected to see him in person. A guy at his level wouldn't go to Lübeck to check out the transfer of a handful of heroin packets smuggled in the lining of a purser's oilskin. It had to be a big consignment, and supervising didn't necessarily mean the drug baron had to wait all day on the quayside.

There would be at least one hardguy, if not more. What the Executioner hoped to do was identify these, locate the merchandise and allow one or the other to lead him to Asticot.

The longshoremen were wearing yellow oilskins or jeans and donkey jackets. Bolan felt conspicuous in his trench coat and tweed. He hurried back to the hotel, found a maritime outfitters a couple of blocks from the dockside and returned to join the waterfront idlers in a watch cap and pea jacket.

The Greek ship was small, not much bigger than a coaster. The wooden cases had all been off-loaded and the hoists were starting on the skins as the final nets of fruit were lowered to the wharf. There were several flatbeds stacked with the cases now; uniformed officers were prying open one or two at random next to one of the customs sheds. Bolan saw radio chassis, cathode-ray TV tubes, electric motors to power dishwashers.

He didn't rate the consignment as cover for a drug shipment, even though the legend Heckler-Asticot Maschinenfabrik GmbH was lettered on the truck doors.

Crated electrical components, cases stenciled Machine Parts—they were such obvious fronts for smuggled narcotics or small arms that they had become a thriller writer's cliché. No, the truth would be that Heckler-Asticot GmbH was the innocent front for the drug baron himself. It gave him a valid reason for being in Germany, in Lübeck, on this quayside at this time.

Flayed animal skins or citrus fruit, on the other hand...

Some of the customs men promenaded sniffer dogs. Bolan recalled Sally Ann's revelation that freshly baked bread disguised the odor of marijuana smoke, and if anything was going to put those highly trained animals literally off the scent, surely the sharp, acrid aroma of lemons, oranges and tangerines or the stench of uncured skins would do the trick.

Shallow trays of fruit, nevertheless, left very little room to maneuver if you wanted to hide a quantity of stuff, unless the fruit itself was split open and stuffed with the contraband, which would be one hell of a job. So Bolan's hunch tipped the skins as the most likely hiding place. A good number of packets could be hidden in a single hide.

The trucks laden with crates were beginning to move away; the fruit was being stacked in one of the freight sheds. Should he follow the last truck? He reckoned not; it was more likely to lead him to a straight storage depot than to any place Asticot would be. In any case, if Asticot was running a regular company as a front, the address would be in the phone book.

He decided to stay with the skins.

Six-foot stacks of them were still being swung off the freighter and onto the quayside; the rancid stink of the uncured pelts washed toward him with the squalls of icy rain blown inland by the wind from the Baltic. Maybe, if they were left in one of the sheds overnight, he would get a chance to check them out. If not, he would follow them when they left.

Except that there seemed to be a complication. The skins were being transported to a shed all right—dockworkers were already loading them onto a train of trolley cars hauled by a small diesel tractor—but the shed was a customs shed, and there were uniformed men stationed by the roller doors, opening and closing them between each delivery. It looked very much as if the skins were being held in bond.

For whom? In transit? And if so, en route for what destination?

Bolan frowned. He pushed himself upright from the steel gantry against which he had been lounging and sauntered toward the freighter. Work on the Finnish ship had stopped; most of the longshoremen had left the wharf when the rain had started to fall more heavily. The last thing he wanted to do was attract unwelcome attention. Maybe the comments of the guys unloading the skins would give him a clue.

He stood near the stem of the *Aegean Queen*, the collar of the pea jacket turned up against the rain, his chin tucked into his chest, staring out beyond the quay, across the expanse of sullen gray water at the flat shoreline on the East German side. There weren't many buildings there. Virtually the whole of Lübeck was concentrated on the left bank of the estuary.

The stevedores' dialogue didn't help him much.

"Fucking rain. Makes these bastards twice as heavy to handle."

"Can't get the stink out of your hair for days."

"They'll stink worse when they've been processed!"

"How come?"

"Leather pants to keep the Vopos' asses out of a sling!"

Laughter. And then, "Why don't they take the fuckers by road? We wouldn't have to load and unload the damn things twice, then."

"This way they get an escort of Soviet nuclear subs!"

"For Chrissakes, pack it in, you guys, and load the shit. You think I want to sit on this goddamn tractor all night?"

Bolan walked away and found partial shelter between the stacks of lumber off-loaded from the Finnish ship. It wasn't until midafternoon that he learned the answer to his question.

The cargo had all been discharged, the crew had come ashore, the skins were locked away in the bonded merchandise shed and the wharf was deserted. Somewhere among the confusion of cranes and derricks surrounding a nearby dock basin a donkey engine rattled, and a tug hooted out on the sound.

Half a dozen officials in watch caps and belted blue raincoats emerged from a glassed-in single-story shack beyond the customs sheds and gathered at the top of a flight of stone steps that led from the dockside to a landing stage below.

From his vantage point Bolan looked out across the water. The sky was now a sulfurous yellow and the rain was turning to sleet. Out beyond the hulls of berthed freighters a launch flying the ensign of the German Democratic Republic was slicing the steel-gray surface of the sound into dirty white foam.

The craft nosed into the landing stage and four men—three uniformed officials and a civilian—climbed the stairway to the dock, leaving an East German naval officer in charge of the boat. There were salutes and handshakes. The whole group then hurried to the glassed-in office shack. Through the misted windows

Bolan could make out papers being exchanged, read, signed, stamped. A West German customs man was punching out a number on a desk phone. He began to speak.

Ten minutes later two of the customs officials escorted the East German civilian and one of his uniformed colleagues to the bonded warehouse. The doors were unlocked and rolled back a few feet and the four men went inside. While they were there a black Mercedes limo appeared between two sheds farther down the dock and rolled slowly to a stop outside the warehouse. A chauffeur climbed out and opened the rear door.

Bolan caught his breath. The man who emerged was short, with thinning hair and slightly protuberant eyes above a thin-lipped lizard mouth. He was wearing a belted camel topcoat with a homburg.

Arvell Asticot.

The Executioner's fingers itched. He could have whipped out the Beretta and blown the guy away then and there; Asticot was no more than sixty feet away. But there was more to learn still, and the soldier wanted this particular scumbag to know that his sins had caught up with him before he was sent to hell.

The chauffeur opened an umbrella and conducted Asticot the few yards to the customs shed. The light was fading fast and illumination from inside the shed cast streamers of yellow radiance across the wet asphalt of the quay. Asticot vanished through the open doors.

Now Bolan was in possession of all the pieces and could assemble the puzzle.

The *Aegean Queen* had indeed been directed to Lübeck because one part of her cargo, the skins, was destined—was now in transit—for East Germany. The officials from the launch must have come across to complete the necessary export-import formalities. They were now in the customs shed, presumably with the East German consignee, to check that the cargo was as advertised. Asticot would be there as the guy who had organized the deal, and the civilian was presumably the buyer.

But was he simply buying the skins, as the stevedores had implied, to turn into leather garments for the Vopos, the East German *Volkspolizei*? Or was he part of a larger, and far more profitable operation that would flood the GDR with hard drugs? If he was merely being used unknowingly as a front, a fall guy for the importation of narcotics, who was Asticot's real contact in East Germany?

One thing was certain: even if they had been given a little "encouragement" on the side to help the transfer go through smoothly, the customs men probably weren't aware of the skins' real purpose.

If Bolan could get next to Asticot and choke the truth out of him, and at the same time expose the filth hidden in the skins, there was a good chance he could tip off the authorities on both sides and wrap up the whole vile conspiracy. But he would have to work fast because, again according to the dockers, the skins were being transferred to East Germany by boat, perhaps tonight, instead of making it the long way around, past the two road frontiers in a convoy of trucks.

And there was, of course, the additional complication that Bolan, as a presumed murderer on the run, could hardly knock on the chief port officer's door and tell him about the drugs. But there wasn't a chance in a million that he could locate Lattuada, choke the truth out of *him* and straighten that one out in time.

There was, nevertheless, an unexpected link that took him totally by surprise. Asticot and the officials came out of the warehouse, and the drug baron summoned someone from the interior of the limo while the customs men were relocking the doors.

Clearly this was the sidekick delegated to oversee the actual transfer of the skins from the business's rather than the authorities' point of view. Asticot's high tenor voice carried clearly to Bolan, where he lurked among the stacks of Finnish lumber.

"Now I don't want any mistakes. The barge will be alongside at dawn. The dockers have been notified. These gentlemen here will officiate at the shipment. But the whole operation must be completed before eight o'clock. I repeat, *must* be completed. Is that clear? The berth is booked for another incoming freighter at that time. I'll hold you personally responsible for the success of the project."

"No sweat, sir," the overseer replied. "All under control. The operation will go ahead exactly as planned."

"It had better," Asticot said. He turned toward the car.

It wasn't the exchange itself that made the Executioner catch his breath—that only confirmed what he suspected already. What fazed him was the identity of the overseer—a short, shaggy man with a blotched red face under the narrow brim of a tweed hat.

With his knee-high boots, breeches and belted jacket, the guy could have been a typical north German farmer. But there was no doubt about it. The man receiving Asticot's orders was Hugo, the doorman from St. Pauli.

CHAPTER FIFTEEN

Lattuada could wait: it was a question of following Asticot and maneuvering to get him alone, or sticking close to Hugo, with the knowledge that at least he couldn't miss out on the transfer of skins to East Germany.

Bolan also wanted to take a look at those skins. It was, after all, only a guess on his part that drugs were concealed inside the consignment. He would bet all the money he had on it, but there was just a slim chance that he *could* be mistaken. And he'd sure feel stupid if he wasted his time spying on the transport of a cargo of regular goatskins!

Geography decided him. He knew where and when the East German boat was due. He knew where the skins were located. He knew where Hugo would be at that time, wherever he was before then. But he had no idea where Asticot was based: if he let him go now, he might lose him altogether. The drug baron might already have completed all the supervising that was necessary. Bolan ran for the BMW, which was parked at the inner end of an empty dry dock behind the customs shed.

Thirty minutes later he was crouched down outside a window, peering through a crack between heavy curtains and trying at the same time to make out an occasional word from the hum of conversation within the room. The window was on the tenth floor of a modern hotel. It was, of course, closed. And double-glazed.

Bolan was on a small stone balcony, trying to forget the driving sleet that was beating on his shoulders. He had gotten onto the balcony via two other balconies and an emergency fire exit at the end of a passageway whose steel door had yielded easily to the Executioner's expertise.

Although Asticot had a small warehouse for his electrical goods, and an office crammed into one corner of the hangarlike lower floor—he had called in there to check out the trucks unloading on his way from the docks—it was clear he had no permanent residence in Lübeck. Following the Mercedes limo through the rush-hour traffic, Bolan had wondered whether the drug kingpin used the city solely as a staging post for a whole series of deals with the East Germans.

Certainly, striding up and down the expensive hotel suite with a tumbler of Scotch in one hand, he seemed on effusively good terms with the civilian from the launch who had accompanied him from the customs shed. But the few words Bolan could hear seemed to be based on nothing more sinister than a normal rag-trade relationship.

"...more supple of course if you chose the lamb," the incisive tenor voice intoned. "But, of course, there is the matter of price...different technique of curing...of course we should be happy to...reversed calf is the toughest, but with your color problems..."

The East German's voice was low-pitched. Bolan could hear nothing of his replies. He noticed the man wasn't drinking.

The rumble of traffic from the streets below diminished as the homeward rush thinned out; the few vehicles that passed hissed greasily through a film of sleet that was fast turning to snow. The shoulders of Bolan's pea jacket were sodden and ice-cold rivulets ran between his shoulder blades.

A taxi swished off the street and stopped at the hotel entrance. The phone in the apartment rang. Asticot answered it. The East German rose to his feet, shook hands and left. Two minutes later, over the rim of the balcony, Bolan saw him get into the taxi.

The Beretta was in his hand. He longed to kick open the window and storm in with flame belching from the muzzle. But caution advised there might be other things to learn first.

There were.

Inside the apartment the phone rang again. Asticot spoke only a single sentence. For a moment, for the Executioner, he was out of earshot. He reappeared wearing a topcoat with a fur collar. Seconds later Bolan dimly heard the chimes of a doorbell. Asticot switched off the lights and went out into a hallway. Squinting, with his cheek against the cold glass and one hand shading the reflections, Bolan saw through the crack between the curtains that he had opened the suite's entrance door.

A man was waiting in the corridor outside. Asticot nodded, flipped a switch, stepped outside and closed the door. Bolan had no more than a second to register the features of the caller before the hallway, too, went dark, but it was enough. The visitor who had come to collect the drug baron was Ferucco Lattuada.

Bolan didn't wait to wonder. He hoisted himself up onto the slippery stone balcony rail, squeezing his eyes shut against the stinging sleet, and leaped for the adjoining one. It took him only four minutes to make the fire escape platform. But the sleet was icing up the holes of the iron grille stairway; each step was a miniature skating rink. By the time he reached Asticot's parking spot in the hotel's underground garage, the Mercedes was gone. He collected the BMW and drove slowly back to the docks.

There were watchmen on the gates, but they weren't checking ID. He left the car in a nearby street and tagged along behind a group of drunken Finnish sailors returning to their ship, peeling off into the shadows beside the customs office as soon as they passed the *Aegean Queen*.

From there he cased the bonded warehouse. Snow was falling fast now. The flakes tumbled remorselessly down through the cones of yellow light cast by the dockside lamps. The dark surface of the wharf was lightening minute by minute, and it was noticeably colder. If he wanted in, if he wanted to check out that consignment before surfaces became too dangerous, or the tracks he left dead giveaways, he had to act fast.

The warehouse had what railroad buffs would call a clerestory roof—a narrow superstructure running the length of the ridgepole, with windows let into the side to provide light for the space below. Bolan reckoned these windows would yield easily enough to the attentions of an experienced penetration agent. The shed, with its tall roller doors and heavy padlocks, was designed to prevent bonded goods from being heisted in bulk—not to keep out the curious who only wanted to look.

The difficulty was making it to the clerestory.

Forty feet of snow-covered roof, sloping upward at an angle between twenty-five and thirty degrees, separated the facade from those narrow windows. And there was no way of reaching the roof in back of the shed. Gantries carrying the mobile cranes were parked on their rails at intervals along the quay. It was from one of these that the Executioner would have to leap to the roof.

The crisscross ironwork was four feet from the corner of the shed. The junction where the upright was married to the horizontal crossbeam was level with the guttering at the foot of the slope.

To a combat veteran with the Executioner's reflexes, in the kind of shape he was in, there was no problem there. Even in the poor light, with the metal grid so cold that his fingers risked sticking to each girder, and the whirling snow fast approaching blizzard proportions, he was able to climb the gantry as easily as a ladder. Easy as falling off a log.

The roof was something else.

The icy slope was too steep to walk up; he would have to lie facedown and inch his way up to the clerestory. And he would be as vulnerable as a fly on a windowpane the whole damn way.

The clerestory had been invented by the designers of Gothic cathedrals to illuminate the nave that ran below it. A medieval intruder, aiming to reach its windows, would be hidden at different times behind spires, towers, balustrades, gargoyles or flying buttresses. The Executioner had no such cover; he would be in full vision the whole distance, if anyone happened to be looking his way.

And someone could be. There was a watch on the *Aegean Queen*'s bridge—a dark shape could be seen in the greenish light from the binnacle—and there would certainly be a lookout on the Finnish freighter beyond.

On top of the gantry, Bolan considered. The leap to the roof was going to make one hell of a clatter. But on the plus side was the fact that the corner itself was masked from the view of anyone on the freighter's bridge by the crane's operating cabin. The hell with it. He jumped.

There was a noise all right. The walls of the customs shed were brick, but the top was a corrugated tin roof. Bolan hit the slope on all fours and slid immediately backward. It was only when his toes lodged in the guttering that he was able to stop himself shooting off the edge and plummeting to the dockside below.

He lay panting. The noise had sounded to him like a galvanized trash can rolling down a concrete stairway, but he heard no shout of alarm, no torchlight flashed, no footsteps raced toward the shed. The sailors aboard the Finnish ship were singing. Away on the other side he could hear the jangle of rock music from a radio. Someone gunned the engine of a truck in one of the basins.

Bolan lay facedown and allowed the snow to cover his back. The whiter he was, he figured, the less chance there was of one of the lookouts spotting him during his hazardous traverse of the roof.

He waited ten minutes, and then began the laborious crawl up to the clerestory windows. It wasn't easy. Sometimes he slipped back more than he advanced. He knew, even if his back was totally blanketed in snow, that this would only reduce the risk of his being seen, not remove it altogether; that the snow he dislodged during his clawing ascent would leave a snail trail as telltale as the sight of a dark body itself. But at last, traversing the ridged metal obliquely, he arrived.

The windows weren't made to open. Bolan knocked out the glass of one with the butt of his Beretta, listened to the fragments tinkle somewhere in the cavernous blackness below, then thrust his head and shoulders through the gap.

He smiled wryly. The last time he had broken a pane of glass and dragged himself through the gap, he had been getting out; this time he was getting in. And the difficulties once he had made it—he shone a penlight down into the shed—were much less this time.

The roof was supported on girders that ran from one side of the building to the other beneath the clerestory. One was immediately below the broken window. And high up against the far wall—he could just make it out at the limit of the tiny flashlight's beam—there was a railed catwalk.

Bolan pulled himself through, shook the snow from his clothes and lowered himself to the girder. It was eighteen inches wide, and although a dark void yawned below, there were no cops waiting for him at the far end and it was relatively easy with the aid of the penlight to negotiate the struts and crossbeams and reach the walkway. After that it was just a question of locating the ladder that led down to the floor.

There was a lot of merchandise in the shed. The flashlight beam revealed bales, sacks, crates, individual cartons and packages between tall stacks of identical wooden cases, an entire container bearing the name of a Swedish tool factory. It was no sweat finding the goatskins: the stench was overpowering in the cold, airless shed.

Bolan walked down one of the aisles separating the bonded goods. The trolleys, a dozen of them, were marshaled in a space at the far end. Holding the penlight between his teeth, the soldier lifted the top skin off a four-foot stack on the nearest, then the next, and the one after that, his fingers probing, exploring, squeezing. He found nothing untoward.

It wasn't until he examined the fourth trolley that he hit pay dirt. There was a different feel to the skins on this one. They seemed even stiffer than those he had handled before. The crackle of the desiccated hide wasn't quite the same; there were unexplained irregularities, as though there might be cysts between the inner and outer layers. Bolan unsheathed his knife and made an incision.

The whole of the inner layer was false. On the side of the pelt away from the shaggy hair, a second layer, cut to size, had been glued in place. And between the two were rows and rows of small oiled silk packets. He slit one open. It contained a little more than an ounce of white crystalline powder.

Twenty minutes later he had discovered that four out of the twelve trolleys were loaded with doctored skins. If each skin in each four-foot stack was similarly packed, several million dollars' worth of the hard stuff was on its way to East Germany, whether or not the guy who was importing the skins knew it.

For Bolan's money the man he had seen in Asticot's hotel suite was a patsy, a blameless importer well-known to the East German authorities, who even, according to the longshoremen, manufactured uniforms for the police there—a guy who was being used simply to get the skins across the frontier. After which, presumably, they would be stolen from his warehouse and the drugs distributed through an underworld network—maybe accomplices of Lattuada and his West German scum.

Bolan bit his lip. How many hundreds, thousands, of young lives would be blighted and destroyed by the white powder concealed in these pelts? How many fortunes would be made by the slimebucket professionals selling it?

The rancid stench of the skins, he thought, was nothing to the stink in the nostrils of the world provoked by Asticot, Lattuada and their kind.

Should he destroy the skins and their vile contents?

No way.

They weren't flammable; it would take a holocaust to incinerate them all. To slit the false layers, remove the packets one by one and empty the contents would take hours, perhaps days, and they were being collected at dawn. Tip off the East Germans, then, once they had gone?

How? An anonymous phone call? No good. Not when the cops received hundreds every day—and the guy with the stuff in his possession was in with them anyway.

The local police? The customs people themselves? Probably the best bet. But again, since he dared not make a personal appearance, and time was desperately short, how could he expect a phone call to galvanize them into activity before the shipment?

It would take him some time to get to a pay phone where he wouldn't be under observation. He listened. From somewhere outside he could hear the chimes of a church clock striking midnight.

And something else.

Far away down the dark alley separating the stacks of merchandise, something moved. A scraping noise, quickly stilled, followed by a subdued pattering.

Bolan cut the penlight and whipped out the Beretta. He sidled into the adjoining aisle and catfooted toward the far end of the shed. The light reflected down from the snow-covered roof through the clerestory windows was very faint, but it allowed him to locate an intersection where an alley at right angles to the main passageways cut a swath through the bonded material. For a brief moment he clicked on the penlight, swinging it right and left. The beam sent gigantic shadows dancing across the warehouse walls and up among the girders supporting the roof. But it showed him nothing.

Somewhere in the darkness above him a bird, startled from its perch by the movement, flapped noisily away. Bolan listened again, holding his breath. Outside the shed a ship's siren bleated once out on the sound. A long way off the rock music was still blaring from the radio. Inside there was silence, until once more that sibilant pattering sound manifested itself, nearer this time, a little to his right.

At the corner of the next aisle.

Bolan made the distance in a tigerish leap, switching on the penlight again as he moved, his trigger finger curled and ready to squeeze. He saw corn falling, sliding from a rent in a bulging sack, a changing pattern of grains on the dusty floor.

Rats!

Bolan grinned. He had better things to do than go chasing after hungry rodents. The customs guys should employ a cat if they were going to keep sacks of grain in bond! As far as he was concerned, there were decisions to make. He moved down the aisle.

Wait! If a rat was going to gnaw a hole in a sack to get at the corn inside, surely the rent would be at floor level, or no higher than the animal itself, standing up on its back feet? The rip from which the corn was still trickling in a steady cascade was hip-high to the Executioner. Some rat!

Overhead the bird flapped again, shifting its position for the second time. The man who had inadvertently ripped open the grain sack with the safety catch of his revolver cursed under his breath. He raised the gun carefully, sighting it on the dark silhouette thrown into relief behind the pool of light cast by the penlight. He pulled the trigger.

Bolan saw the livid green flash just before he heard the shocking detonation of the .38 Police Special. He was diving to the floor before the second shot sent thunderous echoes around the shed. He couldn't, of course, have moved quickly enough to beat that first round, but the gunman had miscalculated. His weapon was throwing high and to the right. The slug streaked past the Executioner's left ear as his ingrained combat sense hurled him into action.

The echoes of the second shot were overlaid by the harsh bark of a 3-round burst from the Beretta. None of the four slugs found a mark, but the rapidity of Bolan's response took the invisible killer by surprise and won the warrior time to worm his way between two rows of wooden cases stacked beside the aisle.

The penlight lay on the floor where it had fallen, illuminating a no-man's-land of packages and crates into which neither of the adversaries dared venture.

For perhaps half a minute there was silence in the shed. Bolan wondered who the gunman could be. A watchman, obviously. A customs guard? Negative. Such a man would have called a warning before he fired. Someone left to protect the dope shipment? Probably. But why wouldn't the man have mown down the Executioner on his way in when he was a perfect target against the clerestory window?

Maybe because he wanted to check, had orders to check, that the intruder was someone specifically interested in the skins, and therefore a lethal danger, and not just some sneak thief breaking into the shed in the hope of picking up something, anything, of value.

Unless the guy with the revolver was himself such a thief, whom the Executioner had happened to disturb....

But if such a man was going to fire at all, and not just lie low until the new arrival had split, surely he, too, would have pulled the trigger the moment Bolan was in his sights?

The silence was broken.

A slither of feet, somewhere over in the next alley, a rustle of cloth as some garment brushed against wood. Bolan thought he could hear breathing, but he couldn't be certain.

He tensed, crouching low in the narrow space between the packing cases. Those on his right, his exploring fingers discovered, were bound with wire, and he could detect the characteristic sour odor of machine oil between the slatted panels.

Machine tools or armament? There was no way of telling. And, for all the good it could do him at the moment, the crates could be packed with MU-50 grenades or Heckler & Koch caseless assault rifles. His strategy must be to tempt the hidden gunman to use up all the rounds in his weapon. He knew this was a revolver, but he didn't know whether it was a six- or an eight-chamber. The guy had fired twice already, so there were either four or six rounds to come before he was forced into the clumsy cylinder-reload routine. At which time Bolan, with his superior magazine charge, would wade in to finish it. Unless, of course, the marksman toted two guns....

That was a risk Bolan had to take.

Lying flat on the chilled floor, he inched his way facedown to the far end of the gap, where he was able to peer each way into the gloom of the aisle. No darker shadow was visible among the bulked masses of merchandise.

He reached to touch the crates on his left. They seemed to be of softer, more friable wood than the wirebound ones on the other side. At the full extent of his arm, he pushed the muzzle of the Beretta against the leading edge of the case nearest the aisle. Eventually a long sliver of wood splintered away with a crisp cracking noise.

The response was immediate. A sharp report, and again that bright muzzle-flash. Bolan reckoned it came from an intersection two rows down, where the trolleys were parked near the Swedish container. The bullet thudded into the crate. From the interior he heard a tinkle of broken glass followed by liquid gurgling. The heavy, aromatic odor of rum seeped into the atmosphere.

Three.

Bolan backed up on elbows and knees until he made the alley behind him. He rose stealthily to his feet and ran across to the far side, sinking down behind a rampart of cloth bales. The two shots followed quickly one after the other. Something twitched the upturned collar of his pea jacket as he lowered himself to the ground.

If the gunman could see that well, down both aisles, he must be high up, above the stacked material, perhaps balanced on top of the skins on one of the trolleys.

The count was now five.

Bolan vaulted up onto the bales. He saw a darker blur against the pale, ridged metal side of the container. Letting loose a three-shot burst, he was rewarded with a cry of pain, a single round that flew wide and the clatter of a body stumbling to the ground.

He leaped down into the aisle, scooped up the penlight and raced for the trolleys. The man was sitting on the floor with his back against a stack of skins. Blood welled between the fingers of the hand clenched over his left shoulder. The revolver was a couple of yards away. Bolan swung the penlight beam.

No surprise. It was Hugo.

The Executioner crouched down beside him and jammed the muzzle of the Beretta into the soft flesh at one side of his throat. "All right, you little snake," he growled, "now's the time to talk if you want to live long enough to get that shoulder mended."

Terrified eyes blinked against the flashlight glare. Hugo's mouth opened, but no words came out.

"You sold me out to Hansie. Now you work for Asticot. What the hell are you playing at?" Bolan grated.

Hugo swallowed. "A man has to live," he choked. "Sure, a fellow has to go where the money is."

"You mean anyone can buy you? You don't even feel loyalty to the scum whose dirty money you take?"

"I took your money, didn't I?" he said craftily. "When you wanted to locate Dagmar."

"Sure you did, and you passed on the information that I was looking for her to Lattuada, so he had plenty of time to frame me for the killing when he wanted to get rid of her. People like you don't deserve to live," Bolan said disgustedly.

"No, no. You got it wrong. You don't understand why—"

"I understand about the dope inside those skins. I understand Asticot is using them, and the East German importer, as a front to get the stuff over there, and that Lattuada, or his friends, will hijack it once it's there and start a new market in the East. I understand why a two-faced bastard like you has been hired to watch over the consignment in case any honest customs man tumbles to the dirty deal that's planned." Bolan's voice rose as his disgust was fueled by anger.

Hugo's eyes were staring. He shook his head wildly, flinching as the gun barrel cut into his flesh. "You got it all wrong!" he cried. "You *don't* understand. It ain't like that at all. The way they doped it out—"

His words were cut off by a thunderous explosion, a concussion whose blast threw Bolan to the floor and sent reverberations echoing around and around beneath the high roof of the customs shed. To Bolan's stunned senses the searing orange flash seemed to come later.

He shook the ringing sound from his blocked ears and sat up groggily. He had been blown ten yards away from the trolleys and was now in among a collection of individual packages. He heard the tramp of many feet, a squeaking metallic rumble as the shed doors were rolled back, a subdued issuing of orders. Combat-honed, his fighter's instinct told him that what he had heard was the detonation of a rocket grenade, probably fired from an RPG-7 launcher or something similar, which had destroyed the locks and bolts securing the shed doors without buckling them so much that they could no longer be pushed open. He could see, in the light from a spot on the quay outside, the brownish-yellow smoke that was still roiling in the entrance.

A dozen men ran down the aisle to the trolleys. Two more stood in the shattered doorway, cradling submachine guns. "Move it!" one of them snapped. "Fucking grenade'll have the cops here any time, for Chrissakes. You know which ones. Move your goddamn asses."

Torchlight flickered on the trolleys. They rolled this way and that. Men panted and strained. Then one of the trolleys separated, three of the men shoving it toward the entrance. It was followed by a second, and then the last two of the quartet with doctored skins. The first two were already out on the quayside.

Bolan stayed where he was, down among the packages on the floor. He had heard no sound from Hugo. The Executioner wondered if the weasel had been knocked out by the blast or fainted from loss of blood.

What puzzled the Executioner even more was the raid itself. He was pretty sure the guy at the door was Hansie Schiller, and that meant the Team, which meant Lattuada.

So why would the mafioso hijack his own stuff, for which he had just fixed trouble-free transport to the far side of the Iron Curtain? Unless, of course, it *wasn't* his stuff. Unless, despite the hotel meeting, Asticot was playing a lone hand on this deal and Lattuada was muscling in.

If that was true—and Bolan recalled that Hugo was telling him he had it figured wrong when the grenade had exploded—then the East German he had seen in Asticot's suite had to know about the dope in the skins after all. Because *he* would have to be the distributor for the Eastern bloc.

Another alternative: the East German was the principal. He had negotiated with Asticot for the dope supply, inspected it, paid for it and was about to take delivery, collecting it for transfer to the East. But Asticot had taken the money, and then hired Lattuada to steal the stuff back for him before the East German boat arrived.

That figured all right. On the whole, it was the most likely. It would be typical of Asticot. That way—Bolan smiled involuntarily—the bastard would have his coke and eat it!

But where did it leave *him*? What were his priorities now? Eliminate Asticot. Nail Lattuada for Dagmar's murder and get himself off the hook. Somehow stop the hell cargo buried in those skins from being distributed, East or West. But in what order?

And where the hell was the wounded Hugo?

The last question was soon answered. All four of the trolleys were now out on the quayside. The second man with the SMG had gone with them. Only Hansie remained. He took a couple of steps inside the shed. "Hugo?" he called. "You there, Hugo?"

"Here," a voice answered weakly from the far side of the shed. "I was told to stay put while the stuff was bein' shifted." He limped up the aisle toward the entrance. "I have to tell you, Hansie, that bastard plugged me, but the boss said to keep my mouth shut until—"

"Quite right, Hugo," Hansie interrupted softly. "The boss still wants you to keep your mouth shut...for a very long time."

Flame stabbed the darkness, and the earsplitting yammer of the SMG spit out as Schiller raised the weapon and emptied half the magazine down the aisle at the approaching Hugo. The man was knocked off his feet by the terrible impact of the 9 mm slugs and slammed against a stack of wooden crates. He slid lifeless to the floor. The hood walked out onto the dock, and Bolan heard his voice calmly issuing orders once more.

Seething with anger at the unnecessary slaughter, he hurried over to the dead man. The whites of Hugo's sightless eyes still gleamed in the half-light. Bolan thumbed them shut, and shook his head.

From the shadows inside the smashed doorway he stared out at a bizarre scene. Two flatbed trucks stood beside the shed, and twelve men were frantically transferring the skins from the trolleys to these, tearing each one off its stack and hurling it up onto the flatbed while the torpedoes with the SMG's stood guard.

For the second time, witnessing a raid that didn't directly concern him, Bolan heard the approach of distant police sirens.

Right now he had written himself out of the scenario. He didn't know the full story. It would be pointless, taking on fourteen armed thugs with a single Beretta whose magazine was partly exhausted. And even if by some miracle he defeated them all, he had no means of annihilating their lethal cargo before the police arrived. Apart from which, if he was caught on the scene, he'd end up with the whole thing pinned on him, especially when they found out who he was. He had decided to try to inch away, pick up the BMW and follow the trucks when the unexpected happened.

There was a shout from the far side of the wharf. A clatter of feet, and a party of men in dark combat fatigues erupted from the stone stairway that led to the landing stage and fanned out over the quayside. They were armed with machine pistols and they started firing as soon as they hit level ground.

Hansie and his partner yelled. The spotlight, mounted on the cab of the truck nearest the shed, was cut. The members of the Team scattered, ducked down behind the vehicles, flung themselves flat. But already several somber shapes lay prone on the whiteness of the snow carpeting the dock.

The newcomers found cover behind posts, a crane gantry and the stacks of lumber off-loaded from the Finnish freighter as Hansie's men blazed out return fire from handguns and SMGs.

From one end of the wharf to the other there was pandemonium beneath the fast-falling white flakes. The noise of gunfire was deafening. Muzzle-flashes sketched a hellish pyrotechnic display between the berthed ships. Sailors crowded the bridge of the *Aegean Queen* and bawled drunken encouragement from the deck of the Finnish freighter. Gunners advanced, retreated, screamed, fell.

Beneath one of the trucks two guys set up the grenade launcher. There was a hiss, a roar, a streak of flame and a violent explosion among the lumber stacks where most of the attackers were concentrated. It was then that Hansie gave the order to split.

The truck engines roared to life. One of the trolleys was still only partially unloaded, but the remaining members of the Team leaped up onto the flatbeds, firing from behind the heaped skins as the vehicles started to move. The last to jump aboard were the two men with the RPG-7. They launched a final round as the truck moved out from over them, scrambling up over the tailgate seconds after the finned five-pound terror bomb burst among a group of attackers advancing from the lumber.

The soldiers in the black combat suits spilled sideways like pins in a bowling alley. One bundle of bloodied rags flopped a few yards and then lay quivering in the snow. Another rose half upright and fired a single shot before collapsing. The bullet took one of the RPG-7 duo between the shoulder blades. He fell backward off the tailgate and lay with outflung arms as the truck accelerated away.

And then suddenly there was no more firing, just the whine of gears, shouting from the boats and an angry bullhorn voice over the dying groan of sirens down at the entrance to the wharf. There were three green-and-white patrol cars there beneath an arc light, with a line of grim-faced cops barring the exit, each with an SMG held ready.

The trucks rumbled toward them. Nearer the customs shed, three of the attackers—the only ones still left on their feet—ran for the abandoned trolley, snatched a couple of skins each and raced for the steps that led to the landing stage. A moment later Bolan heard the bellow of an exhaust, and a powerboat nosed out from the dock and arrowed away into the snowfall over the sound.

The voice from the bullhorn blared again, but neither of the trucks slowed. Bolan saw twinkling points of flame as the cops opened fire. Automatic arms rasped as the hoods fired back.

And then the police were scattering. The leading truck slammed into a four-foot gap between two patrol cars, sending each one crashing over onto its side in a fountain of snow. The driver of the second flatbed must have been hit, because the vehicle veered suddenly out of line, rammed a stone post, slewed sideways and tipped over the edge of the quay. At the same time a red glow from beneath the hood burst into a blazing fireball, suppressed at once when the truck hit the water with a noise like an exploding rocket. A column of steam and white water rose into sight over the quayside and then subsided.

Bolan was already running.

Flames from burning gasoline still licked the dark surface of the water and breathed lurid red light over swirling snowflakes. Five of Hansie Schiller's soldiers lay dead on the quayside and at least three more would have perished with the burning truck. Three of the attackers had gotten away; the rest were strewn about the dock or decimated among the splintered lumber stacks.

The Executioner was sprinting for the lumber, too, where his tracks would be lost among the carnage staining the trodden snow. He had no time to try to work out what the hell had happened. He only knew that he had to get out before the cops waded in to clear up the mess, and that Hansie Schiller had successfully busted through the cordon with three out of the four loads of concealed dope stacked safely on his truck.

Bolan wanted to be free to follow that truck.

Beyond the lumber stacks, he crossed a strip of virgin white, swarmed down a ladder into the empty dry dock, climbed out the far side and headed for a wall that flanked the street where his BMW was parked. There was a tar-paper shack built against the wall, and it was no sweat hoisting himself onto the roof, straddling the brickwork and dropping to the cobblestones below. Three minutes later he was parking the BMW beneath the hotel.

Since there was no direct access to the hotel from the garage, he walked up the ramp to the street. Treading through five inches of freshly fallen snow to the entrance, he happened to glance upward at the fourth-floor corner of the building where his room was situated.

He stopped. Light was showing through a crack between the curtains. He had left the room in darkness, and no hotel personnel would be checking out the sheets, the towels or the soap in the bathroom between one and two in the morning.

For the second time that night the Executioner made use of a fire escape—up this time rather than down. The door at the end of the passageway was no problem for a professional. The door to Bolan's room was closed. Locked.

With the Beretta in his right hand, he unlocked the door, kicked it open and leaped into the room in a combat crouch. He flattened himself against the wall, the muzzle of the autoloader questing left and right.

Nobody.

Bolan rose to his feet, trod softly to the far wall, sidled to the bathroom door, flung it open.

There was nobody.

He listened, but heard nothing. Large flakes of snow patted soft paws against the windowpane. The heat was up high, the air too dry to breathe.

Bolan pulled up the bed covers. There was only a three-inch gap between the bottom of the bed and the floor. He opened the door of a huge old-fashioned wooden clothes closet.

The door was pushed wide against his hand. A limp body slid halfway out and lay with head and shoulders on the carpeted floor. A short man with thinning hair, protuberant eyes and a lizard mouth. The blackened mascara-edge of a close-range bullet hole stared like a third eye from the center of his forehead.

Arvell Asticot had played both ends against the middle once too often.

CHAPTER SIXTEEN

So what the hell had happened? Okay, some person or persons unknown had jumped the gun and done the Executioner's job for him. But why transport the body to Bolan's room? Clearly because they wanted it to look as if he had killed the man himself.

Plenty of folks would want Asticot killed, and obviously he had been deeply involved in some kind of double cross tonight. But how many of those folks would want Bolan blamed for it? And of those, how many would know he was in Lübeck? And the hotel where he was checked in?

How many would have the means, and the nerve, to smuggle a corpse into a hotel room in the middle of the night?

For Bolan was certain Asticot hadn't been killed there. Sure, the body was still warm and there was no rigor mortis. But there was no smell of gunsmoke, either. And he could find no slug embedded, no trace of blood, although there was a fist-size exit wound in back of the murdered drug baron's head.

Those questions suggested a shortlist of one—Lattuada. The mobster would have had the opportunity; he hadn't shown up at the dockside during the hijack scene. He had the necessary callousness, and the nerve. It would suit him to have the murder pinned on Bolan: the fact that the Executioner was already tagged as a killer would deflect any suspicion and take the heat off

Lattuada himself. It was conceivable, if he had the kind of spy network Charlie Macfarlane had described, that he could have been tipped off that Bolan was in town, and where.

The stumbling block in his case was motive. Because it was clear as a bell that, tonight at least, he had been working with Asticot. It must have been Asticot who had filled him in on the East German drug deal, who suggested, or ordered, the hijack. So why would he want to take the guy out? To avoid sharing the spoils, maybe, and keep all the profit for himself? That, of course, was always a possibility.

Otherwise the only believable candidate was Kraul. And he only qualified because he probably knew or guessed Bolan would be in Lübeck. There were no links between him and Lattuada, certainly none with Hansie Schiller. And if he had wised Bolan up on the fact that Asticot and the mafioso were both in the northern seaport, it was precisely because he hoped Bolan himself would eliminate Asticot. Why then should he suddenly decide to do the job himself?

Not for the first time on this screwball mission the warrior's head was spinning. Too many alternatives and not enough evidence. Meanwhile he had to get out. If the killer was Lattuada, it would be in line with his normal MO to tip off the law again. Hastily Bolan started to gather his stuff.

He was scooping up shaving gear from the bathroom when he heard the noise. What was it? A footfall? The creak of a door? A garment brushing against furniture? No way of telling, but something, some small unexpected sound alerted him. He ran back into the bedroom.

He had searched no farther once Asticot's body was revealed. Now he saw his mistake: an alcove where extra clothing could be hung on a rail was hidden behind a heavy velvet drapery. He hadn't pulled back that drapery, but it was pulled back now. The bedroom door was open, and the polished surface of the night table, where he had laid out a leather wallet containing all his papers, was bare.

Bolan swore. He ran through to the hallway. The hotel's one ancient elevator was groaning down to street level. He dashed to the end of the passage and raced down the back stairs.

No wonder the body had still been warm: he had actually interrupted the thugs who had delivered it! But why had they stolen his papers? They couldn't have been instructed to do that, because it was only by chance that Bolan had left them out on the night table those few seconds.

Spur-of-the-moment decision, then? Could be, although that presupposed one of the bosses had been there, because the hired help didn't customarily mess with that kind of deal on their own.

Lattuada, on the other hand, didn't customarily do the dirty work himself. So maybe the delivery boys *had* been told to get the papers...off Bolan himself. And they'd seized the unexpected opportunity to avoid a direct confrontation.

Why would the gang boss want them? To push Bolan deeper into the shit by leaving them at the scene of some future outrage? Maybe. In any case, they wouldn't be necessary to link him with the Asticot killing, not with his description, a Lattuada tip-off to the police and the fact that he was wanted already.

Whatever, it was vital to the Executioner to get them back. Apart from the passport in the name of his other fake cover, Mike Blanski, and certain other documents he would need, there were, despite the fact that passport and press card had been stolen from his original hotel room, papers that would justify the Mike Belasko cover if he should need it again.

He ran across the hotel lobby. The night clerk was on his feet behind the reception desk, staring. The glass entrance doors were still revolving.

Bolan flung himself into the street. It was still snowing. The tire tracks in the roadway were almost obliterated, and the sidewalks stretched untrodden in each direction. But he could hear hurrying footsteps down the parking ramp. He unleathered his Beretta and gave chase.

There were two of them, a fat guy and a short, wiry man wearing a fur hat. The fat one jerked open the driver's door of a car at the far end of the underground lot and climbed inside. Bolan ran for the BMW; it was too long a shot for the Beretta, and if he missed they'd be away, leaving him standing there.

The car was an Opel Manta coupe. The thin guy was dragging his door shut and the car was accelerating up the exit ramp by the time Bolan got the BMW started. He emerged from the lot three hundred yards behind.

The snow had eased off slightly by the time they hit the outskirts of town, but it was still drifting in the hollows, and occasional squalls of wind sent unexpected flurries streaming toward the headlights on the way back south. The highway surface had been plowed and salted, though there were wide margins of icy slush on the shoulder and bordering the central strip. Bolan was forced to tread hard on the pedal, maintaining the speedometer needle hovering around ninety, to keep up with the Opel.

Ten miles south of the city the fat man rocketed the coupe down a turnoff and took to a network of country roads around Bad Oldesloe. It was here that the driver showed how good he was.

The Opel wasn't as fast as the heavy BMW, but it was more maneuverable. The guy was able to take every curve in a controlled slide, and he knew just how much boot to give the car to keep it at the maximum possible speed in these conditions without losing the front wheels. It was all the warrior could do to keep him in sight along the twisty lanes with their icy surfaces and snow-piled hedges.

Despite the biting cold, he was sweating, trying to keep up with the hoods as they skated right and left at minor intersections, racing ahead to try to conceal which road they were taking at a fork on the far side of a ridge. They roared through only one village, a single sleepy street in a bone-white landscape of farms and stubbled fields. In fifteen minutes there hadn't been one vehicle going in the opposite direction. But at the exit from this village the scriptwriter decided to inject an element of drama.

The Opel suddenly spurted onto a straightaway that ran for almost a mile along an embankment crossing a marsh. The roadway was wide enough for two cars, and Bolan drove as fast as he dared, aiming to overtake and then swing in directly ahead, slowing as abruptly as he could to force the Opel to a standstill.

Gradually the distance between the two cars lessened. The BMW swayed slightly on the packed ice, but the tires were biting. The lighter Manta zigzagged crazily from side to side as the speed increased. Soon the details of the coupe, which had been just a darker blur against the nocturnal paleness of the snow, became clear in the illumination of Bolan's headlights. He saw that it was colored mustard-yellow; the single *H* on the left-hand side of the license plate told him that it was registered in Hannover.

Halfway along the embankment, Bolan leaned more heavily on the gas pedal. The muffled roar of the engine climbed a few semitones up the scale. The BMW's front fenders approached the sliding rear of the Opel. He shifted the wheel to pull out and draw level.

They had maybe three hundred yards to go before the road swerved sharply right around a skeletal wood. And it was then that the fat man upstaged the warrior, preempting his plan by veering suddenly left to block the road and stop him passing. Bolan swore, hitting the brakes and running the sedan into the rough snow piled along the roadside.

But the driver of the Opel was doing almost sixty, still on the wrong side of the road, when a West German army convoy headed by a six-ton troop carrier trundled around the corner ahead of him.

After that there was nothing Bolan could do but watch him die.

For once the guy's nerve failed him. He panicked, overcorrecting to urge the car back onto the right side of the road. The rear end broke away, and then he lost it completely. In any case, he was driving far too fast to take the corner on that icy surface.

The Opel skidded wildly, turned through 180 degrees, cannoned into the side of the second truck in the convoy and then bounced back to hurtle over the side of the embankment and drop from sight. A vivid flash illuminated the cloud of snow flung up by the plummeting coupe. It was followed an instant later by a dull, thumping explosion and an orange fireball tinged with black that gushed up beyond the bank and mushroomed into the sky.

The convoy shuddered to a halt. Bolan heard men shouting. He was already out of the BMW and running toward the wreck. Soldiers in uniform piled out of the vehicles in the convoy and plowed down through the waist-deep snow covering the bank. But there was no hope of saving the occupants, or salvaging the papers, which, face it, the Executioner was more concerned about. It was impossible to approach within fifty feet of the blazing Opel. The gasoline tank must have ruptured with the initial impact, spilling fuel on the overheated engine. Now the car was lying on its back in the center of an inferno. The tires on all four wheels were alight, and steam from melted snow hissed up to join the oily flames leaning furiously away from the wind.

A sergeant detached himself from the ring of helpless men surrounding the holocaust. "What the hell happened?" he asked Bolan.

The warrior shrugged. After the penetrating cold, the searing heat was unbearable. "Must have been drunk," he said in German. "Or stoned out of his mind. I'd been following him for several miles and he was all over the road."

The sergeant took off his forage cap and mopped his brow. "Some people!" he said, shaking his head. "Poor bastards, roasted alive. But nobody but a crazy man would drive that fast on this road."

"Hopped-up kids," Bolan offered, thinking of the cargo the fat man's boss had gotten away with, and the young lives it would ruin.

A series of sharp, individual reports penetrated the dull roar of the flames. "That sounds like ammunition going off," the sergeant said.

"Teenage gangsters," Bolan agreed. "Probably stole the heap, hoping to sell it to pay for their shit."

The German clapped the cap back on his head. "There's nothing we can do here," he said. "The thing is, well, we missed the road in this goddamn snow and we're running late...."

Bolan got it. An official report meant official papers to fill in, meant official bullshit, meant time wasted that could more profitably be spent drinking. The last thing he himself wanted was to be roped in as a witness, but he could hardly take off just like that, not while the soldiers were there.

"Don't concern yourself with the formalities, Sergeant," he said. "I have business with the burgomaster at Bargteheide tomorrow morning. You can leave the matter in my hands. I'll report the matter to him. It wasn't your fault. Doubtless he'll make the necessary arrangements to send out a salvage team."

The sergeant looked grateful. "I'm obliged," he said. "We're already running late. You're very kind."

"Think nothing of it," Bolan said. He added fulsomely, "The least a civilian can do is offer help, however trivial, to the men defending the fatherland."

The sergeant stepped back, saluted and tried to click his heels in the slush. He shrilled his whistle and shepherded his men back to the convoy. The big diesels roared to life and rumbled away.

As soon as they were out of sight, Bolan hurried back up the bank. The Opel would burn for some time, and he didn't want to be there when villagers from the far end of the embankment, alerted by the pulsing red light, came out to investigate.

Temporarily he was left not only without papers but also without a lead. But he was convinced the hijacked narcotics, and their eventual distribution, would be centered on Hamburg. And he was determined, whatever the risks, to do his damnedest to wreck the plan. He got back behind the wheel of the BMW and headed for the E.4 motorway, the quickest route back to Hamburg.

THE HOTEL WAS in a residential street in the Hamburg suburb of Barmbek, northeast of the Alster. Fashioned by the union of three separate nineteenth-century row houses, it was an ultrarespectable, no-liquor establishment run by three Calvinist spinsters in their late sixties. The frosted glass transom above the central porch bore the name Shangri-la.

The clientele, as far as Bolan could tell, seemed to be permanent—retired colonials, professional folks in reduced circumstances. Widows exiled from the health spas that had grown too expensive for them shuffled along the creaking, heavily carpeted corridors as slowly as the aging waitress who served bratwurst and stewed fruit among the catsup bottles in the dining room. He figured the place was a near-perfect cover.

Once he had checked in, he left the small grip he had bought on his way into town by the brass bedstead in a fourth-floor single and went out again to replace the stuff he had left in Lübeck. He also bought a newspaper.

The lead story trumpeted the success so far of East-West disarmament talks in Berlin. On the right-hand side of the front page was a lurid account of a gangland battle in the heart of Lübeck's dockland. Rival gunmen, the story said, had fought with brutal ferocity over a consignment of smuggled narcotics, leaving no less than fifteen dead on the quayside before one of the gangs had made off with part of the consignment.

Police who had tried to intervene had suffered five wounded, two of them seriously, and customs officials had captured more than sixty pounds of cocaine and heroin, with a street value of millions of dollars, concealed in a shipment of goatskins from Greece.

In another part of the city, Bolan read, a suspected drug trafficker had been found shot dead in a hotel room occupied by an American named Mike Blanski. No mention was made of the fact that one of the gangs was East German, nor was it revealed that the goatskins had already fooled customs inspectors before the battle had taken place.

He threw the paper into a trash can and returned to the Shangri-la. Before he did anything else, he had to snatch a few hours' sleep.

IT WASN'T UNTIL the afternoon of the following day that Bolan was certain the hotel was being watched. Waking at dusk on the day of his arrival, he had discovered the snowstorm had increased to blizzard force, virtually marooning him indoors. Now another thaw had set in and there was a cold rain pockmarking the deep snow blanketing the front yards along the street.

From the window of his room, he noticed a Volkswagen Golf, a tiny soft-top Fiat 500 and a Renault sedan parked on the opposite side of the street against the dirty white rampart thrown there by the snowplow. In each case the driver affected to be reading a newspaper, waited an hour and then moved off.

How had they known? Charlie Macfarlane's Black Hand Mafia?

He went to the window once more for a final check. Nobody was parked across the street, but the Golf was back, on the near side this time, a couple of houses away but still in full view of the old janitor shoveling snow off the front steps of the hotel.

Bolan went to a bathroom in back of the building and looked out the window. Beyond strips of backyard, most of them planted with bare trees or shrubs in pots, a lane ran along the rear of the block. On the far side of the wall bordering this he could see the soft top of a small car. He didn't need to walk out into the lane to know that the chrome strip outside the louvered hood covering the pint-size two-cylinder rear engine would read Fiat 500.

There was only one thing he could do: find another base, a hole where there wouldn't be a Volkswagen Golf, a Renault sedan and a tiny Fiat parked outside. It could be done two ways: leave openly, draw them after him, then lose the tail someplace, or attempt to leave without them knowing and start over.

Number two was the better bet. They might make the snatch—and he knew that was what they'd try to do—right here in front of the hotel if he left openly, giving him no time to evade the shadows.

As darkness fell, he drew the curtains in his room but left the lights burning. Stuffing as many of his new purchases as he could into the capacious pockets of his trench coat, he left enough bills on top of the night table to settle his account, then slipped into the corridor. He had very little money left now, and he couldn't change any more American Express checks, not with Mike Belasko's name in all the papers. So, if he could prevent the elderly Shangri-la personnel from reporting the strange disappearance of a guest to the local police station, so much the better.

The first part of the escape was no sweat. The hotel's clients were all in the funereal dining room, waiting to drown their slices of warmed-over pork in catsup. Most of the staff was occupied there or in the kitchen, and the three spinster owners would be eating in the office behind the reception desk. The back stairs, designed for servant use, led past the kitchen to a basement laundry room that opened directly onto the yard, an area spanning all three of the hotel's "houses."

Bolan's plan was to scale the wall dividing the hotel from the next-door property, cross the yard there and climb the next wall, and finally let himself out into the lane several houses behind the Fiat.

One of his chief problems was the weather. Rain had been falling all day, and now darkness had brought mist again. The sooty surfaces of brick and stone would therefore be slippery and treacherous, especially where they were still coated with thawing snow. But what the hell—it was time for action.

He stole down the dimly lit stairway, treading on the inside of each step to minimize the risk of creaks, and paused outside the bar of illumination streaming through the open kitchen door. A cook in white coveralls was standing in front of a stove with her back to him. Otherwise the place was empty. He tiptoed past and hurried downstairs and out into the yard.

Making it over the first wall was easy. There was a row of garbage cans lined up by the exit door, and all he had to do was climb them, sit astride the brickwork and drop down on the far side. The yard there had been turned into some kind of patio, with French windows leading from the basement to a flagged terrace ornamented with potted plants. The garbage was kept in a bin just inside the door that opened onto the lane. This was too close to the waiting Fiat for Bolan's comfort.

He was encumbered by the heavy trench coat and the cargo in its pockets, but he figured he could make it via a shack built against the wall near the house. Using a wooden tub as a springboard, he jumped for the snow-covered roof of the shack.

He landed successfully, but his foot brushed against something as he hoisted himself up, something that shifted and then dropped into space. There was a shattering crash.

Bolan froze, spread-eagled on the slanting roof.

Light lanced the darkness of the yard below him as a curtain was jerked aside. A broken flowerpot lay in the snow by a small mound of earth and leaves. A sash beside the French windows was flung up, silhouetting a man's head and shoulders. "Those damn cats!" a voice called angrily. "There's another of the begonias gone!" The man clapped his hands loudly, muttered something under his breath, then slammed down the sash. The light, and the falling rain it revealed, vanished.

Bolan released his breath in a long sigh of relief. Being nailed as a prospective burglar didn't figure in his plan of action at all. He continued his climb to the wall.

The next yard gave him no trouble, nor the one after that. It was stacked with lumber, and the descent was as easy as walking down a stairway. If the house owners saw his tracks before the rain melted enough snow to obliterate them, let them work out the scenario for themselves. Cautiously the warrior unlatched the door in the end wall of the final yard and let himself out into the lane.

The Fiat's twin red taillights were three houses away. Bolan turned up his trench coat collar and hurried toward a tree-lined square at the far end of the lane.

He was passing under a streetlight twenty yards from the exit when he heard the Fiat's two-cylinder engine cough to life. Glancing over his shoulder, he saw the little soft-top turn around and accelerate toward him. Even in his rearview mirror, the tail must have recognized him, which meant it had to be someone who knew him—the vulture-faced thug, for instance, or Hansie himself. Bolan broke into a run and cut across the small public park in the center of the square.

As the Fiat raced around the perimeter, he sprinted over the far roadway and plunged beneath an arch into a pedestrian mall that sliced the block diagonally and led into a shopping street bright with window displays. By the time his pursuer had driven around the block and negotiated the lights, Bolan had crossed the street and jumped a bus turning into the Adolph-Schönfelder Strasse.

The Fiat tailed the bus past a condominium development and up the Oberaltenallee but was forced to abandon the chase by the Alte Wöhr S-Bahn station when Bolan hopped off and ran up the stairs as a train glided alongside the platform.

The Executioner made it into the last car just before the automatic doors closed. Through the glass he saw the Fiat abandoned in the station yard, the driver—it was, in fact, the vulture-faced thug—bounding up the stairs in a vain attempt to get aboard.

Bolan rode three stations to the Wandsbeker Chaussee interchange, dived underground to the U-Bahn subway, changed trains again at Lübecker Strasse and took the U-2 line back north to Barmbek, only half a dozen blocks from the hotel he had escaped from less than a half hour earlier.

There were no barriers, no controllers, conductors or ticket men operating in the Hamburg subway network. Strictly an honor system. Computerized automatic dispensers informed travelers of the route they should take and how much their ticket cost. Bolan saw no railroad police. He walked out the station and headed east, away from the wet sidewalks crowded with late shoppers.

He had no clear idea how he was gong to locate Lattuada with both the police and the underworld after him; he wasn't exactly certain what he would do once he did contact him. But find him he must, or face the thought of remaining a hunted man with a trumped-up murder charge hanging over his head. But first he would have to find a safe base from which he could mount his clandestine operation. The least dangerous place to look for this, he reckoned, and the one least likely to be patrolled by the men who wanted to kidnap him, was the very neighborhood he had just fled. He knew there were numerous rooming houses and cheap hotels even more anonymous than the Shangri-la in the suburban wasteland between Barmbek and Rahlstedt.

Veils of mist swathed the streetlights as he crossed the Adolph-Schönfelder Strasse for the second time that evening. But this time the roadway was deserted, the sidewalks gleaming emptily where lighted storefronts were reflected in the moisture varnishing the swept pavement. He walked toward a roofed recreation center and then turned in under an arch framing the entrance to a lane leading farther east.

The arch pierced a big nineteenth-century office block. Halfway through it was the side entrance to a tavern. Bolan looked at the pink light behind the mullioned windows, listened to the chatter and laughing inside and wished he could take time off to go in there, too. As he passed, the door opened and a man came out, buttoning the collar of his raincoat. Bolan saw him clearly in the illumination flooding the arch from the bar behind him. It was Wertheim, the homicide sergeant working with Fischer.

The recognition was mutual. For an instant the two men froze, and then, as the policeman yelled, "Stop! Just a minute, you," Bolan pushed past him and broke into a run.

Wertheim shouted something and dashed after him. A police whistle shrilled. Bolan sprinted for a turn in the lane. The Beretta was in its quickdraw rig, but he wasn't going to exchange shots with a cop and have that chalked up against him, as well. The sergeant, on the other hand, didn't have to worry about scruples. He shouted another warning, and immediately afterward two shots rang out.

Bolan was unscathed. Luckily the element of surprise had probably blunted the German's professionalism. He had fired on the run, and missed. If Wertheim had stopped, dropped into a combat crouch and steadied his gun arm with his left hand, the warrior would have been lying on the wet cobblestones with a couple of slugs from a Police Special letting air into his back.

He pelted down the lane and turned into a narrow street. The sergeant's footsteps pounded behind. The whistle blew again. Bolan lengthened his stride to increase his lead. He reached an intersection, ran across a wide roadway shining with the remains of old streetcar tracks and continued along the narrow street. For the third time the whistle shrilled. Wertheim was falling behind. But this time there were answering blasts off to one side and dead ahead.

Bolan's breath rasped in his lungs as he turned left into a paved walkway, and stopped in his tracks. The walk was only about fifty yards in length, and it ended in a blank brick wall.

Small modern houses lined the cul-de-sac. By the area railings outside one of the nearest, a tall, dark young woman loitered beneath a streetlight. She was wearing a shiny black raincoat, tightly belted, and a set of keys dangled from the ring she held in her hand.

"All right," Bolan panted in German, "any price you say. But let's make it fast, huh?"

For a moment she stared at him, registering the approaching footsteps and the chorus of whistles. "Name your price," he urged again.

This time she smiled. "Come on then!" she said.

She ran up the steps, unlocked the front door and pushed it open. Bolan slid inside as Wertheim reached the end of the walkway and stopped, peering right and left. The young woman eased the door shut, took Bolan's hand and led him to a room at the far end of a dark hallway. She switched on a light.

It was a pleasantly furnished room, with corn-colored easy chairs afloat on a sea of sage-green carpet. She was beautiful, Bolan saw. Not as young as he had thought—she must be well over thirty—but with good bones beneath the makeup and finely modeled features. She unfastened the belt of her raincoat and smiled again.

"Hate to disappoint you, really I do," she said in excellent English, "but I'm afraid I'm no hooker. Since you're here, though, the least I can do is offer you a drink.'' She walked across to an oak cabinet standing against the wall. ''Do you prefer Scotch or schnapps, Mr. Belasko?''

CHAPTER SEVENTEEN

Bolan stared at the young woman. He didn't get it. "How the hell...?" he began.

She smiled for the third time. Good teeth, wide brown eyes crinkling at the corners, a lot of lipstick, shining in the light. "Wouldn't you like something to drink?" she repeated.

"Sure," he said, collapsing into a chair. "Make mine Scotch." He got up again and stripped off the wet trench coat. "Look," he said, "pardon me for asking, but how in hell did you know who I was?"

She was busy with bottles and glasses at the oak cabinet. "I read your description in the paper."

"Ah, c'mon," Bolan protested. He began to pace up and down. "That description could have fitted thousands of guys."

"Very well. I read the stories. I get around. I didn't figure you for a killer. And when I see a man who answers to that description running from the police, a man speaking with an American accent, well, I just knew. You have to in my business."

"All right," Bolan said, "I'll buy it. For the moment. Just what is your business?"

"I run a nightclub."

"A nightclub? Isn't that a tough business for a woman? I mean, well, in this town, especially right now, with the shakedowns and all."

"Shakedowns?"

"The protection racket. They tell me it's all the rage this side of the Atlantic. Pretty hard for a woman to duck that kind of routine, I'd say."

She shook her head. Her dark hair was short, with a natural wave to it. "Not if you know what you're doing."

Bolan took the glass that was handed him. "What's that supposed to mean?"

"A woman can please several kinds of customers at once, ugly customers included," she said. "A man could never get away with that. I can and I do. I play my cards right, and I hold them close to my chest."

He dropped back into the chair. "Lucky cards," he said.

She ignored the intended compliment. "I did draw lucky ones to begin with," she said seriously. "But you still have to play them right. The Coliseum—"

"The Coliseum?" Bolan was very interested now.

"That's the name of my club."

"What kind of a club? A clip joint? A strip palace? Something ritzy with a floor show?"

"If you'll stop throwing questions at me for five seconds, I'll tell you," she said sharply.

Bolan noted the touch of color in her cheeks, her flashing eyes. "Sorry," he said.

She sat down opposite him and knocked back a sizable jolt of what looked like half a tumbler of straight Scotch. "The Coliseum's kind of special," she told him. "I aimed for a particular mixture of people and I got it. We serve excellent food. There's a good five-piece on-stage. The floor show's just one act, but it's always a headliner. And, of course, it costs."

Bolan said nothing. She was going to tell him, anyway, because obviously she was proud of the place. The

whisky went down well after the run through the cold
rain.

"But it's the clientele itself that's the real attrac-
tion," she went on. "I get the top people from lots of
different walks of life, and most of them find it kind of
intriguing to be among the others. Three out of the five
NATO top brass are regulars, for instance. But so are the
brains behind the off-track betting syndicates and gang
leaders from several cities. I get sportsmen from the
Atlantic Grill and most of the big noises in football and
boxing, along with a sprinkling of columnists and the
spenders in show business, and, of course, the socialites
who get a kick out of rubbing shoulders with the underworld. That's a very chic thing to do right now!"

"No scientists, politicians or literary geniuses?" Bolan
quipped.

"No," she said, "I don't have any of those. But I do
get movie directors and some big-time lawyers. That's
what I mean when I say I get around. No cop's going to
trip me up on the licensing laws when his boss may be at
the next table, and some villain at the bar could tip him
off to a bank raid planned by a rival. No mobster's going
to put the bite on me when I run a place that's going to
varnish him with a coat of respectability. Up and down,
whichever way you look at it, people are snobs."

"You're just a simple altruist, wanting to do the best
for everyone."

She shrugged, drained her glass and got to her feet. "I
make it my business to cash in on that snobbery, that's
all."

Bolan grinned. "Playing all the angles. Pretty sharp."

She laughed, a deep sound, slightly husky, more of a
chuckle actually. "A girl has to make a living," she said,

unbuttoning the raincoat and throwing it over the back of a chair. "Let me get you a refill."

For a moment Bolan didn't reply. He'd realized there was no circus freak under the raincoat, but the stiff rubberized material had concealed the clues. The girl was magnificent, big-hipped, full-breasted, radiating animal vitality. She was wearing a cream silk shirt and a tweed skirt with tan boots that went halfway up her calves. The short hair, which looked as if it had just been ruffled, had been cut by an expert, expensive hand.

He cleared his throat. "No thanks. The last one took the chill off nicely. I guess I don't have to introduce myself. But I didn't catch...?"

"Zuta Krohn," she said. Bolan learned later that her parents had come from East Prussia, but they had fled to Berlin just ahead of the Russian invasion at the end of World War II. She had been born and brought up there, but the family had moved again, to Hamburg, when the Berlin Wall was constructed in 1961. The father, a big-time restaurateur, had been killed in an air crash in the late seventies. Everything she'd learned from him, and everything she'd inherited from him, had gone into the Coliseum when she'd started it four years ago. Now it was one of the most successful night spots in town.

If you really want to see him, you could try the Coliseum, of course. One of the gay chorus boys had told him that in a bar near the Opera aeons ago. Hansie!

"Look, Zuta," he said. "I'm going to be inquisitive again. But first I have to apologize for thinking you were—"

"Taking me for a hooker?" She laughed. "Forget it. With this black coat, hanging around there outside a door with a house key in my hand, I could hardly blame you!''

''That's what I was going to ask. Why *were* you, I mean, how did you happen to be hanging around like that, just at that time?''

''Oh, that's no secret,'' Zuta said. ''I heard police whistles blowing and the sounds of a chase...someone running in my direction. Naturally I waited to see what was going on. Wouldn't you?''

''Why didn't you turn me in when you realized...''

''When I realized who you were? Why do you think?''

Bolan shook his head. He had his suspicions, though.

''Three reasons,'' she said. ''One, I was on my way home from a hoteliers' association meeting. Two, after reading the newspaper stories about you, I wanted to hear the full story firsthand.''

''And the third reason?''

They were standing by the liquor cabinet. She moved closer to him, looked him straight in the eye and picked a thread from the sleeve of his jacket. ''I like tall men,'' she said.

Maybe the liquor helped. Maybe, Bolan thought later, it was just his day. He never knew. He did know that the whole of that evening was kind of hazy, but that at some point he and Zuta found themselves in a pretty hot embrace. And if ever he'd thought Dagmar Schroeder's mouth was promising, he had to admit now that it was strictly minor-league material.

After a time, though, even with a body as pliant as Zuta's draped against a guy, the mind goes on working, the thoughts spiral up through the quickened breathing and whisky fumes. She'd started a bell ringing a while back there. Hansie Schiller. The iron fairy in the velvet glove, as someone had quipped.

Sometime later, Bolan asked casually, "You said some of the mobsters use your club. Ever see a character there by the name of Hansie Schiller?"

She raised her eyebrows. "Another queen, though you wouldn't think it, looking at that face. Yes, he comes in from time to time. Why do you ask?'

"He's been written into my script," Bolan said. "I figure him for the bad guy in the Dagmar Schroeder case. Did you know her, too?"

"The blond pusher? The one you were supposed to have killed?" The deep voice was suddenly dismissive. "I knew her by sight. I had to have her thrown out of the club a couple of times. Even with my clientele, I have to be discreet. I mean, you know..." Zuta shook her head. "I'm afraid she was a little tramp," she said.

"And Ferucco Lattuada?"

"The Yank, as they all him?" She shook her dark head again. "I've heard about him, of course, but I never laid eyes on him. I don't think he's ever been to the Coliseum. Why, is he part of your story, too?"

"You could say that," Bolan said grimly.

"Have you eaten dinner this evening?" she asked, changing the subject abruptly.

"I can't remember the last time I ate something," he told her, getting up from the sofa.

"I'll call a cab and we'll go eat at my place, all right?"

"I thought I was in your place," Bolan said.

"This house belongs to me, but I don't live here," she said. "I have an apartment over the club. That's where I feel really at home. And I can get them to send up something nice from the kitchen. How does that grab you?"

Bolan nodded. Since he'd come to Hamburg, he'd been betrayed and lied to by a lot of people—Dagmar,

Sally Ann, Hugo. But now he fervently hoped Zuta wouldn't join the list. She was his ticket to the Coliseum, though, and he'd trust her for the moment.

They grabbed a taxi and in no time were seated at a table with a white cloth, silverware, tall Czech crystal glasses and a wine bottle in a cradle.

Bolan ate heartily—T-bone steak, french fries, soup, salad. Zuta sat across from him, holding a glass of red wine. She had changed into a gold housecoat. Soft music played in the background—Duke Ellington's "Sophisticated Lady." The lights were low, and the mood romantic. He hadn't felt this relaxed in ages.

It must be a dream, Bolan thought. But suddenly everything sharpened into focus and all the edges became crystal clear. Her teeth were a dazzling white. Her smiling lips were the reddest he had ever seen. Her eyes were the darkest in the world. The glass he raised reflected all the colors of the spectrum from its elegant base. He squinted at her across the pool of light isolating the table, and the shapes of furniture humped in the shadows around him vanished into the unknown reaches of the strange room.

"Finish your steak," Zuta said. "If what you've been saying is more than a boast, you're going to need your strength later."

CHAPTER EIGHTEEN

A soft, warm body rolled on top of Mack Bolan, wedging a thigh between his legs. He felt the gentle weight of breasts against his chest. He opened his eyes, wincing at the bright light cast by a lamp. Zuta was supporting herself on her elbows, chin resting on cupped hands, staring at him with an amused smile on her face.

"Something funny?" he asked groggily.

She laughed. It was a lovely sound first thing in the morning. "Poor baby," she said. "I'll go fix you some strong black coffee and orange juice. You stay put."

"A tank couldn't budge me," he croaked.

A few minutes later Zuta brought in breakfast. She sat on the edge of the bed and dunked a bread roll into a large cup of café au lait. Bolan sipped his own coffee, his eyes feasting on the striking woman. She was wearing a crimson silk kimono with a black dragon embroidered across the back. He looked at the parts of her it wasn't covering. It was a pleasure.

In daylight, with no makeup, her face was handsome rather than beautiful: the skin was maybe a little coarse and the jaw was determined. He guessed it had to be, given the business she was in. Anyway, with a mouth and body like hers, who cared?

"Look, Zuta, I have to make plans," Bolan said, draining the coffee cup. "There are things I have to do."

"Later," Zuta said. "I'll do anything I can to help. But first you need more sleep. You're bushed, Mike."

"Can you tell me one good way I could get back to sleep?" he asked.

She lifted the covers and slid in beside him. "Yes," she said, "I can."

She was right, too. It wasn't until one in the afternoon that he finally surfaced again. The curtains were open, and he lay looking up at small patches of blue among the clouds. He swung his feet to the floor, stood and walked to the window.

The apartment appeared to be on the third floor. He stared down at a gray street lined with young, bare chestnuts. There was still snow on the sidewalks and frozen gray slush banked at the side of the roadway. Drifts of fallen leaves, yellow, orange and brown, showed where the areas of redbrick row houses across the street had been swept clear of snow. Below the window and to one side, a red-striped canopy projected over the sidewalk. It seemed an odd place for a nightclub. There was no traffic in the street. He could see no stores, just a big building that looked like a hospital, and there were very few cars parked between the canopy and a T-junction with traffic lights beyond which he could see more trees.

He saw no Golf, no Renault sedan and no baby Fiat among the cars.

Zuta came into the room. She was dressed in jade-green lounging pajamas with wide pants and a loose jacket. "My God," she said, "I know we made sweet music together, but did I do that?"

She was staring at his naked body. He glanced down and saw that bruises he had received during the beating administered by Hansie had now blossomed into a pattern of blue, purple and dirty amber. He grinned. "I've been waltzing with bad company a lot these days."

"Poor love. I'll have them send up some lunch, then I'll give you a liniment rub while you tell me all about it."

"Swell," Bolan said. "Is the club open for lunch, then? By the way, where are we exactly? I've been trying to pinpoint the location, but I can't come up with it. It looks more like the outskirts of town than clubland."

"I wanted my club to be different," Zuta said. "I didn't want to be running just another joint in the square mile."

"The square mile?"

"St. Pauli—the square mile of vice, so-called. I wanted to be out of that. Which helped me with the no-shakedown situation, incidentally. No competition means no trouble. I wanted to be in a neighborhood that was easy to get to, but where clients could always find parking space. And I also wanted a place that wouldn't attract wandering drunks, tourists, soccer supporters and visiting firemen. Folks don't come to the Coliseum by chance. They come because they know it's there and because they want to come. The trees you can see at the end of the street there are by the Wandsbek-Markt U-Bahn station, where there's a big parking lot. To answer your other question, yes, we do open for lunch. And it'll be here in about three minutes, so you better shower and get shaved quickly."

Lunch was a dozen oysters followed by smoked salmon and a bottle of vintage German white wine. It was served by a guy in a white mess jacket whose face looked like a train wreck.

"Are they all like that?" Bolan asked when the character had swung off from branch to branch. "Or is it just our friend in the white jacket who's doubling for a gorilla in a new Tarzan movie?"

"A woman running a late-night club has to have a certain amount of muscle around," Zuta said, "or people will try to take advantage of her. If you can get strong men who are also good waiters—and that one is— then you're halfway home. Now pour me some wine and tell me all about this mess you got yourself into."

He poured the wine and gave her the complete rundown, telling it the way it was, right from the first time he'd seen Lattuada. The only thing he left out—women, he figured, were unknown quantities in some matters— was the fondness he'd had for Dagmar Schroeder. He pretended the meet with the unfortunate Dagmar was arranged simply in the hope of finding some lead that would get him nearer to the Yank.

"The whole works, in fact," Zuta said when he was through, "arose because you had a hunch, a hunch that this man Lattuada was in some way tied in with the crime scene here."

Bolan nodded. "I was right, too. There's a story there. But following it up landed me the star part in a bigger story. And I can't write the end to that before I get to Lattuada and choke the truth out of him. Which should wrap up the first story, too."

"Before you get to Lattuada? How do you think you'll do that?"

"Go on doing what I was doing. Find a new base. Stick around until I pick up a lead. Follow it through and then—"

"Belasko!" Zuta interrupted. "You're crazy! You wouldn't last a day the way things are now."

"How do you mean, the way things are now?"

"I made a few, shall we say, discreet inquiries this morning," she told him. "I sent up a few balloons and waited to see who would respond."

"And?"

"And you can't step outside this apartment, darling. That's the truth. You're on the spot two different ways. First, the cops, having missed you last night, are putting everything they have into the murder hunt. And, of course, the Team's after you, too. Word's gone around in the underworld that there'll be money paid to anyone who turns you in, and a beating given to anyone who recognizes you and doesn't. I promise, the moment you leave here you'll be surrounded by so many snitches, you'll think you're—"

"But I can't stay here," Bolan cut in. "I have to—"

"Why ever not? There's something wrong with the food? You have some fault to find with the...service? You don't like the company?" Her eyes flashed danger signals through the mascara.

"You know it's nothing like that," Bolan said.

"*If* this man Lattuada's around," Zuta said, "and *if* he's doing what you say he is, then you'll see him all right, a lot quicker than you expect, if you leave here. Only it won't be on your terms. It'll be on his. And if there's any choking to be done, it'll be your neck rather than his."

Bolan sighed. She made sense.

"Stay here with me," she said. "A place like this— downstairs, I mean—I can put out feelers, sound folks out. You can do a hell of a lot more for yourself working on the information I bring you than you ever could on your own."

"Yeah," Bolan said doubtfully. "You could be right. But would there be any intel? I mean, you know, I'm in a spot. I have to get to the bottom of this frame somehow, and that means facts and it means proof, which in turn means some kind of legwork. It has to. Do you really think you'd be able to—"

"You don't know the people I know," Zuta said. "You don't know what influence a girl in my position can have. Trust me, Mike. I'll do everything I possibly can. I promise. Meanwhile, well, there could be worse ways to keep out of jail, don't you think?"

That evening Zuta changed into a clinging black crepe dress with a red rose on one shoulder, and went down to play hostess in her club. She had shown the place to Bolan earlier, in the off hours between six and eight when the afternoon drunks had gone home after their hard day's work in the boardroom and the sugar daddies hadn't yet shown up to wine and dine their mistresses.

It was a ritzy place, all right. A single line of tables surrounded a small sunken dance floor. There were two more rows behind a balustrade a couple of feet above this. On a third level another balustrade partitioned off the tables for guests from the wrong side of Zuta's tracks, and a long bar stretched between the entrance stairs and a door leading to the washrooms. The band occupied a postage-stamp-size stage at one side of the shallow stairway linking the three levels.

They had entered the place through double padded doors with circular windows like classical oriels. On the way down they had passed an office floor full of accountants sorting through bills and invoices in an attempt to con the local tax people that Zuta was losing money. Above that was the apartment, and above the apartment there was an attic floor used for supplies.

Bolan had looked around at the white tablecloths, the cream-and-gold chairs and the crimson carpet. Midnight-blue paper spangled with stars covered the ceiling; Doric columns supported a pediment above the bar; and there were Greek vases here and there in niches to complete the amphitheater motif. Bolan had been happy to see that the waiters were dressed like waiters, not gladiators.

"This is a hell of a place to find in a residential street," he'd told Zuta. "Even in Wandsbek. What's the exterior look like?"

"Apart from the canopy over the sidewalk," she'd said, "you wouldn't know it was here. It's built inside three of the row houses knocked together. There's no electric sign, no neon, not even an nameplate. From the outside it looks exactly like the rest of the street."

He'd nodded. "Just like the Shangri-la, except for the catsup bottles."

Alone, now, in the evening, behind a distant buzz of conversation, he could hear faint strains of music. The five-piece band, Zuta had told him, mostly played quiet, intimate stuff, ballads and subtle torch numbers spiced with a little Latin-American.

The most persistent sounds, however, were the slamming of car doors and the gunning of engines in the street outside. Anyone who could believe the Coliseum wasn't doing good business, Bolan thought, needed his head examined, or maybe a job as a tax inspector.

To help pass the time, he scanned a pile of newspapers and magazines that Zuta had sent up. The news hawks were still discussing disarmament. They traded priorities for the other page-one stories—an earthquake in Turkey, two more UN hostages kidnapped by Arab extremists in Lebanon, an expected rise in the price of gasoline. The *Frankfurter Zeitung* ran a feature on a French woman cyclist who had been stripped of her championship status because urine tests after her latest record-breaking run showed positive for anabolic steroids.

Only one tabloid mentioned the Dagmar Schroeder killer. Three people had recognized him boarding the Denmark ferry at Grossenbrode—for the second time!—but when Danish police later boarded the vessel, the suspect had disappeared. Clearly Sergeant Wertheim wasn't making any press announcements about his encounter with the wanted man the previous evening.

But that didn't mean he was doing nothing about it. Zuta came upstairs to have a drink with the Executioner when the simian in the white jacket delivered a casserole of coq au vin and a bottle of wine around ten o'clock. "Don't say I didn't tell you," she began, "but you can thank your lucky stars I persuaded you to stay with me today."

Bolan smiled, but didn't reply. He would just as soon have had a hamburger. "So what's new?"

"Kunstler, one of the police bosses, was in," she said. "There's a cordon around this neighborhood as tight as a hair net. When they lost you last night, they knew you must have gone to ground somewhere in the quarter. It seems they had every street and alleyway covered within a half hour. If you'd gone out this morning, you wouldn't have lasted a minute."

"So, okay, I stay here until the heat's off. There are problems, though. I need fresh clothes and I need cash. Do you know any way I can pass American Express checks without it being a dead giveaway? I hate to ask you, but, well, I guess I mean illegally."

She smiled. "No problem. We cash them here. Give them to me and I'll put them through myself."

"Thanks. That's terrific. It won't get you into trouble, though, will it?"

Zuta shook her head. "I'll predate the transaction, make it look as though you cashed them here before the cops were after you, before that girl was killed. I can fake a duplicate restaurant bill to make it look better still."

"Zuta," Bolan said, "you're a treasure."

"As well as a treasury? I have to go stroke the big spenders now," she said. "I may not be back until after two, but don't you dare be asleep."

He didn't dare. But it was nearly 5:00 a.m. before he finally got the chance. In the intervening hours, seasoned bedtime warrior that he was, Bolan was alternately astonished and delighted by the big brunette's insatiable sexual appetite and by the adventurousness of her demands. Finally she fell asleep herself with one heavy thigh over his hip.

CHAPTER NINETEEN

The Executioner had been shacked up with Zuta Krohn for several days, and although she had come up with a stack of interesting material on other subjects, the Lattuada file remained at zero.

Bolan began to chafe at the inactivity. He was feeling constricted in the apartment, much as he was enamored of its voluptuous owner. The police cordon had been withdrawn days ago, and he wanted out.

Zuta was adamantly against it on account of underworld gossip insisting the warrior was still very much a target. If he went out, she argued, even if he wasn't nailed, they might follow him back to the apartment, and his cover would be blown once more.

At first he went along with her reservations because he didn't want the Team to associate her in any way with him. The Coliseum might not be on their visiting list right now, but if they knew the boss was sheltering their number one target, things could get tough for her.

Eventually they compromised and went out a couple of times together in a rental car that took them to a dine-and-dance joint somewhere southwest of the city. It didn't bring Bolan any closer to Lattuada, but it let fresh air into his lungs.

They figured on repeating the performance that Sunday, when the Coliseum was closed, but it turned out to be one of those days when northern Germany showed itself in its true colors, all thirty-six of them gray. To make matters worse, the temperature dropped another ten degrees and it snowed as if there were no tomorrow. So they spent the day in bed.

The next day, however, there were patches of blue again, an arctic wind had blown away the snow and the Executioner had itchy feet once more.

Zuta had gone out for the whole day, reordering at wine merchants, butchers and the like. Bolan was staring down at the icy remnants of the blizzard still veneering the street, wondering if he dared risk bringing the wrath of Hansie down on his hostess, when he knocked his billfold off the edge of a bureau as he reached for a bottle of beer.

The leather wallet containing his papers had been stolen in Lübeck, but the billfold had still been in his pocket. He stooped now to pick up the contents fanned over the floor—hundred-mark bills, two American tens, an address book, a sheet of airmail stamps, a small rectangle of pasteboard.

A rectangle of pasteboard? What was that? A business card? He turned it over and read: Heinrich J. Alberts. Day and night taxi service. And beneath, two telephone numbers. He frowned. How come such a card was in his billfold? Then he remembered. Of course—the sharp cabbie who had helped him tail Lattuada back near the beginning of the whole mess.

Seeing the card gave him an idea. With transport available, he could visit one or two of the places he wanted to go to while minimizing the risk of being picked up. As far as compromising Zuta was concerned, he could wait until he was dead sure he was clean before he was driven back to the apartment. And if it came to losing a tail, what could be more anonymous than a local cab?

He punched out the first number on the card, the one written in ink. There was no reply. At the second number, the cab stand on the south side of the Atlantic Hotel, a gruff voice told him that Alberts had taken a fare to the airport at Fuhlsbüttel.

"When will he be back?" Bolan inquired.

"Search me. Depends what he picks up at the airport, don't it?"

Bolan left the apartment number and asked for Alberts to call him as soon as he returned. In fact, it was less than twenty minutes before he rang.

"I'd like to hire you for the rest of the day," Bolan said. "Stop, wait, start, stop again, stuff like that. Do you know the Coliseum?"

"Yes, very well." He chuckled.

"Okay. Be there in ten minutes, and we're on our way."

Nobody noticed Bolan leave the Coliseum. The waiters were setting up tables for dinner, the bar was closed, and he slipped through the padded doors and out the entrance like a ghost.

He was waiting fifty yards down the street when the cab arrived, and he told the cabbie to take him straight to the Andreas Bernersstrasse. He aimed to retrace his steps during the first day he'd hit St. Pauli, and maybe try to scare one or two folks in the cheaper dives into talking. He even had a crazy idea he could con them into believing he was an FBI or CIA operative tracking Lattuada, and that they'd be better off singing rather than getting involved in a big-time investigation with its attendant publicity. With the cab waiting, he figured he could always take a powder if the going got tough or he walked into the wrong joint.

The way it happened, none of that was necessary.

He told Alberts to park at the corner of the cul-de-sac
where he and Dagmar Schroeder had escaped from the
alley in back of the Coconut Grove. At the far end was
an arch leading to the court where he had last seen the
mafioso.

Looking into the cul-de-sac was like seeing a favorite
movie the second time around in an all-night house.
There was a panel truck with the doors open and a guy
delivering a rack of clothes to some rag-trade show-
room. There was a snow-white Cadillac with maroon
trim, tinted windows and whitewall tires, waiting with
two wheels up on the sidewalk. And there was Ferucco
Lattuada walking through the archway.

It seemed the most natural thing in the world to see
him there: a reverse shot of the scene Bolan had witnessed before. There were just two alterations to the
screenplay during the rerun. This time Bolan recognized the Cadillac as the car he'd been roughed up in,
and this time he knew who'd be sitting in the back. This
time, too, there was a short extra scene.

Lattuada opened the rear door of the convertible and
got in. The car moved off, turned right and headed south
along the Andreas Bernersstrasse.

"Change of plan," Bolan said to the cabdriver, sliding aside the glass partition separating the front from the
rear. "I want you to follow that car. But for Chrissakes,
do it discreetly. Those are tough characters in there."

"*Jawohl, Meinherr!* All aboard for today's mystery
tour!" The cabbie shoved the gearshift into first, pulled
out in front of a truck and threaded his way through the
traffic in the narrow, congested street in pursuit of
Bolan's quarry.

Bolan glanced out the window as they passed the end
of the alley above the club where he had first seen

Dagmar Schroeder. There was a new sign above the yellow door now. The barker on the sidewalk was wearing an Australian bush hat, and blue lettering beneath the neon lighting announced: The Outback—Come Down Under for a Real Aussie Welcome!

A couple more pieces of the puzzle had fallen into place. If any confirmation was needed of the links between Lattuada, Hansie and the Team, Bolan had it. Secondly the events of that afternoon when the Coconut Grove had been wrecked were now a little clearer.

Lattuada might well have done the same thing that day, too. He would have walked through the arch, climbed into the Cadillac and sat there waiting... for what? For Hansie and his goons to report that the job had been done. For Dagmar—his own ex-girlfriend who'd been cheating him on the dope pushing—to be hustled out the rear entry and delivered to him. Nobody seemed to know what was supposed to have happened to her after that, but it wouldn't have been pleasant. It must have shaken them up to see her walking past the car hanging on to the warrior's arm.

Maybe, Bolan thought as the cab circled the park surrounding the domed tower of the Bismarck monument, that was when Lattuada had decided he'd better run a check on Bolan and find out who the hell the man was. Maybe it was then that he'd gotten the bright idea of killing the girl and saddling the interloper with the murder.

There remained the enigma of Charlie Macfarlane's last words to Bolan: if Lattuada wasn't the brains of the organization, who did he take his orders from? Fischer and Wertheim, too, had said the American had been hired to mastermind the Team's operations. Charlie, again, had suggested the motive for Dagmar's murder might have arisen from a meeting with this mysterious Mr. Big on the night she refused to see Bolan. But if her dope connection was already blown wide open, what could they have had to quarrel about?

Heinrich Alberts shadowed the Cadillac skillfully through the Brauerknechtgraben quarter, past the hop market and across the Baumwall bridge to the dock area south of the river. Soon the big car pulled left across a line of trucks and semis, turned into a side street and stopped.

"Don't follow it," Bolan said. "Wait until we see what gives."

Alberts borrowed fifteen feet from a bus stop and cut his engine. Hansie Schiller, the scarred vulture man and two other guys with faces like cesspools crossed the side street and piled down a flight of steps into an areaway. There was some kind of sign over the areaway gate, but from where he was Bolan couldn't decipher the wording. He noticed that Hansie was pulling on a pair of gloves as he walked. Lattuada remained with the driver in the Cadillac.

It was about ten minutes before they reappeared. Two of them were straightening neckties and adjusting jackets as they approached the car. One had a rip in his sleeve. Bolan didn't need a pocket calculator to work out what had happened in that basement.

The Cadillac made a U-turn and continued toward the eastern part of the city. It stopped at Harburg and Meckelfeld and at three different places in Hammerbrook, and then went on via Nettelnberg to Bergedorf. Most times the routine was the same: the car waiting with idling engine, the goons vanishing into sleazy premises for a few minutes, the fast getaway. An ambulance with siren shrilling passed the cab in the opposite direction within a few minutes of the convertible quitting one location.

Twice it was Lattuada himself who crossed the street, alone, returning a few minutes later with a nod and a satisfied smile.

The Executioner didn't need a guide to work that one out, either. The Caddie was evidently on what protection racketeers called a milk run—collecting a rake-off from those already intimidated, Lattuada's job, or making with the muscle to show those who hadn't yet come across the error of their ways.

Alberts knew most of the places, at least by reputation, although they couldn't always park nearby in case Lattuada's driver tumbled. Some of them were neighborhood drinking clubs, others illegal betting shops or clandestine strip palaces.

"These joints in the classier districts," the cabdriver said as they approached the outer suburbs, "are probably undercover gambling dives." He shook his head. "I haven't seen one yet that I'd care to go into myself without an escort of your U.S. Marines."

Bolan nodded. "I wouldn't quarrel with that," he said. But after Bergedorf, with Lattuada still heading out of town, he began to wonder.

This was strictly commuter country, with flowering shrubs in the snow-covered front yards of neat little rows of brick villas. Farther on, there were trees lining the streets, the houses were set back from the roadway with big picture windows full of indoor plants and an occasional shopping mall sprawled over a sizable acreage.

What the hell was the mobster doing out here in the stockbroker belt?

Soon they were in a stretch of open country with black stubble sticking up through the snow and crows speckling the pale sky above ridges of close-packed pines. The clouds were blowing away, and the odor of woodsmoke was sucked into the cab through the heating system.

As the traffic flow thinned out, shadowing the Cadillac became increasingly difficult. Alberts was a quarter mile behind, and he was lucky to catch the turn-off when the convertible swung suddenly into a gravel driveway between white gates.

"There's a gas station around the corner," he said, "and I need to fill up. Maybe you'd like to walk back and check the place out while I do that?"

Bolan nodded. He got out of the taxi. It was good to stretch his legs, anyway. Two hundred yards down the road there was a gap in the trees, and he could see on a rise to the south a row of stables with a clock tower in back of a substantial redbrick building with outhouse wings flanking a three-story central block. The Cadillac was parked between a Range Rover, a Chevrolet Blazer and two smaller cars. Five men were walking slowly toward a portico with white pillars.

"What's that place?" Bolan casually asked the grease monkey fueling the cab when he returned to the forecourt. "Some kind of hotel?"

"General Hunziger's?" He shrugged. "New people. Moved in a couple of weeks ago. They sold the horses when they took over from the general. They say it's going to be some kind of country club." He spit on the ground and shook his head. "More like a whorehouse if you ask me. I've seen some of the broads they got in there!" The kid shook invisible drops of water from the tips of his fingers.

"Maybe they'll keep them in the stables," Alberts jested.

"Some riding school!" the kid said.

Bolan was intrigued. It looked as if Lattuada was broadening his activities to include classier material. Since Hunziger's place had just changed hands, and since Lattuada himself had gone in as well as the four thugs, this was probably an exploratory visit, just a softening-up operation before the screws were turned. He wondered where the next stop would be.

It was no more than three miles away, and they almost missed it. Alberts had been watching for the Caddie, and when it left the redbrick house, he was already moving, several hundred yards down the highway before it turned through the white gates.

He stayed ahead as the road twisted through a shallow valley and then climbed uphill again through pine-woods laced blackly against a clear sky in the east. They sped along the foot of an embankment, where an access road spiraled up to a small railroad station. "Aumühle," the cabdriver said. "It's the S-Bahn terminus, though the tracks run right on past the East German frontier. Nights, there are freight trains that go all the way to Berlin."

Opposite the embankment the ground fell away beneath immensely tall cedars to a lake surrounded by dense woods. "The Mühlenteich," Alberts said. "It's all public property now, but until the Nazi years it was part of the Bismarck estate. The property goes almost up to the damn Baltic! There's two thousand acres of forest around that lake, with wild boar and deer, even wolves, some say, prowling around among the trees. In the summertime folks come out here from the city for the fishing and boating."

Bolan peered out the taxi window. The lake was picturesque, about half a mile long, fringed with willows at the narrow end. There was a weir where it widened out, and an old mill that had been turned into a hotel-restaurant. Two more sizable buildings had been constructed between the road and the water's edge—a stone block with steep gables and a long, low, half-timbered place surrounded by a boardwalk.

"That's the Fischerhaus," Alberts said. "Built by the Bismarcks in 1760. Place is a hotel, too, now, though it's open only in the summer months. So's the third one. Shit!" He stood on the brakes, and the old Mercedes slewed to a halt half across the road.

Bolan was thrown forward. "What gives?" he asked, straightening himself.

Alberts was staring into his rearview mirror. "Fucking Caddie's disappeared!"

Bolan twisted around and looked out the rear window. The roadway behind them was empty.

"Must have gone down that dirt road that leads past the millhouse," Alberts said, "and then over the bridge crossing the weir. Must have. There's no other road he could have taken."

"Where does the dirt road go?" Bolan asked.

"On into the woods. It's just a forest trail really. Peters out half a mile on in a glade where people picnic in good weather. Come to think of it, I heard they were building a fourth hotel someplace out there."

"That'll be it," Bolan said. "Can we follow them?"

"Be a dead giveaway," Alberts said. "I mean, it's not a through road. It doesn't go anyplace. I'm real sorry. My fault."

"It happens," the warrior said.

"Tell you what, though. There's a forest clearing beyond the far end of the lake. I could pull the taxi in there and park. Then maybe you could cut across through the woods until you hit the trail and take it from there on foot.''

"Let's do it," the Executioner said.

It wasn't easy going. A marsh with man-high reeds fed water into the lake behind the willow screen, and when that had been skirted Bolan found that steep banks, rock outcrops and sudden hollows in the forest floor made it tough holding a fixed direction beneath the closely packed trees. It was a good half hour before he hit the trail leading from the old mill.

Two hundred yards farther on, around a sharp curve, he saw a movie still of Porsches, Alfa Romeos, Bentleys and customized Mercedes convertibles parked on a gravel sweep in front of a low white stucco building. The place was designed around three sides of a central patio with a pool, springboards, diving towers and summer garden furniture stacked under a tarp. The Cadillac was outside the glassed-in main entrance.

Advancing cautiously, Bolan saw that the driver was still at the wheel. He stepped quickly back in among the trees. He couldn't risk being seen here at this time, at least not until he had checked out the reasons for Lattuada's visit.

Formal gardens had been landscaped around the building, and it was some time before the warrior worked his way around to a position on the far side of the glade where the white stucco walls hid him from the guy in the Cadillac. The patio pool was iced over and there were still traces of snow on the tarpaulin and along the roof of an outbuilding behind the main block. But the ground here was clear and Bolan was able to tread noiselessly, swift as a shadow from tree to tree on the deep carpet of pine needles.

By the time he reached a vantage point with enough cover to satisfy him, he guessed from the slamming doors and the sound of gunned engines that most of the parked cars had taken off. He had heard, too, over the soughing of the cold wind among the branches overhead what could have been raised voices, a hubbub of angry exchanges.

He raised his head above the screen of bushes where he was crouched. There was nobody in sight. The windows on this side of the clubhouse were shuttered. Checking that the Beretta slid easily in its shoulder rig, he bent double and ran between leafless raspberry canes and a row of bean sticks toward the building.

There was a final stretch of lawn to be crossed, a rose garden spined with heavily pruned bushes, and then he was flattened against the wall beneath the eaves. He sidled toward the entrance. As he approached the corner, doors slammed again and he heard the deep, thrumming exhaust note of a multicylinder engine. He peered around. The Cadillac was accelerating away toward the mill.

Bolan shrugged. What the hell. He hadn't a hope of getting back on their trail now. By the time he regained Alberts's cab, and the cabdriver backed up and turned onto the highway, the Team could be in the outskirts of the city.

He walked openly around a gable end and crossed the deserted patio. It would soon be dusk. Crows were cawing among the treetops, and there was a smell of woodsmoke in the air once more. Peaceful country scene, Bolan thought. Time for a quiet drink by the evening fireside. Sure.

"Call the police, Helmut," a woman's voice said angrily. "Who the hell do they think they are? Frightening away customers, acting like—"

"Ah, cut it out, Helga," a man interrupted. "What's the use? You know as well as I do..."

Bolan looked along the inner facade of the clubhouse. French windows stood ajar just beyond the pool. He crept toward them.

"That fucking fairy!" the woman shrilled. "That bitch! If I could get my hands—"

"Don't make yourself silly, sweetheart. What could the cops do? What evidence do we have? They could put us out of business—" fingers snapped "—like that, and you know it. All they have to do is sneak in some teenage hophead, some underage kid from that snob private school at Reinbek who takes a drink, and then tip off the law... and our license is gone."

"Yes, but—"

"All they have to do is stage a few drunken brawls and rough up a couple of clients and, look, no customers! All they have to do in these woods is wait for the wind and start a little fire, and there's our capital gone up in smoke. Apart from that, you know as well as I do that no place like this is run strictly on the level. There's the girls, the bedrooms, the three sets of books. They could easily find—"

Bolan pushed open the French windows and stepped through. "Pardon me."

He was in a small oak-beamed bar with paneled alcoves and a wall-to-wall red carpet. A woman of about thirty-five with short platinum-blond hair and a lot of makeup was standing by an overturned chair holding the torn edges of a silk blouse together. Behind her a thick-set man with a heavy mustache was leaning over the bar as if he had a bellyache. Maybe he had at that, because when he raised his head to stare at the intruder, Bolan saw that there was dirt on his face and all down the front of his suit and shirt. His lips were split and one of his eyes was almost closed. "Who the hell are you?" he demanded thickly. "What do you want here?"

Bolan had an answer ready. The previous dialogue had given him a lead, and it would explain his American-accented German. "Forgive me for bursting in," he said in what he hoped was a scholarly voice. "I teach languages at the school in Reinbek. Two of our lads are temporarily missing, just playing hooky, most likely, but they were seen coming this way. I just thought I'd ask if you'd seen—"

"For God's sake!" the woman cut in. "We have enough troubles of our own without running a bureau for missing brats!"

"Easy, Helga," the man said. "Watch it now." And then, turning to the warrior, he said, "Naturally, sir, we discourage any member of the school from coming here. If any boy did come, we'd refuse to serve him and ask him to leave. But, in fact, none have so far, and I certainly haven't set eyes on any today."

"I didn't really think you had," Bolan said truthfully. "But I figured it might be worth asking. If you *should*, perhaps you would be good enough to telephone the director at Reinbek?"

"Sure," the man said. "Of course."

Bolan murmured his thanks and backed out. He'd seen and heard all he needed to. As he walked away, he heard the woman say, "I still think we should call the police."

And the man answer, "Forget it. Look, just forget it, will you?"

Since the Cadillac and its occupants were gone, there was nothing to stop Bolan taking the dirt road back to the mill and then walking along the highway until he reached the forest clearing where the cab was parked.

It took him five minutes to reach the bridge over the weir. Lights showed through the windows of the old millhouse, where tailcoated waiters were setting silver for the evening meal. The sky was still clear, but it would soon be dark.

He walked past the Fischerhaus and the hotel beyond it. There was no sign of the Caddie. Perhaps they had already been visited. Or maybe they had nothing to hide, were too "respectable" to make worthwhile targets.

Beyond the lake Bolan quit the highway to make a diagonal cut through the wood to intersect the clearing. He was fifty yards along a narrow trail when the shotgun blast sent pellets screaming through the leaves just above his head.

There was game in the forest, and dusk was open season for bird hunters, but the Executioner wasn't taking any chances. It *might* have been a shot from an inexperienced, or irresponsible, gun. But in the circumstances...

He was flat on his face on the forest floor, the Beretta cocked in his right hand, before the crows preparing to roost in the treetops had flapped angrily into the sky.

A second shot decided him. The charge stripped leaves from the evergreen bushes bordering the trail where he had been only an instant before. There could be no doubt: someone was gunning for him right here in these woods.

Supporting himself on his elbows, he glanced swiftly around. The trail ran for another fifty yards before it veered away past the huge bole of an ancient oak. The

evergreens grew thickly on either side, although they
seemed to be spaced farther apart near the old tree. The
shots—from the deafening quality of the reports, Bolan
figured they must have been fired no more than twenty
or thirty yards away—originated somewhere between the
trail and the highway. Basically there was only one way
to go.

Still facedown, he edged back beneath the bushes on
the far side of the trail from the highway. Behind them
a thick undergrowth overlay the pine-needle carpet, and
after that the ground dipped toward the reeds and the
marsh. He was worming his way through the undergrowth when the shotgun roared for the third time—
nearer, he guessed, though the gunner was wide of the
mark.

He heard the swish of branches, the rustle of leaves,
but he could see nothing through the tangle of stalks
surrounding him and the green canopy above. Crablike, he tried to hurry toward the reeds.

Once again the shotgun blast made his ears ring. And
then there were two more reports, sharper, dryer cracks,
more like the amplified snapping of a twig. Medium-
bore handguns, probably .32 caliber.

And they came from two different places.

So there were at least three killers hunting him in the
woods.

Two of the handgun slugs zeroed in uncomfortably
close, one plowing into the earth only inches from his
nose, the other zipping through leaves near his gun hand.
The marksmen must be sighting on branches that Bolan
couldn't help stirring as he moved, and then firing just
below. He shoved himself backward as hard as he could,
levering with his elbows on the iron-hard ground until

the surface sank beneath him and he slid feet first into the reeds.

At that moment there was a concerted volley of shots, and the reeds, swayed, nipped, scythed down by the deathstream, died all around him. The handguns, he could tell now, were automatics, and he was almost certain there were more than two of them, apart from the original shotgun guy.

Icy cold gripped Bolan's ankles. His feet were immersed in water. He half turned, eyes straining through the twilight to catch a glimpse of a moving figure between the tossing stalks.

Nothing.

But the movement set the tufted tops of bull rushes nodding. Both barrels of the shotgun and three-shot burst from the automatics homed in on the motion. Lead peppered the water between the stems. Bolan flattened himself farther still and wriggled back until the clammy embrace was around his waist.

His toes gouged the muddy floor of the marsh, and touched something solid, hard, immovable. Twisting his head, he looked over his shoulder. It was then that he saw, bulked against the sky, the unmistakable silhouette of a dory—a small, flat-bottomed boat that had been run aground among the reeds. It was the hull of this that his foot had run up against.

Gasping with the cold, Bolan plunged thigh-deep into the marsh water, shoving the dory out into the channel with all his strength. More gunshots pockmarked the surface of the water, and wood splintered as the boat's timbers were savaged.

But now he could see the bright flashes against the somber mass of trees. And he had been right—there were four of them. One of the handguns was fifteen feet above ground, wedged into the fork of a gnarled oak.

Bolan swung the dory around once it was fully floating so that it was between him and the hunters. The Beretta, which he had reholstered when his feet reached the water, was once more in his hand.

This time he drew their fire deliberately, feinting an effort to hoist himself up over the gunwale and into the boat. He had dropped back and forced his way through the water to the stern when the guns blazed again.

And this time, his sight line already vectored on the oak, he lined up on the muzzle-flashes as the sniper triggered a long burst and choked death from his own autoloader. He heard a strangled cry over the reverberations of the cannonade, then the snapping of a branch and a crashing of leaves as a heavy body plunged into the bushes below.

The dory was being carried away toward the main channel that fed into the lake. Bolan gripped the stern post and allowed himself to be towed after it. When he could no longer touch the bottom with his foot, he hauled himself up and over into the boat. But there was still enough light for his pursuers to oversee the maneuver, even though the dory was caught at that moment in an eddy and twirled out of sight behind another reed bank.

Bolan heard the rasp and crackle of orders transmitted through the UHF transceiver. The guy with the shotgun, who seemed to be the boss, was telling someone to go down to the willow screen where the marsh drained into the lake, for that was where the dory had to go, too. There were no oars, no pole, and Bolan's arm, paddling over the side, wasn't forceful enough to counter the current.

The shotgunner himself, together with the remaining hood, was advancing toward the reeds. The Executioner could hear the suck and squish of their feet on the marshy ground as they thrust their way between the rattling stems in an attempt to sight the boat veering from channel to channel between islanded clumps of the tufted rushes.

He wondered who the hell they were. There had been no sign of Lattuada's Caddie. Had they left an outrider who had somehow gotten onto the warrior's trail? It didn't seem likely. He would stake all he had on the fact that nobody had seen him approach the clubhouse. He didn't think the goons in the Caddie knew they had been followed. That left the possibility that someone had seen him leave the building, someone who knew who he was . . . and feared him.

So, again, who? The voice on the transceiver was nothing like Hansie's. But he reckoned there had to be a connection. Nothing made sense otherwise. It baffled him just the same, the way the scenario had developed. Because they couldn't possibly have known . . .

The current speeded up; the reed banks closed in on either side. The uneven strip of pale sky above was definitely darkening now. But the spiderweb of bare willow branches at the entrance to the lake was still silhouetted at the far end of the channel, and it was advancing fast. Beyond that, Bolan would be as much of a sitting duck as the waterfowl whose squawks he could hear as they settled down for the night.

Scanning the close-packed vegetation, he saw a furtive movement among the reeds on his left. At once the Beretta barked. A 9 mm messenger of death smashed through the stems. He fired again. There was threshing ten or fifteen yards away among the marsh grasses. A hoarse voice cried out, "Bastard winged me! Fucked up my right arm!"

"Use the left," the voice from the transceiver grated. "We don't leave here until the bastard is blown away."

Light suddenly flared above the fringed reed heads, a yellow glow that was transformed into a double shaft that swept across the wood on the far side of the marsh. Someone was maneuvering an automobile among the reeds.

Were the killers calling up reinforcements?

Bolan tensed, every nerve quivering, his eyes squinting through the thickening dusk, alert for the smallest movement as the muzzle of the Beretta traced an imaginary sightline along the reed bank. Now he could hear the grinding of gears, a laboring engine. A second pair of headlight beams scoured the darkness below the trees. Bolan lay flat along the dory's duckboards.

Through the stems he saw a brighter light moving. A spotlight, perhaps mounted on one of the cars, was quartering the marsh. He gritted his teeth. Within the next few minutes, things were going to get kind of rugged.

They did, but not the way he expected.

A sudden fusillade, shocking in its ferocity—a rasping, tearing, earsplitting barrage that stunned the senses—ripped apart the dusk. Bolan jerked upright. Submachine guns—three, if not more!

A second deadly volley hammered his ears. One of the handguns fired a burst. The shotgun blasted twice.

He didn't get it. None of that lethal hail was coming his way. The dory floated serenely toward the lake. At the edge of the marsh, men were shouting. The SMGs spit fire a third time. He heard a heavy splash. The voice from the transceiver was killed in midsentence. There was a massive rustle of wings, a flapping along the surface of the water as all the birds on the lake took off. A three-shot burst from the handgun was drowned by the clamor of a single SMG. Then there was silence.

After the flickering incandescence of muzzle-flashes, the approaching darkness seemed denser than ever. Bolan saw the dim tracery of willow branches pass overhead. Turning slowly, the flat-bottomed boat drifted into a stretch of open water. In the distance, the lights of the millhouse restaurant mirrored themselves on the leaden surface of the lake. Nobody opened fire on the Executioner.

There could only be one explanation. The history of the Lübeck operation was repeating itself: one gang of killers was being jumped by another.

Yeah, but there was one big difference: in the Baltic port there had been a million-dollar prize of smuggled narcotics. And here? No prizes, unless the Executioner himself was of value to the second group, alive rather than dead.

The dory eddied toward the lakeshore and grounded gently in a grassy inlet behind the hotel next to the Fischerhaus. Bolan shivered. Frost had already rimed the blades of grass. He rose upright and was preparing to jump ashore when a tall, dark figure materialized from a clump of bushes ten feet away. Bolan's hand streaked toward his shoulder rig.

"Don't shoot. I'm unarmed," a voice said quietly.

The voice carried conviction. Bolan believed it. When the owner of the voice held out a hand, he grasped it and leaped from the dory to the grass. He saw with astonishment that the man standing before him in the gloom was the East German civilian who was supposed to have been the consignee for the doctored goatskins in Lübeck.

"No questions," the man said before the warrior could voice his surprise. "You have become involved, Herr Belasko, in something that doesn't concern you. I bear you no ill will, but I have to warn you that this tolerance cannot indefinitely be extended if you persist in your...investigations."

"Just give me a lead," Bolan said. "Or at least satisfy one point that's bugging me. How come you—"

"No leads," the East German interrupted firmly. "Be content with your good fortune. The persons hoping to kill you have all been...eliminated."

"So thanks. But why should they, I mean, why should you—"

"You're soaking wet, Herr Belasko. And no doubt quite cold," the East German said. "I have a car, two in fact, available. Allow my driver to take you a few hundred yards along the highway and into the woods, where I understand you have a taxi waiting...."

CHAPTER TWENTY

"My *God*, Mike!" Zuta exclaimed. "What happened? Where have you been? I've been back for hours, out of my skull because I was afraid the police had you. Nobody even saw you leave, for heaven's sake!"

"I'm sorry, Zuta," Bolan apologized. "But I had to get out."

"You *know* I think you should stay here," Zuta said tartly. "At least for the moment. It's not safe for you to be around, and it's certainly not safe for you to go out through the club when there are clients there. You never know who might see you. What got into you, Belasko? Where did you go?"

"I went to Aumühle."

"Aumühle!" She stared at him. "But that's out in the country. Why did you go there?"

"For just that reason, because it *is* out in the country, at the end of the S-Bahn line. That way nobody could possibly recognize me. Besides, I wanted to take a walk." He was suddenly sore. He didn't like being nagged as if he were a hooky-playing schoolboy.

At first he had intended to give Zuta a rundown on the whole trip, to ask her opinion on the alternatives suggested by the sinister events of the afternoon, but her own irritation made him decide to clam up and stall.

He'd been eager to trace Lattuada, to complete the puzzle, to solve the mystery from the comfort of a safehouse, trying to work it out on the basis of intel fed to him by a woman, a woman he'd allowed to talk him out of action because it might be dangerous!

Danger was his business; danger was his life.

So where was the one-man wave of destruction whose implacable campaign of retribution against evil had earned him the title of the Executioner?

It was in Aumühle—where the peril had actually stimulated him—that the question had finally posed itself, that he had finally gotten wise to the fact that a week, a whole goddamn week, of inactivity hadn't fazed him one little bit!

It bugged the hell out of him. Face it, the only battles he had fought in the past few days had been in the sack. That wasn't Mack Bolan's style.

As soon as Zuta left, he crept downstairs intending to sneak out through the club entrance while the waiters were setting up for lunch. But this time the padded doors with their porthole windows were locked, and he couldn't get through from the apartment to the club.

That threw him some. They hadn't been before. Then he saw the waiter who normally served food in the apartment, the one with the face like a side of spoiled beef. He knocked on the glass to attract the guy's attention and mimed that he wanted out.

The waiter shook his head and wagged a negative finger. Bolan rapped again and gestured authoritatively. "I have to go out for a few minutes," he called out when the man was close to the window. "Do you mind unlocking these doors?"

The ape shook his big head again. "Miss Zuta says it isn't safe for you to leave today. Better you should stay in the apartment, okay?"

"I'd like to go down the road to buy some cigarettes."

"I'll get you some cigarettes from the bar. What brand do you want?"

Two misses and one to go. "Also," Bolan said, "I have to hit the post office."

"I'll send a boy with the message."

The warrior shrugged his shoulders. He went back upstairs. Short of breaking down the doors, there was nothing he could do. Even then the gorilla in the white jacket might consider it his duty to stop him. In any case, Bolan didn't know how wise the waiter was to his own situation, and he didn't want to screw things up for Zuta. She'd done a lot, even if she was overdoing the baby-sitting bit.

Mulling over the events of the past few days just made Bolan angrier. Baby-sitting, hell! More like protective custody. Zuta the jailer, he thought. It was time to break out.

He started to think. These were old houses. There had to be a servants' stairway somewhere in back. Perhaps it had been blocked off from the apartment and the accountants' floor when the transformation was made. He figured it was worth climbing up to the attic floor to check. Leaving the apartment, he walked up instead of down.

It was some kind of public holiday, so the accounting floor below was in darkness. As Zuta had said, the topmost level was devoted to storage and supplies—stacked tables and chairs, an upright piano covered by a sheet, two obsolete refrigerators, cartons of canned food and cases of liquor. There was a back staircase, too. He found out that it bypassed the accounting department, the apartment, even the club, and led straight to the kitchen in the basement. But there was no point in the Executioner playing Santa Claus among the chafing dishes; he'd still have to surface in the club to get to the street.

What the hell, he thought. Maybe he would just wait until Zuta returned. He didn't want to implicate her by drawing attention to himself. He didn't want Zuta to end up like Dagmar.

He was on his way back up to the apartment when his foot kicked something on one of the steps. He stooped to pick it up. In the dim light filtering through a frosted window that most likely looked on an air shaft, he saw that the object was a matchbook, the sort of thing given away to advertise hotels, bars and restaurants. Then, straightening, he noticed for the first time a narrow door on one of the stairway's half landings.

It was painted the same color as the wall, flush-fitting, with a latch and mortise lock. At one side of the door frame a key hung on a nail.

Bolan was curious. He unhooked the key and pushed it into the lock. It turned easily. He opened the door and saw a long passageway. Walking along it, he struck a match now and then to light the way. There were no doors and no windows, but after around fifty feet there was a right-angle turn. He felt his way along a farther doorless and windowless section, longer than the first, and found himself at the top of a steep flight of stairs. At the foot of this was an unlocked door. He opened it, and discovered he had walked into a broom closet.

It seemed a long way to come just to keep the club's storerooms swept. He struck another match. Sure enough—brooms, mops, an ancient Hoover, shelves of polish and cleaning fluid, a galvanized pail. Bolan frowned.

Striking another match, he saw another flush-fitting door at right angles to the stairway. He opened this and stepped into the hallway of a comfortably furnished small house. Through an arch he could see chocolate easy chairs on buff broadloom, with an expensive component stereo in a mahogany cabinet against one ivory wall.

Someone's house? Frowning again, he turned and walked into a kitchen that was as bare and sterile and unused as a shot glass in a Calvinist church vestry. Beyond the virgin refrigerator, one more door opened on three steps that led down into a closed garage. In the gloom the dim shape of a large, long automobile filled most of the floor space. He felt for a light switch, found none and lit a final match from the violated book.

For the first time the gold words printed on the shiny black laminated matchbook cover registered with him: Die Mühlenteich—The Millpond. Dining. Dancing. Swimming.

He struck another match and looked at the parked car. It was an ivory Cadillac with whitewall tires, tinted windows and maroon trim. The number on the license plate was HH777-CDE.

CHAPTER TWENTY-ONE

Bolan read the score this way. Zuta Krohn ran an expensive club patronized by bad as well as good guys, and nobody was putting the bite on her for protection. Other club owners, and folks who ran dives of various kinds, in and out of Hamburg, from the smartest to the cheapest, were paying through the nose to an organized gang led by Hansie Schiller and masterminded by Ferucco Lattuada. These two paragons of the consumer society, accompanied at times by certain lieutenants, visited their victims in a large and distinctive automobile. The last of these trips had been to the Mühlenteich Club at Aumühle.

Zuta Krohn lived in an apartment above her club, but she also had a small house nearby. The two were joined by a passageway that, if it wasn't secret, was at least concealed. In that corridor he had found a matchbook emblazoned with the name of the Mühlenteich Club. And at that club he had seen the car that was now in Zuta's garage, the car in which he himself had once been taken for a ride.

Bolan figured the Cadillac belonged to Zuta, and she had made the trip to Aumühle with the others, remaining hidden by the tinted windows except at the Mühlenteich, where Bolan hadn't been watching, anyway.

He remembered the words of the angry blonde. *That fucking fairy! That bitch! If I could get my hands...*

He'd thought the second epithet, like the first, referred to Hansie Schiller, the way gays are sometimes characterized as feminine. But he'd been mistaken. The blonde had been talking about two separate people.

Inescapable conclusion: the mysterious big noise, the boss to whom Lattuada and Hansie were answerable, the brains behind the racket, was Zuta.

She was also the woman who'd taken him in and saved him from the cops, the "legman" who'd supplied him with all the underworld gossip, his protector from Hansie and his playmate of a thousand faces.

How come? How could all that stack up?

Bolan left the garage and went back to the house's living room. He sank into one of the chocolate chairs and tried to straighten out his thoughts.

If Zuta was the boss, then apart from hiring Lattuada and planning the racket that put the whole of the Hamburg underworld in her hands, she must also have been the one who had decided Bolan's investigations were an embarrassment, the kind soul who'd ordered the Dagmar Schroeder killing and fixed the frame that had saddled him with it.

It must have been Zuta who had put the word around St. Pauli that the warrior was to be brought in after he had escaped from the courthouse. Zuta who had briefed Hugo to finger him for Hansie. Zuta who had ordered the day-and-night watch on the Shangri-la. And probably Zuta who had persuaded Arvell Asticot to doublecross, with Lattuada's help, the East German buying the narcotics.

So why did she take in Bolan like a long lost brother when he ran into her during his third escape...from Wertheim? Why didn't she go through with her original plans and hand him over either to Hansie or to the law?

Yeah, why?

He heard himself asking the same kind of questions about Dagmar. And in his memory he could hear Charlie Macfarlane's answer. *People aren't simple. This was a complicated girl . . . a bit of a nympho.*

Could this be the answer with Zuta, too? It sounded screwy, but he reckoned it was possible. Was she telling the truth that time when she'd taken him in. Had she decided on the spur of the moment to keep him under wraps? Because she, too, was "a bit of a nympho," because she liked tall, lean men, and because she hadn't, up to then, actually set eyes on the man she was hunting?

In a crazy way it figured—pride in the all-around success of the Coliseum, the two houses linked by a secret passage, the oversize American automobile, the female gang boss routine, the continuous role playing in and out of bed. Didn't it all add up, quite simply, to an old-fashioned power complex? And if it did, what could boost that kind of ego more than a captive lover whose future, even if he didn't know it, lay completely in her hands?

All Bolan knew for sure at the moment was that Zuta was a dangerous lady who could decide at any time that his future was short.

He got to his feet. Perhaps a search was in order. Carefully he investigated every nook and cranny of the house. The drawers and closets in the kitchen were empty. A buffet in a small dining room was equally bare. Likewise with the bathroom. Before trying the living room, he checked the car in the garage. But all he found there was stale cigar smoke.

Bolan suddenly remembered that there was a surprising lack of papers or stationery in the apartment above the club. But a smart businesswoman like Zuta must check out her accounts someplace—her personal accounts, that is, not the stuff for the auditors that was processed between the apartment and the club.

It was clear now that half the time she was supposed to be purchasing supplies for the club, she was, in fact, riding around in the Cadillac with Hansie and selected members of the Team, waiting in the car while they pulled their strong-arm stuff. Maybe she spent the other half here in the house. Or the house she'd been standing in front of when he'd first run into her. Whose house had that been, anyway? Hers, too? Or maybe Lattuada's? He had to live somewhere. That made sense. Maybe she'd been waiting for the Yank. Whatever the case, her papers had to be someplace.

A smart woman like Zuta would have a safe somewhere. He still had the living room to check. On one wall in that room he noticed a framed painting of a bank safe. He removed the painting. Sure enough, a wall safe! Next problem: how to open it? He could blow it if he had some plastique. But, no, that would be a dead giveaway, anyway, and he didn't want to tip his hand just yet. Along with other talents, Bolan had a pretty fair knowledge of safecracking. It took him a while but, with a lot of sweat and patience, he finally got the thing open.

Inside, he found ledgers, day books, canceled checks, invoices, bank statements, stock certificates, insurance policies, bundles of letters and sheaves of typewritten documents. He picked out a couple of typescripts at random. One was a list of names, addresses, occupations and estimated incomes. He didn't recognize any of the names, possible "subscribers" to something. Possibles, anyway. The second document was similar, but there were fewer names, and after the estimated income of each was written in ink the name of a club, tavern, café, dive or whatever, followed by a thumbnail sketch of the person's tastes, amusements, spending habits and vices, with notes on particular weaknesses, tax evasions, dubious contacts, liaisons, undercover activities and the like. Bolan didn't need a crystal ball to figure out the score now.

The outrage, the self-reproach and the anger hadn't crystallized yet. But he was pretty certain he had usable material here, material that he might be able to turn to his advantage, stuff he could use to link the Schroeder killing to Zuta and get him out of the mess he was in.

Given the power complex he had imagined, and given the kind of person exercising it and the means employed, wouldn't it be true to form for such a person to celebrate, indeed, to perpetuate, her cleverness? Wouldn't someone like Zuta want folks to see how smart she was? Wouldn't such a person want to write it all down, just for the record? And in what form would such a lesson for posterity be?

By this time Bolan had sifted through most of the safe's contents. Among the stacks of paperwork, he came up with the answer physically before the word formed in his mind. Staring at him in the back of the safe was a thick diary, gold-tooled, gilt-edged and closed with a hasp and lock linking the front and back covers across the pages.

Was the book blank, or packed with damaging confessions? He was wondering how he could tease open the lock without leaving telltale marks when he heard the slamming of a door and Hansie Schiller's characteristic, lisping voice.

He jumped for the window. Damn, the torpedo was paying off a cab at the end of the walkway and heading for the front door! Bolan didn't know what the world record was for replacing a diary, locking a safe and racing to a broom closet, but he reckoned he must have clipped three-tenths of a second off it that day before he heard the hood's key grating in the lock.

He was still out of breath when he arrived a couple of minutes later at the bottom of the stairway leading from the apartment to the club and thumped the portholes to attract the attention of the gorilla waiter. "I changed my mind," he panted when the guy came to the doors. "Send me up a large Scotch from the bar, okay?"

It was while he was downing the whisky, and examining the apartment more carefully now that he knew just who its owner was—that he solved one of the puzzles that bothered him the most. He found something to explain the inexplicable: his own lack of dynamism and initiative during the past week.

It was in a jumble of lipsticks, eyeliners and mascara pots beneath the lid of a black japanned box that Zuta used for her makeup—a tiny plastic-capped glass vial half full of small pink-and-white capsules. He looked at the label. A trade name in German. But he saw from the formula that the capsules contained one of the CNS-depressant drugs, a benzodiazepine derivative. And this would, he knew, have the effect of minimizing anxiety, fear, tension and any sense of urgency, without diminishing sexual interest or drive. If Zuta had been secretly feeding him the stuff, it would account for his recent lethargy, and his compensating energy in the sack.

And it must be secret, too, hidden away in that makeup box. If the drug was for her own use, surely it would be in the medicine cabinet along with everything else.

The vial was half-empty. He replaced it carefully and closed the box. When his lunch was sent up later, he dumped the whole lot into the john, wine included, and flushed it away. It was unlikely that the kitchen personnel would be in on the deal, but he wasn't taking any more chances.

Once the dishes had gone, he went back downstairs to the porthole doors. They were still locked. The bar was crowded, and there were still a few tables occupied by late lunchers. He had to break out. Surely the gorilla waiter wouldn't dare resort to strong-arm tactics in front of patrons. What excuse could he give? The idiot son escaped from the attic?

Considering how dumb he'd been, Bolan thought bitterly, he wouldn't be far wrong at that! Then, through the window, he saw Hansie drinking at the far end of the bar with a kid of about twenty who looked like the son of King Kong. All they'd have to do, even if the boy was just Hansie's latest piece of rough trade, would be to follow him out into the street and take him there. Because the hood would know for sure that Zuta was keeping the warrior upstairs, was probably laughing up his sleeve about it.

Bolan decided that since he was being used as a pawn in the sultry gang boss's private chess game, he'd take the pawn's way out just for now and move one square back. He returned to the secret passageway and let himself out the garage window of the house at the far end.

He made two calls from the first phone booth he saw. One was to call up Heinrich Alberts and his taxi. The second was to Freddie Leonhardt.

The newsman was surprised to hear Bolan's voice. "My dear old boy," he spluttered, "I didn't, that is to say, I never thought I'd be, I mean, I imagined you were still, uh, on the run."

"It's no thanks to you that I'm not, you double-crossing bastard," Bolan said. He paused, then added, "I guess you contacted the Windy City and discovered I really am Mike Belasko?"

"Oh, God, yes. I'm *frightfully* sorry about that. Really I am." Leonhardt sounded confused. "Ghastly trick to play on a fellow, what. I mean, when I say trick, well, the fact is those policemen were awfully persuasive, and—" He cleared his throat, suddenly aware that the weight of excuses was going to push him deeper into the shit.

"Okay," Bolan cut in. "Okay. I know the way cops can feed you ideas and get the right answers to loaded questions. Forget it. There are more important things to talk about. You can make up for it, in any case, if you have a half hour to spare. Do you?"

"Well, I, uh, yes, of course, old boy. I...what can I do for you?"

"Two things. One, get over to the U.S. consulate in the Harvesterhuder Weg, the annex that is, not the main consulate in the Alsterufer. How you do it, I leave to you, but I want you to contact the cipher clerk there and collect a printout I'm expecting from Washington. I can't go myself thanks to the situation I'm in. Plus I want you to ask the guy to send a service message and then wait for the answer." Bolan dictated the message.

"Got it," Leonhardt said. "And the second thing?"

"Do you believe I killed that girl?"

"My dear chap! No, no, certainly not. Good God, no!"

"Thousands wouldn't believe you, but I do. I guess I have to. Okay, call up Fischer, the cop in charge of the murder investigation, the guy you spoke to before, and tell him to expect a message of some kind from me within the next couple of days. Tell him it'll settle the question of who really did murder Dagmar Schroeder, and that it won't be a hoax. It really will be from me. Will you do that?"

"Of course, old boy. Where are you calling from? Can I call you back?"

"With your record," Bolan said, "do you imagine I'd tell?"

"Yes, but the answer to your message—how shall *I* tell *you*?"

"Don't call me," the Executioner said. "I'll call you."

He hung up and pushed his way out of the phone booth. Alberts's cab was waiting twenty yards down the street.

BOLAN HIT PAY DIRT at the second St. Pauli tavern he visited. He was sitting on a stool up against a mahogany-and-frosted-glass partition dividing the bar into two separate rooms, nursing a beer and keeping his ears open. He paid no attention to the bulky shadow on the far side of the art nouveau curlicues festooning the glass until he heard the voice that went with it.

"Gotta make it to those two dumps at Aumühle this afternoon. The boss figures the second creep, the one with the blonde, may shell out. But we'll have to knock around the character at the cathouse a sight more before he comes across." Then there was a hoarse chuckle.

The baritone growl with the hint of a lisp on the sibilants could only belong to Hansie Schiller. And if Bolan thought he'd hit the mother lode with that statement, the reply showed him the genuine nuggets shining in the bottom of the pan.

"Yeah," the second voice said. "I guess it'd be smart to put the arm on the guy PDQ. The follow-through is what counts when folks open up a territory, see. Cut the time in half again for the next approach, then make with the muscle, huh?''

Bolan smiled. And that was the inimitable Ferucco Lattuada.

It was only a confirmation of what the Executioner knew already, but he needed that confirmation. He had to have proof that his deductions were correct before he took the next step. The warrior shifted his position and stared over the barkeep's shoulder.

There was a mirror behind the tumblers and bottles ranged on the shelves. The bartender was filling a shot glass with schnapps from a dispenser inverted in front of those shelves; a waitress was pulling the flowered china handles of a draft tap. Between them Bolan caught a slanted, cubist view of the drinkers on the far side of the partition—Lattuada's lean, blue-jowled face tilted across a bottle of Glenfiddich and a crystal decanter of crème de menthe; Hansie's shallow hat crowning a tall German beer stein decorated with a colorful hunting scene.

"I gotta meet with the Wallmann mob in Bremen," the mafioso said. "Have to talk some sense into their fuckin' mouthpiece and get them to play ball, or we'll have to—" The remainder of the sentence was lost as an argument about the disarmament talks in Berlin broke out behind Bolan.

"You can't trust them. The whole thing's a con. Without that nuclear umbrella, I'm telling you, we'll be swamped within a year."

"Zoltan, you're too damned cynical. If the Russians feel—"

"No, he's right. The Reds'll be over that wall like rats up a—"

"Cynical, hell. I just see things the way they are."

"They don't want war any more than we do. If you would just—"

Bolan swiveled on his stool and leaned his head against the frosted glass, but it wasn't until the arguing men moved away that he was again able to hear the two voices beyond the partition. Even then the conversation was only in fragments.

"Fuck him over until he...long as we stop short of...the way Kraul's boys croaked Becker. But squeeze the bastard dry, because, shit, with all those broads..." He heard Schiller growl.

"Back from Bremen on Thursday, 7:35 at the main station...get the idea—act tough and then *be* tough!" Lattuada said.

Bolan tried his stare-into-the-mirror number again, hoping he wasn't going to meet the flinty gaze of one of the hoods. But they had turned their backs on the bar, crowded into a corner by a party of newcomers shouting ribaldries about the whores in the Eros Center on the Reeperbahn. A few minutes later they left.

Bolan went back to Alberts and his cab. "Between Reinbek and Aumühle," he told the cabbie. "The white gates just before that gas station."

"I had you figured for a private eye or something," Alberts said as they headed for the autobahn and the bridge over the Elbe. "Maybe even a...what is it they call them? G-man?"

"That's a little out of style," Bolan said, smiling.

"Whatever. I'd have bet my shirt on it. But now I've had time to think and I see I was wrong. You're a reporter, right?"

"We can't all be cabdrivers or own a white Cadillac," Bolan said.

"No, sir. And we can't all remember the stories we read in the papers. Or the descriptions they print. Or the photos they're running now. But some folks do." Alberts pulled into the fast lane to pass a convoy of semis hauling containers from the docks, then added slowly, "A tall, lean man with an American accent, claiming to work for a newspaper. I wouldn't stick around in a crowd too long if I were you."

"There are two of us in town," Bolan said after a pause. "The cops picked the wrong one to tag with a killing, that's all."

"You don't need to worry," Alberts said. "I know an honest man when I see him. You learn to make judgments in my business. But I'd hide that face of yours, at least while you're in town. There's a newspaper on the back seat."

"Herr Alberts," Bolan said warmly, "you're a friend in need!"

He picked up the paper, unfolded it and held it open in front of his face, just a businessman scanning the latest stock prices on the way to his office. It was the German edition of the *International Herald-Tribune*.

He turned to pages four and five. The main heading on the right-hand side told him, via a three-deck pyramid, that the Berlin disarmament talks—preliminary session—had reached a successful conclusion. France was dubious, the story said, but an agenda had been agreed upon. A separate story was headlined: TOUGH BARGAINING EXPECTED IN SECOND ROUND NEXT MONTH. And there was a paneled think piece subheaded: Will the Wall Come Down? Berliners Divided.

Bolan was idly glancing at the other items when his eye caught a headline in a box on the left-hand side: CARGO

SEIZED IN DOCKSIDE BRAWL. With quickened interest, he read:

> Armed thugs last night attacked a warehouse in the Fischmarkt area of St. Pauli, smashing through the doors with a bulldozer and overpowering the watchman. The hoodlums were ransacking a part of the building reserved for tannery supplies when they were surprised by a second group of miscreants wielding iron bars, blackjacks and knives. A pitched battle ensued in which shots were exchanged. At least one of the original raiders is thought to have been killed and two more wounded.
>
> Police, alerted by anxious neighbors, were soon on the scene. But by the time they arrived the battle was already over and casualties removed. Sources close to the underworld recalled early this morning that there were striking similarities between this raid and a recent hijack in Lübeck.
>
> The warehouse manager, called from his bed in the middle of the night, told our reporter that, as far as he could see on a preliminary inspection, the only loss suffered was a small consignment of goatskins checked in last week.

Bolan's pulse quickened. The way he read the situation, the East German who had ordered the smuggled narcotics wasn't taking the loss of his paid-for cargo lying down. He had traced the skins, raided the place where Lattuada had them stashed and seized them back, beating off a counterattack by the Team while doing it.

What this had to do with the gunfight in the woods at Aumühle he couldn't say. But he was damn sure it was the same two gangs fighting out something... with the

Executioner at that moment innocently playing Herr In-Between.

Near the big house with the white gates he paid the cabbie. "Should I come back later, maybe pick you up?" Alberts asked.

Bolan fingered his jaw. Zuta wasn't due back from Hannover until nine o'clock that evening. He nodded. "Yeah, you'd be doing me a favor. Let's see..." He glanced at his watch. "Meet me at the gas station at eight o'clock, no later. Okay?"

"Whatever you say." Alberts waved cheerily, made a U-turn and headed back toward the city. Bolan pushed through a spiny hedge and took to the fields surrounding the knoll on which the property was built.

It was a damp, cold, overcast day with moisture glazing the roadway. The snow had gone, but frost still clung to the hedgerow grasses and transformed the plowed field on the far side into a skating rink.

Bolan circled the property at a distance of about a quarter of a mile. The fields were big, some stubbled, some plowed, others pricked through with winter crops. Hawthorn hedges, split-cane fencing and an occasional oak tree gave him plenty of cover from which to case the joint.

The grounds covered maybe six acres, surrounded by a high brick wall, planted with firs, pines and a couple of cedars near the house. Windows stared across the winter landscape from all around the main structure, but in back of the place Bolan saw that he would be hidden by the stables until he was within fifty yards of the boundary wall.

He approached warily, using hedges, isolated trees and a stand of willows in the corner of a field as cover. When he was no longer shielded by the stable block, he lowered himself into a cut that ran toward the knoll. He could hear voices and an occasional burst of radio music now. Two cars approached along the entrance driveway and then stopped. Doors slammed. Laughter, footsteps, more voices.

Long grass beaten flat by the recent snow lay between the plowland and the cut, which was half covered by the dead brown stalks of wildflowers. Beneath this screen a thread of water gleamed.

He made his way toward the knoll very slowly, bent almost double, ducking every few yards to peer through the stems and check out any signs of movement at any of the windows. He saw nothing.

As the ground began to rise, he saw that the wall itself would shield him now from all but the topmost windows. Unleathering his Beretta, he crawled from the ditch and ran across the frosty furrows until he was up against the brickwork directly behind the stables.

The wall was eight to ten feet high. Bolan jumped, hooking his fingers over the top. But moisture there had congealed into ice and he was unable to hold on. He tried a second time, and again his fingers slipped. It wasn't until he moved farther toward the gates, where a pine sheltered the brickwork from the frost, that he could make it with a firm enough hold to hoist himself up and over.

He skirted a vegetable garden, followed a box hedge enclosing a slope of lawn and arrived behind the stable block. A flagstoned pathway led from the rear of the yard to the house. It was laid out beneath a wooden trellis draped with leafless climbing roses, but Bolan reckoned it would be visible from half the windows in the kitchen wing. He prowled toward the far end of the block, where tall gates separating the yard from the entrance driveway stood open.

At the top of the driveway, cars—a Mercedes, an Opel, a Porsche, a Lincoln Continental—were parked on the gravel sweep in front of the white-pillared portico. He peered around the gatepost. A couple of Jeeps shared the yard with a Citroën station wagon and a Polish-built Fiat sedan.

Noiseless, swift as a shadow, he slipped into the yard. Crouching down, he sped from vehicle to vehicle, the gun in his right hand, every nerve tensed, on the alert for the slightest movement, an unexpected sound.

He could have walked up to the front door, asked if the place was a club, what were the membership requirements, how much did it cost, so on. But he had a hunch that wouldn't be smart. Hansie had said the place was ritzy; the grease monkey at the gas station had called it a high-class cathouse. Folks that ran such places didn't always welcome unexpected callers. Bolan preferred to check first.

The hunch paid off. He stopped and hunkered down behind the Citroën. A dozen stable doors closed off the old horse stalls. Three of them had been left with the top section open. Bolan listened. Distant music. Distant voices. Nothing near. Above his head, the clock on the stable tower struck four times. It was growing very cold; the frost was already making the lobes of his ears tingle.

The stable roof hid the half-open doors from the house. He catfooted to the first and peered into the dark hay-smelling interior. The stall was empty. So was the next. But beyond the third stall, with a double-door entrance at the far end of the block, was a large barnlike space, and here Bolan could make out the shape of a long automobile partly covered by a tarp.

He caught his breath. The roof, windows, trunk and most of the hood were hidden, but enough of the lower half was visible to tell him that the car was a Russian-built ZIL limo... with East German plates.

The wide double doors were locked, but there was a pass door on the left-hand side and this opened easily. Bolan tiptoed into the barn.

The ZIL's radiator was cold, but the limo had been used recently because the concrete floor was dark with moisture beneath the doorsills and fenders. Bolan eased open the driver's door. No keys. Nothing in the glove compartment. A faint odor of gasoline, a hint of smoke from strong black tobacco.

Wait.

There was something else. Fainter still but at once familiar, a rancid smell that could constrict the throat if it was stronger. He ran to the rear of the car, pushed aside the tarp and opened the trunk. Goatskins.

The huge trunk was jam-packed with them. Nearby a ladder led to the hayloft. And here, behind a row of trussed straw bales, the rest of the consignment was stacked.

The discovery put his own visit in a very different perspective. He had reckoned he could always bluff his way out of the place the way he had at the Millpond if he happened to be discovered lurking about the grounds. But not now. This was dangerous material. It was dynamite. There were secrets here that had already cost many lives. He had no illusions: if he was caught this time, his own name would be added to the list.

He replaced the tarp and let himself cautiously out of the pass door. There was shrubbery between the stable block and the house. Bent double, he dodged from bush to bush, below the windows of the kitchen wing, and approached the main facade.

Beneath the low cloudfront, night would fall fast. The northern twilight was already thickening, and lights were lit inside the house. Bolan passed under two windows, daring to straighten momentarily outside the third, which was much wider. With a hasty glance he took in what seemed to be a salon—wall-to-wall carpet, cream paintwork with gold trim, modernistic nudes in gilt frames, a crystal chandelier.

Two girls in shiny low-cut cocktail dresses sat on high stools talking to a white-coated waiter behind a plush bar. A third, dressed in a fringed twenties-style robe that revealed most of her large breasts, was straightening the necktie of a dark-suited, distinguished-looking man with gray hair. As the Executioner watched, she took him by the hand and guided him through a doorway at one side of the bar. A busty redhead wearing high-heeled boots and a black leather pantsuit came into the room with a diffident-looking elderly man and approached the bar.

Bolan dropped out of sight and headed for the next window. He was about to risk another quick glance when he heard the entrance doors beneath the portico open. "Come again soon, darling," a soft woman's voice intoned. "You know we love to see you anytime."

The warrior dropped flat behind a laurel bush. A man murmured something inaudible, hurried down the steps, waved once and got into a white Porsche. The doors closed. The Porsche started with a crackle of exhaust, backed up, then headed for the gates, scattering gravel.

Bolan waited thirty seconds. The cold was biting into him. Somewhere on an upper floor there was a sudden peal of feminine laughter. He rose half upright and continued his tour of the house. On the far side of the portico there was a lighted window that was the twin of the one he had looked through into the salon. A hum of men's voices came from behind it.

Once more, from behind a bush, he popped up. He saw book-lined walls, leather armchairs, a log fire burning. A stout silver-haired man wearing pince-nez sat behind a giant desk covered with ledgers, box files and sheaves of paper. Bolan wasn't really surprised to see that the guy who stood facing him, gesturing with a manicured hand, was the East German civilian who had rescued him from the ambush in the marsh. Or, to be precise, not exactly a civilian. Bolan's memory bank supplied a name and a uniform to go with the face that had always had for him a disturbingly familiar aspect. It was the context of drugs, smuggling and dockside brawls that had fooled him until now.

The man was Colonel Gottfried Benckendorff. He was in charge of a political division of the East German secret police.

It all made sense, of course. As the kid at the gas station had guessed, the place was indeed a high-class whorehouse. It was, as Hansie had said, ritzy as all get out. And it seemed, now, to be acting as a front for some kind of East German penetration of the Federal Republic.

Unless, of course, the Eastern-bloc presence was temporary and Benckendorff wasn't using the place as a base but merely a convenient, and unlikely, hideout while he was here.

Whatever, it was clear that, having been cheated of his drug consignment in Lübeck, the secret-police chief had won it back the previous night and was now preparing to take it home as planned. If he couldn't make it one way, he would make it another, and it was unlikely that a se-cret-police official driving a Russian automobile would have too much trouble with the Vopos or the customs people when he crossed the border.

What wasn't clear was how he had known where to send his heavies to steal back the hijacked drugs. And what the swamp battle, presumably also directed against Lattuada, had been about. Especially since it took place well *before* the raid on the warehouse.

One of those questions was answered almost at once. A dark-skinned, slender girl wearing her hennaed hair in a crazy Afro came into the room carrying a tray of drinks. She was dressed in thigh-high silver boots, black wool tights and a flame-colored sweater.

Sally Ann! You could rely on her to do—and be—the unexpected.

But what was she doing *here*?

The answer suggested itself in the way she looked at Benckendorff, picked a thread from his sleeve, and pouted impishly in reply to something he said.

Not a double, as Kraul had claimed, but a *triple* agent....

CHAPTER TWENTY-TWO

Mack Bolan frowned. If Sally Ann was, as he guessed, working primarily for East German intelligence, running errands for the Team and at the same time liaising with Kraul, that would certainly explain a lot of things.

The fact that the East Germans, for instance, had been alerted—almost—in time to foil the hijack of the goatskins in Lübeck, the fact that Benckendorff knew where they had been stashed in Hamburg in time to make his second, successful, attempt, and the fact, maybe, that he had been on hand to take the heat off Bolan himself during the swamp ambush.

It might also explain the girl's apparent invulnerability during the battle at the snowbound crossroads and the subsequent attack on Kraul's headquarters as well as certain inconsistencies in her behavior before and since.

But the big question remained.

Why should an East German intelligence chief mastermind the transfer of an illegal narcotics shipment into his own country?

The question provoked a follow-up. Were Benckendorff and his killer squad in West Germany just to organize the drug transfer? Were they part of an existing network? Or had they been sent specifically to set up a new spy ring, of which the drugs were in some way an important part?

Bolan had to find out. He determined to force an entry into the house and see what he could dig up. The time had come for action. Silent as a ghost, he made his way to the corner of the building and turned to recon the facade that was farthest from the stables.

This time there were no fire escapes. But there was a yew tree at one side of a sunken garden, and a jutting branch that brushed the wall near a window that looked as if it could belong to a second-floor hallway.

Bolan made for the tree. There was only one lighted window to pass at ground-floor level. Behind it he could hear laughter and three voices—two women and one man. The curtains were drawn, but not right across. Through the gap he glimpsed pale flesh, a brass bedstead, a tangle of limbs. The people in there wouldn't be listening for the scrape of combat boots on the bark of a tree.

It was a prickly journey, making it to that branch, but the warrior found it firm and solid. From the far end he was able to step down easily onto a wide window ledge. The window was a casement and the catch was fastened across. Bolan unstrapped the knife from his left ankle, inserted the blade between the two halves of the frame and pushed until the catch sprang back. He eased up the lower section and slid into the house.

A wide hallway. More carpet. Subdued light coming from a chandelier above the stair head at the far end. The doors, four each side, were cream, with the panels picked out in gold. One of them opened as he passed, and a brunette holding the edges of a bathrobe together peered out. "Tell them to bring another bottle," a man's voice called from inside the room.

The girl stared at Bolan. "If you're looking for the john, dear," she said, "it's the other corridor, right at the stairs. Greta should have told you."

He murmured something that could have been a thank-you and kept going. Fortunately the gun, held close to his thigh at arm's length and screened by his coat, was on the side away from her.

The stairwell was circular. Two shallow flights curled down, one on each side, to an entrance lobby floored with black-and-white marble. The hallway he had just left was mirrored by another on the far side of the wall, again with four doors on each side. He took a passage leading to the rear of the house. Ten steps, one more door each side—the place was certainly wired for action if all those rooms were for girls' use—then a T-junction with corridors running left and right.

Bolan turned left because the kitchen wing and the stables were that way and there had to be back stairs in a house this size. There were, past the open door of a linen closet, past a king-size blue-tiled bathroom with a sunken tub, past a woman humming and the whine of a vacuum cleaner. The stairs themselves led past a huge kitchen bright with copper, glass and stainless steel to cellars beneath the house. An electric kettle hissed steam quietly at the kitchen window, but there was nobody to be seen.

He stepped into the room, eased open a padded door blocking off the living quarters and found himself in a long corridor that ran the length of the house's rear facade.

This was the area of maximum risk because he reckoned the place was divided into two separate spheres of influence characterized by the salon and the library— areas, respectively, of physical and moral corruption— and if he wanted to eavesdrop on the people peddling the latter he would have to make it to the far side of the house. For it was clear that this side, where the bar, the kitchen and the blue bathroom were located, was the preserve of the high-class hookers who made such a convenient front for Benckendorff. And, possibly, if their "clients" were big wheels in the army or the administration, a useful base from which secrets could be funnelled eastward.

Bolan was a third of the way along the passageway when he heard footsteps clack on marble, a rumble of wheels and a faint tinkle of glassware. He froze. The noises were coming from behind a door that separated the corridor from the entrance lobby. He glanced swiftly around him and saw another door. Opening it quickly, he slipped in and pulled it shut behind him.

He found himself in a cloakroom among rubber boots, tweed hats and mackinaws hanging from hooks on the wall. His hip pressed against the cold curve of a small sink. The noises grew louder. He heard a door open. Crouching down, he put his eye to the keyhole.

The white-jacketed waiter from the bar was wheeling a trolley stacked with cups, saucers and dirty dishes toward the kitchen. Bolan waited until he heard the guy begin unloading the stuff into the dishwasher. Waiting, he realized suddenly and clearly that his own self-imposed mission, too, was now dividing into two separate spheres of action: one, to destroy the Zuta Krohn-Ferucco Lattuada conspiracy, clear himself of the murder charge and incidentally clean up some of the filth that was tainting the city; two, to unveil the secrets of the East German spy ring, if that's what it was, and above all to bust wide open whatever plans Benckendorff had for the distribution of the hell dust concealed in the smuggled goatskins.

The secret-police chief was the link that joined the two together, but for the Executioner they were two sepa-

rate objectives, two targets that he could no longer hope
to drill with a single shot.

He eased open the cloakroom door, cased the
passageway and stepped out. Thirty silent paces later he
reached the passage that led to the front of the house.
Then he rounded the corner. The library door was at the
far end, past Teutonic-looking busts on plinths and
nineteenth-century seascapes on the wall. There was no
cover for someone who wanted to listen, but Bolan recalled Sally Ann's entry with the drinks: she hadn't appeared through this door but from the side of the room,
so there had to be another door somewhere.

Yeah, as he approached the deeply recessed library
doorway, he saw a flush-fitting door, colored cream like
the passage wall, between two of the gilt-framed oil
paintings. He leaned his head close to the library door
and listened. Was Sally Ann still in there with the two
men? One male voice…two…the first again…a higher,
lighter pitch, a gurgle of laughter.

Positive.

Bolan turned the handle of the flush-fitting door and
went through. He was in a small kitchen. The usual
equipment, very modern. Two doors, one to the library, one that obviously led toward the central entrance lobby. Spiraled around a steel shaft, an open
ladder-stairway giving access through a circular opening to a room on the floor above.

The Executioner hesitated. He figured the room up
there would be private, very private, indeed, and—as far
as the girls using the house and their clients were concerned—secret. Entry strictly reserved for Benckendorff
and his confederates.

He had to go up there and take a look. But if, as he
suspected, the upper room was blocked off from the rest

of the house, he'd be trapped the moment anyone left the library.

What the hell. It had to be done. He tiptoed to the library door, bent down and used the keyhole again. The silver-haired guy with pince-nez was still behind the desk. Sally Ann lay back in an easy chair nursing a glass of something. Benckendorff wasn't in view. Bolan guessed he was pacing up and down in front of the window, because the volume and clarity of his voice varied according to whether he was facing the door or had his back to it. The door was solid, heavy and thick. Even at their clearest, Benckendorff's sentences came to Bolan in fragmentary form.

"Distribution essential well before the next session... time to set up and subvert the chosen... Western connection immediately and unquestionably verifiable... in time for the media to..."

"Will the ring be unmasked by your own—" the man with the pince-nez began.

"No!" Benckendorff came into view, halting in front of the desk. "Of course not. We can leave that to the Vopos and the normal security people. We can't even be connected with the tip-off." He started pacing again, and Bolan lost a great deal of the following dialogue because the man lowered his voice. But the snatches he did hear were enough to set his pulse hammering.

"Straight from the Department A duty officer at the First... although this had to be without the knowledge of the Fourth Department evaluators in Moscow..."

The pince-nez man behind the desk asked a brief question that Bolan couldn't catch.

"Certainly not," Benckendorff replied. "If any member of the present Politburo were to guess... even in Berlin Ulbricht would never have...but several of the Directorate chiefs feel that we ..."

Sally Ann laughed. "Too bad for the stuffed shirts in the Fourth Department."

Bolan straightened. He strode to the spiral stairway and swarmed up it into the room above. If what he now suspected was true, he would need confirmation, some independent verification, preferably documentary, that would confirm his own analysis of the scattered half sentences he'd heard in the library below.

He found it.

The room at the top of the spiral was part office, part bedroom. A small bathroom led off it, but there was no other door. Bolan guessed it was here that Benckendorff holed up when he was in the Federal Republic.

Opposite the stairway entrance a desk stood beneath a window of opaque glass. The top of the desk was covered with papers. He walked across and ran a practiced eye over them. The official press release detailing the results of the inaugural round of disarmament talks in Berlin. A copy of the joint communiqué signed by Eastern and Western leaders. Photocopied digests of speeches made by delegates during the talks. A buff standard-size office folder. A map of East Germany, annotated in blue marker pencil, with certain towns ringed in red.

Bolan opened the folder. He found a score of paper sheets, each with a color snapshot stapled to the top left-hand corner and a dozen or more lines of text centered on the page.

The photos were all head-and-shoulder portraits. Some of them were grainy, probably shot with a telephoto lens without the knowledge of the subject; others looked like reproductions of passport pictures. Three were mug shots with police ID numbers. Only two had evidently been taken with the approval of a smiling sitter.

The subjects were all young, between eighteen and twenty-five years old, Bolan guessed, kids of both sexes who shared a kind of flower power look seasoned with the intensity of the ecologically minded Green Party. Beards and an occasional earring for the boys; headbands, straggling hair and immature mouths in the case of the girls.

The text in each case had been printed by a dot matrix computer printer. Bolan riffled through the sheets. They reminded him of the typed documents he had found in Zuta's safe, for each contained a thumbnail personality breakdown relating to the subject of the photo above: name, address, place and date of birth, interests, background and so on.

Despite the wide differences in their backgrounds, the kids all had three things in common. All of them were citizens of NATO countries, all of them were attending temporary courses at East German universities or polytechnics, and every one of them had some past connection with drugs, from a simple caution through possession of marijuana to registered addiction and, in the case of the mug shots, conviction for pushing the hard stuff.

Bolan's eyebrows rose. He added together what he had learned and what he knew already.

Department A meant only one thing to him. It was the section of the KGB's First Chief Directorate, on Moscow's Dzerzhinsky Square, which was responsible for the worldwide dissemination of "disinformation." The Directorate's Fourth Department had specific responsibility for West Germany and Austria.

Benckendorff had spoken of subversion, of a Western connection, of the media. The guy with the silver hair had asked questions about the unmasking of a "ring." The term "tip-off" had been mentioned, and both Sally Ann and the East German police boss had implied some kind of action that bypassed the Fourth Department.

Bolan read it this way. The KGB, with a vested interest in keeping East-West relations at cold-war level, was dissatisfied with the current *glasnost* climate and particularly with the probable success of the Berlin disarmament talks. Certain top-echelon types of the organization had therefore decided to torpedo the second round of those talks with a disinformation campaign activated through part of the East German intelligence network. The campaign was secret, inasmuch as it was mounted without knowledge or approval of the Politburo and bypassed the First Chief Directorate's special West German section.

The operation involved the use of the smuggled drugs ordered through Arvell Asticot. But the cocaine and heroin wasn't, as Bolan had first thought, to be used by Benckendorff to make money through a newly organized ring in the East. The ring was to be set up, sure. But the members, whose dossiers the Executioner had under his hand at this moment, subverted or with the stuff simply planted on them, were all patsies. The ring was being created with one purpose: to be blown.

Foreign students, typical of their decadent imperialist society, were being used in an integrated attempt to destabilize Communist youth, the Eastern-bloc papers would cry. Suspicion would be provoked. The next round of the talks would be compromised. Would you buy a used disarmament treaty from these people, and similar questions.

Small wonder that the KGB wished to funnel an operation through a third party that ran directly counter to Gorbachev's thinking; no surprise if Benckendorff, the man charged with planning the conspiracy, was adamant that his unit was in no way connected with the exposure of the "Western ring."

But there was an additional factor, something that Bolan suspected but could in no way prove. Benckendorff, he believed, was using the fact that he had been chosen to mastermind this disinformation campaign to set up quite a different operation.

This would involve the creation of a permanent spy ring in the Hamburg area, with a mandate to report not to the KGB but to Benckendorff himself in East Germany. He could lay the groundwork while he was officially here on other business. And the secrets the ring would relay would filter through two main sources: the honey trap provided by the girls working this particular house, and the network of protection contacts set up by Ferucco Lattuada and Zuta Krohn. Through these contacts, Benckendorff's agents would be able to put the bite on Western diplomats and industrialists, most of whom would be members of the Coliseum.

It was all, Bolan thought, very neat and very predictable—once you knew the key factors on which the deal was based. And he himself, he was forced to admit, must have been one of the factors taken into account at some late stage in the planning—the joker dealt suddenly who could be different things to different players in the game.

The East German, like Kraul in his turn, was using the Executioner as a weapon to destroy Lattuada and the Team so that their carefully engineered racket could be modified and turned around to serve quite a different purpose. And the warrior was caught by the short hairs, because if he failed to assist Benckendorff in this way he would automatically abort his own priority mission. . . .

He sighed, putting the Beretta down on the desk as he replaced the sheets of paper exactly as they had been before in the buff folder.

"This is only .22 caliber," Sally Ann said, "but it can kill you as efficiently as a .45 if the person firing it knows exactly where to place the shots."

Bolan whirled. She was standing on the spiral stairs, her elbows resting on the edge of the circular hole cut in the floor, the nickeled automatic she held in her two hands trained on his chest.

"And I do know exactly where to place the shots," Sally Ann said, "so I think you better raise your hands."

CHAPTER TWENTY-THREE

The light was very faint, filtering through a barred grating high up in the cellar wall from some uncurtained window in the facade of the house above. Bolan was shivering with cold. He lay on his back on the damp concrete floor with his feet raised high in the air. The rope that bound his ankles was attached to one of the grating bars; his wrists and elbows were lashed together behind his back.

It was a simple and ingenious way of immobilizing a captive. Tied to a chair, a prisoner could use his feet to lever or shuffle himself into a different position; even if the legs were drawn up and bound so that the feet didn't touch the floor, the chair could be rocked. Roped hand and foot and lying on the ground, a man could roll. But with the feet way up off the ground and the weight of the body increasingly blocking the circulation in the arms, it was strictly a no-go situation.

There wasn't even anything the Executioner could *try*: the floor of the cellar was bare, nothing stood against the walls, the rope was drawn tight enough to kill any lateral movement however much he thrashed from side to side.

There were no options here. The only thing he could do was wait, and hope there would be an opportunity for some kind of break when they came to fetch him back upstairs. They would do that, he reckoned. If they aimed to shoot him like a dog here in the cellar, they would have done it as soon as they had brought him down rather than waste time with the rope number.

In any case, there would be an interrogation. That was for sure. He imagined they simply wanted him out of the way while Hansie Schiller played his tune. *We'll have to knock around the character at the cathouse a sight more,* the big thug had told Lattuada when he'd announced that he was going to visit the two Aumühle prospects that afternoon. *Squeeze the bastard dry, because, shit, with all those broads... Fuck him over until he...* And Lattuada had agreed to that. Yeah, they had to act tough and *be* tough if the owner of the place, presumably the silver-haired man, was to come across.

Benckendorff wouldn't want the Team's top man to know that he had stumbled on the opposition headquarters in his search for fresh victims. With Bolan out of the way he would allow Schiller to make his play cold, and then what? Make like he was scared, beginning to crumble and stall until the goatskin operation was through? Eliminate Hansie and risk having the Team descend on the property in force, which could definitely compromise the disinformation campaign if it brought the police in?

Whichever, one thing was certain: if Schiller did tumble to the place's connection with the smuggled narcotics, his expectation of life would be even shorter than Bolan's own.

And Bolan's expectation? Well, all he knew was that it would be tough taking advantage of a break, if there was one. The faces of the three storm troopers Benckendorff had called in to escort the warrior to the cellar had been stony enough to make Hansie look like Little Lord Fauntleroy. And all 240 pounds of each man had been hard muscle.

"I warned you, Herr Belasko," Benckendorff had said. "We could still, perhaps, have made use of you, with or without your knowledge, if you hadn't persisted in your meddling. But I won't tolerate people spying on my private business. That's totally unacceptable."

"The towns ringed on your map," Bolan had said, "Magdeburg, Dresden, Leipzig, Karl-Marx-Stadt, Rostock and, of course, Berlin, are these the places where your dupes, those poor kids you aim to set up, will have the stuff unloaded on them?"

The East German's lips had tightened. "Belasko," he'd said, "you just signed your own death warrant." And then, with a wintry smile, he added, "St. Pauli Blonde Killer Executed by Vigilantes—that would make a nice headline for the capitalist rag you claim to work for, wouldn't it?"

It was then, before Bolan could reply, that they'd heard the scrape of heavy tires on gravel; then, that the white Cadillac had passed through the band of light streaming through the library window; then, that the silver-haired man had said, "Sally Ann, my dear, if you would keep that weapon trained on our...guest, I'll summon the staff to help him to his quarters."

Now the quarters grew colder every minute. Bolan's teeth chattered. He rolled his shoulders, jerking with his legs at the rope in an attempt to keep his circulation pulsing so that he would be in shape when an opportunity came to make his play. The cords were already cutting into his flesh so much that his limbs were numb.

And those teeth! There was now an almost metallic sound....

Hold it!

The noise, the extra noise that wasn't there before, came from somewhere beyond his feet. He writhed left and right, grimacing with pain as the movement ground his near-paralyzed arms into the concrete floor, and then arched his back and twisted his head so that he could look up past his knees.

There was a shadow outside the grating, something that moved beyond the bars. A gloved hand came through—an arm. An indistinct, nebulous shape hung heavily from the iron grille. A small metallic object clattered to the floor. The shadow withdrew and the light behind the bars brightened again.

Bolan gritted his teeth. Snakelike, he twisted the upper half of his body this way and that until his fingers could touch whatever it was that had been thrown down. They closed around it and he felt a familiar shape—the flat-bladed throwing knife taken off him while Sally Ann had held him at gunpoint.

He didn't trouble asking himself who, or why, or how. He gripped the haft and rolled himself as far as he could over onto his left side. Maneuvering the knife so that the blade was against the cords lashing his wrists together—and would stay that way—was one of the most infuriating physical tests he had ever come up against. With his legs up in the air, the movement of the rest of him was severely restricted. And there was very little chance of sawing the cords against the razor-sharp edge unless the knife itself was firmly anchored somehow.

If he lay on the knife, there was no room for one hand between the blade and the floor. There wasn't enough freedom of movement for him to hold the knife and jockey the tip between his wrists. The only workable system was for him to turn the knife on its side, wedge the hilt beneath his hip so that the blade was canted slightly upward and squirm his bound arms around until his wrists were over the blade.

But he had no purchase and no leverage. The blade only slanted upward if the knife's hand guard was between it and the floor, and the very weight of his body tended to shift it with the slightest motion of his arms or torso. Even if he could roll far enough over for the guard to be free of his weight, he was so precariously balanced that the haft kept slipping from under his hipbone.

The blood was flowing hotly from his lacerated wrists within minutes, and it was a full half hour before the last strand of the rope binding him parted. Even then his upper arms had to be freed before he could jackknife forward and slice through the rope attaching his feet to the grating.

Fortunately the strands restraining elbow movement passed around his chest, and once his hands were free he could bring them around to the front of his body and work the bonds up and over his shoulders so that they could simply be lifted off above his head. If the hoods had thought to lash his arms together at biceps level, he would never have been able to reach the cords binding his feet.

Once he was free he stamped up and down the empty cellar to warm himself and restore the circulation, wincing at the agonizing nerve reaction as the blood flowed back into the numbed arteries and veins. It was another ten minutes before his wrists stopped bleeding. He occupied the time taking stock of his prison.

The cellar was about fifteen-by-twenty-five feet. Opposite the grating three steps led up to the only door. It was closed with an ordinary farmhouse latch. Cautiously he pressed the tongue. The latch lifted, but the door moved only a half inch. There was a metallic rattle from the far side. Probably a hasp and padlock. He crossed the floor to the wall with the grating, reaching his hand up to check out the indistinct shape hanging from it. As soon as his outstretched hand touched it, he had to repress an exclamation of surprise...and pleasure. Draped over the iron bars was his quickdraw shoulder rig, with the Beretta in its holster! He eased it down very carefully, strapped on the rig and checked over the autoloader. The full magazine was still in place.

Who was the unseen rescuer? Sally Ann? He didn't think so. She could easily have wavered, could even have allowed him the opportunity to make a break before she shepherded him back to the library if she'd wanted to help. But she had kept a steely grip on the situation, the little .22 rock-steady in her hand right up until the moment he was hustled away by the storm troopers.

Who then? Clearly neither Benckendorff nor the silver-haired owner of the club. And certainly not Hansie. Bolan refused to waste time speculating. He had no idea how they proposed to deal with Schiller; the hoods could be sent to fetch him back at any minute.

There was no way of getting to the grating, even if it could be moved. So it had to be the door. As a last resort he could shoot off the padlock hasp, but it would take several rounds since he couldn't see precisely where the anchorage was. Plus he had no notion of the layout on the far side; he could easily be caught like a rat in a trap if the sound of the shots brought the hoods quickly enough. He took the knife and started working on the edge of the door at the height he figured the padlock to be.

The old wood was dry and it split away fairly easily at first. Within a few minutes he had carved away a crescent-shaped notch. Sixty seconds later the tip of the blade struck against the iron hasp. He pried away more wood until he could poke a forefinger through and touch the metal. Moving it slightly, he found that the hasp was screwed to and hinged from the door; the iron loop over which it fitted, to be secured with the padlock, was set in the jamb.

Bolan began scraping away wood on the other side. Here it was harder work. The jamb was tougher, moister than the door. The scrape of the knife blade seemed louder, and the splintering crack each time he levered away a chunk, positively deafening.

From time to time he paused, listening. Sometimes, faintly, he could hear muffled footsteps from above. No voices were audible, but there was still a hint of music swelling and fading on the cold night air, and once he heard a door slam and a crackle of exhaust as someone gunned the engine of a roadster. Among the trees in the back of the house an owl hooted sporadically.

Bolan had exposed the threaded shaft of a screw securing the plate to which the iron loop was fixed when he heard the hoods returning. There could be no mistake about it: heavy steps treading down a stone stairway, brutish voices that he recognized, echoing between the walls.

He cursed softly. He was almost finished. Leaning on the door as hard as he could, he saw the screw shift imperceptibly in its wooden bed, but the plate-padlock-hasp combination held firm.

Crouching, he put his eye to the irregular gap he had gouged away. He saw a dimly lit passageway, an arched opening in the wall with the stairway curving up behind it, and the corridor continuing beyond the arch with more doors on either side.

Wait until they open the door and then jump them, hoping the surprise element will get him past before they have time to react? Or shoot away the padlock now and take his chance on finding an out at the far end of that passage? He dismissed the first option: they would see wood shavings on the flagstoned floor outside the door, which would eliminate the element of surprise.

Bolan slid the knife back into its ankle-strap sheath, whipped the Beretta from its leather and shoved the muzzle into the gap little more than an inch from the padlock hasp. He pulled the trigger.

In the confined space of the cellar the noise was deafening. The ringing in Bolan's ears was almost enough to drown the shouts of outrage and the feet scrambling on the stairway.

He charged the door and it burst open to send him reeling into the passage. Three steps took him to the archway. The leading hood was just appearing around a curve in the stairs, a Combat Master flourished in his right hand. He fired at the same time as the Executioner, but Bolan knew roughly what he was going to see and where; the hood didn't.

The goon's shot, triggered wild and without considered aim, flew wide and chipped plaster from the side of the arch. Bolan's slug took the hardman in the thigh, just above the right knee, and sent him sprawling headfirst down the remainder of the stairway, yelling with pain. The other two, piling down after him, were forced to leap over his body as they hit the corridor.

Bolan was already halfway to the door at the far end. He ignored those on each side of the passage, figuring they would lead into small rooms with no exit. He whirled once as he reached the door, while the two hoods were still off balance, and let loose two more shots from the Beretta.

Once again the underground walls reverberated with the deafening sound of the reports. One of the shots scored, drilling a gorilla through the upper arm. He staggered back with the impact and sat down hard while his companion dropped to one knee and blasted off a single round from a Browning automatic. Bolan felt the wind of the slug as he dived through the doorway. The cellar was the twin of the one where he was imprisoned, only this one was used as a storeroom. Huge stone crocks, wooden cases of liquor and slatted shelves aromatic with the scent of apples and tomatoes lined the walls. Beneath the grating there was an old-fashioned, brassbound steamer trunk with a domed lid.

Bolan leaped for it and thrust upward against the grating with all his strength. The iron grille fell outward with a heavy clang, and he jumped for the opening as the last hood fired again.

Something twitched his pant leg, and he felt a jarring blow on his left heel, as he hoisted himself through the gap. A third slug splatted against a bar of the grating, thrumming the ironwork at the moment the Executioner spilled out into the open air.

By the time Benckendorff's killer had made the steamer trunk and leaned through the opening to channel a deathstream Bolan's way, he was in some shrubbery beneath a plantation of elms, and the bullets shredded harmlessly through the leaves above his head.

Bolan lay facedown on the frosty ground, making a swift recon of the terrain. The cellar he had escaped from was at the rear of the house; the shrubbery bordered a lawn stretching between the two wings. Light from a window on one of the upper floors glinted on the sloping roof of a greenhouse behind a box hedge at the end of the kitchen wing.

And on the far side of that wing was the stable block.

The warrior was determined to get there and do his damnedest to destroy the goatskins and their lethal cargo, however much muscle Benckendorff deployed against him.

The strength of the East German's forces showed almost at once. Alerted by the gunfire, Benckendorff was already out in the garden on the other side of the building, shouting orders. A door in the wing that Bolan hadn't checked out opened. The light, momentarily printed against the night, was killed and men streamed out across the lawn.

"Cordon off the house," Benckendorff yelled. "Search every inch of the grounds. This man is dangerous. He must not get away!"

Bolan thought quickly. Only the hood in the cellar knew roughly where he was, and the guy was pulling himself out through the gap where the grating was. The man was a sitting duck, but if the Executioner blew him away, he would reveal his position to the others. He guessed there were six or seven of them at least, and at the moment he had one thing in his favor.

Benckendorff would naturally expect the escaped prisoner to be taking it on the lam. The search would therefore be concentrated more on the outskirts of the property; they wouldn't figure Bolan was aiming to return to the outbuildings.

If he could silence the man from the cellar without firing a shot, he would at least have a head start over the posse. The guy was on his feet and running, heading for the shrubbery. "This way!" he shouted. "I saw the mother—" The words choked in his throat as Bolan leaped for his back, shoving the blunted blade of his knife hard in between the man's ribs. Blood bubbled in his throat and he died, slumping to the ground while Bolan ran.

"Which way? Where?" a voice shouted from the far side of the lawn. But there was no reply and the Executioner was already halfway to the box hedge sheltering the greenhouse.

He thought he had it made to the end of the structure, but his silhouette must have shown up momentarily against some reflected brightness because there was a shot, followed at once by two sharp bursts from what sounded like submachine guns and several more single shots from heavy-caliber handguns.

Crouched behind the box, Bolan was unhurt, but all along the side of the greenhouse rectangular panes disintegrated with an appalling clatter in a thousand gleaming fragments of reflected light. He was through the irregular hole blasted in the side of the building while jagged shards were still dropping from the splintered wooden frame, dodging between stepped shelves of potted plants to race for a door on the far side that he could dimly make out in the indirect illumination.

The hoods, fanning out across the lawn behind the hedge, fired again, a ragged volley that shattered more glass as Bolan's feet crunched over the shivered splinters already strewing the floor. Then he was wrenching the door open and racing for the vegetable garden through which he had made his original entry. He was hoping to make the far end of the stable block and turn into the yard, but two of the hoods were pounding along the flagstoned pathway that led from the kitchen wing to the doorway in back of the yard, and he was forced to hurl himself to the ground behind a row of brick-built cucumber frames as they opened fire.

The dual deathstream slammed into the brickwork. Bolan rolled out sideways and lay behind the heaped earth of a bean row, sighting the Beretta on the head of the nearest thug, visible against the reflected glare from the house. He clicked the Beretta into three-shot mode and fired two bursts, rolling again to distance himself from the muzzle-flashes.

One of the mobsters dropped with a choking cry, his chest smashed open by two of the 9 mm flesh-shredders. Bolan heard the heavy body clatter to the flagstones and a gun skitter away over the hard ground. The second man was hit, but not seriously. Cursing, the hood leaped for the cover of a small wooden shack, getting off a single shot as he moved.

Bolan saw his shape etched momentarily against the pale wall of the stableyard, and he triggered an isolated round with hairspring reaction. The slug climbed high, coring the gunman's skull and splattering the wall with dark blood. He dropped from sight like a poleaxed bull.

Snapping bean stalks, the Executioner lurched to his feet. The posse from the far wing was rounding the end of the greenhouse. He ran, bent double, toward the body on the flagstones. A glint of metal nearby revealed the location of the dead man's gun, and Bolan had to have the weapon. He was using the fifteen-round magazine on the Beretta; ten of those rounds had already gone, and he had no spare clip.

He scooped up the gun—it was a stainless-steel Makarov automatic—and sprinted for the corner of the block. Behind him, the pursuit crashed through the vegetable garden. Two of the hoods stopped, sank to a combat crouch and fired. But Bolan had made it past the corner, and that side of the block, hidden from the reflected glare of the house lights, was in total darkness.

He felt the hot breath of one slug fan his neck, but the rest flew wide. He ran on, limping slightly because the heel of one shoe had been shot away when he'd escaped from the cellar. The thugs pounded after him, shouting as they ran. Bullets gouged dust from the wall.

Panting, the warrior turned the far corner, breath misting in the frosty air as he passed for an instant through the light welling from the windows in the front of the mansion, and plunged into the blackness of the stableyard.

The cobblestones were icy and he slid wildly, careering between the Citroën and the other cars parked there. The leading hoods reached the entrance to the yard when he was level with the first of the half-open stall doors. Gunfire blazed. Glass tinkled onto the stones. The Citroën moved slightly, settling as the air blew out of a tire.

Bolan turned, holstering the Beretta and shoving the Makarov into the waistband of his pants. Sprinting as fast as he could in the few yards available, he took a running dive over the lower half of the stable door, hit the straw-covered floor, shoulder-rolled and came up within a couple of yards of the tarped ZIL limo.

Outside he could hear excited shouts, the milling of feet, orders yelled from a distance by Benckendorff. The East Germans reckoned it was all over. They thought they had him cornered; they wouldn't know that he was wise to the contents of the ZIL's trunk.

But the warrior hadn't dashed into the yard and dived over that particular half-door by chance. Cornered he might be, but he would worry about that later. Right now he had something important to do.

He dropped to one knee, groping with his left hand beneath the king-size limousine's rear fenders until he found the cold, curved surface he was seeking. Then, snatching out the Makarov, he pumped three quick shots into the bottom of the ZIL's gas tank. The acrid, pungent odor of the volatile liquid filled the barn and tickled his nostrils as fuel gurgled out of the three holes and spilled across the floor.

Bolan figured the limo would tote a fifteen- or twenty-gallon tank. And if they were planning to shift the goat-skins right away, it would almost certainly be full. He backed off toward the big double doors closing off the barn, waiting for enough gasoline to flood from the tank to leave a mixture of explosive vapor above the sinking level of fuel.

It was a maneuver he had used before, but this time it was doubly difficult because there was no light inside the barn, and he had to act before the leaking fluid spread across the floor as far as his own feet.

Breathing hard, he waited. Over the gurgle of fluid he could hear low voices in the yard. The hoods were planning to rush the stables through all three of the open half-doors, firing as they came. He compressed his lips. Let them rush.

Now.

He couldn't wait any longer. The floor in front of him was still dry, but the gasoline stink was overpowering. He imagined the thin, dark tide sweeping over the concrete floor toward him—concrete in which, he had noted when he'd seen the place in daylight, there were flints embedded.

With his back against the pass door, he stretched his right arm down and fired the Russian pistol in a trajectory almost parallel with the floor, bouncing the steel-jacketed slugs off the concrete in ricochets that whined beneath the ZIL and clanged off the heavy metal of its chassis.

It wasn't until the fifth shot that he struck a spark. Instantly, with a *whoomp* that blocked his ears and sent him reeling, all of the spilled gasoline ignited. A sheet of flame filled the inner part of the barn and enveloped the ZIL in a roaring maelstrom of fire. Bolan jerked open the pass door. The inrush of cold air boosted the blaze into a searing inferno that boiled upward and set alight the rafters and wooden floor of the hayloft. The straw bales around the remainder of the goatskins flared.

The limo was consumed. Windows imploded like shrapnel. Metal screamed and buckled. Burning tires belched out choking black smoke. And then the heat exploded the vapor inside the tank, tearing the car apart to send flaming fragments all over the barn.

Outside there was pandemonium. Bolan could hear Benckendorff's frenzied voice bawling orders. He barreled through the open pass door below waist height, a gun in each hand. There were three men outside, but they didn't know what hit them. He straightened up, spitting death. One of the men keeled over, with blood spouting from the hole in his throat. Then the Executioner was past them and running. He raced down the curving driveway toward the white gateposts, secure in the knowledge that Benckendorff's desire to save his precious narcotics would outweigh any thoughts of catching the intruder who was wrecking his whole campaign of disinformation.

"Get that car out of there! Pull out that goddamn ZIL! Kill the flames in the loft!" the secret-police chief screamed.

No way.

In the stableyard, gasping thugs played useless garden hoses on the holocaust. Others, shielding their eyes with upflung arms, staggered back from the incandescent heat after vain attempts to penetrate the stables. The ZIL couldn't have been hauled out anyway, even if they could reach it, because the pass door was open but the double doors around it were locked and the key was still in the house.

Bolan looked over his shoulder as he rounded the last curve in the driveway. Scantily dressed women and their clients crowded the brightly lit portico, staring awestruck at the spectacle. Benckendorff was backlit by the glare, waving his arms like a madman. Seconds later the roof of the stables collapsed, and a huge column of flame, spurting red sparks and smoldering fragments of wood, whirled into the night sky.

Bolan was approaching the deserted gas station when two fire department trucks with sirens shrieking thundered up the road from Aumühle and turned into the driveway. He grinned. They had about as much chance of saving the stable block as Benckendorff had of rescuing his grilled heroin and cocaine.

There was no sign of Heinrich Alberts or his cab at the gas station. Bolan glanced at his watch. The luminous digital figures told him that it was 8:22. He frowned. Their date had been for eight, but he would have thought the guy could have waited at least a half hour. Maybe he'd had a late fare and hadn't shown yet.

Bolan waited until 8:30, watching the pulsating glare outline leafless trees around the high ground on which the house was built. When Alberts still hadn't shown, he set off on foot for the S-Bahn station at Aumühle. It was only a half-hour run back into the city, but he couldn't afford to be out of the apartment when Zuta returned.

One half of the mission was successfully completed, but the more difficult part was still to come, and he didn't want to alert the woman that he was wise to her before he decided how to handle it.

Several cars passed him on the way, but none stopped when he tried to thumb a ride. Two hundred yards down the road a white Cadillac was parked on the shoulder. He approached it warily, squinting through the dark.

In the red twilight from the distant fire he made out distinctive trimwork with a monogram on the driver's door. And whitewall tires. Somebody was asleep in the front passenger seat.

Gripping the Makarov, he jerked open the wide door. In the illumination from the overhead light, he saw the vulture man, the mobster with the broken nose and the scarred face, grinning up at him—a broad, toothless grin, yawning blackly beneath the guy's stubbled chin. His throat had been cut from ear to ear.

No need to ask questions now about how the silver-haired man would react when the Team tried to put the bite on him. Hansie Schiller could congratulate himself that, in the absence of his boss, he had sent in a deputy.

Bolan took a quick look around the Cadillac's spacious interior. Nothing of interest. He was withdrawing his head and shoulders when he saw that the East Germans obviously liked to make doubly sure. There was a bullet hole in the center of the dead man's forehead. Maybe fired from the Makarov the Executioner himself was holding? Maybe not. Just the same, he wiped the butt clear of prints and tossed the gun into the car. You never knew. And he figured one murder rap already hanging over his head was enough.

He closed the Caddie's door quietly and started running. There was a train in the station waiting to leave. He made it as the automatic doors were hissing shut, sinking into a seat with a gasp of relief.

The car was empty, but there were people in the next one. Looking idly through the glass windows of the doors separating them, Bolan saw a familiar face, intent above cupped hands shielding a match that was lighting a cigarette.

It was Ferdie Kraul.

CHAPTER TWENTY-FOUR

Zuta didn't return to the apartment until ten-thirty. She was dressed like a smart businesswoman—black kid gloves, a classic two-piece in clerical gray, a frilled white blouse. Looking at the artfully, not-quite-concealed curves beneath the suit, meeting those wide dark eyes that were only just beginning to wrinkle at the corners, Bolan found it hard to believe what he had discovered in the house beyond the secret passage.

The lies that could be framed by those sexy lips!

She was sitting at the table, demolishing a steak. Almost without realizing what he was doing, he shook his head and ran his fingers absently through her short, springy hair.

Zuta shrugged him off a little impatiently. "Not now, darling," she said. "I had a late session at the beautician's and I have to go soon to chat up some big-time types at the bar. Be a lamb and fetch my purse from the sofa, would you?"

Bolan's eyebrows rose. Was it his imagination, or had her ardor cooled significantly. Was the prize bull about to be demoted and put on the shelf reserved for fatted calves? He stopped pretending to paw the ground and went to get the purse.

He feigned sleep when she came to bed around three o'clock. She made no attempt to wake him. In the morning she was gone.

The next day was colder and equally damp. But there was no wind, and by the time he had showered and shaved, the atmosphere had thickened to a fog that was dense enough to hide the traffic lights at the end of the street. Looking at the halos around the still-lit street-lights, Bolan junked the idea of another fact-finding walk around the saloons of St. Pauli; it would be simpler, and quicker, if he hired a native guide.

He took his billfold from his hip pocket to look for Heinrich Alberts's number. The billfold was empty. The cabbie's business card was gone. So was the rest of his money.

He frowned, tapping the thin leather envelope against his teeth. She must have taken it while he'd slept. What the hell—Alberts would take one of his remaining American Express checks. He'd simply look up the guy's home number in the phone book.

He sat down by the breakfast table and opened the fat Hamburg directory. He was leafing through the *A*'s when glasses and cups on the table jingled and the whole room vibrated as a jetliner flying very low roared overhead. Poor bastard, Bolan thought, glancing out the window at the fog veiling the streetlights. Rather him than me, heading for the short Fuhlsbüttel runway in this shit. Then, looking back at the phone book, his eye fell on a newspaper lying beyond it on the far side of the table. The paper was folded back to an inside page, an early edition of the current daily, and there was an item at the foot of column six lightly ringed in pencil. He saw the modest head, HAMBURG CABDRIVER'S MYSTERIOUS DEATH, and picked up the paper. His German was good enough for him to translate:

Hamburg police were today seeking clues to the attacker or attackers responsible for the death of Herr Heinrich Alberts, 48, the owner-driver of a city cab. Herr Alberts's body was discovered in a secluded part of the botanical gardens by a patrolling police officer whose suspicions had been aroused by the sight of an empty taxi abandoned in a nearby street with the engine running.

The cabdriver had been brutally assaulted and then battered to death with an iron bar. The police captain in charge of inquiries told our reporter, "Assaults on cabdrivers, here, as in the rest of Europe, are on the increase. But this seems an apparently motiveless killing. Alberts had no enemies and there was a considerable sum of money in his cab. Yet the attacker must have been a professional wearing gloves, for there were no fingerprints on the murder weapon." Herr Alberts, who worked from a cab stand outside the Atlantic Hotel, leaves a widow and a daughter aged 18.

Bolan's fingers were shaking as he put the paper down. The muscles in his jaw rippled in anger.

The gloves, of course, spelled Hansie. But who gave the orders?

He didn't know if the paper had been deliberately left there for him to see, or whether it was an oversight. He wouldn't gamble on Zuta being forgetful; he figured she did very little that wasn't premeditated.

He went into the bedroom and took his jacket off its hanger. The big wallet in which he kept the few papers he still had was in place in the inside pocket. But it was as empty as the billfold. The American Express checks,

along with the rest of his folding money, had vanished.
So had the few coins he kept in the ticket pocket.

As a man wanted on a murder charge and hunted by
the underworld, the loss would imprison him, in the
sense of restricting his movement, almost as much as a
locked door, even if he was wise, unknown to Zuta, to
the secret of the attic passage.

Why was he suddenly being written out of the script?

Because he wasn't sticking to the rules. Her rules. Although he hadn't told her what happened there, she
knew he had been to Aumühle, even though she had
"advised" him to stay put in the apartment.

Since he had made no accusation at the time, she
should also know that he couldn't have seen her getting
in or out of the Cadillac at the Mühlenteich Club.

But she couldn't be one hundred percent certain.

And, as he was beginning to find out, odds of ninety-
nine to one weren't short enough to qualify as a dead
certainty in the lady's book. They just qualified the
runners as dead.

That must have been the reason why Alberts had been
killed the night before, not because they knew he was to
pick up Bolan by the gas station at eight o'clock, but *in
case* the Executioner had confided in him, *in case* the
two of them had seen her at the club, *in case* the cabbie
could make the link between Zuta, Lattuada, Hansie
and their racket.

Which left him where? He wasn't positive, but most
likely in the doghouse.

So what kind of event, he wondered, was the high
jump, and how long was the drop? About as far as it was
to the quicklime beneath the trapdoor in the death cell?

Were they, in other words, simply aiming to hand him
back to the law in a neatly tied package and hope he'd go

down for Dagmar's murder? Or was some more sinister
end in view, the kind that involved a secluded part of the
botanical gardens?

There was a more immediate question. How the hell
was Bolan to react when Zuta came back up to the
apartment? Would he be expected to perform as if
nothing had happened? Or was he supposed to have
taken some kind of hint from the newspaper story.
Maybe, like him, Fräulein Krohn was trailing a decoy....

There seemed to be something special on at the club.
The band was there, unusual for lunchtime, louder than
usual, too, jazzier. The street was choked with cars,
never mind the fog. The gorilla brought lunch at midday, which Bolan tossed down the john, and told him
Zuta would be occupied with special guests until late that
night. In fact, she never returned to the apartment at all.

Hell, Zuta wasn't actually sadistic; she was just busi-
nesslike. She didn't watch the animals destroyed when
they had outlived their usefulness; she rang the vet and
went out for the day.

Bolan was in a quandary. The obvious thing was for
him to make a break for it. But he had to have *some*
money. Maybe he could put the bite on Freddie Leonhardt, promising that the magazine would repay him.

Bolan returned to the phone. The line was dead. No
amount of jiggling would produce a dial tone. Evidently the wires had been cut or a plug had been pulled
out someplace. And he didn't even have coins for a
public pay phone!

Final surprise: the Beretta and the throwing knife had
vanished from their customary hiding place beneath the
clothes in his dresser drawer. That did it. Okay, the

Executioner thought grimly, so this is where we move into the open-warfare phase.

What was being planned for him? Well, he wasn't going to wait and see. It was time for the condemned man to bust out. But first he was going to take a long, hard look at that red leather diary.

He crept up to the attic floor and made his way along the concealed passageway to the house. This time he gave the whole place the once-over before he settled down. The garage was empty, but there was a smell of coffee in the sterile kitchen. They must have had it sent in from outside.

Upstairs Bolan found two bedrooms. One was unused; in the other there was a king-size unmade bed with rumpled sheets. The bathroom was still misted with condensation and the steamy air was heavy with the scent of expensive cologne. No prizes, he thought, for guessing where his hostess had entertained her "special guests."

There was a cabinet-size portrait in a leather photo frame standing on the night table. "For Zuta—my love!" read the heavily inked dedication slanted across the lower right-hand corner. And the face staring soulfully out at Bolan was the face of Ferucco Lattuada.

So much for all that innocence. So much for the pretense of knowing nothing about "this man Lattuada." So much for those persistent "inquiries" among the know-it-alls at the club, none of which, strangely enough, had produced anything specific.

When he got the safe open, as far as he could see, and he had rigged some telltale pointers, the red leather diary was exactly as he had left it. That indicated that Zuta didn't make entries everyday.

He determined to break the lock. Hell, he was getting out, anyway. He went into the kitchen and found a knife. Slipping the blade beneath the lock and levering, he popped open the hasp. When he opened the book, he saw at once that he had struck oil.

There was a spread of two pages for every day of the year. Many of them were blank; more still were covered with Zuta's obsessively neat, back-slanting handwriting. He had guessed right, too. She hadn't been able to resist the "what a clever girl am I" routine, and it was all down there—dates, places, figures, details of operations—in an easily decoded personal shorthand. Plus identifiable initials for the cost.

He flipped through the past few weeks, catching a line here and there.

Coconut Grove taken apart by HS plus four. Visited Blue Lagoon with L: 2,500DM. HS returned to Grove to collect 1,000DM. L thinks we should talk C.McF into letting us have a piece of Tondelayo's.

The sums quoted weren't enormous—one thousand deutsche marks was less than six hundred bucks—but if the collection was weekly, if there were several dozen contributors, and if you added tied-in liquor sales and the huge profits from drug distribution, the total would be, well, interesting. He turned more pages.

HS on milk run delivers two warnings (Club Hawaii and Bobbies). The Millpond: L suggests we triple our normal demand. 3,000DM collected from Becker's widow. L thinks we should attempt to bring Bremen into line.

Suddenly Bolan stopped reading. What was somebody trying to pull? Because he remembered: Lattuada couldn't have spent the afternoon in bed with Zuta, in this or any other Hamburg house. He *was* in Bremen. Bolan had overheard him talking to Hansie about it in the saloon. *I gotta meet with the Wallmann mob in Bremen. Have to talk some sense into their fuckin' mouthpiece.* And then: *Back from Bremen on Thursday, 7:35 at the main station.*

Today was Wednesday.

Since the mobster wasn't due back in town until 7:35 p.m., all at once it looked to Bolan as though that love nest number up in the bedroom was some kind of setup.

Of course she could have allowed herself a siesta with just Lattuada's photo for company. After all, she liked tall, lean men. Or she could have jumped in the sack with someone else and not troubled to remove the picture, except that Zuta, however crooked she might be, always did things with a certain style and that wouldn't be cool. No, now that he thought about it, that Sicilian mug gazing out over the artfully mussed covers, with the used bathroom beyond, was just a little too pat. Something smelled. And if it was a case of walking open-eyed into a setup that looked suspicious even before things started to move, then Bolan wasn't going to play. The setup couldn't relate to him, okay, because Zuta didn't know that he knew about the secret passage and the house beyond it. But whatever it was, he wanted to stay clear.

More research among the pages of the diary—even if, as he hoped, they threw light on the fate planned for him—would have to wait. He would take the book back to the apartment and do a few more minutes of reading before he finally split. Backing out of the obsessively neat living room, he made for the broom closet.

That was his first mistake.

He got wise to the second as soon as he was back in the apartment, sitting down at the bureau with the diary. Opening the red leather book he saw ruefully that, whatever happened, he wasn't going to be able to replace it and pretend it had never left its home base in the safe. Forcing the lock with the kitchen knife had buckled the thin gold locking plate that closed over the pages.

The knife!

All the blood in his body seemed to drain down to his feet, the way it does when the organism is brought face-to-face with the realization that it has made some especially dumb play.

He had left that damning knife on the polished top of a small table in the hallway outside the kitchen. Stuffing the dairy under his mattress, he hightailed it back to the attic corridor like a swallow that had missed out on the migration. Hansie Schiller was waiting in the hallway when he opened the closet door. Three men built like diesel trucks stood behind him.

"Been expectin' you, sweetie," the big thug jeered. "Fancy pulling a stroke like that without even letting the boss know you knew! Never mind. Me and the boys got exactly what you need."

He held up one hand, the forefinger and thumb pincered over the bone handle of the kitchen knife. The fingers of the other hand were wrapped around the rubber-covered butt of a blackjack.

IT WAS DARK when he came to, and the inside of his head was hammering like a shipyard on overtime. But a beating at the hands of the bad fairy didn't entirely account

for the taste in his mouth or the feeling behind his eyes
when he sat up on the bed and swung his feet to the
floor. He knew from experience that his current state of
mind wasn't just the result of a simple KO. He had been
drugged and kept under sedation for some time.

Which meant he was being kept under wraps. But for
what?

Bolan looked around. Everything was familiar. He
was in the apartment above the club. He stood up shak-
ily and fought his way through the colored stars to the
living room and the entrance door. As he expected, it
was locked, and it opened inward, so there was no point
charging it with his shoulder. He pulled at the handle,
but it came away in his hand and left him worse off than
before.

The phone was still dead. He went to the window and
pushed up the sash. Halos circled the streetlights again
and the air was moist and cold. But this time there was
no row of bricks below the window ledge, no strip of
stone jutting out from the facade, just a sheer brick face
dropping forty or fifty feet to the sidewalk. The nearest
drainpipe was yards away.

It was when a newsboy walked under one of the lights
with his placards flapping that Bolan got the message.
EUROPEAN CUP—HAMBURG VS PRAGUE: RESULT, the red
letters on one side spelled out. And on the other he read:
RITTER HERO OF HAMBURG SUCCESS.

He caught his breath. The soccer match, and the local team's chances of winning it, had been headlined in
Wednesday's paper. It was to be played, one hour ahead
of local time, in Czechoslovakia on Thursday afternoon.

If the game was already over, and the result printed,
this must be Thursday evening. Bolan had been trapped

by Hansie Schiller early Wednesday **afternoon**: he had been out for the count for twenty-eight hours or more! He looked at his watch. Yeah, it was already six o'clock.

So, once more, what the hell?

He remembered the one card left in his hand, the one thing they didn't know. He'd brought the red leather diary with him, the first time he'd returned to the apartment the previous day. And, luckily, he had hidden it before he'd walked back into Hansie's welcoming arms. If he had any luck at all left on his side, Zuta wouldn't have missed it yet.

He went back to the bedroom and felt beneath the deep mattress where he'd stashed the book. Lady Luck still smiled on him. The diary was there all right.

Reluctant to advertise the fact that he was conscious and alert again, he resisted the temptation to switch on the apartment lights. He took the diary into the bathroom, where there was no window, and pulled the cord operating the fluorescent lights in there. He opened the book and began to read.

The material between those red covers was an eye-opener.

For starters, it was obvious that Lattuada had been Zuta's lover from the day he'd hit town over a month ago. And although—reading between the lines—the torch had cooled down some, she still liked tall, lean guys and she kept the bed warm for him when there was nothing more exciting around.

Which wasn't to say that Lattuada had the same freedom. Bolan recalled his hostess calling Dagmar Schroeder a little tramp. It was clear from the entries dated a couple of weeks earlier that she'd been savagely jealous of the blonde, even after Lattuada's liaison with her was over. On the day Bolan rescued Dagmar from the Coconut Grove there was a short entry that read: "L is seeing the tramp again. He says because he is sore over some business deal. I wonder."

Bolan turned the page. The entry for the day he wanted to date Dagmar, the day she refused to see him, was underscored. He read: "Caught them together! I heard her apologize for some kind of double cross and then proposition him. The tramp must go."

He knew then what he was going to find next, but he didn't expect it to be quite so casual. Among a collection of details about club membership, bulk buying and audit problems appeared the laconic line: "HS settled the tramp affair. Useful for eliminating MB?"

For MB read Mike Belasko? Yeah, that was Zuta all right: take the decisions but keep the hands clean. Nice lady.

There were no further references to the warrior until the day he escaped from the courthouse: "MB outwitted police. Team to survey." And then later: "HS instructed—seek and capture." There was only one entry for the day he finally met Zuta. It read: "MB! L will learn that two can play his game!"

The Executioner grinned wryly. So much for Mack Bolan's electric charm. What it came down to was that he'd been taken on a whim to make a mafioso jealous.

On impulse he leafed back to the day he himself had hit town, reading: "Distributors must learn that it doesn't pay to pocket the proceeds. EM to be eliminated publicly as a lesson to others."

EM?

Hell, yes! Another piece of the puzzle clicked into place. Edwina Mueller, the young woman shot down in front of him outside the Black Tie. The beginning of it all. The cops had found nothing, but it seemed she was a drug pusher who had succumbed to temptation and kept some of the income for her own use. Silly girl.

And talking of puzzles—he flipped pages until he came to the Monday of the current week—there remained that one burning question: what were members of the Team doing in the woods at Aumühle *after* their bosses had left the Millpond Club? And how come Benckendorff's men had been there to rescue Bolan when he was attacked?

The answer was spelled out in Zuta's handwriting: "Precocious child reports that B may try to retake the shipment and channel it to Berlin by rail. Second Unit to keep watch in woods."

Precocious child was presumably Sally Ann, confusing things as usual and probably ordered to lay a false trail so the Team wouldn't get wise to the fact that they were prospecting two places in a sensitive area, one of which was actually their enemies' HQ.

Bolan knew that freight trains still went through to Berlin on the Aumühle line at night. What Zuta called the Second Unit must have been left in place, waiting for more intel, with the hope of intercepting any attempt to smuggle the drugs out of West Germany. And their scouts had happened on an intruder prowling the woods and apparently casing the bosses' meal ticket, so they had opened fire. After that it wasn't difficult to work out why Benckendorff had intervened.

There was no mention anywhere of Kraul. Bolan read on, skipping the stuff he knew because he had been involved in it, and then suddenly he was sitting bolt upright on the edge of the tub, rereading a detailed instruction, or the blueprint for one, which left him gasping, even after what he had discovered already.

It was no less than a plan to get rid of *him* and lover boy Lattuada in a single move!

He read the entry for the third time. Now he understood the bedroom setup in the house behind: it was just that he had stumbled the day before on a dry run for the real thing. Now he realized why he had been kept on ice for over twenty-four hours. Now he knew why Zuta hadn't handed him over to the law once she'd tired of him.

That was much too crude a move for her kind of endgame. What she had worked out was this: a man's body was to be found beaten to death outside that steamy bathroom at the foot of that cutely rumpled bed. Bolan's.

Zuta had been having an affair with him, the story would run. She was, as everyone knew, a red-blooded woman. She had no idea, of course, that he was a wanted man. But there would be plenty of witnesses from the club that they *had* been living it up together. Then, suddenly, bingo, the cast-off boyfriend, Lattuada by name, returns from an out-of-town trip, finds them in bed together and kills the interloper in a fit of mad jealousy.

Distressed though she was, the lovely club owner, one of the few clean people in a dirty business, would tearfully be able to give an eyewitness account, a blow-by-blow description, of the killing. Others would no doubt testify to hearing the sounds of the struggle, voices raised in anger, a woman screaming and so on.

Result: Bolan out of the way for keeps, Lattuada sent down for his murder, and Zuta, now that the hood had set up the organization she hired him for, would be able to run the racket on her own. With no need to cut him in, and no inconvenient witnesses to how it was set up and how it worked.

Would such a crazy plan work? The way it was planned, Bolan figured it would. It bore the same trademarks, evidenced the same thinking, as the Dagmar Schroeder setup, and that had worked only too well. Lattuada wouldn't have a chance. Not with such a respectable lady, with such highly placed connections, saying she actually saw him do it; not with the perjured testimony she'd fix; not with his record; not the way it had been planned down to the last detail. They had even remembered not to mark up Bolan's face so that the wounds, when they were inflicted, would stack up with the time of death. The intended murder weapon probably had Lattuada's fingerprints on it already. Bolan almost felt sorry for the poor bastard.

He stood up abruptly. The time of death? Damn, that was *his* death! The hell with mobsters: what about *this* poor bastard?

The frame would be fixed for around a half hour after Lattuada's train hit town—just time, in theory, for him to come home and find Zuta in the sack with a stranger.

And the train pulled into the central train station at 7:35.

Another time check. The digital figures read 6:23. He had an hour and twelve minutes in which to save both their lives.

On foot, with no money to weigh down his pockets, a man in shape would need a minimum of thirty minutes to reach the train station at a run. And the man was securely locked into a third-floor apartment northeast of the Alster.

Don't panic, he told himself. There's still one thing in your favor: they don't know that you know. So you still have a chance to get out of here.

But how? He couldn't just throw up the window and yell for the cops. Not with a murder rap hanging over him.

No, but he could call the fire department.

CHAPTER TWENTY-FIVE

It didn't take long once Bolan had decided to do it. In any case, whatever the odds were, they would be better than trying to take on Hansie's hitters.

Zuta kept a bottle of lighter fluid in the drawer of the night table, and there was a patent cleaner, probably benzene or carbon tetrachloride, behind the built-in wall closet. Bolan uncorked one, unscrewed the cap of the other and poured the liquid from both bottles over crumpled newspapers, silk sheets from the bed, the filmier clothes in the closet and anything else that looked as if it would burn nicely.

He placed one pile of flammable material against the locked entrance door and pushed a pale oak dressing table over it. The doused clothes were heaped on the closet floor. Then he struck a couple of matches and stood back.

The fumes rising from the pile beneath the dressing table ignited with a soft thump, and a moment later flames from burning paper and silk were licking against the oak. The fire in the closet was slow to start, but soon the cleaner he'd sprayed around in there was ablaze, too, incinerating two hundred thousand dollars' worth of feminine glamor from the hem upward.

Bolan waited until smoke was billowing out from the crowded dress racks and the odor of scorched varnish had been replaced by the smell of burning paint from the door. Then he did the one thing you're supposed to avoid at all costs in case of fire: he threw open the window.

The cool, moist air streaming in, sucked upward by the heat, fanned his homemade fire. It might not have stood comparison with the gutting of Benckendorff's stables, but it was impressive in terms of growth just the same.

The draft whistled in under the door, creating a minor inferno that quickly set the dressing table and door panels alight. Next to catch was the molding and wallpaper, and a few seconds later the closet floorboards were burning. By now there was choking black smoke billowing from the flaming garments. He hurried to the open window and leaned out over the sill.

He knew there was a fire station less than two blocks away, and he was gambling on their efficiency to get him out. But it was getting hot as hell, and he crossed his fingers, hoping he hadn't overplayed his hand.

Gesticulating silhouettes appeared in the lighted windows of houses across the street. At least two of them were dialing frantic emergency calls. The newsboy had run into the middle of the roadway, pointing up at the apartment, and there were waiters and club members milling around on the sidewalk beneath the entrance canopy.

The flames had begun to snarl, but it was another two minutes before Bolan heard sirens. Three fire trucks skidded around the corner and raced up to the Coliseum. The crews were still fixing their chin straps as the heavy scarlet machines maneuvered broadside-on to the street between parked cars. The men scattered, uncoiling hose, running for the fire hydrant, operating the motor to rotate the ladder.

The Executioner's clothes were smoldering. He heard the fire chief shouting orders over the whine of machinery. He could also hear shouting from the far side of the burning door.

Zuta and Hansie would be in a jam. A roasted Bolan would kill their plan. They couldn't frame Lattuada for the death of a guy in a fire, especially if the mafioso was on a train at the time. On the other hand, if they tried to bust down the flaming door and drag him out, the blaze would funnel through to the stairway and likely burn down the whole building. Even if they could get through. A third option—dramatic rescue and Bolan off the hook—might not occur to them at first, not unless they realized he had started the fire deliberately. But once they heard the alarm bells they'd be wise to the possibility and they might try to do something to foul it up. It was Bolan's aim to get the hell out before that happened.

He couldn't wait while they telescoped the ladders out and winched a man up to rescue him. There was another way. He stood silhouetted against the flames and waved his arms as if he was in a panic.

He was black with soot, the heat seared through his smoking clothes and he could feel his skin begin to shrivel. He climbed out onto the window ledge and crouched there, covering his face.

Behind him the snap, crackle and pop of the fire settled down to a steady continuous roar. Below, the chief was waving his arms around. Some of the guys left one of the trucks and hustled out crablike onto the sidewalk, stretching a wide disk of canvas taut between them. The chief signaled urgently for Bolan to jump.

That signal was what he'd been waiting for. Clutching Zuta's diary, which he had stuffed beneath his jacket, he jumped.

A rush of blessedly cold air, a confused succession of noises, an impact not much harder than a collision with a Mack truck, and then he was bouncing to rest on the canvas escape sheet.

The chief helped him off it and asked if he was okay. Bolan mumbled his thanks, brushed aside the offer of an ambulance and pushed his way through the crowd to the far side of the street.

He figured his only chance was to intercept Lattuada as he got off the train, show him the dairy as proof of Zuta's duplicity and persuade him to sing to the law. That way the mobster could get protection against the Team and save his life at the expense of extradition to the U.S. to face those old tax charges, and incidentally clear Bolan, actually Belasko, of the Schroeder killing with his testimony.

There were just a couple of difficulties in the way of his plan. Bolan had to get to Lattuada before the Team did. And there had to be some cops for him to sing to.

Plus it was vital that he make a couple of phone calls first.

And he had no money.

He hated to do it, but there was one way—and one way only—that he could grab some fast. The newsboy's stand was just across the road from the Coliseum—an upended packing case supporting a headline newsbill in a wire frame, a stack of papers and an old hat in which customers who wanted a copy while the guy was absent could toss a coin and help themselves.

Bolan helped himself to a handful of marks. He scooped up the coins and ran.

Somewhere in the crowd the newsboy yelled in outrage. Over his shoulder, Bolan saw a fireman at the top of the fire truck ladder being swiveled toward the apartment window, directing the jet from his hose at the blazing interior. Floodlights had been set up, and in their livid glare Bolan saw the unmistakable shape of Hansie Schiller leaning out the stairway window, scanning the crowd below. As he saw the Executioner, pointed and then vanished abruptly, the church clock in the square at the end of the street chimed seven times.

Thirty-five minutes.

It was possible. But there were two calls to make. And it wouldn't be enough to be at the barrier and hope to buttonhole Lattuada as he walked off the train; Bolan would have to check out the place, find a corner where he could see without being seen and distance himself completely from the pursuers who would be sent out from the club any second now.

And the direct route to the train station, the only sensible way for a man on foot, lay through a neighborhood of small-time shopkeepers, pizzerias and delicatessens, many of them Italian-owned—a quarter, Charlie Macfarlane had told Bolan, where the Team was working a Black Hand-style racket, using their muscle to scare the little men into acting as lookouts, informers and, if necessary, confederates.

Racing toward the traffic lights and the square, Bolan could see Zuta in the entrance lobby of the club, her face a mask of anger as she spun the dial of the pay phone on the wall. He guessed she was even now phoning instructions ahead to block him while Hansie rounded up a posse. They would use cars, of course. But many of the streets were one-way for traffic *leaving* the station, and

the rush-hour flow was dense enough to kill any attempt to drive against the flow.

Did they know he was heading for the station? They
would if Zuta had missed her diary. But had she? Would
there have been time? No way of telling. They would, in
any case, quarter the area, and Hansie had seen the way
he was running.

A crowd of travelers stood around a sidewalk information kiosk outside the entrance to an S-Bahn station
on the far side of the square. They were watching a television screen in the window. As the warrior sprinted
past, he saw the face of a local anchorman and heard the
guy say, "Here is a special announcement from Bonn.
We are interrupting our programs so that the Herr
Chancellor..."

He remembered. The West German chancellor was to
make a countrywide TV and radio broadcast on the
subject of the disarmament talks.

Bolan pounded past a fruit-and-vegetable store on the
corner of a narrow street. From the interior he heard the
chancellor's familiar tones: "I want to speak to you
frankly because this affects all of us..."

Fifty yards on there was a cross street, and he heard
the voice again, coming from an open window above a
sandwich bar. "I ask you to approach the subject with
an entirely open mind. Many of you, I know, will have
fears..."

A big, blue-chinned guy in a white apron, holding a
cleaver, erupted onto the sidewalk ahead of Bolan.

Once he had decided Bolan was the man he had been
told to stop, he stood blocking the way like an ape, feet
planted wide and arms spread to catch him whichever
way he swerved, shifting hairy fingers on the handle of
the weapon.

The guy was pretty obvious, telegraphing the way he expected Bolan to run. The Executioner ran straight at him, planting a foot in the center of his unprotected belly. He was caught off balance with his weight on his heels and crashed over backward with a roar of rage, cracking his head against a metal crate full of empty wine bottles. One down, Bolan thought.

The street was almost empty. A few doors beyond the restaurant Bolan could hear a phone ringing. Zuta was evidently calling the next goon in her address book. Maybe he could afford to bypass that one with a one-block detour. He dodged into an alleyway and raced through to the Kirstenallee. Behind him, a dark blue Golf GTi halted by the no-entry sign at the cross street. A big American car pulled up behind it: a white Cadillac with tinted windows. So they had recovered it—and the body of the vulture man—from Aumühle.

The Kirstenallee was two stories of grimy brick above pants pressers, felt blockers, a tailor's workshop, a cobbler and the steamed-up front of a cheap laundry. On the far side of the lane there was a gas station, but it was closed, the concrete forecourt deserted, the pumps unlit. The pavement was empty, too—no cars, no bicycles, no trucks, not even a pedestrian crossing the pools of lamplight between the sleazy facades. There was just an echo of the chancellor's voice filtering through an uncurtained window above one of the storefronts.

"Our German brothers in the East . . . grave mistake not to treat seriously . . . perhaps a genuine desire for peace . . ."

And a glass-paneled public phone booth beyond the service station. Bolan hurled himself inside and punched out the free emergency call number.

A click, then a man's voice said in German, "Police emergency. Can I have your name, please?"

"The hell with that," Bolan snapped. "This is urgent. Get—"

"Your name, please, *Meinherr*."

"You've got to be kidding! Mike Belasko."

"Thank you. Would that be one *L* or two, sir?"

"Help yourself to as many as you want!" Bolan shouted. "I want to get a message—"

"And the address?" the unruffled voice queried.

The warrior choked back a retort. He guessed they were obliged to follow their routine. "The train station," he said as calmly as he could. "Get this message to Kriminalkommissar Fischer at the police headquarters, fast. Tell him I'm meeting the 7:35 train from Bremen. Tell him to be there if he wants to solve a murder and stop another. He'll be expecting a message from me, but tell him to hurry." Bolan slammed down the receiver before the guy could reply, then dug out the newsboy's money from his pocket. He needed it for his second call.

He fed the right amount into the box and stabbed the buttons. Freddie Leonhardt had to be at home, because if he wasn't...

He was. The receiver was picked up almost at once. "Leonhardt."

"Belasko. This is urgent. Did you pass on those messages?"

"My dear old chap," the affected would-be Brit drawled into his ear, "of course I did. The police fellow seemed a bit dubious, don't you know, but—"

"Never mind," Bolan interrupted. "Just so long as you made contact. And the rest?"

"I called by the annex, as you asked. The printout had arrived. Do you want me to read it?"

"Forget it," Bolan snapped. "The subject met with a fatal accident." A rundown on Arvell Asticot's Hamburg connections was the last thing he needed now. "What about the service message, the one concerning Lattuada?"

"I waited for the reply, like you said. It was short. Quote. Your mistake. Stop. There are two brothers. Stop. Roberto repeat Roberto is the hit man. Stop. Ferucco is the organizer. Stop. He plans dirty deals, but so far no suspicion of killings. Unquote."

"Right," Bolan said. "That's what I wanted to know. Thanks."

"Look, old lad, if there's anything I can do to—"

"You already did." The warrior banged down the receiver. Now for the stretch, he thought as he burst out into the street again.

CHAPTER TWENTY-SIX

There was a T-junction blocking off the Kirstenallee at the next intersection. Either he had to turn right, take the main drag, lose time and risk the Golf and Cadillac, or run back into the narrow one-way street and make the train, at the expense of whatever shit Zuta would throw in his way. For *her* phone, he knew, would be busy, too. He turned left and went into high gear.

Stores were still open along the street: delicatessens, grocers, an ice-cream parlor and a milk bar as well as a fruit-and-vegetable market with cases of apples and oranges stacked outside the window. Customers in the deli and folks on stools at the milk bar stayed as rigid as the subjects of a painting as he pelted past each radio or TV, the chancellor's words swelling and fading in his ears: "You must believe me when I say...no question of altering the status of Berlin...guaranteed by four-power agreement...no mention of unification on the proposed agenda..."

One of the paintings jerked itself into a movie. Three guys came out of the fruit-and-vegetable market and spread across the sidewalk and roadway. They were dark, sturdy types with tough chins and curly Mediterranean hair. But they didn't look like professional hoods; they were just neighborhood muscle carrying out the boss's orders.

Once again Bolan banked on the belief that they would be dumb enough to figure him for dumb. Instead of trying to force his way through or outflank them, he jumped up on the ranked displays in front of the shop. His feet squelched through tomatoes and pears, skidded on beets and squashed melons. He turned his ankle on a tray of potatoes and kicked cabbages, bananas and a huge basket of onions tumbling to the sidewalk. By the time the boys were plugged into the change of plan, the sidewalk was jumping.

One of them tripped and fell. Another smashed his shin into a wooden crate and staggered off balance toward the warrior. The third, the nearest to the storefront, got his hands on the edge of Bolan's jacket.

The warrior whirled toward him, chopping at his neck with the flat of one hand as he came down off the displays. The guy grunted and swung a huge fist. The blow caught the Executioner high up on the left side, just over the heart. It didn't hurt him, but it knocked him off his stride and allowed the goon to wrap his arms around Bolan's thighs and bring him down among the winter produce.

For a moment they thrashed around in the salad, grappling for an advantage. Then the guy who had fallen threw himself down with the aim of smothering the quarry with his weight. At the same time the third man picked up the crate he'd run into and swung it at Bolan's head. The teamwork would have been great, if the Executioner hadn't kneed his adversary in the balls and rolled aside at the crucial second. The second man dropped on the character who had floored Bolan, and then had the crate splinter over his head. By the time they sorted themselves out, Bolan was on his feet ten yards away and running.

They started after him, yelling, "Stop, thief!" There was noise farther back down the street, too. And Bolan

knew that Hansie and the prowling cars could material-
ize anywhere.

There were still five, maybe six blocks to cover before
he reached the comparative safety of the crowded
Steindamm, and at the end of that wide stretch of asphalt was the bus terminal and the train station.

He ran as fast as he could. The blood was roaring in
his ears, and his feet were beginning to feel as if there
were lead weights attached to the ankles. As he raced
past, a husky Italian was moving reluctantly toward a
shrilling phone inside a low-ceilinged store hung with
sausages, hams and wicker bottles of Chianti. Behind
him a fat woman sat at a cash register, frowning in the
direction of a small television screen that showed the
mournful face of the chancellor in close-up.

Bolan thanked his lucky stars that it took time to dial,
speak, replace the handset, wait for another tone and
then call again, even for someone as determined as Zuta.
He was over the next cross street before the big man
made the sidewalk. A block away down the cross street
he saw the rear end of the Cadillac vanish around a corner.

"One has to give in order to receive," the chancellor's voice thundered from the interior of a cabbie's
shelter. "I would ask you, therefore, to approach these
proposals with an open mind..."

Two more intersections, a row of brightly lit stores
and the Hansa Theater separated the Executioner from
the glass-canopied entrance to the train station. About
a quarter of that distance lay between him and the thugs
clattering up the narrow one-way street in pursuit. Two
men ran out of the shelter and headed across the street
toward him. The phone must have been ringing in there,
too.

They could have been running for the line of empty cabs parked by the curb. But Bolan couldn't afford to take chances. He put the palm of his hand on top of a low iron railing and vaulted over onto a small triangle of grass in front of a café-bar standing back from the road. "And now," a radio just inside the open door of the bar told him, "I will summarize what has been suggested: it is not a world-shattering about-face, but it is worth . . ."

A shot, the first fired in anger since Bolan had quit the blazing apartment, rang out behind the railings. He heard the sonic crack as the slug zipped past him. Glass tinkled and fell among cars parked beyond the bar. The pistol, which sounded like a heavy-caliber revolver, fired again. This time a ricochet screeched off the brick wall of the building.

Blackened and disheveled, the warrior's scarecrow figure caused people to stop and stare as he dodged, panting, among groups moving from the bus station toward the theater. He ran across the Steindamm under the yellow lights, glancing over his shoulder at the red, amber and green traffic signals winking on and off along the wide perspective to the east. Three streets away, behind a truck, a bus and a bunch of taxis, the white Cadillac appeared, pulling over to the wrong side of the road and laying down rubber on the damp pavement, roaring toward the station.

Bolan turned and sprinted for an alley that ran behind the theater. He raced between long lines of buses standing at the terminal and headed for a side entrance to the station. The minute hand of the giant clock on the tower jerked onto the half hour.

Scaffolding surrounded the arched pedestrian entrance where restoration work on the wall of the building was in progress. Bolan ran between tall wooden partitions and joined a crowd of raincoated commuters passing beneath the arch. He figured he would be safe from lead poisoning now. They had to be pretty desperate to fire at him out in the open like that. Then he saw six or seven heavies, including the guys with the guns, threading their way between the buses. They must have seen him come in.

The station concourse was crowded with travelers, porters, officials, workers, most of them listening to the broadcast over the public address system.

"So I ask you," the chancellor's voice cried out from bookstalls, pillars, baggage checks and the tops of gantries beneath the great glass roof, "not to dismiss this relaxation of the Soviet attitude out of hand as a shoddy political maneuver. The policy of *glasnost* merits serious consideration, and perhaps a little faith, on the part of all those who sincerely hope for peace in our time. In the case, therefore, of an eventual referendum on the disarmament proposals, I say to you again: think before you vote. And now I wish you all a very good night . . . and thank you for listening."

Reactions to the broadcast were mixed. "Bloody Russians," a porter growled as he pushed a cart loaded with suitcases toward the cab stand. "Expect us to junk our weapons, and keep their own hidden behind their backs. Mark my words!"

"You have to trust *some*body, *some*time," a woman said.

"I suppose it's just possible they might really mean—"

"It's all right for the fucking politicians. They'll all be safely in their fallout shelters when the time comes!"

Bolan was standing beside a baggage trolley stacked high with sacks of mail. His pursuers were checking out the commuters crowding the ticket offices and news-stand. "I'm happy to see, Herr Belasko," a quiet voice said behind the Executioner, "that you're still, as you Americans say, on the ball."

Bolan swung around. A square-jawed, soberly dressed man wearing a gray topcoat was regarding him through slitted eyes.

"Kraul!" he exclaimed. "What the hell are you doing here? How did you—"

"You forget that I have friends in the enemy camp." The mobster's voice was suave. "And so, my friend, have you."

Bolan grinned in spite of himself. Sally Ann was a walking news bulletin! "That's right," he said. "You were at Aumühle. I saw you on the train. Are you telling me you're in cahoots with Benckendorff now?"

"Let's just say I serve in an advisory capacity. A long time ago, a very long time ago, I was a Party member. I found the capitalist way of life more...rewarding. But I keep in touch, and Gottfried and I both have an interest in the dismantling of a certain organization, although admittedly for quite different reasons."

"You, so that you can get your hooks back into the Hamburg underworld. Benckendorff, so that he can torpedo the disarmament talks, and make use of an existing network, perhaps with your help, for his espionage activities." Bolan's voice was accusative, harsh with disgust.

"It seems," Kraul said blandly, "that there was a fire. Unfortunate. However, my half of the arrangement should still work out successfully." He smiled. "Thanks to you."

Bolan compressed his lips. It was true. The harder he nailed the Lattuada-Schiller-Krohn team, the more it would benefit Ferdie Kraul. And there was nothing he could do about it.

"You know what you can do with your—" he began. But the rest of the sentence was drowned by a fresh outburst from the public address system.

"The train arriving on track six is the 7:35 express from Wilhelmshaven, Oldenburg, Bremerhaven and Bremen. Will passengers please..."

"It was you who dropped my knife into the cellar, wasn't it?" Bolan said. "And hung the shoulder rig over the grating? It had to be you."

"Yes," Kraul said. "I was visiting. And it was necessary for me to be out of the way while they attended to some illiterate gorilla sent by Schiller to put the bite on the management. I considered it more helpful to my private affairs to keep you alive."

Bolan resisted the temptation to hit him. No barriers blocked off track six as the huge diesel-electric locomotive slid to a halt in its bay. Friends and relatives surged forward; doors opened all along the length of the train; passengers carrying their baggage dropped to the platform, hurrying toward the exits to secure a porter, grab a taxi, a phone, make the U-Bahn before it became too crowded.

Running, Bolan heard Kraul call after him, "Sally Ann tells me your man had a reservation in car 44."

He fought his way against the tide. It wasn't very easy, locating one human being in that crush, but he couldn't afford to stand still and let Lattuada come to him. There were at least a dozen hoods in the concourse, all looking for the same guy, with orders to stop Bolan getting to him first at all costs. And Lattuada himself wouldn't know that his accomplices were now his enemies.

The first car, immediately behind the locomotive, was numbered 32. That meant that car 44 would be at the other end of the train. Bolan shouldered his way onward, agonizingly aware of his vulnerability.

He was aware suddenly of separate sounds. Footsteps, hundreds of them on the moist platform. Doors slamming. A hiss of steam from somewhere. An incomprehensible announcement over the public address system. The gunning of a taxi engine.

His ears registered shouts, then Italian accents calling through the groundswell of voices. There was another sound, too, and Bolan knew then that that was no taxi engine he'd heard. The rasping exhaust note was accompanied by the dying warble of a police siren. He saw the car, a green-and-white Mercedes with an illuminated sign on its roof, maneuvering among the baggage trolleys on the far side of the empty bay beyond Lattuada's train. A bell trilled somewhere out of sight. The doors of the car swung open. Fischer, Wertheim and two cops in uniform spilled out and began clambering over the tracks in the empty bay. At the same moment the Executioner saw Lattuada.

He was climbing down from the last car of the whole train, a tall, lean figure carrying a pigskin valise and wearing a brown raincoat. There was a cellophane cover shielding his wide-brimmed hat.

Summoning his last reserves of strength, Bolan accelerated his stumbling run. He was happy to see that Fischer had taken his message seriously, and that he had gotten there so damn fast, but he had to see the mobster himself, alone, first. Behind him he heard a yell. "There he is! Get him! Nail the motherfucker!"

Hansie Schiller.

They were even more desperate now if they were going to risk an open chase in confrontation with the law. Bolan was aware of the rush of feet, angry complaints from passengers as they were jostled or their baggage overturned, curses from the Team and their henchmen. Fischer was shouting, too. Hansie's screech had focused the German policemen's attention on the warrior. But the cops had a greater distance to go.

Bolan pulled up in front of Lattuada. He'd halted by the open door at the end of the car, narrow brow furrowed, the sallow face with its stubbly lantern jaw alert. Maybe he'd recognized Hansie's voice; maybe he'd tumbled to the fact that it was something to do with him; perhaps he just wondered what the hell was going on. "Get back in there," the Executioner snapped at him. "Fast!"

The mobster's eyes widened, staring at Bolan's wild, unkempt figure. But urgency must have lent the warrior's voice authority, because the mafioso turned obediently and climbed back onto the step. It was only when Bolan shoved him into the corridor that he said, "What the hell—"

"Move, if you want to live," Bolan ordered. "Move!"

"Who the hell are you?" the hood demanded. But he moved.

"Get into the washroom, Lattuada, or you're a dead man." Bolan hustled the guy into the tiny cubicle at the end of the car, slammed the door, swung the lock over and leaned his back against the flimsy panels. Maybe because the use of his name surprised him, the mafioso had gone along with Bolan so far. But now his right hand hovered between the lapels of his raincoat. "Look, asshole,'' he snarled, "I don't know who the fuck you are, but—''

"The name's Belasko. Mike Belasko." The Executioner saw recognition flare in the hood's cold eyes, then he rasped, "Don't be more of an idiot than you've already been. Junk the iron unless you want me to ram it down your throat." The car rocked slightly as heavy feet stamped along the far end of the corridor.

Lattuada hesitated, then plucked a short-barreled .38 Police Special from a shoulder holster, looked around, shrugged and dropped the gun into the toilet bowl. It was too big to fall through the hole. Bolan slammed the lid shut and leaned one foot on it.

"Just what the fuck are you playing at, mister?" Lattuada said softly. They were jammed together pretty tightly. His breath smelled of mint with a slight scent of liquor.

"Down there. Try the toilet," a voice called from outside the door.

"Listen," Bolan said. "We've only got a few seconds. You know Zuta's handwriting, don't you?"

"Sure I do," the mafioso said, scowling. "What the hell has that—''

"Then read this, and read it well...patsy." Bolan pulled the diary out from under his jacket and handed it over, opened to the page where the mobster's fate, and his own, were blueprinted. "MB is me," he said.

A heavy hand explored the grooved brass knob on the other side of the door. The panels against Bolan's back shifted to an inquiring shove.

"Holy shit!" Lattuada said. He flipped back a few pages, more to convince himself that what he read was part of a continuing plan than because he doubted the authenticity of the dairy. "The dirty stinking bitch," he said. "The whoring goddamn—"

"Sure," Bolan cut in. "In spades. Me, too. Thing is, are you going to play ball?" He lurched forward a little as the door behind him heaved violently. Luckily their toilet door was the one parallel to the corridor and not the one set diagonally at the end of the car, which would have given the besiegers more space to maneuver.

"What's the pitch?" Lattuada finally asked.

"The cops are out there, as well as Hansie and his muscle. There's nothing against you in this country. No charge has been made. The cops know what you set up, but they don't even know your name."

"So?"

The door shivered and shook to a heavier charge. There had to be two of them there now. Bolan said, "So forget your connection with the Team and the racket you organized. Turn yourself in and plead guilty to those old tax charges back home. Have them extradite you. Get the hell out." He hated to allow any scum tied in with the Mafia off the hook. But knowing that however dirty his hands, Lattuada wasn't the killer he had thought—that it was Hansie who had murdered Dagmar—made the play at least morally more digestible.

"The IRS will crucify me. Three to five, most likely."

"You should worry. Zuta will crucify you for keeps. We'll both be sitting ducks if we stay here. Listen, they'll even tangle with the cops to get us!"

Sounds of cursing and struggles were audible outside now. Feet stamped the platform. What Bolan didn't know was that Kraul had sent in his two bodyguards, Nils and Georg, to mix it up a little while the Executioner made his play. In the car, the toilet door was splintering and Bolan's back was getting bruised.

Lattuada's sullen expression tightened. He had made up his mind. "Okay," he said, nodding.

"You'll have to wise them up some on how the Team works if you want the free pass. That includes the low-down on the Schroeder killing."

The mobster nodded again. From below the frosted toilet compartment window, on the tracks, Fischer called out, "Give yourself up, Belasko! You can't get away!"

Leaning his back for the last time against the disinte-grating door, Bolan launched himself forward with one leg held stiffly out in front of him, pushing the frosted glass out of its frame and down onto the rails. "Coming!" he shouted.

Ten minutes later he was squashed, together with the mafioso, in the back of the patrol car with Kriminal-kommissar Fischer, waiting for the lights to change so that the driver could turn into the Glockengeisser Wall. Wertheim was in front, nursing a black eye and a split lip. Three of the Black Hand guys had been arrested for disorderly conduct and taken away. Hansie and his Coliseum muscle, more professionally, had melted into the crowd as soon as Lattuada and the warrior had escaped through the broken window; there was no percentage risking good soldiers when the prize was already in the hands of the enemy.

"I'm not going to pull the 'justice is above us mere mortals' line on you," Fischer said to Bolan. "Corners are sometimes there to be cut, and the Minister of the Interior is rather busy at the moment. I'll need statements, depositions and signatures, of course, particularly this man's testimony on Schiller and the Schroeder killing. But if you're prepared to skip certain formalities and waive certain rights, I think we can arrange everything to our mutual satisfaction." He cleared his throat. "Only thing is, you'll have to be out of the country pretty damn quick, and by quick I mean within twenty-four hours. Tomorrow's papers are going to be full of the chancellor's speech, but after that they'll be looking for copy and questions will be asked."

"Suits me," Lattuada said.

Bolan shrugged. Both his objectives had been gained, at the expense, he hated to admit, of giving Ferdie Kraul back his stranglehold on the St. Pauli underworld. But if he was going to try to break that one, it would have to wait until another time.

The lights flashed green, and the car surged forward. "Don't think," Fischer continued, "that I'm handing out favors, but the police commissioner, Kunstler, has been laying for these mobsters a long time, watching and waiting. Your two statements should give us the lever we need to move in and nail them." He shook his head and tapped the diary Bolan had handed over. "And you say this proves the mastermind behind it all is the Krohn woman? My God, there'll be some red faces at city hall when that comes out. The Coliseum's a favorite haunt of a lot of big wheels." He chuckled happily.

"If I do give you the lowdown on the whole deal," Lattuada said, "how do I know you won't go back on your word? I mean, like drag me back to stand trial with the others, use my own stuff against me?"

"You don't know," Fischer said. "You have to take a chance, but you should be used to that. Even if the others snitch on you, and they will, the most we could go for would be conspiracy and uttering threats. And with you singing like a bird, the sentence wouldn't be worth your transportation to the court. There'll be nothing else against you if you can help me put Schiller away for killing that girl."

The car stopped at another red light. "Of course," Fischer said, "if you don't want to take my word, you're free to get out now and take your chances with the boys. No warrant's been sworn out for you, and there's nothing I could do to stop you." He paused, eyebrows raised, his fingers resting on the door handle.

"Forget it. Let's hit the station and get it over with, huh?" Lattuada growled.

Bolan had the impression Fischer was hiding a smile. "As for you, *Meinherr*," he said, "it's fortunate that you were able to, shall we say, remove yourself from the court's jurisdiction before you pleaded. I'd never have been able to fix things myself once you'd been indicted. And, believe me, you would have been."

Bolan smiled wryly. "How do you like that? When it's a question of *my* word, I get pushed around and shouted at like a long-term con. But on the word of a convicted hood that I've been framed and, in fact, am in the clear, suddenly I'm *Meinherr*! Maybe, Herr Kriminal-kommissar, you, too, should take a chance from time to time. Like on the word of, well, let's say an American newspaperman."

Fischer shook his big head. "We never take chances."

The police car continued cruising down a wide street toward the city center when a white Cadillac convertible came steaming past at about seventy miles an hour. Zuta was driving it herself, with Hansie in the passenger seat beside her. The windows were down and four or five of the local muscle were jammed in the back beneath the car's soft top.

As the Cadillac passed, its tail end shook as the tires hit the wet remnants of old streetcar tracks protruding through the asphalt in the middle of the roadway. Then, just before a half-completed underpass that took the center lanes beneath a busy intersection, Zuta swung the wheel hard right and cut across the patrol car's front.

That had probably been her intention, at least, either in an attempt to force the police car into the curb and dispose of its occupants there by hand, or in the hope of a shrewd, glancing blow that would tip the car on its roof and eliminate them that way. Bolan saw Hansie's malicious smile, and he saw Zuta's furious scowl. And beyond them he saw what they were too hooked on his destruction to notice.

A twenty-ton dump truck trundling up the slope from the unfinished tunnel.

The truck surfaced and bounced onto the road at the very instant the Cadillac was turning at a sharp angle in front of it. The driver didn't have a chance. The Caddie was still traveling at around fifty, and the massive steel pushbar in front of the dump truck's giant wheels slammed into it just aft of the rear wheel.

With the impact hurling it one way and the steering and engine another, there was only one thing, dynamically, for the car to do. It leaped into the air and crashed down onto its soft roof, cartwheeled into a steel sand bin on the edge of the sidewalk and then bounced back across the road to smash, still upturned, into the iron railing protecting the entrance to a subway station.

Police drivers should have quick reactions in traffic. But Fischer's man, Bolan thought, could have beaten an electric current from the switch to the lamp. Faced with a bus, a panel truck and three sedans coming toward them, he swerved the Mercedes neatly to the right, ran between the sand bin and a plane tree and nudged the hood to rest against the shutters of a closed jewelry store. By the time they had piled out, the Caddie was blazing from end to end.

Hansie Schiller was lying on the pavement with his head at an original angle and glass sparkling in his hair. The rest of the gang was still inside the wreck, but Bolan didn't hear any screams.

Fischer looked from the skid marks to the blood splashes and broken glass and then back at the flames. He shook his head. "Maybe I won't need to trouble you gentlemen for a statement after all," he said.

EPILOGUE

The ship, registered in Galveston, Texas, was a freighter with accommodation for a dozen passengers. She was on a coastal run, unloading and taking aboard cargo at Rotterdam, Le Havre and Genoa before heading through the Suez Canal to India and the Far East.

Lattuada, escorted by police, and Bolan were taken aboard at dawn, shortly before the ship sailed. The faceless officials who made such things tidy on paper had probably worked late at city hall that night.

"Pan Am, TWA and Lufthansa are all booked solid on the transatlantic run," Fischer told the Executioner. "And if we pull people off at a small field like Fuhlsbüttel, it's going to cause the kind of talk we want to avoid." The two Americans, he said, would be put ashore at Rotterdam and taken by U.S. embassy staff car with a Marine Corps escort to the international airport at Schiphol, near Amsterdam.

Fischer stood with the warrior on the pint-size promenade deck as the Elbe widened toward the North Sea. It was bitterly cold, and yellowing clouds over the city promised a fresh fall of snow.

"We'll put them all away," the policeman said. "Once they know the racketeer bosses have croaked, every person who ever had the bite put on them is going to come up with damning testimony."

"Exit the Team," Bolan said, "leaving a clear field for Ferdie Kraul. That's what bugs me."

Fischer sighed. "He's going to be a tough one," he admitted. "He's got connections in high places, and can afford to buy his way out." And then, with a quizzical smile, he added, "You wouldn't care to take a leave of absence from your 'journalistic' career and accept a short-term engagement, seconded to a West German police force, with special responsibility for straightening out the rackets in St. Pauli?"

Bolan shook his head and grinned. Obviously Fischer wasn't buying his Belasko cover. Not surprising, considering his actions during his stay in Hamburg. "Like they say, you have to put your own house in order. But I have something here that could help."

He dug into his pocket and produced a manila envelope. It had been waiting for him when he'd collected what remained of his gear and checked out of the Hotel Oper. With it there was a card, which he had destroyed, bearing the penciled message: "With so many thanks for your help." The card was Ferdinand Kraul's. Inside the envelope was a thick wad of hundred-mark bills.

"This is dirty money," Bolan said. "I haven't counted it, but there's a lot in there. I want you to take it and give one of these bills to the newspaper vendor outside the Coliseum, okay?"

Frowning in puzzlement, Fischer nodded.

"Divide the rest in two equal parts," Bolan continued. "Half is to go to a man named Charlie Macfarlane, a guy who lost the use of his legs. He's in a hospital near the botanical gardens."

"And the rest?"

"A donation to the Hamburg police department. I'd like to think this money could be used in some way—paying off informers, outbidding Kraul—against the guy who collected it in the first place."

Fischer took the envelope. "Very well, Herr Belasko. You may be sure it will be used precisely in the way you specify."

Before the warrior could say anything else, an American-accented voice called across the water, "Goodbye to our friends from Galveston. We wish you Godspeed and a pleasant voyage. Please come to visit us again soon."

He turned in surprise. They were passing the suburb of Blankenese. The voice, relayed by a loudspeaker above a long, low clapboard building on the right bank of the Elbe, was followed at once by a recording of "The Star-Spangled Banner" that blared across the river; at the same time the Stars and Stripes was run up a flagpole.

"The *Willkommhöft*, a local tradition," Fischer explained. "That is the Schulau ferry station. Every vessel entering or leaving the Hamburg docks is greeted with the national anthem and flag of its home country, along with a message in the appropriate language."

"I'm sure it's appreciated," Bolan said, turning again as a young deckhand approached, carrying a strip of paper. "Radiogram for Mr. Belasko, sir," the boy said, saluting. "Text reads, 'Urgent. Take first available plane for Hawaii.' The message is signed Uncle Hal."

"There is something wrong?" Fischer asked, concerned.

Bolan smiled. "Just a playful editor. Must be a big story breaking in Hawaii."

The policeman stared ahead as the bow lifted to the incoming swell from the estuary. The icy wind stirred his hair. "Hawaii? A paradise, no? Certainly warmer than here. Of course, Herr Belasko, I imagine you'll make it even hotter."

Trouble erupts for Nile Barrabas and his men when an undersea Soviet war base pits them against their most deadly enemy.

THE BARRABAS WAR

JACK HILD

A full-scale war is about to break out when suspected acts of Turkish terrorism result in furious Greek retaliation. Barrabas and his elite mercenaries discover a state-of-the-art command station and a sinister Soviet plot lurking beneath the Aegean Sea!

The line between good and evil is a tightrope no man should walk. Unless that man is the Executioner.

BLOWOUT $3.95 ☐
Framed for murder and wanted by both sides of the law, Bolan escapes into the icy German underground to stalk a Mafia-protected drug baron.

TIGHTROPE $3.95 ☐
When top officials of international Intelligence agencies are murdered, Mack Bolan pits his skill against an alliance of renegade agents and uncovers a deadly scheme to murder the U.S. President.

MOVING TARGET $3.95 ☐
America's most powerful corporations are reaping huge profits by dealing in arms with anyone who can pay the price. Dogged by assassins, Mack Bolan becomes caught in a power struggle that might be his last.

FLESH & BLOOD $3.95 ☐
When Asian communities are victimized by predators among their own—thriving gangs of smugglers, extortionists and pimps—they turn to Mack Bolan for help.

Total Amount	$ _____
Plus 75¢ Postage	.75
Payment enclosed	$ _____

SMB-3